PRAISE FOR SANDRA BROWN AND
FAT TUESDAY

"[Brown] is a masterful storyteller, carefully crafting tales that keep readers on the edge of their seats."
—*USA Today*

"Author Sandra Brown proves herself top-notch."
—Associated Press

"Sandra Brown has continued to grow with every novel."
—*Dallas Morning News*

"Brown's storytelling gift is surprisingly rare, even among crowd-pleasers."
—*Toronto Sun*

"A novelist who can't write them fast enough."
—*San Antonio Express-News*

"Brown has few to envy among living authors."
—*Kirkus Reviews*

"A taut, seamless tale of nonstop action...A revel not to be missed."
—*BookPage*

"Sandra Brown is a master at weaving a story of suspense into a tight web that catches and holds the reader from the first page to the last."
—*Library Journal*

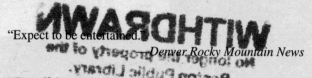

"Expect to be entertained."

—Denver Rocky Mountain News

"Fast pacing and tricky plotting."

—Publishers Weekly

"Brown's novels define the term 'page-turner.'"

—Booklist

FAT TUESDAY

NOVELS BY SANDRA BROWN

FAT
TUESDAY

SANDRA
BROWN

GRAND CENTRAL
PUBLISHING

NEW YORK   BOSTON

Copyright © 1997 by Sandra Brown Management, Ltd.
Excerpt from *Seeing Red* © 2017 by Sandra Brown Management, Ltd.

Grand Central Publishing
Hachette Book Group
1290 Avenue of the Americas, New York, NY 10104
grandcentralpublishing.com
twitter.com/grandcentralpub

Originally published in hardcover by Grand Central Publishing in June 1997
First mass market edition: June 1998
Reissued: April 2018

Grand Central Publishing is a division of Hachette Book Group, Inc. The Grand Central Publishing name and logo is a trademark of Hachette Book Group, Inc.

The publisher is not responsible for websites (or their content) that are not owned by the publisher.

The Hachette Speakers Bureau provides a wide range of authors for speaking events. To find out more, go to www.hachettespeakersbureau.com or call (866) 376-6591.

ISBN: 978-1-5387-1267-2 (mass market reissue), 978-1-5387-1266-5 (trade paperback), 978-1-4555-4630-5 (ebook)

Printed in the United States of America

OPM

10 9 8 7 6 5 4 3 2 1

FAT TUESDAY

Chapter One

"He'll walk." Burke Basile extended the fingers of his right hand, then formed a tight fist. This flexing motion had recently become an involuntary habit. "There's not a chance in hell they'll convict."

Captain Douglas Patout, commander of Narcotics and Vice of the New Orleans Police Department, sighed discouragingly. "Maybe."

"Not 'maybe.' He'll walk," Burke repeated with resolve.

After a moment, Patout asked, "Why did Littrell assign this particular assistant to prosecute this case? He's a newcomer, been living down here only a few months, a transplant from up north. Wisconsin or someplace. He didn't understand the...the nuances of this trial."

Burke, who'd been staring out the window, turned back into the room. "Pinkie Duvall understood them well enough."

"That golden-tongued son of a bitch. He loves nothing

better than to hammer the NOPD and make us all look incompetent."

Although it pained him to compliment the defense lawyer, Burke said, "You gotta hand it to him, Doug, his closing argument was brilliant. It was blatantly anti-cop, but just as blatantly pro-justice. All twelve jurors were creaming on every word." He checked his wristwatch. "They've been out thirty minutes. I predict another ten or so ought to do it."

"You really think it'll be that quick?"

"Yeah, I do." Burke took a seat in a scarred wooden armchair. "When you get right down to it, we never stood a prayer. No matter who in the D.A.'s office tried the case, or how much fancy legal footwork was done on either side, the sad fact remains that Wayne Bardo did not pull the trigger. He did not fire the bullet that killed Kev."

"I wish I had a nickel for every time Pinkie Duvall said that during the trial," Patout remarked sourly. "'My client did not fire the fatal bullet.' He chanted it like a monk."

"Unfortunately, it's the truth."

They'd tramped this ground at least ten thousand times—ruminating, speculating, but always returning to that one irreversible, unarguable, unpalatable certainty: The accused on trial, Wayne Bardo, technically had not shot to death Detective Sergeant Kevin Stuart.

Burke Basile wearily massaged his shadowed eye sockets, pushed back his unkempt wavy hair, smoothed down his mustache, then restlessly rubbed his palms against the tops of his thighs. He flexed the fingers of his right hand. Finally, he set his elbows on his knees and stared vacantly at the floor, his shoulders dejectedly hunched forward.

Patout observed him critically. "You look like hell. Why don't you go out and have a cigarette?"

Burke shook his head.

"Coffee? I'll go get it for you, bring it back so you don't have to face the media."

"No, but thanks."

Patout sat down in the chair next to Burke's. "Let's not write it off as a defeat yet. Juries are tricky. You think you've got some bastard nailed, he leaves the courthouse a free man. You're practically assured an acquittal, they bring in a guilty verdict, and the judge opts for the maximum sentence. You never can tell."

"I can tell," Burke said with stubborn resignation. "Bardo will walk."

For a time, neither said anything to break the heavy silence. Then Patout said, "Today's the anniversary of the Constitution of Mexico."

Burke looked up. "Pardon?"

"The Mexican Constitution. It was adopted on February 5. I noticed it on my desk calendar this morning."

"Huh."

"Didn't say how many years ago. Couple of hundred, I guess."

"Huh."

That conversation exhausted, they fell silent again, each lost in his thoughts. Burke was trying to figure out how he was going to handle himself the first few seconds after the verdict was read.

From the start he'd known that there would be a trial. Pinkie Duvall wasn't about to plea-bargain what he considered to be a shoo-in acquittal for his client. Burke had also known what the outcome of the trial would be. Now that the moment of truth was—if his prediction proved correct—approaching, he geared himself up to combat the rage he knew he would experience when he watched Bardo leave the courthouse unscathed.

God help him from killing the bastard with his bare hands.

A large, noisy housefly, out of season and stoned on insecticide, had somehow found its way into this small room in the Orleans Parish courthouse, where countless other prosecutors and defendants had sweated anxiously while awaiting a jury's verdict. Desperate to escape, the fly was making suicidal little *pflats* against the windowpane. The poor dumb fly didn't know when he was beaten. He didn't realize he only looked a fool for his vain attempts, no matter how valiant they were.

Burke snuffled a self-deprecating laugh. Because he could identify with the futility of a housefly, he knew he'd hit rock bottom.

When the knock came, he and Patout glanced first at each other, then toward the door, which a bailiff opened. She poked her head inside. "They're back."

As they moved toward the door, Patout checked the time, murmuring, "Son of a gun. Ten minutes." He looked at Burke. "How'd you do that?"

But Burke wasn't listening. His concentration was focused on the open doors of the courtroom at the end of the corridor. Spectators and media streamed through the portal with the excitement of Romans at the Colosseum about to witness the spectacle of martyrs being devoured by lions.

Kevin Stuart, husband, father, damn good cop, and best friend, had been martyred. Like many martyrs throughout history, his death was the result of betrayal. Someone Kev trusted, someone who was supposed to be on his side, furthering his cause, backing him up, had turned traitor. Another cop had tipped the bad guys that the good guys were on the way.

One secret phone call from someone within the division, and Kevin Stuart's fate had been sealed. True, he'd been killed in the line of duty, but that didn't make him any less dead. He'd died needlessly. He'd died bloody. This trial was merely the mopping up. This trial was the costly and time-consuming exercise a civilized society went through to put a good face on letting a scumbag go free after ending the life of a fine man.

Jury selection had taken two weeks. From the outset, the prosecutor had been intimidated and outsmarted by the defense attorney, the flamboyant Pinkie Duvall, who had exercised all his preemptory challenges, handpicking a perfect jury for his client with hardly any argument from the opposition.

The trial itself had lasted only four days. But its brevity was disproportionate to the interest in its outcome. There'd been no shortage of predictions.

The morning following the fatal incident, the chief of police was quoted as saying, "Every officer on the force feels the loss and is taking it personally. Kevin Stuart was well respected and well liked among his fellow policemen. We're using all the resources available to us to conduct a complete and thorough investigation into the shooting death of this distinguished officer."

"It should be an open-and-shut case," one pundit had editorialized in the *Times Picayune* the day the trial commenced. "An egregious mistake on the part of the NOPD has left one of its own dead. Tragic? Definitely. But justification to pin the blame on an innocent scapegoat? This writer thinks not."

"The D.A. is squandering taxpayers' money by forcing an innocent citizen to stand trial for a trumped-up charge, one designed to spare the New Orleans Police Department the public humiliation that it deserves over this incident. Voters would do well to take into account this farce when District Attorney Littrell comes up for reelection." This quote was from Pinkie Duvall, whose "innocent citizen" client, Wayne Bardo, né Bardeaux, had a list of prior arrests as long as the Lake Pontchartrain Causeway.

Pinkie Duvall's involvement in any court case guaranteed extensive media coverage. Everyone in public service, every elected official, wanted to hitch a ride on the bandwagon of free publicity and had used the Bardo trial as a forum for his or her particular platform, whatever that might be. Unsolicited opinions were as lavishly strewn about as colored beads during Mardi Gras.

By contrast, since the night of Kev Stuart's death, Lieutenant Burke Basile had maintained a stubborn, contemptuous silence. During the pretrial hearings, through all the motions filed with the court by both sides, amid the frenzied hype created by the media, nothing quotable had been attributed to the taciturn narcotics officer whose partner and best friend had died from a gunshot wound that night when a drug bust went awry.

Now, as he tried to reenter the courtroom to hear the verdict, in response to the reporter who shoved a microphone into his face and asked if he had anything to say, Burke Basile's succinct reply was, "Yeah. Fuck off."

Captain Patout, recognized by reporters as someone in authority, was detained as he tried to follow Burke into the courtroom. Patout's statements were considerably more diplomatic than those of his subordinate, but he stated unequivocally that Wayne Bardo was responsible for Stuart's death and that justice would be served only if the jury returned a guilty verdict.

Burke was already seated when Patout rejoined him. "This can't be easy for Nanci," he remarked as he sat down.

Kev Stuart's widow was seated in the same row as they, but across the center aisle. She was flanked by her parents. Leaning forward slightly, Burke caught her eye and gave her a nod of encouragement. Her return smile was weak, suggesting no more optimism than he felt.

Patout waved to her in greeting. "On the other hand, she's a trouper."

"Yeah, when her husband's gunned down in cold blood, you can count on Nanci to rise to the occasion."

Patout frowned at Basile's sarcasm. "That was an unnecessary crack. You know what I meant." Burke said nothing. After a moment, with forced casualness, Patout asked, "Will Barbara be here?"

"No."

"I thought she might come to lend you moral support if this doesn't go our way."

Burke didn't wish to expound on why his wife chose not to attend the proceedings. He said simply, "She told me to call her soon as I know."

Vastly different moods emanated from the camps of the opposing sides. Burke shared Patout's estimation that the assistant D.A. had done a poor job of prosecuting the case. After lamely limping through it, he now was seated at his table, bouncing the eraser end of a pencil off a blank legal tablet on which was jotted not a single notation. He was nervously jiggling his left leg, and looking like he'd rather be doing just about anything else, including having a root canal.

While at the defense table, Bardo and Duvall seemed to be sharing a whispered joke. Both were chuckling behind their hands. Burke would be hard pressed to say which he loathed more—the career criminal or his equally criminal attorney.

When Duvall was distracted by an assistant from his office and turned away to scan a sheaf of legal documents, Bardo leaned back in his chair, steepled his fingers beneath his chin, and gazed ceilingward. Burke seriously doubted the son of a bitch was praying.

As though he'd been beckoned by Burke's hard stare, Bardo turned his head. Connecting with Burke's gaze were flinty dark eyes, which he doubted had ever flickered with a twinge of conscience. Lizard-thin lips parted to form a chilling smile.

Then Bardo dropped one eyelid in a wink.

Burke would have come out of his chair and lunged toward Bardo if Patout, who'd witnessed the insolent gesture, hadn't grabbed Burke by the arm and restrained him.

"For chrissake, don't do something stupid." In a tense undertone he said, "Fly off the handle, and you'll be playing right into the hands of those bastards. You'll lend truth to every negative allegation they made about you during this trial. Now if that's what you want, go ahead."

Refusing to honor the reprimand even with a comeback, Burke yanked his arm free of his superior's grasp. Smug grin still in place, Bardo faced forward again. Seconds later, the court was called to order and the judge resumed the bench. In a voice as syrupy as the sap that dripped from summer honeysuckle, he admonished everyone to conduct himself in an orderly "maunnah" when the verdict was handed down, then he asked an aide to summon the jury.

Seven men and five women filed into the jury box. Seven men and five women had voted unanimously that Wayne Bardo was not guilty of the shooting death of Detective Sergeant Kevin Stuart.

It was what Burke Basile had expected, but it was harder to accept than he'd imagined, and he had imagined that it would be impossible.

Despite the judge's instructions, spectators failed to restrain or conceal their reactions. Nanci Stuart uttered a sharp cry, then crumpled. Her parents shielded her from the lights of the video cameras and the rapacious reporters who swarmed her.

The judge thanked the jury and dismissed them; then, as soon as court was loudly and formally adjourned, the ineffectual prosecutor quickly stuffed his blank legal pad into his new-looking attaché case and walked up the center aisle as though it had just been announced that the building was on fire. He avoided making eye contact with Burke and Patout.

Burke mentally captioned the expression on his face: *It's not my fault. You win some, you lose some. No matter what, the paycheck comes on Friday, so get over it.*

"Asshole," Burke muttered.

Predictably, there was jubilation at the defense table and the judge had given up trying to control it. Pinkie Duvall was waxing eloquent into the media microphones. Wayne Bardo was shifting from one Bally loafer to the other, looking complacently bored as he shot his cuffs. His stone-studded cuff links glittered in the TV lights. Burke noted that his olive-complexioned forehead wasn't even damp. The son of a bitch had known he had this rap licked, just as he'd beaten all the others.

Patout, acting as spokesman for the NOPD since the

incident involved his division, was busy fending off reporters and their questions. Burke kept Bardo and Duvall
in his sights as they triumphantly worked their way
through the crowd of reporters toward the exit. They
dodged no microphones or cameras. Indeed, Duvall cultivated and relished publicity, so he basked in the spotlight.
Unlike the prosecutor, they were in no hurry to leave and
in fact loitered to receive the accolades of supporters.

Nor did they avoid making eye contact with Burke
Basile.

On the contrary, each slowed down when he reached
the end of the row where Burke stood, right hand flexing
and releasing at his side. Each made a point of looking
Burke straight in the eye.

Wayne Bardo even went so far as to lean forward and
whisper a hateful, but indefensible fact. "I didn't shoot
that cop, Basile. *You* did."

Chapter Two

Remy?"

She turned and pushed a strand of hair from her forehead with the back of her gloved hand. "Hi. I wasn't expecting you."

Pinkie Duvall strode down the aisle of the greenhouse and took her in his arms, kissing her hard. "I won."

She returned his smile. "So I gathered."

"Another acquittal."

"Congratulations."

"Thank you, but this one was hardly a challenge." His expansive grin belied his humility.

"A less brilliant lawyer would have been challenged."

Pleased by her praise, his grin widened. "I'm going to the office to make a few calls, but when I come back I'll be bringing the party with me. Roman had everyone on standby. In fact, I noticed the catering vans arriving when I came in."

Their butler, Roman, and the entire household staff had

been on alert since the trial began. The parties Pinkie hosted to celebrate his legal victories contributed to his notoriety as much as the flashy diamond ring he wore on the small finger of his right hand, from which he'd derived his nickname.

His post-trial bashes were as much anticipated as the trials themselves and were well documented in the media. Sometimes Remy suspected jurors of voting for an acquittal just so they could experience firsthand one of Pinkie Duvall's famous fetes.

"Is there anything I can do?" Of course there wasn't, and she knew that before asking.

"Just show up looking as gorgeous as always," he told her, sliding his hands down her back and giving her another kiss. After releasing her, he wiped at the smear of dirt on her forehead. "What are you doing out here, anyway? You know I don't like a lot of traffic in here."

"There hasn't been a lot of traffic. Only me. I brought a fern from the house because it didn't look healthy and I thought it could use some TLC. Don't worry, I didn't touch anything I shouldn't."

The greenhouse was Pinkie's domain. Horticulture was his hobby, but he took it seriously and was as much a stickler for neatness and precision in the greenhouse as in his law practice and in every other area of his life.

He took a moment now to survey proudly the rows of plants he had cultivated. Few of his friends, and even fewer of his enemies, knew that among Pinkie Duvall's other passions were his orchids, in which he specialized.

Extreme measures were taken to maintain the delicate balance of the environment inside the greenhouse. There was even a special enclosure within the greenhouse to house the equipment that monitored and controlled the climate. He'd done an exhaustive study of the topic and attended the World Orchid Congress every three years. He knew the precise light, humidity, and temperature conditions in which each particular group flourished. Cattleyas, laelias, cymbidiums, oncidiums—Pinkie nurtured them with the attention of a neonatal ICU nurse, providing each with proper potting, drainage, and aeration. In return, he expected his plants to be exemplary and extraordinary.

As though they didn't want to disappoint their master, they were.

Ordinarily. But now he frowned as he moved toward a grouping of plants labeled *Oncidium varicosum*. The stalks were heavy with blossoms, although they weren't as profuse as some of their neighbors'. "I've been pampering these nonas for weeks. What's the matter with them? This is a very poor showing."

"Maybe they haven't had time to—"

"They've had plenty of time."

"Sometimes when—"

"They're inferior plants. That's all there is to it." Pinkie calmly picked up one of the pots and dropped it to the floor. It broke upon impact with the stone tiles, creating a mess of fern root, shattered crockery, and bent pedicels. Another soon joined the first.

"Pinkie, don't!" Remy crouched down and cradled one of the tender plants in her hand.

"Leave it alone," he said with detachment, even as he sent another of the plants to its doom. He didn't spare a single one. Soon the entire group lay in shambles on the tiles. He stepped on one of the stalks and ground the blossoms beneath his heel. "They were ruining the appearance of the greenhouse."

Remy, upset over the waste, began scooping up the plants. Pinkie said, "Don't bother with that. I'll send one of the gardeners in to clean up."

He left with her promise that she would leave soon and start getting dressed for the party, but she didn't leave immediately. Instead, she stayed to sweep up the debris herself, being careful to put away everything she had used and leaving the greenhouse in pristine condition.

The pavestone path leading to the house meandered through the lawn. Carefully tended flower beds were sheltered by a canopy of moss-draped live oaks. The trees had been there for centuries before the house was built; the original building dated back to the early nineteenth century.

Remy entered through one of the back doors and took the rear stairs, avoiding the kitchen, butler's pantry, and dining room, where she could hear the caterer issuing terse orders to her corps of assistants. By the time Pinkie and his guests began arriving, everything would be ready, and the food and beverage service would be seamless.

Remy barely had allowed herself enough time to dress, but preparations had been made to speed up the process. A maid had already drawn her bath and was there awaiting further instructions. Together they discussed what Remy would wear and, after having laid everything out, the maid left her alone to bathe, which she did quickly, knowing that she would need extra time with her hair and makeup. Pinkie expected her to look her best for his parties.

Fifty minutes later, she was putting on the finishing touches at her vanity table when she heard him enter the master suite. "Is that you?"

"It sure as hell better not be anyone else."

Leaving her dressing room, she joined him in the bedroom and thanked him when he whistled appreciatively. "Can I fix you a drink?"

"Please." He began removing his clothes.

By the time she'd poured him a scotch, he was down to his skin. At fifty-five, Pinkie was impressively fit. He kept his body hard and compact with rigorous daily workouts and deep muscle massages by a masseur he kept on retainer. He was proud of the physique he'd maintained despite his fondness for exceptional wines and New Orleans' notable cuisine, including its famous desserts like bread pudding with whiskey sauce and creamy pralines chock-full of pecans.

Kissing Remy's cheek, he took the highball glass she offered and sipped the expensive scotch. "I brought you a present, and you've exercised enormous restraint by not mentioning it, although I know you saw it."

"I thought you should choose the time to give it to me," she said demurely. "Besides, how was I to know it was for me?"

Chuckling, he handed her the gift-wrapped box.

"What's the occasion?"

"I don't need an occasion to give my beautiful wife a gift."

She untied the black satin bow and carefully removed the gold foil paper. Again Pinkie laughed softly. "What?" she asked.

"Most women tear into packages with unbridled greed."

"I like to savor a gift."

He stroked her cheek. "Because you didn't receive many when you were a little girl."

"Not until you came along."

Inside the gift wrap was a black velvet jewelry box,

and inside that, lying on white satin, was a platinum chain on which was suspended an emerald-cut aquamarine, surrounded by baguette diamonds.

"It's beautiful," Remy whispered.

"It caught my fancy because the stone is the same color as your eyes." Setting his drink on the nightstand, he lifted the pendant from the box and turned her around. "I think you can dispense with this for one night," he said as he unfastened the cross she always wore. He replaced it with the new pendant, then propelled her toward the eighteenth-century cheval glass that had once dominated the Parisian boudoir of a doomed French noblewoman.

Critically, he assessed her reflection from over her shoulder. "Nice, but not yet perfect. This dress looks wrong now. Black would be much better. Something low-cut, so the stone lies directly against your skin."

He unzipped her dress and pushed it off her shoulders. Then he unhooked her brassiere, and pulled it away. With the stone now nestling in her cleavage, Remy averted her eyes from the mirror and crossed her arms over her chest.

Pinkie turned her to face him and pushed her arms aside. As he gazed at her, his eyes turned dark. His breath rushed over her skin. "I knew it," he said in a rough voice. "That's the perfect setting for that stone."

He pulled her toward the bed, ignoring her mild protests. "Pinkie, I'm already dressed."

"That's what bidets are for." He pushed her back onto the pillows, then followed her down.

Always potent, Pinkie's sex drive was never as strong as following a successful trial. This evening he was particularly urgent. It was over in a matter of minutes. Remy still had on her shoes and stockings, but her hair and makeup had suffered his aggressive lovemaking. He rolled off her and reached for his drink, finishing it as he left the bed. Whistling softly, he crossed the bedroom and went into his separate dressing area.

Remy turned onto her side and stacked her hands beneath her cheek. She dreaded beginning the dressing procedure all over again. In fact, given a choice, she would go to sleep where she lay and skip the party altogether. She had started out the day feeling tired, and the lethargy was still weighing her down. However, the last thing she wanted was for Pinkie to notice her lack of energy, which she'd been hiding from him for weeks.

She forced herself to get up. She was filling her tub with another bath when he emerged from his dressing room, freshly showered and shaved, dressed in an impeccably tailored black suit. He looked at her with surprise. "I thought you'd be ready."

She raised her hands helplessly. "It's easier to start over than try and repair. Besides, I don't like using a bidet."

He pulled her close and gave her a teasing kiss. "Maybe I left you in that convent school a semester too long. You developed some awfully prissy habits."

"You don't mind if I'm a little late making an appearance, do you?"

He gave her fanny a pat, then released her. "You'll be ravishing and well worth the wait." At the door, he added, "Remember to wear something sexy, black, and low-cut."

Remy lingered in her second bath. Downstairs, she could hear the musicians tuning their instruments. Before long, the guests would start to arrive. Until the wee hours, they would gorge themselves on rich food and strong drink. There would be music, laughter, dancing, flirtation, and talk, talk, talk.

Just the thought of it made her sigh wearily. Would

anyone notice if the mistress of the house decided to stay in her room and skip the party?

Pinkie would.

To commemorate his courtroom victory, he'd bought her another beautiful piece of jewelry to add to a collection that was embarrassingly considerable. He would be offended to know how much she dreaded attending his celebration or how little value she placed on his gift. But deriving any real joy from his generosity was impossible, because his lovely and expensive gifts were poor substitutes for all that he denied her.

With her head still resting on the rim of her tub, she turned to look toward the dressing table, where the new treasure lay in its satin-lined box. The beauty of this particular stone escaped her. It radiated no warmth and, indeed, looked cold to the touch. Rather than shooting off sparks of fire, the facets glittered with an icy light. It called to mind winter, not summer. It didn't make her feel happy and fulfilled, but hollow and empty.

Silently, Pinkie Duvall's wife began to cry.

Chapter Three

Pinkie made much ado over Remy when she came downstairs. Possessively taking her arm, he announced that the party could officially begin now that she had joined it. He guided her through the crowd, introducing her to the guests she didn't know, including the bedazzled Bardo trial jurors.

Many of the guests were infamous for their association with scandal, crime, or combinations thereof. Some were rumored to belong to the Metropolitan Crime Commission, but since the membership of that by-invitation-only group of blue bloods was secret, no one could be sure. The group's unlimited funds were exceeded only by their unlimited power.

Some of the guests were politicos who wielded self-serving influence over voters. There were movers and shakers among the *nouveaux riches,* while others hailed from established, old-monied families who exercised despotic control over local society. A few had connections with organized crime. All were Pinkie's friends, associates, and former clients. All had come to pay him homage.

Remy endured the fawning of her husband's guests for the same reason they fawned over her—to remain in his good graces. The new pendant was admired and envied, and, to Remy's embarrassment, so was the chest on which it reposed. She was reluctant to be the center of so much attention, and hated being ogled by sly men whose sly wives scrutinized her with barely concealed disdain and jealousy.

Seemingly unaware of their insincerity, Pinkie put her on display like a living trophy. Remy sensed that behind their phony smiles, his friends were inspecting her for the first signs of tarnishing and asking themselves, Who would have thought such an unlikely pairing would have lasted *this* long?

Eventually the conversation turned to the trial and she was asked her opinion of the verdict. "Pinkie gives one hundred percent to every trial," she replied. "I wasn't in the least surprised that his client was acquitted."

"But you must admit, my dear, that this one was easy to predict." The remark was tinged with condescension and came from a society maven whose turkey-wattle neck dripped diamonds.

Pinkie spoke for Remy, countering the woman's comment. "The outcome of a trial is never predictable. This one could just as easily have gone the other way. Anytime you get a policeman on the witness stand, you'd better be on your toes."

"Please, Pinkie," one of the men in the group scoffed. "A policeman's credibility in the courtroom was destroyed forever when Mark Fuhrman testified at the O. J. Simpson trial."

Pinkie shook his head in disagreement. "Granted, Fuhrman did that prosecution more harm than good. But Burke Basile is a different animal altogether. We searched his past for something that would discredit him. His record was impeccable."

"Until the night he shot his own man," one of the guests chortled. He whacked Pinkie on the shoulder. "You really raked him over the coals on the witness stand."

"Too bad the judge refused to let the trial be televised," another guest remarked. "The public would have seen live coverage of cop meltdown."

Another said, "It wouldn't have surprised me if the jury had stopped the trial during Basile's testimony and asked if they couldn't close up shop and go home right then."

"We're talking about a man's death," Remy blurted. She considered their joking and laughter obscene. "Regardless of the outcome of the trial, Mr. Stuart would not have been shot if Bardo hadn't used him as a human shield. Isn't that right?"

The laughter died a sudden death and all eyes turned to her.

"Technically, my dear, that's precisely right," Pinkie replied. "We acknowledged in court that Mr. Bardo was holding the wounded officer against him when he was shot, but I wouldn't go so far as to say that Stuart was being used as a shield. What happened was a tragic accident, but that doesn't warrant sending an innocent man to prison."

Remy had never been invited to attend a trial and see Pinkie in action, but she was well acquainted with the facts of this case because she'd followed the media coverage. Narcotics officers Stuart and Basile had been the first of their unit to arrive at a warehouse where it was suspected that drugs were being manufactured and distributed.

Those inside the warehouse had been alerted that a raid was imminent. When Stuart and Basile approached the building, they were fired upon. Without waiting for backup, Stuart had charged into the warehouse, exchanging gunfire with and killing a man named Toot Jenkins.

Toot Jenkins lay dead; Stuart was badly wounded. His bulletproof vest had deflected potentially fatal shots, but he'd been hit in the thigh, the bullet narrowly missing his femoral artery. Another bullet had shattered his ulna.

"The doctor testified at trial that Stuart was probably in shock, but that he would have recovered from those wounds," Remy said. "They were serious, but not life threatening."

"But your husband destroyed the doctor's credibility."

Pinkie held up a hand as though to say that he didn't need anyone to come to his rescue, particularly since the one challenging him was his own wife. "Put yourself in Mr. Bardo's place, darling," he said. "One man lay dead, another was wounded and bleeding. Mr. Bardo reasoned—correctly—that he had inadvertently walked into a very dangerous situation.

"He thought that perhaps the men outside weren't police officers as they claimed, but were in fact Mr. Jenkins's business rivals *impersonating* officers. Toot Jenkins had been dealing with an Asian gang. These gang members can be extremely clever, you know."

"Officer Stuart was red-haired and freckled. He could hardly be mistaken for an Asian."

One of the guests chuckled and said, "Touché, Pinkie. Too bad for the D.A. Remy wasn't arguing his case."

Pinkie laughed along with the others at the mild put-down, but perhaps only Remy noticed that his laughter was forced. His eyes moved over her. "Remy in a court of law? I hardly think so. Her talents lie elsewhere." As he said that, he ran his fingertip across her low neckline.

Everyone else laughed, but a hot flush of humiliation and anger surged through her. "Excuse me. I haven't eaten anything yet." She turned away from the group.

She had an opinion on what had happened the night Stuart died, but it wouldn't be prudent to air it in front of Pinkie and his friends. They were celebrating his client's acquittal, not his innocence, which weren't necessarily one and the same.

She didn't believe for a moment that Wayne Bardo had been confused when gunfire erupted. He had known exactly what he was doing when he lifted the wounded policeman off the floor of the warehouse and used him as a shield when he went through the dark, open doorway, drawing fire from any other law enforcement agents who might have taken cover outside the building.

Unfortunately, Burke Basile had excellent reflexes, and he was an expert marksman. Believing he was firing at an assailant, he'd gone for a head shot, and his aim had been true. The jury's verdict had laid all the blame for Stuart's death at his feet.

Making good her lie about being hungry, she went into the formal dining room, where, as she had expected, the buffet was a gourmand's delight. Sterling silver chafing dishes were brimming with steaming crawfish étouffée, red beans and rice, and barbecued shrimp steeping in a sauce so fiery that the aroma alone caused her eyes to tear.

Raw oysters on the half shell lay upon trays of ice. A chef was carving slices of ham and roast beef off enormous slabs of meat. There were deviled eggs and deviled crab, along with salads and side dishes and sausages, breads and desserts to suit every palate. The sight and smell of so much rich food didn't pique Remy's appetite, but rather made her slightly queasy.

Glancing around, she saw that Pinkie was now conversing with some of the recently dismissed jurors. They appeared to be enthralled by whatever he was saying, and he loved having an audience, so he wouldn't miss her for a while.

Unnoticed, she slipped through a French door into the relative quiet and seclusion of the backyard. The air was cold enough to make vapor of her breath, but the chill actually felt good against her exposed skin. She moved along the pathway that led to the gazebo. The lacy wrought-iron structure with the onion-shaped dome roof was located in a far corner of the property. It was one of her favorite spots. Whenever she desperately needed seclusion, or a semblance of it, she retreated to the gazebo.

Stepping into the circular structure, she leaned into one of the support posts, practically hugging it while resting her cheek against the cold metal. She was still embarrassed over what Pinkie had insinuated in front of his guests. Comments like that underscored what everyone already believed about her, that she was a pampered trophy wife, with limited intelligence and trivial opinions, whose only purpose in life was to accessorize her flamboyant husband in public and satisfy him in bed.

It also appeared they thought she had no feelings, that their subtle insults bounced off her without leaving a mark. They thought she was happy with the sheltered life she led and had everything her heart desired.

They were wrong.

* * *

Wild horses couldn't have kept him away.

Burke Basile acknowledged that being here was inadvisable. *Inadvisable, my ass,* he thought. It was downright *stupid* that he was lurking in the shadows of a hedge of tall, dense azalea bushes, glaring malevolently at Pinkie Duvall's Garden District mansion.

The house was as fancy and white as a wedding cake, gaudy as hell in Basile's estimation. Golden light from the tall windows spilled onto the lawn, which was as perfectly tailored as a green carpet. Music and laughter wafted from the shimmering rooms.

Burke hugged his elbows to ward off the cool evening air. He hadn't even thought to wear a jacket. Autumn had come and gone. The holidays had passed virtually unnoticed. New Orleans' mild winter was on the wane, but the changing seasons and encroaching spring were the last things on Burke's mind.

Kev Stuart's death eight months ago had consumed him, immobilized him, and anesthetized him to his environment.

Barbara had been the first to notice his preoccupation, but then she would because she lived with him. When his grief evolved into obsession, she had lodged a legitimate complaint. And then another. And another, until she exhausted herself with nagging. Her attitude of late had been indifference.

As Wayne Bardo's trial date approached, it became obvious to everyone within his division that Burke's heart was no longer in his work. He couldn't concentrate on present cases because he was still hung up on the case that had taken him and Kev to that warehouse.

For more than a year prior to that night, they'd been shrinking the size of that particular operation, chipping away at it bit by bit by taking out key dealers one by one. But the really big players had continued to elude them, and were probably laughing their asses off at the bungling and self-defeating efforts of the authorities, local and federal.

To frustrate the division further, their success rate dwindled into nonexistence. Each time a raid was organized, it was foiled. No matter how tight the security, how secret the bust, the criminals were always tipped off beforehand. Drug labs were deserted with the chemicals still cooking. Huge inventories were abandoned moments before the squad arrived for the take-down. These were sacrifices the dealers could afford to make; they simply factored in the loss as a cost of doing business. The next day, they relocated to a new place of operation.

The sons of bitches scattered quicker than roaches when the lights went on. Cops were made to look like fools. After each failed raid, the division was forced back to square one, and the painstaking procedure of rooting out the suppliers started all over again.

Having worked Narcotics for years, Burke knew the drill. He knew to expect setbacks and delays. He knew it took months to build a case. He knew the undercover guys had to cultivate relationships and that these matters took time and patience. He knew the odds against success were overwhelming, and that even when they did succeed, the rewards were few. But knowing all that and accepting it were miles apart.

Patience wasn't one of Burke's virtues. Frankly, he didn't even look upon patience as a virtue. In his opinion, time equated failure. Because for every day it took to do his job right and to collect enough solid evidence for the D.A. to build a case around, kids by the dozens were yielding to the allure of neighborhood dealers. Or a yuppie stoned on a designer drug plowed the hood of his BMW into a van-load of senior citizens on an excursion. Another few crack babies were born. A teenager's heart burst from overuse. Someone else OD'd and died a wretched death.

But because the only alternative was complete surrender, he and the officers in his division kept at it. Painstakingly they built their cases. But each time they thought they were *there,* each time they thought that the next bust would be the mother of all busts, each time they thought they'd catch the bastards red-handed and nail their asses good, something got fucked up.

There was a traitor within the Narcotics Division of the NOPD.

Had to be. There was no other explanation for why the dealers were always a step ahead of them. It had happened too many times to be attributed to coincidence or karma or bad breaks or rotten luck or the devil's handiwork. Someone in the department was working on the side of the bad guys.

God help the bastard when Burke Basile discovered his identity, because it was that cop's betrayal that had turned Nanci Stuart into a widow and had left her two young boys fatherless.

Burke had begged Kev not to go barging in before the van got there with the rest of the squad, equipped with rams, gas masks, and automatic weapons. The two of them had arrived a few minutes ahead of it, the arrest warrants in Basile's pocket. But Kev, frustrated over yet another failed raid, had lost his Irish temper. He had charged the building through the open overhead door. Burke had heard a hail of gunfire, seen the flashes, smelled the gun-powder.

Then screams.

For damn sure, someone was down.

Frantic, Burke had called out to Kev.

Silence.

The longer he waited for Kev to answer, the more anxious he became. "Jesus, Jesus, no, no," he prayed. "Kev, answer me, you goddamn mick!"

Then a man came lurching through the open, black maw of the warehouse door. It was dark; Burke couldn't see why he was walking with such an awkward gait, but his gun was drawn and aimed at Burke. Burke shouted for him to drop the weapon, but he kept coming. Again, Burke shouted for him to drop the weapon and put his hands on his head.

The man fired the pistol twice.

Burke fired only once.

But once was enough. Kev was dead before Bardo dropped his body to the ground.

As Burke raced toward the friend he'd mistakenly killed, he heard Bardo's laugh echoing off the metal walls of the warehouse. He hadn't learned it was Bardo until he was captured by the backup unit arriving in time to see him running through an alley behind the warehouse. There were flecks of Kev's blood and flesh and brains and bone on the face of the repeat offender, but his three-piece Armani suit hadn't even been spattered. He'd walked away clean, literally and figuratively.

The weapon he'd fired was never produced. In those few intervening minutes, Bardo had successfully disposed of it, refuting Basile's claim that Bardo had fired a weapon.

Nor was it ever explained to the court what business

Bardo was conducting in the drug lab with Toot Jenkins. Pinkie Duvall argued that Bardo's presence in the lab was irrelevant to what had transpired, and that it might only serve to prejudice the jury against his client.

No shit, Einstein, Burke remembered thinking. It was *supposed* to prejudice the jury against Bardo.

On that question, the judge had ruled in the defendant's favor. No mystery there. Duvall contributed heavily to the elections of judges. The candidates with the most money backing their campaigns usually won, and then went soft on the lawyers who helped put them on the bench. Duvall had most of them in his pocket.

And that wasn't the only dirty pool Pinkie Duvall played. Wayne Bardo had been in that warehouse that night conducting business for his boss, Pinkie Duvall.

It was an accepted fact throughout the division, although never proved, that Duvall was the primo operator they'd been after for years. He had more connections to drug trafficking than whores did to herpes. Every trail led to him, but ended just short of contact. There was no solid proof against him, but Burke knew the son of a bitch was a player. A big-time player.

Yet, here he was, living it up in his fancy house, celebrating Kevin Stuart's death with a big, blow-out party.

Movement at one of the rear doors interrupted Burke's bitter reflections. He shrank farther back into the foliage so as not to be seen by the woman who made her way along a path to a gazebo.

She was alone. For a time, she leaned into one of the support columns, then she made a slow circuit around the gazebo, trailing her hand along the ivy-covered railing. When she returned to her original spot, she leaned against the support column again, this time placing her back to it.

Burke saw her face for the first time and, although he didn't speak it out loud, he thought, *Wow*.

Her black hair looked iridescent in the cool, bluish light, while that same moonlight made her skin appear as pale and translucent as alabaster. The short black cocktail dress showed off a lot of leg. Her breasts swelled above the scooped neckline.

Burke immediately pegged her as one of the expensive whores who worked the classy hotel bars where conventioneers from out of town were eager to spend huge sums of money for an hour or two of carnality with what they were promised was a genuine, hot-blooded Creole gal.

Burke smiled grimly. He bet this one was higher priced than most. She had a look about her that said *I'm expensive and worth every penny*. She was the kind who could hold out for clients with Duvall's flash and finances.

Not that she would have to hold out. A man with a bankroll like Pinkie Duvall's didn't have to surround himself with ugly women. Maybe this one had been hired only for the night as a party decoration. Or maybe she was the girlfriend of one of the guests. Or she could be a permanent hanger-on who put out routinely for Duvall and his friends in exchange for designer clothes and good drugs.

The keeping of mistresses had been an accepted practice in New Orleans since the city was first settled. Flesh peddling was a major industry in any convention town; New Orleans was certainly no exception. Every cab driver in the city knew the address of Ruby Bouchereaux's place. Her girls were top-notch. Ruby herself was one of the richest women in the state.

But there were also the street hookers who worked the dark corners of the Quarter. They would give blow jobs in an alley for a hit of crack. They were no more selective than the crib girls who had made Storyville one of the most notorious red-light districts in the world. Regardless of the price tag, there was no shortage of work in the Big Easy for a hard-core whore.

But even as the thought crossed his mind, Burke realized that this one didn't look hard-core. Since drug dealing and prostitution often crossed lines with each other, he'd learned a lot from watching these girls. He could size one up and know immediately if she was going to succumb to the life or if she possessed the killer instincts to survive.

He wouldn't put his money on this one to make it. She was classy, all right. But she didn't look rapacious and calculating. She looked... sad.

Still unaware that she was being watched, she relaxed her head against the ornate ironwork and closed her eyes. Then she slid her hands down her body until they met at the center of her lower abdomen.

Burke's mouth went dry. His gut clenched.

The guys working Vice routinely circulated pornographic videos, films, or magazines that had been confiscated for evidence. It wasn't Burke's habit to watch them, but he was as normal as the next guy, and what man, cop or otherwise, could turn away from this scene without waiting to see what was going to happen next.

Actually, nothing did. She didn't remove her clothing. She didn't actually fondle that erogenous zone. She didn't moan or groan or gyrate or breathe heavily through partially opened lips.

Nevertheless, her pose was arresting. Arousing, even.

And apparently he wasn't the only one who thought so.

Burke had been so transfixed by her that he saw the approaching man only seconds before she herself became aware of Wayne Bardo.

Chapter Four

*B*ardo, Basile thought, contempt causing his mustache to curl downward.

He'd mistaken her for a classy chick, when she'd been waiting on Bardo, lord of the lowlives, a career criminal who always beat the rap with the able assistance of Pinkie Duvall.

Did she know that Bardo had killed a prostitute when he was only sixteen? They'd been playing tie-me-up-and-hurt-me when he'd gotten her neck confused with her wrist and strangled her with her own stocking. He'd been tried as a juvenile for involuntary manslaughter and served only a year of his sentence before being placed on probation. If that's the kind of creep this high-ticket whore pandered to, she deserved no better than she got.

Bardo was all over her now, and she was squirming against him. Turning away in disgust, Burke thrashed through the hedge and returned to his Toyota, parked among the Beemers and Jags belonging to Duvall's guests.

* * *

"Taking the evening air?"

Remy's heart jumped when she opened her eyes and saw Wayne Bardo standing poised in the entrance of the gazebo. He had been intentionally stealthy, wanting to startle her. His dark features were heavily shadowed and indiscernible, like a figure in a nightmare.

Instantly she lowered her hands, but she knew he'd seen her pressing them against her body because his grin was even more suggestive than usual. He was blocking her exit. Short of vaulting the railing, there was nowhere for her to run.

Without bothering to conceal her dislike, she asked, "What are you doing out here?"

"I missed you at the party. Came looking for you." He stepped forward. Although it took an act of will not to recoil from him, Remy stood her ground. When he was only inches from her, he gave her an insulting once-over, his eyes lingering on her chest. Lowering his voice to a confidential level, he said, "And here you are."

Bardo was handsome in the way of a silent-movie idol. His black hair was combed straight back from a wide forehead and steep widow's peak. He had a smooth, olive complexion. He was trim and lean, and flashily dressed. But from the day Remy met him, she had mistrusted his suave manner and was put off by the smoldering intensity he affected.

Even before Pinkie was retained to represent him in the Stuart case, they had been associates, so Bardo was a frequent visitor to the house. Remy treated him with cool politeness, but avoided having any close contact. His smoky stares gave her the creeps.

On those rare occasions when she was caught alone with him, usually by his cagey design, he never failed to say something suggestive, his smirk loaded with innuendo. He always acted as though he and she shared a naughty secret.

"Pinkie will be looking for me."

She tried to move past him, but instead of giving way, he boldly splayed his hand over her lower body and stroked her with his fingers. "Why don't you let me take over for you here?"

He had never dared to touch her, and for a moment she was paralyzed by repugnance and fear. She had overheard enough of his boasts to know that he enjoyed all forms of violence, a penchant that logically would extend to his relationships with women. No less importantly, she feared what Pinkie would do if he were to learn that another man had laid a hand on her.

Bardo's boldness tonight was probably due to his delusions of invincibility following his acquittal, and possibly to the alcohol she smelled on his breath. His excitement would only be fanned if she showed any fear. Instead, in a harsh and distinct voice, she told him to remove his hand.

Stretching wider his reptilian grin, he ground his palm more firmly against her. "Or what, Mrs. Duvall?"

Pushing the words between clenched teeth, she said, "If you don't take your hand off me—"

"He was fucking you, wasn't he?"

Unable to stand his touch another second, she shoved his hand away. "Leave me alone." This time when she made to go past him, he roughly took her by the shoulders and backed her against the support column.

"That's why you were late for the party, right? Pinkie was screwing his brains out. If you belonged to me, that's what I'd do. Day and night. All the time, I'd be at you. One way or another."

Lewdly, he rubbed his pelvis against her. "You think Pinkie is good? Until you've had me, you don't know from good, Mrs. Duvall." He stuck out his tongue and wagged it obscenely, then dragged it across her neck. "It's only a matter of time, you know. I'm gonna have you."

She swallowed her nausea and pushed against him with all her strength. She couldn't have physically overpowered him; he allowed her to push him away. When he stepped back, he was laughing at her attempts to stave him off.

"If you come near me again—"

"You'll what? Well, speak up, Mrs. Duvall: What'll you do?"

He placed his hand above her head on the column and leaned into her. His voice was taunting. "You'll what? Tattletale to Pinkie?" He shook his head. "I don't think so. If you told your husband I'd come on to you, he might blame you instead of me. He trusts me, see. And you do have a way of advertising the merchandise."

He reached for her breast, but she slapped his hand aside. "I won't bother telling Pinkie. I'll handle you myself."

"Handle me?" he mocked. "I like the sound of that."

Her voice calm, eyes glittering as coldly as the gem around her neck, she said, "Mr. Bardo, are you under the misconception that you're the only killer-for-hire on my husband's payroll?"

For a fleeting moment, his arrogant grin faltered and his dark eyes lost some of their gleam. Using that momentary lapse in his self-confidence, Remy pushed him aside, and this time successfully escaped him.

She walked quickly and purposefully up the pathway back to the house, hoping that Wayne Bardo couldn't see how unstable her knees were. Because, despite her boast, in a toss-up situation between her and Bardo, she wasn't sure whom Pinkie would believe.

* * *

Barbara was already asleep when Burke got home. He undressed in the dark, not wanting to awaken her. But when he got into bed beside her, she rolled toward him. "Where have you been?"

"Sorry I woke you up."

"It's late, isn't it?"

"A little after midnight."

"Where've you been?" she repeated.

"Working."

"You told me Doug had given you the rest of the week off."

"He did." He wished she would leave it there, but he sensed her unspoken demand for an explanation. "I had to put some closure on it, Barbara. Isn't that the catchphrase these days? Closure?"

She gave a little huff of disapproval. "For God's sake, Burke, Kev Stuart's been dead for months. The verdict is in on Bardo's trial."

"I know all that."

"So get over it," she snapped.

"It's not that easy."

"It's not easy, but you're making it harder than it has to be."

A dozen sharp retorts sprang to mind, but he held them back. He and Barbara had plowed this row countless times. He didn't want to plow it again tonight. Their arguments always left him feeling like he'd been wrung out and hung up to dry. He couldn't take another defeat today.

In a more conciliatory tone, she said, "What happened to Kev was terrible. But the harsh reality is that policemen get killed. The risk goes with the job."

"But it's pretty damn rare that a cop's own partner is the risk."

"It wasn't your fault."

"The jury must've thought so. In any event, they didn't blame Bardo." While subconsciously flexing his right hand, Burke envisioned Duvall's house, lit up like Shangri-La, flowing with liquor, and filled with food and fancy women. "He and Duvall are having a big party tonight in celebration of killing a good cop." He kicked off the covers and sat on the edge of the bed with his hands supporting his head.

Behind him, Barbara also sat up. "How do you know what they're doing?"

"Because I was over there watching them."

Even though his back was to her, Burke imagined her frowning with consternation. "Are you insane? Are you trying to get yourself fired? If Doug Patout is forced to fire you, will that make everything all right? Would losing your job make you happy?"

"It would make *you* happy."

"What's that supposed to mean?"

He shot her a pointed look over his shoulder. "Like you haven't been after me for years to leave the department."

"I don't want you to leave it in disgrace," she said angrily.

He snorted a caustic laugh. "Oh, I see. No wonder you

didn't come to the courthouse during the trial. You didn't want to be associated with the disgrace of the NOPD, which, ironically, is an organization you've bad-mouthed for years."

During the course of their marriage, a recurring argument had been over his work. Barbara wanted him to give up police work in favor of something less demanding and more lucrative. Discussions on the subject started out in a fractious mode and usually deteriorated into shouting matches that resolved nothing, but left in their wake disaffection and resentment on both sides.

Barbara always fell back on the argument that if he loved her, he would take her feelings into account. Burke's argument was that if she loved him, she wouldn't ask that he stop doing what he loved to do. What if he were to insist that she give up teaching? Would that be fair? It was an ongoing debate that neither side could win.

Tonight, Burke was too tired to engage in such a futile argument. He lay back down and stared at the ceiling.

After a long silence, she said contritely, "I didn't mean that the way it sounded. The disgrace part." There was genuine remorse in her voice, but she didn't touch him. He couldn't remember when they'd last touched each other in anything more than a perfunctory way. Not since the night Kev died. Maybe even before then. No, definitely long before then.

He turned his head toward her and said softly, "Forget it, Barbara. It doesn't matter."

Although years of chronic discontent had etched lines into her face, she remained a very attractive woman. Teaching physical education at a public middle school had kept her figure slender and supple. In fact his co-workers often dropped envious, if lewd, comments about her figure. They all thought he was one lucky son of a bitch to have Barbara in his bed every night.

Sadly, Burke couldn't recall the last time they'd done anything in bed except sleep. During the months leading up to the trial, his fractured emotions and heavy workload hadn't left him with the energy even to think about sex. Responding to his moodiness, Barbara hadn't initiated it either.

But now Bardo's trial was over. The issue was history. Kev had died, but Burke hadn't. It was time he began living again. Sex would be rejuvenating. It might make him appreciate that he hadn't been entombed along with Kev.

A woman's softness had healing properties. Her body could provide a man not only physical relief, but surcease from spiritual conflict. Suddenly, Burke yearned for that sense of peace. He was desperate for a few minutes of sweet oblivion. He craved intimacy with something besides suffocating guilt and bitter regret.

Curving his hand around the back of Barbara's neck, he drew her head down for a kiss. She didn't overtly resist, but he felt a tension there, and it wasn't the good kind. He rationalized her lack of enthusiasm. It had been a long time since they'd made love, and he cautioned himself to take his time and not to rush it. Each of them needed a slow and steady warm-up, an easy adjustment, a period of familiarization. Or maybe she was simply being coy. Maybe their lengthy abstinence had damaged her ego and she wanted to be wooed.

He deepened their kiss in the hope of sparking her desire—and his. He fondled her breast through her nightgown, but her nipple didn't respond to his stroking. He slid his knee against the seam of her thighs, but she didn't part them. Between kisses, he whispered her name.

After another few awkward moments, she disengaged herself. "I've got to be at school early tomorrow morning. We begin a volleyball tournament during first period."

He released her. "Yeah, okay."

"I'm sorry, Burke. I—"

"It's cool. Don't apologize."

"I really do have to be up early, but—"

"Barbara, it's no big deal," he said, more sharply than he intended. "Okay? I'm sorry I woke you up at all. Go back to sleep."

"You're sure you're—"

"I'll live, believe me. You don't die from not getting laid."

"Don't blame me, Burke," she lashed out. "You've done this to yourself. You've harbored this grief far too long. It's unnatural. Why is it still eating at you?"

He refused to answer. He couldn't answer.

"All right then," she said. "Good night."

"G'night."

He closed his eyes, but he knew he wouldn't go to sleep, and he didn't. Her rejection had pissed him off, but he wasn't as pissed off as he had a right to be, and that in itself bothered him.

When he was sure she'd fallen asleep, he got up, went into the kitchen, and fixed himself a sandwich. Then he sat down at the table and, holding his head between his hands, stared unseeingly at the sandwich he never ate.

Chapter Five

Double or nothing? She'll stop in front of us and give us an up-close and personal look. Do we have a bet?"

"No." Burke rubbed his temple where a headache had taken root an hour ago and which so far had continued to outpound the drums in the jazz band and defy two analgesic tablets. Maybe he should have taken Patout up on his offer of a paid week off, but he'd rather work than stick around the house where he had too much idle time to think. "I don't want to play anymore, Mac. Give it a rest, okay?"

Mac McCuen flashed his irrepressible grin. "I'm giving you a chance to win back some of the money you've lost to me."

"No thanks."

McCuen would bet on anything from the outcome of the World Series to which cockroach would win the race to the doughnut box. Disappointed by Burke's lack of interest, McCuen turned his attention to the topless dancer who, by God, did stop directly in front of him. Breasts shimmying, she winked at the narcotics cop, who was young and good-looking and who dressed like a *GQ* model even when he wasn't pretending to be a gawking out-of-towner taking in the nightlife of Bourbon Street.

By comparison, Burke looked tired and disheveled and ill-tempered, which was exactly how he felt. He'd been up most of the previous night, alternately wallowing in self-pity and honing his anger over Barbara's rebuff to a razor's edge. They'd mumbled hostile good mornings and goodbyes to each other this morning, and his piss factor had been at a record high all day.

Scowling, Burke watched Mac as he watched the gyrating dancer. What was Mac's real first name, he wondered? All he'd ever heard was Mac. McCuen had made repeated requests to be transferred into Narcotics and Vice before he was actually assigned to it a little more than a year ago. In Burke's opinion the guy was too flashy and effusive to be a good narc.

"I've got a five-dollar bill says her tits are plastic," McCuen said as the dancer strutted away. "What do you say?"

"I say I'd be stupid to lay money on that. How do you propose we determine it? By asking her?"

McCuen couldn't be provoked. Engaging grin still in place, he lifted his glass of club soda and took a sip. "I'm just jacking with you, Basile. Trying to get a smile out of you. Besides, if I went near a chick like that, my old lady would kill me. She's jealous as hell. I've never given her reason to be. I look, sure, but I've never cheated, and we're going on three years together." His record of marital faithfulness seemed to surprise him. "You ever screwed around, Basile?"

"No."

"Not ever?"

"No."

"Jeez, that's impressive. All the women you meet. And you've been married a long time, right? How long?"

"Long enough."

"Happily?"

"Are you a wanna-be marriage counselor, or what?"

"Don't get pissed," Mac said, sounding wounded. "I was only asking."

"Well, don't ask. We're here to work, not to ogle the dancers and not to discuss our private lives. A good way to get killed is to stop thinking about the job and—"

"Our guy just came in," Mac said, interrupting. He was still looking at Burke, still smiling. Maybe he was a better cop than Burke gave him credit for. "He's moving this way. Ass-ugly yellow sport coat."

Burke didn't turn around, but he felt the familiar adrenaline rush he experienced before every arrest.

An undercover cop had been buying from this guy for months. His name was Roland Sachel. He was a nickel-bag dealer, but only quality stuff, and there appeared to be no shortage of his supply. It was believed his drug trade was more for the thrill than for the income it provided. He owned a legitimate business, a handbag factory that produced designer knockoffs that sold to discount stores.

Sachel's turf wasn't the streets, but the trendy clubs. He liked to rub elbows with celebrities, professional jocks, and their groupies. He enjoyed the good life and moved in a circle of acquaintances that availed themselves of it.

Narcotics was operating under the theory that if they could bring Sachel in, even on a petty charge, he might hand over Duvall. The undercover cop working the case had supplied them with information during a secret meeting that morning.

"Sachel is ambitious and greedy. He's all the time grumbling about the 'boss,' and since he's the boss at his factory, I figure he's referring to the boss of his drug business. I think Sachel would hand the boss to us if we offered him a deal."

"Has he given you a name?" Burke had asked.

"Never. Just 'the boss.' "

"But I'd wager my left nut it's Duvall," Mac said.

Patout asked, "You're sure Sachel would go for a deal?"

"He's got a kid who plays football," the undercover cop explained. "Sachel's crazy about him, bragging always. He's going to LSU next year, and naturally Sachel wants to see him play. It would be hard for him to make the games if he's doing time, even for a chicken-shit dealing rap."

Burke hated the whole concept of making deals with people who broke the law. It was a cop-out in the strictest meaning of the term. Sachel would come back to haunt them. As soon as he was free, he'd get right back into business.

But Burke wanted Duvall. He was willing to sacrifice a sleazoid like Sachel in exchange for Duvall.

They had concluded the meeting with the narc telling them that this club was one of Sachel's favorite haunts, which stood to reason since the dancing girls were gorgeous and the crowd upscale. And since one of Pinkie Duvall's dummy corporations owned it.

Out of the corner of his eye, Burke saw Sachel pause to light a cigarette while watching the featured dancer massage her crotch against a vertical brass pole. He seemed totally captivated by her act. After the dancer's simulated orgasm, he applauded enthusiastically, then moved on, wending his way through the smoky room, glad-handing and calling out greetings, seemingly in search of someone, whom he ultimately found occupying a table in a dim corner.

His first customer of the evening was a well-dressed yuppie who was lean to the point of emaciation. His quick motions and darting eyes made him look long overdue for a snort of coke. Sachel signaled a cocktail waitress and ordered a round of drinks.

"Damn!" McCuen exclaimed, coming to his feet. "She was something else, wasn't she? I've never seen anything like that. There's something about a shaved pussy that drives me crazy. I got to go to the can."

He left the table he'd been sharing with Burke and headed for the restroom at the rear of the club. Burke also came to his feet and pretended to review the tab the chesty cocktail waitress had handed him.

When McCuen reached the door that led to the restroom, he dropped a matchbook and bent down to pick it up.

Burke saw the yuppie pass Sachel what appeared to be a folded bill. With a cardsharp's sleight of hand, Sachel slid his palm over the money, while reaching into the pocket of the yellow sport coat with the other.

Burke hurdled several tables and was across the room before the band's next drumbeat. Pistol drawn, he shouted for Sachel to freeze. McCuen was already there, the barrel of his pistol resting on the patch of skin behind the yuppie's right ear.

Two other cops from the division posing as drunken Shriners had been waiting for a signal. They burst through the door leading to the restroom and assisted in the arrest.

As he was read his rights, the anorexic yuppie was trembling and weeping and blubbering that he couldn't go to jail, man, he'd fucking freak out in jail. As Sachel was handcuffed and relieved of the small handgun he was carrying in an ankle holster, he viciously cursed the arresting officers and asked what the fuck they thought they were doing. Obviously they didn't know who they were fucking with. Then he demanded to speak to his lawyer, Pinkie Duvall.

"Ten to one the bastard beats us uptown," McCuen said as he and Burke left the club.

"That's a safe bet, Mac."

* * *

"Lieutenant Basile, it's good to see you again so soon."

"You wouldn't have the pleasure, Duvall, if you didn't have criminal friends coming out your ass," Burke shot back.

As Mac had guessed, the lawyer was already at the department by the time they arrived. A loyal employee of the club must have immediately notified him that Sachel had been caught red-handed in a drug transaction.

"Still carrying a chip on your shoulder over the outcome of Wayne Bardo's trial?"

Burke would have liked nothing better than to ram his fist into Duvall's handsome, smug face and rearrange his expensive smile. Although it was nearing midnight, when one would expect him to look a little rumpled and fresh from bed, the lawyer was wearing a three-piece suit and a stiff white shirt. He smelled of shaving cream. Not a single silver hair was out of place.

Sensing a potential for trouble, Doug Patout stepped

between them. "I'll take Mr. Duvall in to see his client. Burke, they're waiting for you."

He nodded toward an interrogation room where, through the glass, Burke could see the arrested yuppie puffing on a cigarette like it was the last one ever to be rolled.

"What's his name?" Burke asked.

"Raymond..." Patout consulted the label on the file before handing it to Burke. "Hahn."

"Priors?"

"Possession, misdemeanor. He was given probation."

As Burke turned and moved toward the room, Duvall said, "Instead of arresting him, why didn't you just shoot him, Basile?"

Knowing Duvall was trying to goad him into doing something he could file assault charges for, Burke kept moving and didn't stop until he was in the relative safety of the interrogation room, with the door firmly closed and serving as a barrier between him and the lawyer.

He watched Patout escort Duvall into a similar room, where Sachel was waiting. Duvall would advise Sachel to say nothing, which he would. But there would be a time when they had Sachel to themselves. Hopefully they could wear him down and by this time tomorrow night it would be Duvall they were locking behind bars.

Mac McCuen had already grilled Raymond Hahn. So had the cops in the Shriners fezzes. Before taking his turn, Burke poured himself a cup of tepid, rancid coffee, pulled out a chair for himself, and moved it close to the arrested man.

"Talk to me, Ray."

Raising his cuffed hands, the undercover officer took a long drag off his rapidly shrinking cigarette. "It's iffy."

His eyes darted about the room, briefly lighting on all the somber faces staring at him. "He didn't have a lot on him. Right?" he asked, addressing one of the Shriners.

"Couple of ounces. They're stripping down his car, but looks like it's going to be clean."

"So it won't be any big deal," Hahn continued. "Duvall will plead him out of a long sentence. Not much threat, so there's not much for us to bargain with. Can you take these off now?"

One of the officers stepped forward to remove the hand restraints. "Thanks." Raymond Hahn massaged circulation back into his wrists. "Scared me shitless when you charged across that room, gun drawn," he said to Basile.

Hahn still looked edgy. Burke figured he was in reality a cokehead, and that's why he was so convincing to dealers.

"Since this morning, we've talked to several of Sachel's former customers who're doing time," Burke told him. "They're willing to testify against him in exchange for early parole. Those raps, added to delays in trial dates, could keep Sachel out of commission for a long time. Say, long enough for his son to graduate LSU without his seeing a single game except maybe on TV."

"It might work," Hahn said, gnawing on a nub of a fingernail. "But I don't know. He's a turkey with an ego big as Dallas, but he's no fool. And for all his complaining about the boss, I figure he's scared of him. Besides, he could be out on bail while all these delays are taking place."

Patout came in. "Surprise, surprise. Mr. Duvall has advised his client to keep his mouth shut. Hope you've got something solid for us, Ray."

Before the undercover officer could respond, Burke

said, "Know what I'm thinking?" Slowly he came to his feet, rubbing the spot on his temple that was still throbbing. "I'm thinking we were stupid to bust Sachel over a nickel-bag sale. We should have held out until we could raid his factory and warehouse."

"He doesn't do his drug trade out of there," Hahn said. "I've tried to buy from him there. He refused. He makes a point of keeping his two businesses separate."

"A lesson he learned from Duvall," Mac remarked dryly.

"Besides, we've gone that route and got nowhere," Patout reminded Burke. "We've got no probable cause to raid what appears to be a legitimate business. No judge would grant us a warrant."

"All I'm saying is—"

"We blow another bust, we'll never nail Duvall. If it *is* Duvall."

"It's Duvall," Burke said tightly.

"All the more reason for us to keep our asses covered."

"I know that, Doug, but—"

"Littrell won't touch a case unless we've got solid evidence—"

"To back it up," Burke shouted. "I've got it, okay? God knows I've heard the sermon often enough."

"I just don't want another major fuckup," Patout fired back. "This department can't afford one, and neither can you."

Patout's shout reverberated around a sudden and uncomfortable silence. The other officers averted their eyes from the two who were arguing.

"Come on, y'all," Mac mumbled. "Stay cool."

It was well known, especially to Burke, that Patout favored him over other officers in the division. Not only because he considered Burke a good cop, but because the two had started out friends. They'd gone through the academy in the same class. Patout had chosen administration over street work, but rank hadn't made a difference in their relationship.

Until recently. The circumstances surrounding Kev Stuart's death had placed a strain on their friendship. Burke felt it. But he also understood where it was coming from. Doug had to answer to his superiors for the conduct and performance of each of the officers under his command. Being the go-between was difficult at any time, but especially when he was trying to protect the reputation of an officer who was also a friend.

Burke realized that Doug didn't want his career sacrificed to that one dreadful mistake. Doug had gone to the mat for him when his stability and reliability came into question following the incident. Publicly and privately, he'd backed him one hundred percent through the trial. Despite the anger of the moment, Burke understood that Doug didn't want him to lose his head and do something reckless, providing the nervous decision-makers a good reason to seize his badge.

Since the outburst, he and Doug hadn't broken eye contact. His temper now under control, he said, "Give me a shot at Sachel."

"In your present frame of mind, I don't think so," Patout replied evenly. "Tomorrow maybe."

"He'll be sprung by tomorrow."

"We'll drag our feet on the bail hearing."

Burke sighed, rubbed the back of his neck, then gave each of the other officers a sour glance. "Then I'm going home."

"What about me?" Hahn asked.

Patout looked at Burke. "You call it. This is your show."

"Like hell it is," he grumbled. Then, to Hahn, he said, "We'll lock you up for a couple of hours."

"Oh, Jesus. I hate that stinking place."

"Sorry, Ray, but we can't let you be blown or we're really screwed."

* * *

Pinkie stood up and snapped shut his briefcase.

"You're leaving?" Sachel exclaimed in disbelief. "You can't leave. What am I supposed to do?"

"You're supposed to spend the night in jail."

"Jail? *Jail?* When can you get me out of here?"

"I'll start working on a bail hearing first thing in the morning. I'm afraid you're in for the night."

"Well that's just great. Fuckin' great."

"A little cell time will be good for you, Sachel. It might make you think about how stupid you've been."

Sachel stopped his grousing and looked sharply at Pinkie. "What do you mean?"

"I mean you're a fool to get arrested for selling to a customer in the club." Pinkie had kept his temper under control as long as the policemen were in the room, but now that they'd granted him a moment alone with his client, he felt free to vent his rage.

"This guy is no stranger to me," Sachel said in his defense. "He's a regular. I sell to him all the time. I didn't see any harm—"

"Shut up," Pinkie snapped. "Since when did you become a user?"

"Me? I'm not. Never have been."

"But your girlfriend is."

"Girlfriend? What the hell you talking about, Pinkie? I gotta wife. A kid. I don't have a girlfriend."

Pinkie hated for someone to lie to him. He hated it even worse when the lie was so blatantly transparent as to imply that he was too stupid to see through it. "The acrobatic dancer. Frizzy red hair. Skinny ass. Small tits, but nipples the size of saucers. Come on, Sachel, you know the one."

Sachel swallowed hard. Sweat popped out on his forehead and his skin turned a sickly shade of pale that clashed with his bright jacket.

"You've been banging her for three months," Pinkie said softly, almost sympathetically. "She's swapping you sex for dope. *My* dope. You're supplying it to her for free. And that's stealing, Sachel.

"Furthermore, because it's free, she's doing so much of it that about half the time she's too stoned to perform. As you know, she's the club's most popular dancer. Men drink for hours while waiting for her act. They pay well to stay and see her famous back-bend finale, but they go home early if she cancels." Pinkie stepped close enough for Sachel to smell his minty mouthwash. "Your hard-ons are costing me money, Sachel."

Sweat rings had formed around the sleeves of Sachel's yellow coat. "I wouldn't do anything against you, Pinkie. You know that."

"Do I?" He shook his silver head. "I've heard rumors, Sachel. Upsetting talk about you and your ambitions."

Sachel tried to smile, but his rubbery lips didn't quite cooperate. "You can't believe gossip."

"Oh, I believe it. After tonight, I do."

"Wh...whadaya mean?"

"Why would a smart narc like Burke Basile arrest you

over a couple of ounces? He was careless once, but he's too damn clever to screw around with a cheap, smarmy hustler like you unless he wants something from you."

"Like what?"

"Information. Evidence."

"I'd tell them to go fuck themselves."

Ignoring Sachel's self-righteous indignation, Pinkie continued: "They'll let you spend a night or two in jail with the worst of the worst, let you see how really bad incarceration is, and then, when your defenses are down, they'll offer you a deal. My guess is it'll be a dismissal of all the charges against you in exchange for information about your operation."

"I'd never take a deal."

Pinkie smiled. "No, I don't believe you would."

Sachel relaxed. "Hell no. I'd never betray a friend."

"I'm confident you won't." Pinkie's voice was deceptively silky. "Because I'm sure you'd rather do some jail time than have anything bad happen to your boy."

Sachel's bravado collapsed. "My boy? Oh God, Pinkie. No. I—"

Pinkie laid a hand on Sachel's shoulder to calm him and to stop his sputtering. "I look forward to seeing that kid play for the Tigers, and so do a lot of other people." He gently massaged Sachel's rigid deltoid. "Wouldn't it be a shame if he was seriously injured in a freak accident, if his promising career in football was abruptly ended before it even got started?"

Sachel began to cry.

"Wouldn't you hate to see your son fall victim to a tragic accident, Sachel?"

Sobbing like a baby, Sachel nodded.

Chapter Six

Would you like some eggs?"

"No thanks, Pinkie." Bardo glanced over at Roman. "But I'll take a cup of coffee."

After returning home from the police station, Pinkie realized he was ravenous. He'd awakened the butler and asked him to prepare a breakfast. Rather than being disgruntled, Roman was happy to oblige. Having been saved from death row instilled a lot of loyalty.

Roman carried a carafe of fresh coffee and another cup and saucer to the kitchen table. "Will you be needing anything else, Mr. Duvall?"

"No thank you, Roman. Good night."

Over the rim of his china cup, Bardo watched the old gentleman as he went down the hall toward his quarters. "Not too many niggers like that left in the world."

"I wouldn't let him hear you say that," Pinkie remarked as he broke the yolk on one of his sunny-side-ups. "When he caught his wife in bed with another man, Roman took an ax to both of them."

"No shit?" Bardo was obviously impressed. "Hmm."

Pinkie came straight to the point of the unscheduled meeting. "We're going to have trouble with Basile."

"Duh!"

Pinkie's fork halted halfway to his mouth. He looked up at Bardo and was pleased to see that the other man correctly read the meaning behind his dangerous expression.

"Sorry," Bardo mumbled. "Didn't mean to sound like a smart-ass. It's just, you know, I'd already figured we weren't finished with that Boy Scout yet."

"I thought we could take care of him in good time, but I've changed my mind. I don't think we should wait."

"Why? What's up?"

Pinkie told him about Sachel's arrest. "I think it's time we sent Mr. Basile a message."

"Okay."

"A clear message that if he meddles with us, he's begging for trouble. Bad trouble."

"What do you want me to do?"

"Pinkie?" At the sound of Remy's voice, both men looked toward the open doorway where she was standing, wrapped in a robe, her hair tousled, eyes sleepy. "I didn't hear you come in."

"I've been back a while." Pinkie noticed that she had deliberately kept her eyes away from Bardo, and Pinkie couldn't help but wonder why that was. "Mr. Bardo and I had some business to discuss."

"At this hour?"

"Urgent business."

"I see."

"Go back to bed. I'll be there shortly."

Her gaze shifted to Bardo for a millisecond before she looked back at Pinkie. "Don't be long."

Keeping his voice low, he finished his conversation with Bardo. It took no longer than it did for him to finish eating his food. In conclusion he said, "I'd like this taken care of immediately."

"Sure."

"Immediately," Pinkie repeated with emphasis. "The impact should be hard and strong, like a blow to the head. I want this to be a real wake-up call for Basile and everyone in the Narcotics Division."

"I understand."

"As to your fee..."

"The usual?"

Pinkie nodded. "You can leave by the back door, same as you came in."

After Bardo left, Pinkie reset the alarm system, then went upstairs. Remy was in bed, but she was still awake. "What was that about?"

"I told you. Business." He began undressing, but his eyes remained on her. "Are you feeling well, Remy?"

He could tell the question made her uneasy. "Of course. Yes. Why wouldn't I be?"

"You haven't been yourself lately."

She gave him an unconvincing smile. "You know I get a little blue every winter. I'm ready for spring. It seems a long way off."

"You're lying." In their natural state, other men might feel vulnerable and less imposing. Not Pinkie. Nakedness didn't inhibit him. Placing his hands on his hips, he gave his wife a stern stare. "You've been dragging your ass around for weeks."

"I told you, it's—"

"The time of year? Bullshit. Where'd these newfangled ideas of yours come from?"

"What newfangled ideas?"

"The ones you so outspokenly shared with our party guests last night." Dropping his voice almost to a whisper, he said, "You came awfully close to siding with the opposition, Remy."

"That's ridiculous. You know whose side I'm on."

"Do I?"

"You should."

She met his gaze levelly. He could see no equivocation in her eyes, but he wasn't ready to let the matter drop just yet. Her position in his life did not include the voicing of opinions on anything of importance. "I also didn't like the fact that you disappeared during my party."

"I didn't disappear. I developed a headache and had to come upstairs and lie down."

"A headache?" he repeated skeptically. "You've never had headaches before. You've never been this lethargic before either. Are you ill? Maybe I should schedule a doctor's appointment for you."

"No!"

The force of her answer surprised even her. She mollified it with a light little laugh. "It's nothing, Pinkie. I'm fine. Just a little moody, that's all."

He sat down on the bed close to her and stroked her neck. "The one thing I won't tolerate, Remy, is someone lying to me." His fingers ceased stroking her. "Tell me, now, what the hell is wrong."

"All right," she exclaimed angrily. Throwing back the covers, she left the bed, then turned back to confront him. "It's that *man*."

He came to his feet. "What man?"

"Wayne Bardo."

"What about him?"

"He makes my skin crawl." She hugged her elbows and rubbed her bare arms. "I loathe him. I can't stand to be in the same room with him."

"Why not? Has he done something, said something to you?"

"No, no. Nothing like that." Obviously vexed, she expelled a deep breath and pushed her fingers through her hair. "It's just a feeling I get. He gives off vibes, evil vibes. I was hoping that after his trial he wouldn't be hanging around so much. Tonight, I find him at our kitchen table."

Pinkie was on the verge of laughing with relief. Most women thought Wayne Bardo was attractive—until they got to know him better. It pleased him that Bardo's Mediterranean good looks held no appeal for his young, beautiful wife. Her studious avoidance of him was due to repugnance, not attraction.

Hiding his relief, he said, "Bardo does odd jobs for me. He's working off part of his legal fee."

"Well, from now on please conduct your business with him somewhere other than the house."

"Why do you dislike him so much?"

"Isn't it clear? He frightens me."

Pinkie did laugh then as he pulled her into his embrace. "He frightens a lot of people. That's why he's so useful to me."

"You use him to frighten people?"

Above her head, he frowned. She rarely asked him even the most harmless questions about his business dealings. Lately she had expressed more than a passing interest, and that could be dangerous. More than a few of his clients had been double-crossed by spiteful wives or girlfriends who knew too much. "Why are you so curious about my association with Bardo?"

"I'm not, so long as he doesn't come to the house. I don't want him here."

"All right. If Bardo offends you, I'll try and keep you separated."

"Thank you."

"Now that's settled, I want your promise that you'll stop this irritating moping."

"I'll try."

He placed his thumb beneath her chin and tilted her head back. "Do." He spoke softly, but he didn't need to raise his voice for her to catch his drift. "Have I given you any reason to be discontent, Remy?" She shook her head. "Good." He ran his thumb across her lips. "I'm glad to hear that. Because I want you to be happy. I'd hate for us to have another situation like Galveston."

"That was a long time ago."

"But not so long ago that we've forgotten it."

"No, I haven't forgotten it."

"So you're happy?"

"Of course."

He reached for her hand and guided it to his lap. "Show me."

Later, just as he was drifting off to sleep, she said, "A visit to Flarra will cheer me up. I'll go see her tomorrow."

"Good idea. I'll send Errol to drive you."

"Don't bother. I can drive myself."

Pinkie thought about it a moment. His uneasiness hadn't been entirely allayed either by their conversation or their lovemaking. She'd given him a plausible explanation for her recent melancholia, but he suspected there was more to it than her dislike for Bardo.

Doubts could cripple the thinking of a reasonable man. Mistrust and jealousy were weakening and destructive. On the other hand, Pinkie preferred erring on the side of caution to being a fool. Especially when dealing with a woman.

"Errol will drive you."

* * *

"Say, you're sure you're okay with this?"

The woman formed a pouty frown and toyed with the buttons of his shirt. "Of course I'm okay with it. Would I have invited you to my place if I weren't?"

"But we only met an hour ago."

"Doesn't matter. It didn't take me even that long to know I wanted you tonight."

He grinned. "Then what are we waiting for?"

Groping each other along the way, they stumbled up two flights of stairs. The old house had been converted into six apartments, two on each of the three floors. Her unit was small, but nice. The windows in the bedroom overlooked the private courtyard in the rear.

It was in front of these windows that she did a clumsy striptease for him. "See anything you like?"

"Nice," he murmured, reaching for her. "Very nice."

She had absolutely no sexual inhibitions. Either that, or she was too high to care what he did to her. But after a while her appetite was satisfied, and she became tired and cantankerous.

"I'm sleepy now."

"So go to sleep," he said. "It won't bother me."

"I can't sleep with you doing *that*."

"Sure you can."

That earned a giggle from her. "You're sick, you know that?"

"So it's been said."

"You sure you wore a rubber?"

"I said I did, didn't I?"

"Yeah, but I couldn't see. Come on now, really, stop. I'm tired. We'll save it for another time, okay?"

"The night is young, sweetheart."

"Young, hell," she groaned. "It'll soon be time to get up."

"You're just coming down off your high. What you need is a little pick-me-up."

"I can't do any more drugs tonight. I've got to be at work in a few hours. Let's give it a rest for tonight and— hey! That hurt."

"It did?"

"Yes. Now cut it out. I'm not into that shit. Ow! I mean it, goddamn it! Stop that!"

"Relax, honey. The best is yet to come. No pun intended."

* * *

Raymond Hahn drove himself home from city hall, one eye on the rearview mirror all the way. He was good at his job, mainly because he was scrupulously careful. His cover was a job in a three-man accounting office, but his paycheck originated at the NOPD. Ostensibly calling on clients, he moved facilely through neighborhoods, meeting people and setting up networks of drug users and dealers.

It was dangerous work. He could spend months winning the confidence of a paranoid dealer, constantly putting his ass on the line, and then have all his efforts wasted. A prime example was the snafu at the warehouse where Kev Stuart had been killed.

It didn't take a rocket scientist to deduce that somebody in the division was tipping the dealers of impending raids. But that was an inner-office problem. His problem was to stay alive by seeing that his cover wasn't blown.

He'd been working undercover for three years, which may have been too long. He was tired of continually having to look over his shoulder, tired of being suspicious of everyone, tired of living a double life.

Lately, he'd been toying with the idea of relocating and going into another line of work. There was one major drawback: No other occupation would give him easy access to drugs. That was a bonus to his present job, and no small consideration whenever he thought of leaving it.

After making sure that nobody had followed him home, he unlocked the door of his apartment and slipped inside, then secured all the dead bolts. Every time it was necessary for him to be arrested and jailed, it gave him the shakes. He played his part so well that sometimes even he was fooled into thinking that the make-believe was real.

He and Burke Basile were on the same team. Nevertheless, the guy scared the hell out of him. It was frightening to think what Basile would do if he learned about his habit. He wouldn't want to get on Basile's bad side. The guy was all business. So straight-as-an-arrow, in fact, that he hadn't endeared himself to other cops of the NOPD.

Taking graft was the accepted modus operandi. It was the rule, not the exception. Some cops figured that in a crime-crazy society, it made sense to look away from petty malfeasances, and to get tough only on crimes that were a threat to human life.

Burke Basile saw it differently. A law was a law. It was either right or wrong, legal or illegal, period. He didn't preach. He didn't have to. His silent reproach was effective enough to make cops on the take mistrustful of him. Now that Kev Stuart was dead, the only other officer Basile could regard as a friend and drinking buddy was Doug Patout. And being the boss's friend didn't win him any favors among his colleagues, either.

Not that Basile seemed to mind being out of the fraternal loop. In that respect, Hahn thought, he and Basile were somewhat alike. He worked alone, and he liked it that way, just as he suspected Basile did. He doubted Basile ever cried over his unpopularity.

Hahn undressed in the dark. His girlfriend got pissed if he woke her up after she'd fallen asleep. She resented his staying out late and leaving her alone when he went carousing. She thought he was an accountant and didn't understand his penchant for nightclubbing even on weeknights.

Their schedules often clashed, but, actually, the less they saw of each other, the better they got along. Their relationship was based almost strictly on convenience. When she invited him to move in with her, it was more convenient for him to accept than to come up with a reason to decline. Besides, they liked the same drugs. They bonded best when they got stoned together. The rest of the time, they were more or less compatible, but not what you could call intimate except when they had sex.

He knew his main appeal was the drugs he brought home to her, but that didn't bother him. He even suspected her of cheating on him, but since he had to be out nearly every night, he couldn't really blame her. He just hoped she didn't contract a sexually transmitted disease. The public-service announcements on TV warned against relationships such as theirs, but, hell, his odds for getting whacked by a drug dealer he had set up were far greater than his dying of AIDS.

He slid in beside her and was grateful that she didn't stir. He didn't want a scene. Not after everything he'd been through tonight, including a couple hours in jail. What a freaking zoo!

He'd been locked in a cell with two redneck brothers covered in homemade tattoos, who'd opened up a third brother's scalp with a can opener during a family dispute. Their other cell mate was a transvestite who cowered in the corner and wept in fear of the abusive rednecks. He'd cried so hard over their insults that his fake eyelashes had come unglued, and that had brought on another crying jag, which had prompted more shouted invectives.

Raymond never had been a good sleeper, but tonight he found it particularly difficult to relax and shut off his skittering thoughts. After a while, he sat up, thinking that a joint might help relax him.

He reached across his sleeping girlfriend and switched on the nightstand lamp.

What he saw barely registered before he sensed movement behind him.

Raymond Hahn died with a silent scream on his lips.

Chapter Seven

Burke knew something was up the moment he reported for work. The men lurking around the coffee machine mumbled good mornings as he approached, but no one made eye contact, and by the time he had poured his coffee, they had scattered.

At his desk, he shrugged off his jacket but hadn't even had time to hang it on the coatrack when Patout opened the door to his office and called him in. Burke left his jacket on his desk but carried his coffee with him. "What's going on?"

Patout closed the door to give them privacy. "Sit down."

"I don't want to sit down. I want to know what the hell's going on."

"Raymond Hahn is dead."

Burke sat down.

"He and his girlfriend were found in their bed this morning."

Burke took a sip of coffee. "Am I to assume he didn't die of accidental or natural causes?"

"They were murdered."

Patout went on to explain that the woman worked as a teller at a branch bank. She clocked in by six-thirty in order to open up the drive-through window at seven. When she didn't show up and hadn't called in sick, a co-worker went to check, expecting to find her hungover or stoned. She'd failed one random drug test, but had been given another chance on the promise she would get counseling for substance abuse. The co-worker found the apartment door unlocked. She went inside.

"It was... a mess."

"Don't spare me the details," Burke said irritably. "I'm not going to faint."

"Well, the woman from the bank did. The girl sustained several stab wounds. Initial coroner's report is that only one of those wounds could have been fatal. The killer took his time and enjoyed killing her. It appears she'd also been sodomized, but whether before or after she died hasn't yet been established. Hahn was luckier, if you could call it that. He had only one wound in the side of his neck, but it was well placed. The killer knew where to stick him for a quick and silent kill."

Burke left his chair, took his coffee with him to the third-story window, and stared out of it while sipping coffee from his personal mug, which was decorated with multicolored sea horses. Barbara had bought the souvenir mug on a rare vacation to Florida. He didn't remember how long ago that had been. Eons. At least it seemed that long ago. He could no longer imagine doing something as carefree as going on a trip to the beach and shopping for silly souvenirs. Any frivolity in his life had died the night he shot and killed Kev Stuart.

"Clues?"

"The crime unit is on it, but so far it looks clean. Something might turn up in autopsy. The girl's rectum and vagina were bruised and abraded. But there wasn't visible semen on her."

The lab was wasting their time and manpower. There wouldn't be any evidence. Bardo liked knives, and this sounded like his kind of hit. His favorite pastime was rough sex, but even in the heat of his sordid passion, he would have been careful to use a condom. He was too smart to leave a DNA fingerprint behind, although they might get lucky and find a tissue or hair sample.

Burke had sent Hahn to jail last night. Had the undercover officer been wallowing in the drunk tank while his girlfriend was being raped and killed by Bardo? Had he come home and caught them together?

"Signs of struggle?"

"None," Patout replied. "I can't figure how he managed to kill both of them. Did he ice Hahn, then terrorize the girl before killing her?"

"Maybe. Or..." Burke thought about it. "Or he did the girl first, then waited in the apartment until Hahn got home."

Patout frowned doubtfully. "Hahn was undressed and in bed when he got hit."

"Hahn was late coming in. The killer hid until poor Ray was in bed. He probably got into bed without turning on the light. I do it all the time when I don't want to wake up Barbara. Hahn didn't see that his girlfriend was dead. He didn't see the blood or realize that anything was wrong." Burke gripped the coffee mug tighter. "That sounds like him."

"Who?"

"Bardo. Bardo would have thought it was funny that his victim locked him in instead of out."

"Why would you think it was Bardo?"

"We arrested Hahn and Sachel. Duvall shows up here in the middle of the night. We know that Sachel is on Duvall's secret payroll. Bardo is his hired gun. Our undercover man gets hit. Figure it out. It can't be a coincidence."

"Of course it can!" Patout exclaimed. Burke came around to face him, but Patout continued before he could say anything. "You know as well as I do that Hahn was a junkie. It appears the woman was too. The hit could have been over a drug deal gone south. It could have been a love triangle. It could have been—"

"That Duvall knew Ray was ours and wanted to put him out of commission, while at the same time teaching us a sound lesson."

"All right, it could," Patout conceded, coming to his feet. "But I don't want you to take this personally. Like it only happened to you. The whole division will feel shitty about it. We're a team, Burke. We've got to work together. We can't let a few setbacks send us spinning out of control. We must continue to work methodically."

This managerial bullshit speech was uncharacteristic of Doug. He usually reserved the textbook pep talks for when he addressed the entire group. In private, he and Burke were more candid with each other.

"What else?" Burke asked.

"What do you mean?"

"I mean there's more, isn't there? What is it you're dreading to tell me?"

Patout rubbed the back of his neck. He was a slender man, with a high, smooth forehead and a receding hairline. This morning, he seemed years older than he was. "You're too smart for your own good."

"Yeah, I get that all the time," Burke said impatiently. "What?"

"Sachel declined our deal."

"Give me fifteen minutes with him."

"It won't do any good, Burke. He turned it down before we even laid out the terms. He left absolutely no room for negotiation."

"He's going to risk a trial?"

"No, he's going to enter a guilty plea. To all charges."

"Son of a bitch," Burke swore. "Duvall got to him."

"That would be my guess, yeah."

"Jesus, is the guy immortal?" He barked a caustic laugh. "He beats us at every turn."

"Duvall doesn't play fair. We abide by the rules."

Burke gnawed the inside of his jaw, muttering, "Maybe it's time we didn't."

"Come again?"

"Nothing. Say, Doug, I gotta get out of here."

"Burke—"

"Catch you later."

He slammed the door behind him, grabbed his jacket as he sailed past his desk, and headed for the exit, nearly colliding with Mac McCuen. "Hey, Basile. I've been looking everywhere for you. We need to talk."

"Not now." He wasn't in the mood for McCuen. Right now he couldn't stomach McCuen's unflagging optimism and irritating, inexhaustible energy. Without even slowing down, he said, "Later, Mac."

* * *

"Hello, Burke. Come in." Nanci Stuart motioned him inside her suburban house.

After hearing about Hahn and Sachel, it was masochistic to come here today. But after driving around for hours, stewing and cursing, Burke didn't know what else to do with himself. He was supposed to be taking the week off anyway, so why not piss away the whole day?

The Stuarts' house was a brick structure with painted wood trim. The lawn wasn't as well kept as it had been when Kev was alive. He had enjoyed yard work and boasted that his Saint Augustine was the greenest grass on the block. Burke noticed that a shutter on one of the front windows was sagging. The entry-hall rug needed shampooing, and one of the lightbulbs in the vaulted ceiling had burned out. One day soon, he needed to spend a day off helping Nanci with some maintenance and repairs.

"Come on back into the kitchen," she said over her shoulder as she led him down the central hall. "I've started supper. We're eating early. It's open house at school tonight. Would you like something to drink?"

"Coffee, if you've got it."

"Do you mind instant?"

He did, but he shook his head. The kitchen was cluttered and homey. Hanging in a prominent spot was a calendar marking car-pool days, dental appointments, and the open house at school tonight. Reminder notes and class pictures of the two boys were stuck to the refrigerator with magnets shaped like ketchup bottles and mustard jars. A cookie jar in the shape of a teddy bear smiled at him from the countertop.

Following his gaze to it, Nanci offered him some. "They're store bought. I don't bake much anymore."

"No thanks," he said. "The coffee's fine."

She returned to her mixing bowl where she was crumbling saltine crackers into ground beef. Chopped green peppers and onion were waiting to be added along with a can of tomato sauce. "Meat loaf?" he asked.

"How'd you know?"

"My mom made it often enough."

"Your mom?" She looked at him with puzzlement. "You know, Burke, I think that's the first time I've ever heard you mention your family. In all the years I've known you."

He shrugged. "I worried about reprisals, you know, that sort of thing. So I purposefully don't talk much about them. Anyway, it's not much of a family anymore. My dad worked for the railroad. When I was in third grade, he got crushed between an engine and a freight car. So my mom was a working single parent before it came into vogue. She was a telephone company employee until she died of cancer a few years ago.

"Now it's just me and my kid brother. He lives in Shreveport. Has a wife, a couple of kids." He smiled wryly. "Mom must've known three dozen ways to stretch a pound of ground meat."

"I can identify."

"How are the boys?"

"Fine."

He sipped the coffee, which tasted worse than expected. "Are they doing okay at school?"

"The last report cards were good."

"Besides grades."

Knowing that he was referring to their psychological well-being, she hesitated. "They're okay. Considering."

"Well. That's good." He toyed with the salt and pepper shakers on the table, placing them side by side, separating them, pushing them back together. "It's been warm lately."

"I'd like to think that means the end of winter. But we still might get a freeze."

"Yeah. As late as March."

Lately, this lame attempt at conversation seemed the best they could do. They avoided talking about anything substantive or important. Which was strange since the roughest times were behind them.

He'd been the one to bring her the news of Kev's death. Doug Patout had volunteered to carry out the unpleasant task, but Burke had insisted that the responsibility fell to him. He'd been there to support Nanci when she collapsed after hearing the news, and he'd remained a fixture at her side throughout the funeral procedure.

In the ensuing weeks and months, he had helped her sort through insurance papers, file for the inadequate pension she received from the NOPD, set up her own credit and bank accounts, and make other necessary budgetary adjustments.

Responding to a phone call from her, he'd come over the day she cleared out Kev's closet. She offered Burke some of his better clothes, and he'd accepted them. Then he'd dropped them into a Goodwill receptacle on his way home. He couldn't have worn them.

In the fall, he'd checked the furnace and changed the filters for her. At Christmas, he'd set up the tree and helped her decorate it. Kev had been dead almost a year, but Burke still felt compelled to come by every couple of weeks to lend his widow whatever assistance she might need.

Trouble was, it was becoming harder to find things to talk about. With the passage of time, their conversations had become more strained, not less so. Burke avoided talking about anything relating to the police department and the personnel Nanci knew. Since his work was the most vital component of his life, he found himself searching for something besides the weather and the boys' health to fill the increasing stretches of silence.

She always received him graciously, but she had changed, subtly but undeniably. She was more reserved now than she'd been when Kev was alive. They'd shared some rollicking laughs. She could tease and put you down as well as one of the guys. Burke supposed it was easy for a woman to joke with her husband's friend when her husband was there, laughing along with her. It wasn't so easy when he was dead.

They had spent a lot of time speculating on the outcome of Bardo's trial. Now that it was over, now that the final chapter on that dark episode in their lives had been written, what was there for them to talk about?

"Uh…"

"Burke…"

She must have been as uncomfortably aware of the lagging conversation as he, because they began speaking at the same time. He indicated for her to go ahead. "No, you," she said.

They were saved further awkwardness by the boys' arrival. Having seen Burke's car parked out front, they raced into the house, filling it with welcome racket and the unique smell of sweaty little boys. They dropped their jackets and backpacks and crowded Burke, jostling each other to get near him.

After a quick snack, he took them into the backyard. This was their routine. Following his visit with Nanci, he did something with David and Peter alone. The boys got to choose the activity. Today they decided on batting practice.

"Like this, Burke?" the younger, Peter, asked.

His stance was atrocious, but Burke replied, "Just like that. You're getting the hang of it, slugger. Choke up on your bat just a little. Now let's see what you can do."

He pitched a ball that hit the bat, not the other way around. Peter whooped and ran their makeshift bases. At home plate, Burke gave him a high five and a swat on the butt.

"We're going out for Little League. Maybe you could come to one of our games, Burke," David ventured hopefully.

"Just one? I planned on getting a season ticket." The hair he teasingly ruffled was the same coppery red their father's had been. And because the smiles they beamed up at him were replicas of Kev's, a lump formed in his throat. He might have made a fool of himself if Nanci hadn't come to the back door just then and called the boys in to wash up.

"Dinner in fifteen minutes," she told them.

"See ya, Burke."

"See ya, Burke," Peter said, parroting his older brother as they traipsed toward the rear of the house.

"You're great with them," Nanci observed.

"It's easy to be great with somebody else's kids. I understand it's tougher with your own."

"Why didn't you and Barbara have children?"

"I don't know. Just never got around to it. There always seemed to be a good reason to postpone them. First, a shortage of money."

"And then?"

"A shortage of money." He meant it as a joke, but it fell flat.

"I don't know what I would have done without my sons. Kevin is still alive in them."

Solemnly, he nodded with understanding. Then, realizing that his right hand was flexing, he stilled it and said quickly, "I'd better shove off. I wouldn't want to make the Future of Baseball late for open house."

"You're welcome to stay for supper."

It was an obligatory invitation. She always offered, and he always declined. "No thanks. Barbara will be looking for me."

"Tell her I said hi."

"Will do."

"Burke." She glanced down the hallway toward the bathroom, where the boys could be heard arguing. Then, abruptly bringing her focus back to him, she said, "I don't want you to come back."

He didn't think he'd heard her right. "What?" Even after she repeated it, he was dumbfounded.

She drew a deep breath and pulled herself up straighter. Obviously she had given whatever she was about to say a great deal of thought. As much as she had dreaded saying it, she had made up her mind to do so now and was bracing herself for it.

"I can't be around you, can't even look at you, without thinking of Kev. Every time I see you, it's like going through the whole ordeal again. Each time you call or visit, I cry for days afterward. I get angry, feel sorry for myself. It's a setback that I barely recover from before I hear from you and have to go through it again."

She rolled her lips inward and paused to regroup emotionally. "I'm trying to build a life without Kev. I tell myself that he's lost to me. Forever. And that I can live with knowing that. Just when I'm almost convinced, you show up and..." Tears overflowed her eyes. She dug into her pocket for a tissue. "See what I mean?"

"Yeah, I see what you mean." He didn't even try to disguise the bitterness in his voice. "It hurts you to serve coffee to the man who made you a widow."

"I didn't say that."

"You didn't have to." He brushed past her and went through the door.

"Burke, please understand," she called after him. "Please."

He stopped on the walk and turned back. But when he saw her tortured expression, his anger evaporated. How could he be mad? She hadn't made this decision to hurt him. This wasn't about him; it was about her. It was for her self-preservation that she'd asked him not to return.

"Hell of it is, Nanci, I do understand. In your situation, I'd feel exactly the same way."

"You know what you've meant to me and to the boys. We know what you meant to Kev. But I—"

He held up both hands. "Don't lay a guilt trip on yourself over this. Okay? You're right. It'll be best this way."

She sniffed and blotted her nose with the tissue. "Thanks for understanding, Burke."

"Tell the boys..." He tried to think of something she could tell them to explain why he, like their father, was abruptly disappearing from their lives.

A sob shuddered up through her chest. "I'll handle it. They're amazingly resilient." She gave him a watery smile. "After all you've done for us, I hate the thought of hurting you. If it makes you feel any better, this is very difficult for me. I feel like I'm severing my own right arm in order to save my life. You've been a good friend."

"I still am. Always."

Softly she said, "I can't move away from it until I let it go, Burke."

"I understand."

"The same should go for you. When are *you* going to let it go?"

Several seconds ticked by. Then he said, "If you ever need anything, you know where to find me."

Chapter Eight

Barbara's car was in the driveway when he reached home. She would be pleased that, for once, he was home on time, even early. Guiltily, he had hoped that the volleyball tournament or some other activity would have kept her at school for a while. He needed some down time, some solitude.

The day had begun with Patout's double-barreled bad news. Then Nanci Stuart told him, essentially, to get lost and stay that way. Today, even a mild argument with Barbara would be too much to handle. A minor disagreement, one cross word, might upset some delicate balance within him. He feared that on his present emotional yardstick, there would be only a hair's breadth between irritation and outrage.

He entered through the back door, calling her name. She wasn't in the kitchen or in the forward rooms of the house, so he went upstairs. When he reached the landing, he heard the TV set in the bedroom. Water was running in the shower.

But when he went into the bedroom, he saw that he was only half correct. The shower was running. But the voices he'd heard weren't coming from the television set.

Crossing the bedroom, he went through the connecting door into the bathroom. It was foggy with steam. Burke yanked open the glass door of the shower.

Barbara was against the tile wall, eyes closed, mouth open, legs wrapped around the furiously pumping hips of the short, stocky boys' football coach from the middle school.

With a surge of feral fury, Burke grabbed the guy with both hands and jerked him from the shower stall. The coach lost his footing on the slippery, soapy tile and would have fallen had Burke not been holding him by the neck.

Barbara uttered a sharp scream, then clamped her hands over her mouth as she watched her husband slam her lover against the bathroom wall several times before starting to pummel him with his fists. Working like pistons, they hammered into the man's flesh, making slapping sounds against his wet skin.

He was younger than Burke by fifteen years, well muscled and perfectly conditioned, but Burke had the element of surprise on his side. Even so, he didn't fight with any particular stratagem. He was maddened by a need to cause pain, to spread some of the suffering around, to make this rutting son of a bitch hurt as much as he was hurting. There was satisfaction in the crunch of cartilage and the splitting of skin and the giving of soft tissue against his ramming fists.

He had reduced the guy to a quivering, blubbering, begging mass before delivering the coup de grâce. He kneed him in the balls with the impetus of a locomotive, which caused the coach to scream in agony and slide down the wall to the floor, where he lay cradling his injured manhood between his hands and weeping. His battered face streamed mucus and blood and tears.

Breathing hard, Burke bent over the sink. After washing his hands and sluicing his face with cold water, he came upright and saw Barbara's reflection in the foggy mirror over the basin. She had put on a robe, exhibiting some semblance of shame, but she hadn't shown any concern for her wounded lover, which surprised Burke. Didn't she care for him at all? Maybe not. Maybe she'd taken a lover just to get his attention. And maybe he was flattering himself.

"Feel better now?" she asked, heavy on the sarcasm.

"No," Burke replied honestly as he dried his face with a hand towel. "Not much."

"Are you going to work me over, too?"

He turned away from the sink and looked at her, wondering when she had turned so snide and unapproachable. Had she always been that way? Or had years of dissatisfaction and unhappiness made her into the bitter woman confronting him now? Either way, he hardly recognized her as the bride he'd started a life with. He didn't know this woman at all, and he saw nothing there that he cared to know.

"I'm not even going to honor that question with an answer."

"You've abused me, Burke. Just not with your fists."

"Whatever." He stepped around her and went into the bedroom, where he reached beneath the bed for his suitcase, into which he began emptying his bureau drawers.

"What are you doing?"

"Isn't it obvious?"

"Don't think for one minute that you can file for divorce on the grounds of adultery. Our problems began long before—"

"Before you started wall-banging other men in our shower?"

"Yes!" she spat. "And he isn't the first."

"I'm not interested." After cramming a few items from the closet into the suitcase, he latched it.

"Where are you going?"

"I haven't the faintest."

"But I know where I can find you, don't I?"

"Right," he replied, letting it go at that. He'd be damned before defending his work ethic to his cheating wife. "As for 'filing,' be my guest, Barbara. I won't contest any charges you lay on me. Say I'm a sorry provider, a brute, say I'm queer. I couldn't care less."

He glanced around to see if there was anything he'd overlooked, and it saddened him to realize how easily and quickly he had packed. They hadn't *lived* together in these rooms; they had merely *resided*. He was walking away with nothing personal. He had packed only the bare essentials that could have belonged to anyone. He was leaving behind nothing of value to him. Not even Barbara.

* * *

He wasn't even certain the building would still be there. But he found it squatting between similar buildings, all stubbornly withstanding the encroachment of development around them.

The escalating tourist trade was rapidly destroying the uniqueness of New Orleans, which was the attraction that caused tourists to flock to the city in the first place. It was a paradox that defied logic.

Burke would have hated to find this building destroyed, because, for all its signs of aging, it had character. Like a dowager who clung to fashions of decades past, it wore its age with dignity and an admirable air of defiance. A section of the ironwork was missing off the second-story balcony. The front brick walkway was buckled. Weeds sprouted from cracks in the mortar, but there was an element of pride in the pot of pansies on each side of the gate, which squeaked when Burke pushed it open.

The first door on his left was designated as belonging to the building manager. Burke rang the bell. The man who answered wasn't the landlord he remembered from years before, but this one and the one in his memory were virtually interchangeable. The apartment behind the stooped, elderly gentleman was a stifling ninety degrees and smelled of a cat box. In fact, he was holding a large tabby in one arm as he peered curiously at Burke through the rheumy eyes of a lifetime alcoholic.

"Do you have a vacancy?"

The only thing required for leasing an apartment was a hundred-dollar bill to cover the first week's rent. "That includes a change of towels on the third day," he was told by the landlord who shuffled up the stairs in his slippers to show Burke the corner apartment on the second floor.

Basically it was one room. A shabby curtain was a nod toward privacy for the commode and tub. The bed was a double that dipped in the middle. The kitchen amounted to a sink, a narrow shelf, a refrigerator not much larger than a mailbox, and a two-burner hot plate that the landlord believed was in working order.

"I won't be doing much cooking," Burke assured him as he accepted the key.

A black-and-white TV set chained to the wall was

about the only amenity that had been added since he had rented here nearly twenty years ago after leaving his hometown of Shreveport to accept a job with the NOPD. Before he could find more suitable lodging, he had leased a temporary room in this building and wound up staying eighteen months.

His recollections of it were hazy. He hadn't spent much time in the apartment, because he was at the station nearly every waking hour, learning from the veterans, volunteering for overtime, and catching up on the paper-shuffling that was the scourge of policemen around the world. He'd been a young crusader then, committed to ridding the world of crime and criminals.

Tonight a less idealistic Burke Basile drew a hot bath in the antique claw-footed tub and climbed into it with an uncapped bottle of Jack Daniel's black. He drank straight from the bottle, watching dispassionately as a cockroach the size of his thumb scuttled across the water-stained wallpaper.

When a guy catches his wife in flagrante delicto with another man, the first order of business—after beating the shit out of the other man and buying a bottle of whiskey, which he intends to drink from until it's empty—is to reassure himself that he can still get it up.

So, with his free hand, he brought himself erect. Closing his eyes, he tried to replace the image of Barbara fucking the football coach with a fantasy that would sustain his erection long enough for him to enjoy it and bring him to an ego-restoring climax.

In an instant, there she was in his mind's eye: the whore in Duvall's gazebo.

He rubbed every bad thought from his mind and focused on the woman in the snug-fitting black dress, her hair as dark and glossy as a raven's wing, her breasts kissed by moonlight.

Her face was indistinct. In his mind, he brought it closer. She gazed back at him with sultry eyes. She spoke his name. She stroked him with a soft hand. An even softer mouth caressed him. Her tongue—

He came, cursing blasphemously through bared teeth.

It left him feeling weak and dizzy and slightly disoriented, but that could be as much from the hot water and whiskey as the sexual release. It was comforting to know that he was still a functioning male. But on an emotional level he felt only marginally better.

Well on his way to being good and drunk, he climbed out of the tub and, wrapping one of two thin towels around his middle, sat down on the edge of the bed to reflect on his future.

He supposed he should be contacting a divorce lawyer, freezing bank accounts, canceling credit cards, all the things people do for spite and self-protection when their marriage becomes a statistic.

But he lacked the wherewithal to enter that kind of legal fray. Let Barbara have it all, whatever the hell she wanted from the spoils of their life together. He'd salvaged all he needed; a few changes of clothes, his badge, his nine-millimeter.

He reached across his pile of discarded clothes on the bed and picked up the pistol, weighing it in his hand. It was from this gun that he'd fired the bullet that had killed Kevin Stuart.

His personal life was for shit. So was his career. He no longer nursed illusions about valor and duty. Only fools believed in that crap. Those standards were outdated and didn't apply to contemporary society. When

he enrolled in the police academy, he had fancied himself a knight, but the Round Table was history before he even began.

Burke Basile was a pariah, an embarrassment to the Narcotics Division for shooting one of his own men, then for demanding justice when no one else seemed to give a damn.

Wayne Bardo was free to kill again, and he had.

Duvall was ensconced in his ivory tower with his servants, and his rich friends, and their expensive whores.

Meanwhile Burke Basile's expressions of sympathy were being rebuffed and his wife was screwing younger men in his own house.

Again he hefted the pistol in his palm. He wouldn't be the first cop, dejected over the futility of his work, to eat a bullet. How long before he'd be missed? Who would miss him? Patout? Mac? Possibly. Or, secretly, maybe they'd be glad he had solved their problem for them.

When he began to stink up this horrible little room, when the landlord's cat began scratching at the door, they'd find him. Who would be surprised that he'd taken his own life? He had destroyed his marriage, they'd say. Gossip would get around that he had caught his old lady, the one with the great body, doing the wild thing with another man in Basile's own shower. Poor schmuck. They would shake their heads and lament the fact that he had never fully recovered from killing Stuart. That's when all his troubles had started.

While Stuart's widow struggled to keep food on the table for her children, unscrupulous lawyers and criminals threw lavish parties to celebrate their lawless successes. Ol' Burke Basile couldn't take that. He couldn't handle the guilt anymore.

So, bang. Simple as that.

It occurred to him that he might be suffering a bad case of self-pity, but why the hell not? Wasn't he entitled to a little self-analysis and regret? He'd been deeply wounded by Nanci Stuart's decision, although he admitted it was the right one for her. She was holding on to her life with both hands. Eventually the pain of Kev's death would abate; she would meet someone else and remarry. She didn't blame him for the accident, but his visits were bound to stoke her most painful memories.

He wanted to think of Barbara as a cheating bitch who'd been unwilling even to try to understand the hell he'd gone through over his partner's death. But that wasn't entirely fair. She certainly wasn't without flaws, but he hadn't exactly been an ideal husband either, even before the fatal shooting incident and certainly not since. The marriage should have ended long ago, putting both of them out of their misery.

He'd made lousy choices all around. Bad choice of wife. Bad choice of career. What the hell had all the overtime hours and all the hard work been about? He had accomplished nothing. *Nothing*.

Well, not exactly nothing. He had killed Kev Stuart.

Damn, he missed that mick! He still missed Kev's quiet logic, and his stupid jokes, and his unshakable sense of right and wrong. He even missed his bursts of temper. Kev wouldn't have minded dying in the line of duty. Actually, that was probably how he would have preferred to go.

What he wouldn't be able to tolerate was that his death had gone unavenged. The criminals responsible for it had gone unpunished by the system of law that Kev had dedicated himself to uphold. Kevin Stuart would have had a hard time accepting that.

And that was the thought that sobered Burke Basile like a cold shower.

He set the bottle of Jack Daniel's on the rickety night-stand, and, alongside it, his pistol. Removing the towel from around his waist, he stretched out on the lumpy bed and stacked his hands beneath his head. For hours he lay there, staring at the ceiling and thinking.

Although there really was nothing more to think about.

He knew now what he had to do. He knew who he had to kill. And it wasn't himself.

When he finally fell asleep, he slept as he hadn't for months—deeply and dreamlessly.

Chapter Nine

Quitting?"

"Quitting," Burke repeated.

For a moment Patout was speechless. "Just like that? For chrissake, why?"

"It's not 'just like that,' Doug. And you know why."

"Because of Kev?"

"Primarily. And Duvall, and Bardo and Sachel. Shall I go on?"

"How can you do this?" Patout left his chair and began to pace the area behind his desk. "If you quit a job you love because of them, they win. You're making it too damn easy on them. You're giving them control over your life."

"It might look that way, but it's not. I wish my reasons were that simple and clear-cut."

Patout stopped pacing and gave him a sharp look. "There's more?"

"Barbara and I have split."

Patout gazed down at the floor for several seconds, then looked at Burke with regret. "I'm sorry. Is this a trial separation?"

"No, it's for good."

"Jeez. I sensed that you two were having problems, but didn't know that things had unraveled that completely."

"Neither did I," Burke admitted. "Until last night. I won't bore you with the details, but take my word for it that we reached the point of no return. I moved out and told her to file for divorce on the grounds of her choosing. The marriage is kaput."

"I'm sorry," Patout said again. He wasn't any more sorry than Burke that his bad marriage had finally ended. The real regret was in the timing.

Burke said, "I'm fine with it. Really. It had been coming for a long time. As for the other, the job, that's been coming for a long time, too. I'm burned out, Doug. In my present frame of mind, I'm no good to you."

"Bullshit. You're the best man in the division."

"Thanks, but this is the right thing for me to do."

"Look, we've just come off a disappointing trial. You're upset about you and Barbara. Not a good time to be making a career decision. Take a week off..."

Burke was shaking his head before Patout finished. "That's not what this is about. A week off would be like using a Band-Aid when I need open-heart surgery."

"So maybe a desk job for a while," Patout suggested. "Work in an advisory position. Something that would relieve the pressure a bit."

"Sorry, Doug. My mind's made up."

"At least let me place you on suspension with pay. You can come back when you feel like it. The job will be waiting."

That alternative was tempting, but Burke considered it for only a few seconds before stubbornly shaking his head. "If I had that umbilical cord, I might use it. A few weeks later I'd be right back where I am now. No, Doug, it's gotta be a clean break."

Patout had returned to the chair behind his desk. He ran his hand through thinning hair. "I can't believe this. I'm the head of this department, but you're the heart of it, Burke."

He made a scoffing sound. "Trying a new tactic, Doug? Sweet talk?"

"It's the truth."

"I appreciate the compliment, but that doesn't sway me."

"Okay," Patout said, making an impatient gesture with his hand. "Forget the division. What about *you*? Have you really thought this through? What will you do with yourself?"

"That's one of the perks of quitting, Doug. I don't have any plans."

That was the first time Burke had ever lied to his friend.

* * *

The brothel was as imposing a structure as a branch of the public library.

It was set well off the street behind an iron picket fence in a grove of spectacular magnolia trees. The house had been built by a wealthy Creole family who had grown and imported cotton prior to what was commonly known as the War of Northern Aggression.

During that conflict, the Yankees had seized all the family's ships and warehouses, burned their plantation upriver, and commandeered this, their home in the city, to be used as quarters for Union officers. It was this final insult from which the family never recovered.

Following the Civil War, the house had fallen into ruin because no one could afford to own it and pay the property taxes. In the early 1880s, a northern entrepreneur fell in love with the mansion. He poured money into the refurbishing of it until it surpassed its original splendor. That lasted until his grandson and heir was caught swindling his partners and lost not only his family's fortune, but his own life in a suspicious shooting "accident" beneath the Dueling Oaks.

The house again sat vacant until the 1920s, when a group of investors converted it into a speakeasy. The upstairs rooms saw as much, if not more, action than the elegant salons on the ground floor. Flesh was peddled as actively as bootleg liquor. Soon the madam had made enough money to buy out her partners. Under her management, the business flourished.

When she died, the business was passed down to her daughter, and now, the present owner, Ruby Bouchereaux, was the third-generation madam. The elegant establishment had been under Ruby's control since the sixties. She had outprospered even her enterprising mother and grandmother.

Ruby Bouchereaux's house was part of the Big Easy's mystique. Local law enforcement had an understanding with Ruby. She was allowed to run her business without any interference, except where drug trafficking was involved.

Occasionally one or more of Ruby's girls saw a way to make a little extra cash on the side while promising a client heightened sensitivity and staying power with the help of a controlled substance. Ruby didn't like the temporary interruption in business that a raid created, but she liked even less the prospect of being permanently shut down if one of her well-heeled clients died of asphyxiation or heart attack while in the throes of ecstasy. Nor was she too keen on her girls having an enterprise of which she got no percentage. So she regarded the occasional raid as a necessary evil and remained on good terms with the authorities.

Burke had been to the house twice in the line of duty. Naked men, clutching their three-piece business suits and Rolexes, were pulled from the luxurious beds and shaken down with no more deference than hollow-eyed junkies who begged for coins around Jackson Square. If one of Ruby's customers was caught using drugs to spike his sex, Burke didn't have any compunction about arresting him no matter how wealthy he was or which public office he held.

The door was answered by a bouncer who greeted Burke with a suspicious scowl. "Please tell Miss Bouchereaux that Burke Basile would like to see her."

"Aren't you a cop?"

"You got something to hide?"

He closed the door in Burke's face and left him standing on the threshold for five full minutes before reappearing. "She'll see you," he said, sounding none too pleased about it.

He led Burke to an office that could have belonged to any hardworking, overachieving executive who delegated little and insisted on exercising absolute control over everything. It was equipped with a multiline telephone, two fax machines, and a computer. Prostitution had gone high-tech.

The woman seated behind the desk motioned him into a chair. "This is an unexpected pleasure, Lieutenant Basile."

"Thank you for seeing me without an appointment."

She offered him something to drink, which he declined. After dismissing the bouncer, she said, "I hope you've come to establish a line of credit with us. My girls will be thrilled. Your rugged good looks, especially that attractive mustache, haven't gone unnoticed whenever you've graced us with your presence, even if it was to carry out your unpleasant duty."

She was a diminutive woman, no more than five feet tall, with platinum hair that was said to be natural. Her skin, it appeared, had never been exposed to sunlight, because it was as white and smooth as a gardenia blossom. Rumor had it that she had undergone a face-lift without anesthesia so that she could oversee the surgeon's work and make certain he was acting on her precise instructions. But the story was a little too farfetched to be believed, even for Ruby Bouchereaux, about whom rumors abounded. In any event, she was stunning.

Since he entered the office, her lavender eyes hadn't wavered from his. She was old enough to be his mother, and he knew her art of flirtation had been perfected over years of practice. Nevertheless, he felt himself blush at her compliment.

"I'm afraid I can't afford your services."

"We've made allowances for other city officials." Eyeing him with interest, she toyed with the strand of pearls around her neck. "I'd be pleased to discuss several discount options with you."

He smiled, but shook his head. "Sorry, no. But I appreciate the offer."

Her lips formed a rueful pout. "The girls will be disappointed. And so am I." Then, folding her small hands together on top of her desk, she inquired why he had come to see her.

"Pinkie Duvall."

The change in her expression was so subtle, only someone with Burke's experience in gauging people's reactions could have detected it. "What about him?"

"You two were partners in a club down in the Quarter before you had a falling out a couple years back."

"That's correct."

"What happened?"

"Off the record?"

"Entirely."

"Pinkie wanted one of my girls to come dance in the club. She wasn't interested, and politely turned him down. Shortly after that, Wayne Bardo paid us a visit and requested this girl. After an hour with him, she couldn't even walk, much less dance."

"Bardo was sent by Duvall to teach her a lesson." When Ruby agreed with a slight inclination of her head, he asked if he could please speak to the girl.

"I'm afraid not, Lieutenant. Two days after her session with Bardo, she took a razor to her wrists. She didn't believe that her face would ever look the same, and, frankly, neither did any of the doctors we consulted. She was a gorgeous girl. Mr. Bardo ruined her not only for this profession, but for any other where meeting the public is required."

"I don't suppose you reported this to the police."

"A whore getting assaulted in a whorehouse?" she said with a harsh laugh. "How sympathetic do you think the authorities would be? I couldn't prove that the assault had taken place here, or that Bardo was the culprit, or that he was carrying out Pinkie Duvall's directive.

"Besides, it would have been bad for business. I don't advertise our mistakes and misfortunes. Anytime a girl goes into a room alone with a man, she runs the risk of being hurt. I and my staff do everything to prevent that sort of thing from happening, but we can't be in the rooms to guarantee that it won't. It's a hazard of the profession."

Burke leaned forward slightly. "Ms. Bouchereaux, as a former partner, do you know anything about Duvall's sideline businesses?"

"I assume you're referring specifically to drug dealing."

"So you're aware of it?"

"Of course, but I couldn't prove it, any more than you can. He's incredibly shrewd. Pinkie and I only discussed business relating to the club we held in common. He didn't pry into my other interests, and I didn't pry into his."

"You see my dilemma?" Burke said. "District Attorney Littrell won't touch Duvall without hard evidence, and there's not a chance in hell that he's going to make a mistake and give us any room to maneuver."

"What has all this got to do with me?"

"I was hoping that you'd be willing to cooperate with the Narcotics Division. Help us out, maybe work out an arrangement."

"Like no more raids for a while if I help you catch Pinkie Duvall?"

"Something like that."

She gazed at him unflinchingly while still fiddling with the strand of pearls. "You're in no position to be making deals on behalf of the Narcotics Division. You no longer work for the police department."

Caught, there was no point in denying it. Expelling his breath, Burke sat back, appraising her with heightened respect. "It was worth a try. I'm sorry."

"I thought it was very strange for a policeman to come calling before noon. While you were waiting to see me, I placed a call."

"I turned in my badge this morning."

"Why?"

"I'm going after the bastard on my own."

Her eyes narrowed slightly. "How intriguing. A personal vendetta."

"I suppose you could call it that."

"No doubt because of Stuart's death. I followed the story."

He nodded, but didn't elaborate. "I knew the partnership between you and Duvall had gone sour, and figured there would still be some animosity. Even so, I took a chance by coming here. If something unfortunate were to happen to him, I'm trusting you to forget that I was here."

"You have my word on it, Mr. Basile."

"Thank you."

"How can I assist?"

"You're willing? Even though I tried to trick you?"

"Let's just say that I appreciate passion in all its forms."

Returning her smile, Burke sat forward eagerly. "Where does Duvall keep his records? Not for his law practice. His personal records."

"Here," she said, tapping her temple. "There won't be any records of what you need to know, either written or on computer disks."

"You're certain?"

"As certain as I can be. This is no small undertaking you've chosen for yourself. After the incident with my girl, I tried to think of a way to repay Pinkie. Blackmail. Embezzlement. I even considered killing him." She laughed musically. "I guess I'm trusting you with secrets, too, Mr. Basile."

"You have my word that I'll never recall this conversation to anyone else, either."

Her smile gradually faded. "I never got my revenge. I devised a dozen schemes, but abandoned them all because they left me too vulnerable."

"You see, that's the beauty of this," Burke told her. "I've got nothing to lose. Absolutely nothing."

Looking deeply into his eyes, she said softly, "You may surprise yourself."

"I don't think so."

"I hope you're wrong." A moment passed before she stood up and crossed the room to a cabinet where glasses and liquor were stored. "You're determined to have your vengeance?"

"Whatever the cost."

"It might be more costly than you think. From here on, trust no one."

"Including you?"

He meant it teasingly, but she responded seriously. "Including me. Pinkie keeps his former clients indebted to him. When they fall behind on their payments, he lets them work off their fees. Since he deals with criminals of all types, I can't stress to you enough how deadly he can be."

"I'm aware of the danger."

Burke had resolved last night that he was going for broke. He didn't care if he lived or died, as long as he took

Duvall and Bardo with him. Nevertheless, he would be a fool to dismiss the madam's advice.

She poured two shots of bourbon and brought one to him, which he accepted and thanked her for, even though he'd declined a drink earlier. Thoughtfully, she sipped from her tumbler. She tapped her fingernail against the crystal as she held it to her lips. "There might be a way, Mr. Basile. Pinkie's one Achilles' heel is his Remy."

Burke tossed back his shot. The whiskey stung his throat, his eyes. He coughed. "What's a *remy*?"

Chapter Ten

Remy, I don't think I need remind you that this makes the third episode this semester."

"No, Sister Beatrice. I'm all too aware of my sister's infractions." She smoothed her skirt, an unconscious gesture of contrition held over from her days at the academy. "I agree that Flarra's behavior is unacceptable."

"Not only are we responsible for our girls' educations," the nun continued, "but for their spiritual harmony and emotional stability. Here at Blessed Heart we take very seriously the responsibility of guiding our students in every area of their lives."

"It's because of those high standards that Flarra is enrolled here."

"Yet she seems determined to break the rules, which are in place for her safety, as well as to instill self-discipline. If something like this happens again, we will be forced to expel her."

"I understand," Remy said, feeling soundly chastised herself.

Although it had been twelve years since she graduated from Blessed Heart Academy, the few lectures she'd received for disobedience or poor performance were embedded in her memory. For all the benevolence of their profession, the boarding school's administrators knew how to magnify a minor infraction until it seemed a cardinal sin.

"May I see my sister alone now, please?"

Sister Beatrice stood. "Certainly. You may have use of the office for fifteen minutes. Please give my regards to Mr. Duvall and thank him on behalf of the faculty for his latest endowment. His generosity never ceases. God will bless it."

"I'll tell him."

As Sister Beatrice moved past, she paused and laid her hand on Remy's arm. "How are you, Remy?"

"Very well."

"Happy?"

"Certainly."

The nun had taught Remy English literature before becoming principal of the school. She could be stern when required, but she was as kind as she was strict. Her life and her career had been devoted to education, but she might have been equally as successful as a psychologist. Or a detective. With unsettling perception, she peered deeply into Remy's eyes.

"I still think of you often, Remy. And when I do, I pray for you."

"Thank you, Sister."

"Sometimes I question..." She let the thought trail off without vocalizing it, saying instead, "I love all the young ladies God places in my charge. But I'm human. Every now and then one comes along who touches my heart in a special way. You can't be surprised to know that you were one of those select few, Remy. I doubt I hid my partiality from anyone, especially you."

"I sensed your love, yes. I'm still grateful for the attention you gave me when I needed it most."

"I wanted very much for you to be happy. I would hate to think that your life hasn't been all that you hoped it would be."

"If I seem a little out of sorts today it's because I'm upset by Flarra's latest stunt."

Sister Beatrice studied her face a moment longer, then patted her arm before releasing it. "Don't worry too much about Flarra. Your sister is a delightful girl. A bit more headstrong and impulsive than you."

"Or simply more courageous."

"Perhaps," the nun said with a small laugh. "You came to us much later than she did. You had seen more of the world."

"What I had seen of it didn't hold much allure for me."

Sister Beatrice smiled sympathetically. "Flarra regards that lack of exposure a curse, not a blessing. Her problem isn't disobedience so much as curiosity. She feels constrained." After a slight hesitation, she added, "As much as I'd hate losing her, it might be time for you to consider moving her into another school, where she'll have interaction with other young people and get a better feel for what the world is like."

"I'll think about it."

Sister Beatrice withdrew slowly, gracefully, and silently, except for the whispering of her habit and the clacking of her rosary beads.

In contrast, Flarra flounced in and slammed the door

closed. Her expression mutinous, she threw herself into the chair facing Remy's and glared hard at her older sister. "Well? Are they kicking me out? I hope."

"No such luck for you."

Flarra's resentment lasted only another few seconds before her hauteur collapsed and her eyes filled with tears. "Remy, I can't stand it in here any longer!"

"Is that why you and three of your friends sneaked out?"

"We didn't get very far."

A policeman had seen the girls, recognized them as too young to be out walking past midnight, picked them up in his patrol car, and returned them to the school.

"Where were you off to?" Remy asked.

"The French Quarter."

"At that time of night? Don't you see what an irresponsible and crazy thing that was to do, Flarra? The Quarter isn't safe."

"I wouldn't know. I never get to go."

"Pinkie and I take you there all the time. You've eaten in the finest restaurants, shopped in the best boutiques."

"With you and Pinkie. Big deal. It's not the same as going with a group of friends."

Remy conceded that her sister had a point, and her tone softened. "No, I'm sure it's not."

Noticing the change in her sister, Flarra looked across at her. "Did you ever sneak out?"

"Once," Remy admitted with a mischievous smile. "Two of us. But we didn't get caught. We sneaked back in before we were discovered missing."

"If you confessed to Sister Bea today, she'd probably make you do penance."

"Probably." Remy laughed. "Actually I wasn't so

scared of her finding out as I was that Pinkie would hear of it."

"How old were you?"

"Seventeen. Thereabouts."

"You got married when you were seventeen."

"Hmm. The day after graduation."

"You're so lucky," Flarra grumbled, her chin resting on her chest. "To have a man fall so madly in love with you that he couldn't wait for you any longer. All my friends think it's the most wildly romantic story they've ever heard. How he became your guardian, paid for your schooling here, then married you right away."

At the time, it had seemed romantic to Remy, too. Pinkie had been like a knight in armor who rescued her and Flarra from a squalid life and certain doom. It seemed like a lifetime ago. To be exact, *her* lifetime.

"One day, you'll have a man fall madly in love with you," Remy assured her.

Of the two, Flarra was prettier. Her animated eyes were the vivid light green of springtime buds. Her hair was dark and glossy like Remy's, but Flarra's natural curls were unruly and extravagant. Since they'd had different fathers, neither of which was known to them, and since their mother had no family that claimed her, it was anyone's guess where this curly gene had originated.

Flarra's young body was lithe and slender and athletic, but gently rounded where it should be. The tailored school uniform couldn't completely hide the female form beneath it. That's why Remy shuddered to think of her innocent sister walking the streets of the Vieux Carré late at night where she would be prey for rowdy tourists, drunken collegiates, and countless miscreants with depravity on their minds.

"Who'll have a chance of falling in love with me when I'm locked up in here?" Flarra whined, bringing Remy back to the conversation.

"Only another year and a half, then you'll graduate and be off to college where you'll meet many new friends."

"Remy…" Flarra slid from her chair onto her knees and knelt in front of her sister. "My spirit is dying in here. I've lived inside these walls for as long as I can remember. I want to explore and experience new places. I want to meet new and interesting people. I want to meet *men*. I've never even been kissed."

"You told me your date to the Christmas dance kissed you."

"That?" Her face puckered with disgust. "That doesn't count. He grabbed me and sort of poked his mouth against mine when the nuns weren't looking. It was gross. He was all sweaty and nervous. Rather than turning me on, it made me mad."

She inched closer and lowered her voice to an urgent whisper. "I'm talking about a real kiss, Remy. I want to go on a real date without nuns watching every move. I want—"

"Romance."

"Well, what's wrong with that?" Reaching for Remy's hands, she pressed them between her own. "Please, please, please, let me come live with you and Pinkie and go to a coed school. Just for my senior year."

Flarra was bursting to experience Life in its capitalized form. She was curious about men because her exposure to them was limited to Pinkie, who treated her like a father would—or at least a loving uncle. Like any youth her age, her hormones were raging. That physiological boiling pot was seasoned with Flarra's innate zest for life, her active imagination and natural exuberance, and her curiosity.

Remy could understand her sister's restlessness, but she couldn't exactly relate to it. She had been an adolescent when she was admitted to the academy, but it hadn't seemed a restricting place. It had been a refuge. For her, it had been a clean, quiet, and restful haven.

Within its ivy-covered walls she had enjoyed a sense of safety and serenity that she hadn't known was possible. Music amounted to the hymns sung at mass and benediction, not a radio blaring at all hours of the day and night. No frightening characters drifted toward the alcove where she slept. There were no sly looks to fear and avoid, no drug-related rages, no filthy language, no frantic coupling on unmade beds or on any surface that wasn't being otherwise utilized. There was no hunger, and no crying baby for which she was solely responsible.

Remy gave one of Flarra's springy curls an affectionate tug, her heart swelling with love for that sickly, crying baby who had depended on her for everything—food, caring, love, and protection—when she was little more than a baby herself. Despite that stunting first year, Flarra had grown into an incredibly intelligent and beautiful young woman. Remy had protected her from harm when she was a newborn, and she would continue to protect her until her dying breath.

"I'll speak to Pinkie about it."

"Promise?"

"I promise to speak with him," Remy emphasized. "I don't promise that our decision will be what you want."

"Pinkie wouldn't mind if I came to live with you, would he?"

"His favorite sister-in-law?" Remy scoffed.

In fact, Pinkie *had* objected to Flarra's living with them when they married. She had been living in a foster home while Remy attended Blessed Heart; he said it would be cruel to uproot the child yet again. That was the reason he gave. The real reason, Remy knew, was that he hadn't wanted Remy's time, attention, and loyalty to be divided between him and her sister.

When Flarra was old enough to go to school, he had moved her to Blessed Heart, convincing Remy that Flarra would receive the best upbringing in the boarding school. She'd really had no choice then except to agree, and, looking back on her years of marriage to Pinkie Duvall, she realized that it had been the best arrangement for all of them.

Over the years, Pinkie might have changed his mind about having Flarra with them. Remy didn't know. She hadn't asked. Because she was the one now opposed to Flarra's living under their roof. God forbid that her impressionable and impulsive younger sister come into contact with Pinkie's nefarious associates—men like Wayne Bardo.

Granting Flarra's request was out of the question, but she couldn't tell the girl that without having a battle on her hands. Nor could she tell her the reasons why she opposed it, or discuss with her matters that she wouldn't understand.

She couldn't talk to Flarra about Galveston.

For the time being Remy remained noncommittal. "A lot will depend on how you conduct yourself for the remainder of this semester. Will you behave yourself?"

The sixteen-year-old took that as a definite maybe. She leaped to her feet and executed a graceful pirouette. "I promise on my maidenhead."

"Flarra!"

"Don't freak. That's *all* that's going on with my maidenhead. What about Mardi Gras?"

"What about it?"

"Last year you said that maybe this year I could come to your party."

"That's right—I said *maybe*."

"Reee-my."

"I'll bring it up with Pinkie, Flarra. You're hardly in a position to be asking for favors."

"But you'll ask him," the girl insisted.

"I'll ask."

Then Flarra took Remy's hands and pulled her into a hug. "Thanks, sis. I love you."

Remy hugged her tightly, whispering, "I love you, too."

When they pulled apart, Flarra's face had turned sad. "What do you think she would think of me? Of us?"

Flarra could only be talking about their mother. "Who knows? I don't think about her at all," Remy lied.

"Neither do I."

Flarra was lying too. Naturally they thought about the woman who had given them away without a smidgen of regret. Of course if she hadn't, Flarra probably would have died before her second birthday. As to Remy's fate, she knew what she would have become.

"I must go," she said, moving toward the door. "Pinkie will be getting home soon."

"Does he make love to you every night?"

"None of your business."

"We—my friends and me—think he does. Completely naked and with the lights on. Are we right?"

"Instead of speculating on my sex life, shouldn't you be studying geometry?"

"Remy, are you feeling okay?"

It was customary for Flarra to switch subjects with rocket speed. This time she caught Remy with her guard down. "Am I feeling okay? Sure. Why do you ask?"

"The last few times you've been to see me, you look sort of, I don't know, tired."

"I am, a bit. We hosted a party night before last. I was up late." *Scrubbing off Bardo's touch,* she added to herself.

"If you're sick, don't lie to me."

"I'm not sick."

Flarra's eyes brightened and her voice dropped to a hush. "Could you be pregnant?"

"No, I'm not pregnant."

"Damn. I thought maybe..." She pulled her lower lip through her teeth. "You don't have cancer or something, do you, Remy?"

"No! Of course not. Flarra, I swear, there's nothing wrong with me."

"But if something were wrong with you, something terrible, you'd tell me?"

"I would tell you."

"Because I'm not a kid."

"I know that."

"'Cause if I lost you, I..." She swallowed hard. "I couldn't lose you, Remy."

"You won't," Remy declared with soft urgency. "I swear I'll always be here for you. If something were wrong, I'd tell you, but there's not, so don't worry. Okay?"

Flarra released a gust of breath and flashed her engaging grin. "Okay. I'll see you Friday night."

"No. I'm afraid we won't be taking you to dinner as planned."

"How come?"

From the threshold of Sister Beatrice's office, Remy looked back at her crestfallen sister. "Because you squandered that privilege on your adventure last night."

Chapter Eleven

S on of a bitch," Burke said softly.

He cursed with disbelief. Mrs. Pinkie Duvall was the woman he'd seen in the gazebo. Sitting behind the steering wheel of his car, he watched her enter the exclusive girls' school. Even from half a block away, he couldn't mistake her.

A little more than an hour ago, he had asked Ruby Bouchereaux, "What's a *remy*?"

"Not a *what*. A *who*. Pinkie's wife."

That Duvall was married had been a staggering revelation. Burke didn't recall ever hearing about a wife. Marital bliss just wasn't in his mental character profile of the flamboyant defense attorney.

As soon as he left the brothel, he drove to Duvall's neighborhood and cruised past the estate several times. He didn't really expect to see anything, but he got lucky. While he was making a turn-around down the street, a limousine came from the rear of the property and drove

right past him. Since it was business hours, he assumed
that Duvall was either in court or at his law office downtown. Was the lady of the house in the limo?

He had followed it here, to Blessed Heart Academy,
and watched with dismay as the woman he recognized
alighted with the assistance of the chauffeur. Chauffeur
and bodyguard, Burke thought. After Mrs. Duvall went inside, the man took up his post at the gate. Burke wasn't
surprised by the vigilance. Ruby Bouchereaux had already
told him that Duvall kept an eagle eye on his wife.

"You didn't know he was married?" the madam had
said, gauging his astonishment. "I'm not surprised. Pinkie
keeps her under lock and key."

"Why? What's wrong with her?"

"Nothing," she replied with a soft laugh. "I see her pe-
riodically. She's quite beautiful. As was her mother, until
her lifestyle began to take its toll."

Burke listened raptly as Ruby told him about Remy's
mother, Angel. "She was an exotic dancer in one of the
nightclubs Pinkie owns. This was twenty or more years
ago. Angel Lambeth had talent and a promising career, but
she became pregnant and had to quit dancing long enough
to have the baby. When she returned to work, she was not
only a mother, but an addict. Heroin, I believe. Her performance got sloppy. The drugs took a toll on her looks. So
she was transferred to a club with a less critical clientele.
A dive. You know the kind of place."

"What about her daughter?"

"When she was old enough, Remy became Pinkie's
bride. Beyond that, I know very little of the mysterious
Remy. No one knows much."

"How did Angel fare?"

"Badly. She was eventually demoted from dancing to

running the cash register. Shortly after Pinkie married the girl, Angel died. Supposedly of an overdose."

"Supposedly?"

Ruby Bouchereaux arched her brow eloquently. "Pinkie was a big man around town by then. Would he embrace a drug-addicted mother-in-law who turned tricks to support her habit?"

"You think he disposed of Angel to spare himself embarrassment?"

"Or the cost of rehab. He probably considered Angel a bad investment. In any case, her death was awfully convenient for him, wasn't it?"

Now, his butt growing numb from sitting so long in his car, Burke reviewed the story from every angle, wishing he knew the information that would fill in all the blanks. What was Mrs. Duvall doing here at the school? Did they have a kid?

His stomach growled, reminding him that he hadn't eaten since breakfast the day before. He searched the car for something to eat and found a forgotten Twinkie in the glove box.

What was taking so freaking long? The chauffeur had found a way to pass the time. He was cleaning his fingernails with a pocketknife. Burke saw him cough up a wad of phlegm and spit it into the shrubbery flanking the gate. Nails clean, he folded his arms across his chest and leaned back against the iron post of a gaslight. Burke couldn't see his eyes, but he would bet they were closed and that the goon was taking a nap standing up.

Forty-seven minutes after Remy Duvall went into the school, she came out. She said nothing to the chauffeur until they reached the car, when she paused before getting in and spoke to him over her shoulder. He doffed his cap.

"Yes, ma'am. Anything you say, madam. Kiss your ass? You bet. Jump? How high? Roll over? Play dead? Your wish is my command." Burke's muttering was tinged with contempt as he watched the chauffeur hustle to carry out her orders.

He cranked up the engine of the Toyota and followed at a nonthreatening, nonsuspicious distance as the limo left the Garden District, traveled down Canal Street, and then turned left, entering the French Quarter via Decatur Street.

The driver double parked beside a row of parking meters, all of which were occupied. Straight ahead lay the French Market. The chauffeur got out and went through the routine of opening her door and helping her out.

Burke whipped his Toyota into a space farther down the street, ignoring the stripes marking it as a loading zone. He reached for the duffel bag in his backseat. When he stepped out of the car a few moments later, he was wearing not a sport coat and dress shoes, but a loose rain jacket, Nikes, a baseball cap, and dark sunglasses.

Placing his hands in the pockets of his jacket, he strolled down the banquette looking like an average Joe who had the afternoon off, with seemingly no purpose in mind except to shop the fresh produce of the French Market and to meander among the stalls where vendors sold everything from voodoo dolls to alligator money clips.

He picked through a bin of Vidalia onions while, one row over, Remy Duvall sorted through the oranges. Now no more than eight feet away, Burke got his first close look at her.

There was no cleavage showing today, yet her two-piece suit could have been tailored for a Barbie doll. The skirt was short and snug. Its tightly nipped waistline drew attention to her breasts—his attention anyway. Her heels were high, her earrings flashy. The diamond on her ring finger was the size of a doorknob. She looked like the girls in the get-off magazines, except for her hair. It wasn't long and tangled. It was sleek and smooth. But there was something about the way it brushed her cheek each time she moved her head that was like an invitation to touch. Cherry-colored lips parted into a smile when she lifted one of the oranges to her nose and sniffed it.

Except for the small gold cross around her neck, she couldn't have looked more blatantly sexual if she'd been stark naked and had BOFF ME tattooed on her tits.

Even the fruit vendor was almost too flustered to sack up the pair of oranges she selected. The chauffeur paid for her purchase, but the vendor handed her the sack, placing it in her hands with his profuse thanks.

As she moved away, the bodyguard fell into step with her, his eyes sweeping right and left. Burke thanked the onion vendor but declined to buy any. Instead he ambled across the street, past the stand that sold African artifacts and clothing, toward the kiosk coffee bar where Mrs. Duvall had taken a chair at one of the small, round tables. She opened the brown paper sack and began to peel one of the oranges, her long fingernails digging into the flesh of the fruit.

At the bar, Burke ordered a banana smoothie. He stood elbow to elbow with the bodyguard. The guy's forearm was bigger around than Burke's neck. He picked up Mrs. Duvall's cappuccino with his beefy hand and carried it to her. He returned to the bar only long enough to get his own cup of coffee, but he didn't return to Mrs. Duvall's table. He stationed himself at another one nearby, while she sat alone, eating her orange section by section and sipping her cappuccino.

The banana smoothie was even more obnoxious than Burke had imagined, but he drank it slowly and with feigned, drawn-out pleasure as he watched Mrs. Duvall's reflection in the mirror behind the bar.

She attracted attention from passersby, but she didn't make eye contact with anyone and spoke to no one. For a woman with her looks, a rich husband, a mansion, and a chauffeur-driven limousine, she seemed to make an event out of something as simple as eating an orange. She chewed each section slowly, and waited several minutes before consuming another.

Burke began to wonder if she was waiting for someone to join her. Could Duvall be using her as a courier for his extracurricular activities? But no one came near her, and the guard didn't appear on edge. His head was buried in a tabloid newspaper.

The banana smoothie had melted into a syrupy slush that smelled like suntan lotion before Remy Duvall finished her orange and wrapped the peel in a paper napkin. When she stood to dispose of it in a trash can, the chauffeur closed his tabloid and rushed over to assist. Together, they began making their way back toward the illegally parked car.

"Hey, lady!" Burke cursed himself for acting impulsively, but at that point he was committed. Both Mrs. Duvall and her guard dog had turned back and were looking at him.

The brown paper sack with the extra orange in it was still sitting on the table. He picked it up and jogged toward her. "You forgot this."

It was the chauffeur who snatched the sack from him. "Thanks."

Burke, ignoring him, addressed her. "No problem."

He was close enough to smell an expensive floral fragrance and the essence of orange. For her hair to be so dark, her eyes were an incredibly light shade of blue, almost clear. The red lipstick had been eaten off, but her lips were rouged from the orange's acid sting.

She said to him, "Thank you."

Then the bodyguard stepped between them, blocking her from Burke's view. Although wanting to watch her walk away, Burke turned and ambled off in the opposite direction. He waited until the limo was out of sight before returning to his car, where he sat for a long time, motionless, but breathing as though he'd sprinted a mile.

* * *

"And that's it?"

Errol the chauffeur was sweating under the incisive glare that Pinkie used on clients he knew were lying. "That's it, Mr. Duvall. I swear. I drove her to the school. Then she asked me to take her to the market. She bought a couple of oranges and had some coffee at that little café across the street there. I took her to church. She was in there for half an hour, same as always. Then I brought her home."

"You didn't take her anywhere else?"

"No, sir."

"She was within your sight the entire time?"

"Except when she was inside the school, yes, sir."

Pinkie steepled his fingers and tapped them against his lips, while keeping the nervous bodyguard beneath his baleful stare. "If Mrs. Duvall asked you to take her somewhere, somewhere that I hadn't okayed first, you would refuse to take her and then you'd tell me, right?"

"Absolutely, Mr. Duvall."

"If she went somewhere that wasn't scheduled, if she kept an appointment that I didn't know about, you'd report it to me right away, correct?"

"Right, sir. I don't understand—"

"Because I'd hate to discover that your loyalty had shifted from me to my wife, Errol. She's a beautiful woman. I'm sure you're aware of that."

"Jeez, Mr. Duvall, I'd have to be—"

"My wife could twist any man around her finger. She could get a man to do something for her that she knows would not meet with my approval."

"Swear to God, sir," the chauffeur exclaimed, swallowing hard. "No, sir, that would never happen. Not with me. You're the boss. Nobody else."

Pinkie reprieved him with a wide smile. "Good. I'm glad to hear you say that, Errol. You can go now."

Baffled and looking downcast, Errol slunk from the office. Pinkie watched him go, thinking that he had come down on him a little harder than necessary, but that's how a man in his position instilled and maintained fear in the people who worked for him.

Look at Sachel. He was now a guest of the state at Angola and would be for a while. Was fear a powerful motivator, or what? Pinkie had enjoyed several private chuckles over how quickly Sachel had capitulated when his son's football aspirations were threatened.

Tonight, however, he didn't feel like laughing. Something was going on with Remy, but damned if he could figure out what it was.

For weeks this problem had been nagging him with the persistence of a toothache. Remy had become uncommonly withdrawn. *Uncommonly* being the operative word, because, on occasion, she retreated into herself and nothing could touch her, not lavish gifts, not teasing, not sex, not threats to snap out of it. These spells were usually short-lived and she always got over them. Except for that one character flaw, she was as perfect as a woman can be.

But this period of despondency had lasted longer than most, and it was more profound. When he looked into her eyes, they were shuttered. When she laughed, which was rarely, it seemed forced. She was distracted when he talked to her, and vague when she talked to him.

Even in bed, it seemed he couldn't touch her, no matter how tender or how forceful he was. She never refused him, but, at best, her performance could be described as passive.

Her symptoms were those of a woman having an affair, but that was impossible. Even if she'd met another man, which was highly improbable, she couldn't rendezvous without Pinkie knowing about it. He could account for how she spent every minute of her day.

He doubted that Errol's loyalty had shifted. The man was too afraid of him. But, even supposing Remy had managed to bribe her bodyguard or otherwise put something over on him, someone within Pinkie's wide network of acquaintances would tattle on her. He had already asked the house staff about incoming and outgoing telephone calls. Besides those to and from Flarra, there'd been none. No one had come to the house to see her. She'd received no packages, no personal mail.

Rule out an affair.

Then what in God's name could be the matter? She had everything a woman could want or dream of wanting. Although, he reminded himself, she might think differently.

After they married, she had sulked when he told her that college wasn't in her future. That's when she began taking courses by correspondence and reading every goddamn book she could get her hands on. He'd indulged her quest for knowledge until it became so tiresome he forced her to ration her studies and to read only when he wasn't in the house.

A few years after that, she had become obsessed with the notion of joining the workforce, at least on a part-time basis. That whim had been squelched soon enough.

So was this current mood just another female "passage" that he must endure before she returned to normal?

Or was this something more serious?

On impulse, he pulled up a card from the Rolodex on his desk. "Dr. Caruth, please." After identifying himself, the call was put straight through to Remy's gynecologist.

"Hello, Mr. Duvall."

The broad greeted him tersely, like she had better things to do than take his call. He'd heard from doctors he played golf with that she was a real ball-breaker, the scourge of the hospital. She was one of those women who seemed to work at making herself unattractive and unlikable, especially to men.

Pinkie had never liked her, and he knew the feeling was mutual. But Remy was her patient because he sure as hell wasn't going to give another man, any man, that kind of private access to his wife.

"Are you calling on behalf of Mrs. Duvall?" she asked. "There's nothing wrong, I hope."

"That's what I'd like to know. *Is* there something wrong with her?"

"I can't discuss a patient with you, Mr. Duvall. That would violate professional privilege. As an attorney, you should understand that."

"We're not talking about a patient. We're talking about my wife."

"Even so. Is she ill?"

"No. Not exactly."

"If Mrs. Duvall feels she needs to see me, have her call my office in the morning and set up an appointment. I'll work her in. Beyond that, it would be improper for me to carry this discussion any further. Good night." She hung up on him.

"Goddamn dyke!"

Her abrupt manner made him furious, but the call had told him what he needed to know. Dr. Caruth had always talked down to him. She talked down to everybody. She'd been no different tonight. If Remy had recently been diagnosed with a serious illness, the doctor would have been much more alarmed. She would have put aside her low opinion of him to find out what symptoms he had noticed to prompt the call.

Contacting the doctor had been a long shot, anyway. Remy's problem wasn't health related. It was mental, emotional. There was something weighing heavily on her mind that she wanted to hide from him.

Whatever it was, he would find out. Eventually it would surface, and when it did, he would quell it.

These minor insurrections were of no lasting consequence. They were irritations, like a mosquito bite that itched like hell for a few days, and then it vanished, not even leaving a scar to remember it by.

He could reshape Remy's attitude as easily as he could remold warm clay. With a few words, he could cleanse her mind of any dissatisfaction. He had the extinguisher that would put out any fires of rebellion that might burn in her heart.

Because he knew what she feared most.

Chapter Twelve

Pinkie was reading a legal brief when Remy came from her dressing room and joined him in bed. He removed his reading glasses and set the brief on the bedside table. "Remy, I want to know what's going on with you."

"What do you mean?"

He'd never struck her, but he came terribly close then to slapping the phony innocence off her face. Instead, he reached for her hand and squeezed it hard, but not as hard as he felt like. "I'm tired of this game. I was tired of it weeks ago. It ends tonight."

"Game?"

"Your game of keeping secrets."

"I'm not keeping secrets."

"Don't…" Bringing his raised voice under control, he began again, "Don't lie to me."

"I'm not."

He gave her a long look. "Are you planning to run away again?"

"No!"

"Because if you are, I caution you not to try. I was for-giving before. But I won't be again."

She tried to turn her head away, but he pinched her chin between his fingers and forced her to look at him. He rubbed his thumb across her lower lip, pressing hard. "I wanted you the first time I saw you. I could have had you then. But I was patient. I didn't do what it would have been within my rights to do, did I? Answer me."

"No, you didn't."

"I could have taken you then, but I waited. Even after you were old enough, I didn't have to marry you, but I did. Have you ever thought of where you'd be if you'd tried to steal from somebody else that day, Remy? Hmm? Where would you be if I hadn't been so understanding?"

"I don't know."

"Yes, you do," he whispered, stroking her cheek. "You'd be whoring just like your mother."

Tears sprang to her eyes. "No. I wouldn't."

"Yes, you would. When we met, you were already well on your way to becoming another Angel." His eyes moved over her in a way he knew she hated. "Oh yes, Remy. Even then you were alluring. I bet your mother's cus-tomers were hot to get on you long before I entered your life."

His fingers tightened around her hand. He thrust his face close to hers, but kept his voice soft. "Maybe you would have liked that life. Maybe you wish I hadn't saved you from all those men. Maybe you liked their fondling and heavy breathing better than you like being married to me."

"Stop it!" Yanking her hand free, she left the bed. "What are you threatening to do, Pinkie, report my crime after all these years? I'm not one of your clients. Or one of your lackeys. So don't speak to me as if I were. I deserve better than veiled threats. I'm your wife."

"Well, I want my wife to tell me why she's been slinking around the house like a goddamn ghost!" he shouted.

"All right! Flarra. I'm worried about Flarra."

Flarra? That's all? That's it? She was depressed over something as trivial as her sister? First it was Bardo who was agitating her, now Flarra. He'd been thinking the worst, fearing she might be planning another escape, and here she was telling him that her dejection was over nothing more significant than Flarra. Or was she lying?

"What about Flarra?" he asked brusquely.

Angrily Remy pulled on a robe and haphazardly tied the belt around her waist. As she composed herself, her chest rose and fell, making her gold cross pendant twinkle in the lamplight. He was glad to see her upset. His taunting about her former life had reminded her how fortunate she was.

"She sneaked out again," she said. "I went to see her today for a routine visit, but when I arrived, I walked into a lecture." She told him about Flarra's latest escapade and Sister Beatrice's warnings against any further breaking of rules. "I reprimanded her, but I'm not sure how much good it did."

"Sounds to me like she needs a good paddling."

"She's a little old for that."

"You're too soft on her, Remy. I should take over the discipline. I'll put my foot down and revoke some privileges. That will get her attention."

Her anger having subsided, Remy frowned with obvious disappointment. "Well, that answers that."

"What?"

"Never mind. It—"

"Tell me."

She gestured nervously. "Flarra has been hounding me about something for months. That's what's been bothering me, and I was a fool to think you wouldn't notice my distraction." She shot him a guilty smile. "I want to make my sister happy, but you're my husband and your wishes must come first. I've felt trapped in the middle. Today, I finally agreed to ask you." She wet her lips. "And frankly, Pinkie, I think she might have a good idea. It's a valid request."

He spread his hands to indicate that she still had the floor and that he was listening.

"Flarra wants to move in with us and go to a coed school for her senior year. She wants to live a more well-rounded life. Meet new people. Experience what other girls her age are experiencing. That's reasonable, isn't it?"

He stared hard at her for a long time, stripping her of defenses. Then he moved his hand to the empty place beside him and patted the spot. "Now, Remy."

"What about Flarra?"

"I'll think about it. Now, come back to bed." He uncovered himself, showing her how aroused he was. Her anger had stirred him, but her earnest petitioning had excited him even more.

When she rejoined him, he left no doubt in her mind that she belonged to him. He owned her. Her body, mind, and spirit were his to do with as he wished.

Afterward he told her that Flarra would remain at Blessed Heart Academy through her graduation.

For a moment, she didn't respond. Then she said, "Whatever you think is best, Pinkie."

He stroked her hair. "Your sister is young and doesn't know her own mind. It's up to us—to me, actually, because you're far too lenient—to see that she doesn't make any major mistakes or wrong decisions. I know what's best for her. Just as I knew what was best for you."

"She also asked permission to attend our Mardi Gras party."

"She's got her gall," he said with a chuckle. "That's a very prestigious guest list."

"That's why she wants to come."

"We'll see."

"Be prepared for her to sulk the next few times we're with her."

"She'll get over it," he said, dismissing the warning with a chuckle.

As he drifted off to sleep, he was smiling. *Thank God that's the end of that.*

* * *

Burke went to the university library because it stayed open later than the public library, and he knew he had a lot of material to cover.

For hours he scrolled through microfilms of the *Times Picayune*. Years back, the newspaper had done a profile on the city's most illustrious lawyer. Patrick Duvall had grown up in a middle-class neighborhood, but his parents worked hard to keep him in parochial schools, where he excelled in contact sports as well as scholastics. He received a scholarship to university, worked his way through law school and graduated first in his class, apprenticed in an established firm for nine years before he outgrew it and branched off on his own.

How much was truth and how much was fabrication Burke couldn't guess, but he reasoned that the piece was at least based on fact, because so much of it could be checked out. What came across clearly was that the subject of the piece was an overachiever who had been determined to climb above middle-class mediocrity, and that's what he'd done.

The writer touted Duvall as a philanthropist, but no mention was made of the clubs and topless bars he owned. Listed were the sundry citations he'd received for outstanding citizenship from civic groups and professional associations, but Burke knew of just as many hits Duvall had ordered, including, most recently, Raymond Hahn. Duvall was living the good life while thumbing his nose at the law-abiding public who lauded him.

And therein, Burke realized, lay the mechanism that made him tick.

Drug trafficking wasn't just a means of making money; it was Duvall's primo head trip. He did it because he could get away with it. To him it was a game, and he was winning. His illegal activities allowed him to demonstrate his superiority, if only to himself.

Pinkie Duvall figured frequently in front-page stories. Aside from that, his name routinely appeared in the society columns. But mention and pictures of his wife were noticeably scarce. When she did appear in a rare candid photo, she was usually standing in her husband's shadow. Literally.

Was she camera shy? Or was it impossible to upstage a media-savvy egomaniac like Pinkie Duvall, no matter how gorgeous you were?

What Burke also thought odd was that very little copy had been written about her. She had never been the focus of a write-up. Nor was she ever quoted. So either she didn't have an opinion about anything, or her opinion was so vapid it wasn't newsworthy, or her opinion was never solicited because her verbose husband was always on hand with something printable to tell reporters or columnists.

Mr. and Mrs. Pinkie Duvall were listed on the rosters of several charities, but Remy Duvall didn't hold an office in any of the social or civic women's clubs, nor did she serve on any board or committee, or chair any fund-raisers.

Remy Lambeth Duvall was her husband's antithesis. She was a nonentity.

He stayed until the library closed. They literally locked the doors behind him when he left. He realized he was hungry: All he'd consumed today were a stale Twinkie and as much of the banana smoothie as he could stomach. To help curb the roach population, he kept nothing edible in his apartment. He eschewed a restaurant in favor of a convenience store, where he bought two microwave hot dogs and a Big Gulp.

He drove away from the store with no particular destination in mind.

But he knew where he was going. When he got there, the house was dark except for security lights and a second-story window.

The wieners in the hot dogs were rubbery and the buns stale, but he chewed and swallowed mechanically, without tasting, wondering what Mr. and Mrs. Pinkie Duvall were doing on the other side of that shuttered window.

Talking? From what Burke had seen and read, she was no chatterbox. Was she capable of scintillating conversation only with her husband? Were her opinions and insights reserved for his ears alone? Did she entertain him in the evenings with her witty observations?

Yeah, right, Burke thought sardonically as he wadded

up the hot-dog wrappers and threw them to the floorboard. She'd keep ol' Pinkie stimulated, all right, but about a yard south of his brain.

He belched up the taste of bad hot dogs and washed it down with a swig of his overcarbonated cola.

Poor Pinkie. He was obviously pussy-whipped by this chick and blissfully unaware of the thing she had going with Wayne Bardo. Or maybe not. Maybe Pinkie shared her with his clients. Maybe she was one of the perks he provided for a client when he got away with murder.

The light went out.

Burke continued to stare at the dark window. The graphic images that flickered through his mind bothered him so greatly that he squeezed his eyes shut to try to block them out. His gut felt like lead. He blamed it on the hot dogs.

A half hour passed before he started his car and drove away.

It was clear to him that Duvall was besotted with his wife. She was treated like goddamn royalty. Ruby Bouchereaux had told him that Pinkie kept her under lock and key. He'd seen for himself how well she was guarded and protected.

"What does that tell you, Basile?"

As he let himself into his bleak apartment, he was smiling.

* * *

Remy lay perfectly still, listening to Pinkie's soft snores. She sent up a small prayer of thanksgiving that her ruse had worked. He had denied Flarra's request, never guessing that was exactly what Remy wanted him to do.

This wasn't the first time she had used reverse psychology to manipulate her husband. Most often it failed. But this time she had the advantage of knowing that he wouldn't welcome anyone intruding on them and making demands on her time. Especially Flarra. Pinkie knew how much she loved her sister, and he was jealous of their bond.

Thank you, God, for his jealousy. Keep him jealous.

Be careful what you pray for.

As on many other sleepless nights, Sister Beatrice's advice came back to haunt her. She understood now the lesson the nun had been trying to teach her. As a child, hadn't she begged God for another life, one free of poverty and responsibility?

Well, that's exactly what she had been granted. Little had she known what a tremendous price she would pay for this answer to her naive prayers.

Pinkie slumbered contentedly, his arm around her. The weight of it seemed crushing.

Chapter Thirteen

The men's restroom comprised one side of a square, concrete-block structure. Inside were two rusty sinks, three stained urinals, and a single enclosed stall, the door of which hung by only one hinge. There was no roof, but despite its open-air interior, the public toilet smelled badly in need of cleaning. Burke held his breath as he went in.

It was dark inside because the light fixture had been broken. The vandalism had probably gone unreported to City Park maintenance. There weren't too many men crazy enough to be in here after sundown, and those who were preferred darkness.

When Burke went in, only one other man was in the room. He was standing at a urinal, his back to the entrance. He must have heard Burke come in, but he didn't even glance over his shoulder at the sound of approaching footsteps.

Burke moved to the urinal next to the one being used. The man beside him finished but didn't immediately zip up. He turned his head slightly in Burke's direction and somewhat shyly remarked, "Sort of spooky in here."

Burke zipped his fly and turned toward the other man. "Sure as hell is. Never know who you might bump into."

Gregory James slumped against the wall and grappled with his zipper, groaning, "Basile."

"Aren't you glad to see me?"

"Shit."

"Guess not." Burke took the slender young man's arm and pushed him toward the exit.

Gregory balked. "I haven't done anything. You can't arrest me."

"I ought to take you in just for being stupid. How'd you know I wasn't a Jeffrey Dahmer? Or a redneck out to roll myself a queer? One of these days they'll be spooning your parts into a body bag. You're gonna make a move on the wrong guy and wind up minced meat."

"Don't bust me, Basile," he pleaded. "Swear to God, I've learned my lesson."

"Sure you have. That's why you're lurking around in City Park restrooms in the middle of the night."

"I was just taking a leak."

"Save it, Gregory. You're lying through your teeth. I've been following you, so I know you've been seeing action, friend. Lots of it."

"That's not true! I've cleaned up my act."

"Like hell. The guy you hustled last night looked like a minor to me. If I hadn't been on other business, I would have hauled you in, and they could've thrown a book of felonies at you."

"Oh, Jesus," the young man sobbed dryly. "If you bust me—"

"They'll lock you up and throw away the key this time. You're a menace to society."

Desperate now, the younger man began to beg. "Please, Basile. Cut me some slack. I've done you favors in the past, haven't I? Remember all the times I helped you?"

"To save your ass from arrest."

"Please, Basile, give me a break."

Burke pretended to mull it over, then said brusquely, "Let's go, pretty boy."

Gregory wailed.

"Shut up," Burke ordered, giving him a shake. "I'm not going to bust you, but I'm taking you home and seeing you inside, so at least I'll know your neighborhood is safe for the rest of the night."

Gregory thanked Burke repeatedly as they made their way toward Burke's car. Gregory lived alone a few blocks from the park, in a two-story townhouse that had been fashionably refurbished. The house and courtyard garden were kept in excellent condition—despite the owner's frequent absences when he was serving time for sex offenses.

Burke escorted Gregory past the beveled glass front door and into the foyer. "You don't have to come in with me," Gregory told him. "I'm not going out again. Swear."

"Your parents taught you better manners, Gregory. Offer me a cup of coffee or something."

Tense and jittery and obviously mistrustful of Burke's intentions, he agreed quickly. "Right. Good idea. I should have thought of it myself. Don't know what I was thinking."

"You were thinking of getting rid of me, so you could go out and try to score again tonight."

"You have a suspicious nature, Basile," said Gregory with mild reproof as he led Burke into the kitchen.

"Because I've dealt with too many lying criminals like you."

"I'm not a criminal."

"Oh, yeah?" Burke straddled one of the bar stools backward and watched his host assemble the coffeemaker. "Let's see if memory serves. I recall a child-molestation case."

"He was sixteen, and it was consensual. The charges were dropped."

"Because your daddy paid off the kid's parents. Then I remember a string of public-exposure arrests."

"Nothing serious. I got probation."

"You wienie waggers are a pathetic lot, you know that, Gregory?"

"If you're going to be verbally abusive, I'll file charges of police harassment against you."

"Be my guest. I'll call your daddy, tell him you're up to your old tricks, and he'll stop paying for this swell place he's set you up in."

Gregory gnawed the inside of his cheek. "Okay, you win. But you're a bastard, Basile."

"So I've been told."

Burke didn't enjoy badgering him, but Gregory James had made himself an easy target of derision. His was the classic story of a young man who hadn't lived up to his wealthy family's standards and expectations. His eldest brother, after successfully playing major-league baseball for a few seasons, had assumed control of the family's industrial empire and added millions to its coffers. The second brother was a neurosurgeon of world renown.

Gregory had broken this chain of overachievement. He probably wouldn't have graduated from the university if his father hadn't bought him a degree by making a sizable grant to the school. Gregory then entered the seminary, the consensus being that a cleric was needed to round out the family. They were counting on a cardinal at least.

Gregory endured the seminary for a year and a half before deserting that ambition, having discovered that his penchant for sexual misconduct was incompatible with a life of religious devotion. To distance themselves from his disgrace, the James clan banished him to New York, where he attended drama school.

It was there that Gregory had finally found a niche. He actually had a talent for acting and had performed in several off-Broadway productions before being arrested for performing an indecent act with another man in a public phone booth in Penn Station. Once again his wealthy father interceded, and the charges were dropped. Gregory returned home, shrouded in scandal.

This was the final straw for the Jameses, who washed their hands of son number three, although they continued to pay the bills on this townhouse. Burke figured they'd rather be out the expense than have Gregory living with them and have to confront their singular failure on a daily basis.

Gregory served the coffee. "Would you care for anything in that? Cream, sugar, a liqueur?"

"No thanks, this is fine." Gregory sat down across the bar from Burke, who could tell that the younger man was nervous. "How come you're so jumpy, Gregory?"

"I can't figure out why you're here."

"Consider it a social call. As you said, we go way back."

Gregory James was one of the drug division's best snitches. He was an active participant in the French Quarter's nightlife and circled in the same orbit with drug dealers, although he wasn't a user himself. He had often swapped information in exchange for leniency toward his vice of choice.

"You'd have been a real asset to the department if we could have kept you out of jail," Burke remarked as he sipped his coffee.

"Earlier you called me a criminal. I take umbrage at that, Basile," he said peevishly. "I'm not a criminal."

"Then what are you?"

"A patient. I have a... a problem."

"That's a given."

"I'm suffering an acute emotional disorder that has roots in my childhood. My family's values are skewed. I was forced to be competitive with my brothers when it's not in my nature to be. They were beastly to me."

"Gee, Gregory, you're breaking my heart."

"It's true! The prison psychiatrist said my problem was psychological."

"So was Ted Bundy's."

"It's not my fault!" the younger man exclaimed. "It's an urge I can't control. I can't help it that I ... do ... what I sometimes ... do."

"Uh-huh. That's become a popular defense these days. Because Mommy made me wear white socks and Daddy liked Diet Dr Pepper, I whacked 'em both." Burke sneered in disgust. "Guys like you make me sick. You whine around, blaming everybody else for your actions. You're a grown-up now, Gregory. You *are* accountable for what you do."

Suddenly he came to his feet and grabbed a handful of Gregory's shirt collar. "I've changed my mind. I'm taking you in."

"No! No, Basile! Please. You promised!"

"I did?"

"Yes."

"I don't remember promising."

"You did."

Burke released him slowly and returned to his stool. He fixed a hard stare on Gregory and held it for so long that Gregory began to fidget in his seat. Finally, he looked helplessly at Burke. *"What?"*

"I was just thinking." He continued to stare at the younger man as he took another sip of coffee. Lowering his cup, he said, "Maybe I could conveniently forget that I saw you with that minor last night. Maybe I could overlook that you made a move on me in a park restroom tonight. I might be willing to let it go this time."

"If…"

"If you do me a small favor."

Gregory's expression turned wary. "What kind of favor?"

"I can't discuss it with you until we strike a deal."

"That's not fair."

"Hell, no, it's not fair. But that's the gig, take it or leave it."

"Would I be working with Mac McCuen?"

"Why?" Burke winked at him. "Got a crush on Mac?"

"Fuck you, Basile."

"Not in this lifetime, pal. I've noticed you ogling Mac, but if your heart is set on him, you just as well forget it. He's got a hot-to-trot wife who thinks his cock is a magic wand. Now, do we have a deal or not, because the offer is only good for another thirty seconds."

"If I say yes…"

"You get off the hook this time. Otherwise we go up-town right now, and I book you."

"On what charge?"

"Soliciting me for sex in the men's room in the park. Twenty seconds."

"I didn't!"

"Because I didn't give you a chance."

"So you can't charge me."

"Of course I can. Who're they gonna believe, you or me?"

"Shit."

"Ten seconds."

Gregory dug into his wavy black hair with his fingers. "You give me no choice."

"Not true. You can choose to say no. Maybe jail won't be so bad this time."

Gregory raised his head and looked at Burke with poignancy. "Do you know what they do to guys like me in there?"

Burke did know, and at that moment he hated himself for manipulating the pitiful young man. And in Burke's human eyes, Gregory was pitiful. But he had to view him through a cop's eyes, too. One of his offenses had taken place on a playground. It was hard to drum up compassion for a guy who'd exposed himself to a class of preschoolers.

"Time's up. What's it going to be?"

"What do you think?" Gregory mumbled dejectedly.

"Good." Burke stood up and moved to the coffeemaker to refill his cup, then patted Gregory's shoulder as he returned to his bar stool. "Don't look so glum. This will be a challenging acting job. It could make your career."

"I'll bet." Gregory glanced over at him. "Tell me something, Basile. How in hell did you know about the guy last night?"

It was an honest question that deserved an honest answer. Looking Gregory square in the eye, Burke replied, "I didn't. Lucky guess."

* * *

The following morning, Burke locked the door of his apartment on his way out, turned toward the stairs, and ran into Wayne Bardo's fist.

He landed ignominiously on his backside. Standing over him, Bardo laughed. "Everybody says you're an asshole, Basile. I'm beginning to believe it."

His jaw throbbing, Burke came slowly to his feet. He wanted nothing better than to duck his head and ram it into the son of a bitch's gut. He might get in a few good punches, but he was more curious than angry. For the time being, Burke elected to spar verbally.

"Well at least I don't dress like a faggot. I bet the person who sold you that purple shirt is still laughing about it."

Although Bardo kept his smirk in place, Burke could tell the insult had hit home. He retaliated by saying sarcastically, "Nice digs, Basile."

"Thanks."

Burke didn't bother to ask how Bardo had located him. Duvall had a more sophisticated tracking system than that of the NOPD, the FBI, the DEA, or any other law enforcement agency—local, state, or federal. That's why he would never be convicted in court. There was only one way to stop Duvall and his machine, and Burke was going to do it.

It worried him that they knew where he lived. That meant that they'd been keeping tabs on him. Did they

know he had tailed Mrs. Duvall yesterday? If not, why
was Bardo here so bright and early?

As though reading his mind, he said, "Mr. Duvall wants
to see you."

"Duvall can kiss my ass. And so can you."

Bardo stepped closer. "Good. I like that. You're going
to make this difficult. Please do. I'd purely love to hammer
the shit out of you and leave it here on the landing to
stink."

Burke wasn't intimidated by the threat, but he was curious to know how much they knew. Shrugging, he said,
"Lead the way."

"No, after you." Bardo pushed him toward the stairs.
Burke lost his balance and stumbled down to the first floor.
When they reached the front of the building, Bardo shoved
him again toward the street where a late-model Cadillac
was parked at the curb.

"Hey, Wayne," Burke taunted, "when were you demoted from hit man to errand boy? Did Duvall take away
your knives?"

"Shut up and keep your hands where I can see them."

"I'm not armed."

"You think I'm an idiot?"

"As a matter of fact, yeah."

When they reached the car, Bardo patted him down, then
ran his hands down both inseams of Burke's trousers, finding nothing.

"Told you," Burke said.

"Get in, wiseass."

As he stepped into the car, Burke grinned. "Admit it,
Wayne. That purple shirt is getting to you. You just wanted
to feel me up."

* * *

Pinkie Duvall's law offices were as swank as his house, but entirely different. Here, the decor was sleek and contemporary. His secretaries and paralegals were leggy and gorgeous. No office machinery was visible to visitors and clients, only clean surfaces of marble and polished wood. The telephones didn't ring; they chimed in muted bell tones.

Pinkie was behind his desk when a secretary announced that Mr. Basile had arrived, as though this wasn't a command appearance, as though he was keeping an appointment, as though he hadn't been forced to come here under threat of bodily harm.

Duvall didn't stand when he and Bardo walked in. Burke knew the slight was intentional, calculated to make him feel like a plebeian going before his ruler. Duvall said, "Hello, Mr. Basile."

"Duvall." Petty, maybe, but he got in his slight, too.

Pinkie pretended not to notice. "Have a seat."

Burke took a chair facing the desk, which was slightly larger than a Ping-Pong table. On it, a picture of Remy Duvall was encased in an ornate silver frame. He pretended not to notice it.

"Would you like something to drink?" Pinkie offered.

"Such as hemlock?"

Duvall smiled. "I was thinking more along the lines of coffee."

"I don't want anything."

"Thank you for coming."

"I didn't come. I was brought."

Burke propped his ankle on his opposite knee and glanced over his shoulder at Bardo, who'd taken a seat on the sofa against the wall. Burke disliked having his back to a man he knew was a killer, but he supposed if Duvall had sent Bardo to pop him this morning, he'd be dead by now.

When he turned back at Duvall, he sensed his amusement. He was waiting for Burke to ask what the hell this interview was about. Burke would have petrified before asking. Why give Duvall the satisfaction of seeing his curiosity, or fear? This meeting was his idea. Let him commence it.

After a lengthy standoff, Duvall finally said, "I'm sure you're wondering why I wanted to see you."

Burke shrugged indifferently.

"I've heard some surprising news."

"Yeah, what?"

"You've resigned from the police department."

"Your sources have always been excellent."

"Your resignation creates a large hole in the Narcotics Division."

"I doubt that."

"You're too modest."

"I'm also too busy to sit here all day and bullshit with you about something that's none of your business."

Again, Duvall refused to be provoked. "Early retirement?"

"Maybe."

"Why'd you quit?"

"None of your damn business."

"What do you plan to do?"

Burke shook his head with disbelief and spread his arms wide. "You're forcing me to repeat myself."

Duvall gave him a measured look. "My guess is that you resigned because you're still upset over the verdict of

Mr. Bardo's trial. We won; you lost, and you took the defeat personally. Doesn't the term 'sore loser' apply, Mr. Basile?"

"You'd like to think so, wouldn't you? It would boost your colossal ego to believe that you have that much influence over the choices I make. Well, sorry to disappoint, but you couldn't be more wrong."

Duvall smiled in a way that indicated he knew Burke was lying. "You want to know the point of this meeting?"

"Or not. I really couldn't care less."

"Now that we're no longer on opposing sides, I'd like to offer you a job in my organization."

Burke Basile didn't have a sharp sense of humor. In the mirth and merrymaking department, he never lost control. In fact, it was common knowledge that he seldom smiled. Audible laughter was even rarer than that. It had been the unfulfilled ambition of many of his colleagues to make Burke Basile break up with hilarity.

They wouldn't have recognized the hearty laughter that burst out of him at Duvall's absurd statement. "Come again?"

"I believe I made myself clear," Duvall said, no longer looking amused.

"Oh, I heard you. I just can't believe what I heard. You want me to come to work for you? Doing what?"

"A man of your experience could be valuable to me. More valuable than you were to the police department." Reaching into his desk drawer, he withdrew several sheets that had been paper-clipped together. He held them up for Burke to see. "A copy of your tax return for last year. Shameful, the pittance society pays the men and women who protect it."

Duvall wouldn't have had too much trouble getting

his hands on a copy of his tax return. It could have come to him through anyone from an IRS employee to Burke's postman. He didn't care that Duvall knew how much, or how little, he had earned at his former job. What bothered him was that Duvall had such easy access to him. That, he felt, was also the point Duvall was making.

"I'm no longer a cop," Burke said, "but make no mistake, Duvall. You and I are still on opposing sides. Fact is, we're poles apart."

"Before taking that moral stance, shouldn't you at least hear the job I have in mind?"

"Doesn't matter what it is or how much it pays. For all your fancy surroundings," he said, giving the well-appointed office a glance, "you're maggot shit. I wouldn't piss on you if you were on fire, so I sure as hell wouldn't work for you."

Burke stood up and headed for the door. Duvall ordered him to sit back down. Bardo lunged toward him and would have thrown a body tackle if Burke hadn't thrust his hand into Bardo's sternum, stopping him cold. "You put your hands on me again and I'll break your freaking neck." The warning carried enough impetus to make Bardo reconsider. He remained where he was, but his eyes glowed with hatred.

Burke looked across at Duvall. "I'm not interested in your job."

"Really? That's odd." Unruffled, Duvall folded his hands on top of his desk. He even smiled sympathetically as he said softly, "Because I have very good reason to believe that you might be. Don't I, Basile?"

The two men stared at each other. The distance between them seemed to shrink, until Burke could almost make out his reflection in Duvall's black pupils. It was a haunted man who stared back at him.

He dropped his hand from Bardo's chest. "Go fuck yourself, Duvall."

Duvall's smile widened. "Tell you what, I'll keep the position open for you. Think about it and get back to me."

"Yeah. I'll do that. I'll get back to you." *Just not in the way you expect, you smug son of a bitch.* Burke looked over at Bardo. "No need for you to see me home." Then to Duvall, he added, "I know my way."

Chapter Fourteen

At precisely two thirty in the afternoon, Remy Duvall entered the church. Confession was heard between three and five o'clock, but because the Duvalls were generous contributors, Remy was afforded the courtesy of having her confession heard early. Pinkie had arranged it so that by three o'clock, when other parishioners began to arrive, she was already safely in the limo and on her way home.

Errol stationed himself just inside the church door, where Remy would be constantly in his sight. She moved down one of the side aisles, genuflected at the end of a row, and slipped into the pew. Retrieving her rosary from her handbag, she pulled down the kneeling bench and got on her knees to pray.

Even after her prayers were finished, she remained with head bowed and eyes closed. This half hour spent in church each day was precious to her. Pinkie ridiculed her for being excessively devout, but aside from her

Catholic faith, there was another reason why she regularly came to pray: This was the only time she was entirely alone.

Even when she went to the gazebo, there were always people around the house, full- or part-time workers doing one job or another. Since the day she married Pinkie, she had never been in her house by herself. Before that, she had lived at Blessed Heart in a dormitory with other girls. And before that, she'd shared a single room with her mother. There, she'd been left alone every night while Angel went to work. But on those nights alone, Remy had been too young and too afraid of the raucous noise on the streets and in the neighboring apartments to appreciate the solitude.

Here in the cathedral, she was both safe and alone. She savored the stillness, the quiet. She loved watching the ever-changing mosaic of color that the stained-glass windows cast on the walls. The flickering of the candles and the soft organ music were calming. She loved the freedom from watchful eyes.

Today in her prayers, she asked God for wisdom and courage. She needed wisdom to devise a plan to protect Flarra, and the courage to carry out that plan. For the time being, Flarra was safely ensconced in the academy and would remain there until she graduated. Then what? She placed the problem in God's hands, although she couldn't give over worrying about it.

Finally, she asked for forgiveness, or tried to. The words wouldn't come. She couldn't acknowledge, even in her own mind, the transgression that haunted her and made her appear ill to those around her. Some sins were too great to lay before God. If she couldn't forgive herself, why should He forgive her?

Glancing toward the confessional, she saw that the light had been turned on. The priest was waiting for her. She moved from the pew to the confessional and went in.

"Bless me, Father, for I have sinned. It's been one week since my last confession."

She enumerated a few minor offenses, but she was stalling, trying to garner enough courage to confess the Sin. She hadn't been willing to share it with anyone, not even a priest. She sensed him on the other side of the screen, waiting patiently.

Finally he coughed softly and cleared his throat. "Is there something else?"

"Yes, Father."

"Tell me about it."

Maybe if she talked about it, she would know some peace. But the thought of confiding it caused her throat to compress and her heart to pound. Tears clouded her eyes. Swallowing dryly, she began. "A few months ago, I conceived. I haven't told my husband about it."

"That's a lie of omission."

"I know," she cried softly. "But I...I can't. I'm conflicted, Father."

"About what?"

"The baby."

"The Church is very clear on this. A child is a gift from God. Don't you want the child?"

Staring at the large diamond on her left ring finger, she whispered through her tears, "There is no child. Not anymore."

She had hoped that finally speaking the words out loud would provide instant relief from her guilt, but she didn't experience any such release. Indeed, the pressure inside her chest increased until she thought her ribs might crack.

She had difficulty breathing. Her short, choppy breaths sounded loud in the enclosure.

Quietly, the priest said, "You also know the Church's position on abortion."

"It wasn't an abortion. I miscarried in my tenth week."

He assimilated this, then said, "Then what is your sin?"

"I made it happen," she said in a broken voice. "Because of my ingratitude and uncertainty, God punished me."

"Do you know God's mind?"

"I wanted my baby." Sobbing, she rubbed her abdomen. "I loved it already. But I was afraid..."

"Afraid? Of what?"

Afraid Pinkie would stick to his word and force me to have an abortion.

That was too ugly to confess, even to a priest. Pinkie had made it clear to her when they married that she would not be having children. Period. End of argument. The subject was closed. He didn't want the competition. Nor did he want her to be disfigured, even temporarily. He had said that if she felt the urge to nurture, she could nurture him without becoming grotesquely misshapen.

So when her contraceptives failed her and she accidentally conceived, she didn't tell him. She feared that he would insist on an abortion.

But she was just as fearful that he wouldn't.

What if he had mellowed on the subject of children and changed his mind? What if he had reversed his thinking and welcomed the idea? Did she want her child to be reared under Pinkie's control?

While she was still debating the dilemma, the problem had been solved for her. One terrifying afternoon, when she felt the tearing inside her womb and saw the blood trickling down her legs, she knew in her heart that she had willed it to happen. A precious life had been sacrificed to her cowardice.

The priest repeated his question, asking what she was afraid of. "Of Hell, Father. God knew I was ambivalent about having a baby, so He took it from me."

"Did you do something that caused you to abort?"

"Only in my heart. Please pray for me, Father."

Desperate for understanding and forgiveness, she reflexively reached out, pressing her palm against the screen. Head bent, she wept.

Suddenly, against her palm and fingers, body heat, as though the priest had aligned his hand with hers on the opposite side of the screen. It was a fleeting sensation, and when she raised her head, only her hand was silhouetted against the mesh.

But whether physically or spiritually, she had been touched. A peace she hadn't known for months stole through her. The bands of guilt around her chest dissolved, and she took several cleansing breaths.

Speaking with quiet reassurance, the priest granted her absolution and gave her a penance, which seemed moderate when compared to the enormity of her sin. It would take more than this penance to assuage her guilt, but it would be a start, a move toward redemption, a way out of the morass of guilt in which she had been floundering.

Slowly lowering her hand from the screen, she wiped the tears off her face and left the confessional with a soft, "Thank you, Father."

* * *

The scent of her perfume lingered for as long as Burke remained inside the confessional.

It was time to get out. He mustn't still be in the booth when the priest appeared to begin scheduled confession. Each second counted.

Nevertheless, he was reluctant to leave. In that small confessional chamber, he had shared a strange sort of intimacy with the woman of his fantasies, the moonlit woman in the gazebo.

Who just happened to be Pinkie Duvall's cheating wife. And Pinkie Duvall was the enemy he had sworn to destroy.

Prompted by that thought, Burke forced himself to move. When he stepped from the booth, his eyes swept the sanctuary, hoping for a glimpse of her, but she wasn't in sight. He glanced toward the door. The bodyguard he'd seen her with in the French Market was no longer at his post. She was gone.

He took a handkerchief from the hip pocket of his black trousers and blotted perspiration from his forehead, then from his upper lip, which felt naked without the mustache. A stranger had gazed back at him from his shaving mirror this morning.

Without further delay he left the church through a side exit. Gregory James was already in the car, waiting for him. Burke said nothing as he got behind the wheel and drove away. The car seemed excessively warm. He switched the air-conditioning system from heating to cooling and turned it on full blast. The black shirt was sticking to his back beneath his coat. The reversed collar was bugging him. He tugged at it irritably.

"Didn't it go well?" Gregory asked nervously.

"It went fine."

"The lady showed up?"

"On schedule."

After following Remy Duvall for a few days, it had become clear to Burke that she was never alone. Either she was inside the mansion and completely inaccessible, or in the company of her husband, or with the bodyguard. She never went anywhere unaccompanied. The only time she was by herself was when she went to church to pray.

"Pray?" he had exclaimed when Ruby Bouchereaux told him of the occasions on which she saw Mrs. Pinkie Duvall.

One of the madam's carefully penciled eyebrows arched. "Which surprises you most, Mr. Basile, that she goes to church to pray, or that I do?"

"I didn't mean any offense," he'd muttered abashedly. "It's just that—"

"Please." She raised her hand to indicate that she hadn't taken umbrage at his shock. "I frequently see Remy Duvall at prayer. I've never spoken to her. Nor does anyone. She's not there for show. She appears very devout and is always the first one there to go to confession."

After following Pinkie's wife into the cathedral for several days in a row and verifying Ruby Bouchereaux's information, he had thought, *Perfect*.

What better way to get inside someone's head and learn what she's about than to hear her confession? Did she do drugs like her mother, Angel? Would she confess her affair with Bardo? What sordid sins would she cite to her priest that would be useful to someone out to destroy her husband?

Come Saturday, Burke determined to be in the booth waiting for her. It was a ballsy plan, but brilliant. Except for two hitches: how to sound priestly, and how to forestall the real priest.

The last time Burke had been to confession was the day

following his mother's funeral, and then he'd gone only to honor her memory. He was a little rusty on the drill, although, once trained in Catholicism, one never completely forgot. But even if he could do a passable job, that still left him with the problem of delaying the parish priest.

That's when he'd thought of using Gregory James, who'd been trained both as a priest and as an actor.

"Did you say everything right?" Gregory asked him now.

"You'd been over it with me a dozen times." Burke cursed a slow driver as he whipped around him. "I said everything right."

"She didn't guess?"

The tearful remorse he'd heard in her voice couldn't have been faked. "She didn't guess."

"Good thing she couldn't see that scowl on your face. It hardly looks saintly."

"Well she didn't, so relax."

"I'm relaxed. You're the one who's sweating and driving like a maniac."

Having said that, Gregory sat back, smiling. He tapped his fingers on his knees in time to a tune inside his head. "I did my part great. Waylaid the priest outside the rectory, just like you told me to. I told him I was trying to hook up with Father Kevin, that we'd been seminary students together.

"He'd never heard of him, of course. 'Are you sure?' I asked. 'I'm positive his mother told me that he'd been assigned to Saint Michael's in New Or-*leens*.' Those voice classes I took in New York sure helped cover my accent," he told Burke in an aside.

"Anyway, the priest says that my friend could very well have been assigned to Saint Michael's, but I was at

Saint Matthew's. So then we laughed. I said the taxi driver must've gotten his churches mixed up. 'Or his saints,' says the Father. And we laughed some more.

"To keep him occupied a while longer, I asked if he was a New Orleans native, and he said he'd been here ten years. But he knew all the good restaurants. Not that he could afford them, he rushed to say, but some of his parishioners could, and they were generous enough to invite him out frequently. Duh-da-duh-da-duh-da. So we killed maybe ten minutes. Enough?"

"Plenty. Now will you shut up?"

He didn't want to chat with Gregory. He wanted to reflect on those few minutes he'd been separated from Remy Duvall by only a thin wall and a screen. He'd been close enough to smell her perfume and to hear her soft sobs as she confessed a sin Burke hadn't expected.

Drugs, drunkenness, adultery—none of that would have shocked him. But guilt over a miscarriage? He hadn't expected that, and it had knocked him for a loop.

All the same, he would use it to his advantage. Even while her perfume was making him damn glad he'd never taken a vow of chastity, he'd been in his policeman's mode, wondering how he could apply this confidential information to the job that must be done. In a burst of inspiration—not necessarily *divine* inspiration—he'd dreamed up a penance that fit her sin and worked nicely into his overall plan.

But he wasn't all that happy about it.

He wished he didn't know about the baby she'd lost. That made her human.

He wished he hadn't touched her hand through the screen. That made him human.

"Say, Basile, did you undergo a religious experience or something?"

Drawn from his thoughts by Gregory's question, Burke shot him a dirty look.

"Because you're acting really weird. You came out of the cathedral looking like you'd seen God." Again, Burke gave him a disparaging glance. "Okay, forget it. I guess I'm just not used to you sans mustache, and with your hair slicked back like that. I don't think your own mother would recognize you. The glasses are a nice touch, too."

Realizing that he'd forgotten to remove the square, horn-rimmed eyeglasses, he did so now, dropping them on the console between him and Gregory. The lenses were only clear glass, but it was strange that he hadn't thought to take them off. A guy could get himself killed overlooking a detail like that. Cop or criminal, it was the small stuff that tripped you up.

He ordered himself to snap out of it, whatever *it* was. If he started second-guessing his decision, he might waver in his determination to avenge Kev's death. If he couldn't go through with it, he couldn't go on breathing. It was something he had to do or die trying. His right hand flexed around the steering wheel.

When they reached Gregory's townhouse, he wheeled into the driveway and applied the brakes with such resolve that the car rocked to a halt.

Gregory reached for the door handle. "Reluctant as I am to admit it, it was fun. See you around, Basile. But only if I'm very unlucky."

To his consternation, Burke got out of the car along with him and accompanied him up the brick walkway. "I'm glad you had a good time. Because you're not finished yet, Father Gregory."

Chapter Fifteen

Pinkie cut into his rare filet mignon. "What's it called?"

Remy looked away from the blood-red juice oozing across his plate. "Jenny's House. Named in honor of a three-year-old girl whose mother abandoned her. She was starving when they found her. They couldn't save her."

"That's incredible," Flarra exclaimed. "In America, a nation of overweight people who spend fortunes dieting, a kid actually starved to death?"

"Horrible to think about, isn't it?"

Remy had carefully chosen a night when Flarra was joining them for dinner to broach this subject with Pinkie. She knew Flarra would rally to her side. Her sister was a crusader against any social injustice.

Pinkie swirled his stem of Merlot. "This priest, Father...?"

"Gregory," Remy supplied. "He called and asked if he could meet with me to discuss the special needs of the facility."

"Needs, meaning money."

She conceded with a nod. "He said they're struggling financially to get Jenny's House open and operative."

"Places like that are always begging for donations. How come you're not eating?" he asked, motioning down at her plate.

"I'm not very hungry."

"Your appetite was spoiled by all this talk of starving little girls. My wife, the soft touch." He reached across the table and stroked her hand. "If it'll make you feel better, I'll have my secretary send Father Gregory a check tomorrow."

"That's not good enough," she said, sliding her hand from beneath his. "I want to become directly involved."

"You don't have time to become involved."

Believing that he'd put an end to it, he went back to his steak. But Remy couldn't let the matter drop. This was more than just a need for a hobby. It was a spiritual matter. The priest had said, "Maybe if you did something to benefit children..."

Jenny's House had been a direct answer to her prayers. She'd asked for an opportunity to atone, and it had come in the form of Father Gregory's telephone call this morning. If this is what God wanted her to do, not even Pinkie Duvall could deter her.

Keeping her voice casual, she said, "I have a few hours a week that aren't committed to anything else."

"I think it would be good for her, Pinkie," Flarra chimed in. "She's been so despondent lately."

"I have not," Remy said.

"You've noticed, too?" Pinkie ignored Remy's protest and addressed Flarra.

She nodded, her black curls bouncing. "For months she's been a real drag."

"Thank you."

"Well you have, Remy. It must be true if both I and my favorite brother-in-law noticed." She batted her eyelashes at him. "May I please have some wine?"

"No, you may not," Remy said, answering for him.

"Jeez, no public school. No boys. No wine. I might just as well live on Mars."

"Sister Beatrice would have a fit if we returned you to the convent tipsy."

"I bet Sister Bea takes a nip on the sly. Can we talk about Mardi Gras?"

"Not tonight." Pinkie had let the conversation between her and Flarra go uninterrupted, Remy noticed. He was focused on her, and his hard scrutiny made her uneasy. "What are you thinking, Pinkie?"

"I'm thinking how much I hate the idea of my wife rubbing elbows with riffraff."

"I don't even know what Father Gregory plans to propose," she argued. "He may only want permission to add our name to their list of supporters, or to ask that we encourage our friends to contribute. I won't know until I meet with him, but I'd really like to get involved in this project. At the very least, I'd like to personally present our check."

"Where is this new facility?"

"He didn't say specifically."

"Where did he propose the meeting take place?"

"He said I could pick the place."

His index finger impatiently tapped against his wineglass. "Why is this so important to you, Remy?"

How she answered was critical. For Pinkie to agree, he must hear something he liked. "It's important to me because little Jenny didn't have a Pinkie Duvall appear in her life in time to save her. She wasn't as fortunate as Flarra and I."

"That gives me goose bumps," Flarra said.

Pinkie relaxed and signaled Roman to refill his wineglass. "All right, Remy, you may have your meeting. Here in the house. During the day."

"Thank you, Pinkie."

"Cool," said Flarra.

* * *

Father Gregory hung up the pay telephone and turned to Burke. "Their house, tomorrow afternoon."

During their previous conversation Father Gregory had given Mrs. Duvall the number of a telephone in the men's room of one of her husband's own strip joints. The sounds of bass instruments vibrated through the paper-thin walls.

"Their house?" Burke repeated, rubbing the back of his neck. "I was expecting to meet in a public place."

"Well, no such luck," Gregory said. "So it's no go, right? You have to ditch the plan."

Upon reflection, Burke said, "Actually, this might work out better. What time did you set the meeting?"

"Didn't you hear what I said, Basile?"

"Yes. You said, their house tomorrow. And I asked you what time."

"This is never going to work."

"It'll work. If you keep your cool and do everything I tell you to do, it'll work."

"Maybe you think you know me, Basile, but you don't. Basically I'm a coward. When it comes to choices, I always think of myself first."

"Good. That's good. Think of yourself. If you leave me

in the lurch, or choke up and blow the sting, think of yourself in jail for a very long time."

Gregory moaned forlornly. "Even if something goes wrong that's not my fault, you'll probably blame me."

"No, I won't. I promise," Burke told him, meaning it. "No matter how this goes down, you'll walk away free and clear."

"Free and clear? From Pinkie Duvall?" Gregory snorted scornfully. "I nearly shit bricks just calling his house on the telephone. I remember my folks talking about him around the dinner table when I was still in grade school. He's a freaking legend, one of the most powerful men in this town, if not *the* most powerful."

"I know all about him."

"So then you know he's a damn scary character. It's rumored that he's had people killed if they crossed him."

"It's more than rumor."

Gregory's jaw dropped open with incredulity. "Yet you expect me to walk into his house impersonating a priest, meet his wife face to face, and take money from her?"

"Unless you want to go to jail and become the sweetheart of a guy everybody calls Bull."

"You've used up that marker. I went to the cathedral with you and acted out my scene. Brilliantly, I might add. That squared us."

"I never said that," Burke countered blandly. "I said that if you agreed to play Father Gregory, I'd let you off the hook."

"I assumed I only had to pose as Father Gregory that one time."

"Well, you assumed wrong. What time tomorrow?"

"You're crazy as hell, Basile."

"Probably."

Gregory had him there. This plan of his *was* crazy. Dramatic, yes. Effective, assuredly. Crazy, definitely.

Since hearing Mrs. Duvall's confession, he'd thought the plan through from every angle. There was always a damn good chance that something would go awry, but he was taking every precaution against failure. He'd vacated his apartment and, using a false name, had moved into another place that was equally as disreputable. He'd ditched the Toyota for an older model.

When in the new car, he kept an eye on his rearview mirror. On foot, he checked frequently to see if Bardo, or someone of his ilk, was tailing him. He was fairly certain no one was.

Had Duvall called off his dogs? After Burke declined his job offer, Duvall might have dismissed him as insignificant. Maybe he was too cocksure of himself to fear retribution from a bummed-out, broke, besmirched ex-cop like Burke Basile. If he did expect reprisal, he would be looking for it to be violent.

That's why this just might work.

"Why can't another cop play the priest?" Gregory whined. "How come an undercover cop can't be Father Gregory?"

"Because you're a better actor than anyone in the division." Gregory still thought he was participating in a covert police action.

"Well, I quit," he said, taking a stand. "I don't want to play Father Gregory anymore. I'd rather go to jail than have Pinkie Duvall after my ass."

Burke bore down on him. "If you back out on me now, your skinny ass will be fair game for every pervert in the Orleans Parish jail. I'll see to it." He now had the younger man backed against the stained wall of the men's room.

Teeth clenched, Burke said, "Now, for the last fucking time, Father Gregory, *what time tomorrow*?"

* * *

"What a pleasure it is to meet you, Mrs. Duvall." Gregory James smiled disarmingly as he shook hands with their hostess. "Thank you for agreeing to see us."

She glanced beyond him to the second priest.

"Uh, this is Father Kevin," Gregory stammered. "My colleague and cofounder of Jenny's House."

Burke had chosen his pseudonym in honor of Kev Stuart, which seemed appropriate.

"Thank you both for coming," she said. "I'm flattered that you want to enlist my help."

The solarium into which the butler had shown them overlooked the rear lawn and afforded a clear view of the gazebo. Looking at it, Burke remarked, "You have a beautiful estate, Mrs. Duvall."

He wasn't worried about her recognizing his voice. In the confessional he'd spoken in a muffled whisper and had faked several coughs. Nor would she make a connection between the spit-and-polished Father Kevin and the casually dressed, mustachioed man in the baseball cap who'd retrieved her forgotten sack of oranges at the outdoor coffee bar.

"Thank you. Please sit down."

He and Gregory sat side by side on a wicker settee. She sat in a chair facing them and asked if they would like coffee.

Father Gregory smiled at the butler. "I'd love some. Decaf, please."

"Same for me," Burke said.

He withdrew, leaving the priests alone with Mrs. Duvall. And her bodyguard.

The man's wide shoulders extended beyond the back of his chair, and the wicker seemed to be straining to support him. His dark suit was incongruous with the sunny garden room. He looked as out of place as a monkey wrench in a floral arrangement.

Burke had experienced a heart flurry when he entered the solarium and saw the familiar bodyguard. Mrs. Duvall hadn't recognized him, but the man was supposedly trained to be on the alert. Burke had given him a pleasant smile and a slight nod. He'd grunted a greeting, his eyes registering no recognition. Whatever Duvall was paying the dullard, it was too much.

Mrs. Duvall addressed him as Errol. "You don't have to stay. I'm sure you'll be bored with this discussion."

He thought it over, gave each of the priests a look that could have passed for a stern warning, then stood. "Okay. But I'll be right outside if you need me."

When he left, Father Gregory turned to their hostess. "Is he always like that? Or is he sometimes dour?"

She laughed spontaneously. Burke silently thanked Gregory for putting her at ease. So far the young man was doing an exceptional acting job. They chitchatted easily until the butler, whom she referred to as Roman, returned with a large silver tray and set it on a wheeled cart, from which Mrs. Duvall herself served them coffee and small cakes frosted with pastel icing. Her motions were fluid, effortless, natural. She handled the heavy silver coffeepot as gracefully as she handled her spoon, with which she stirred a single dollop of cream into her coffee.

"I'm anxious to hear all about Jenny's House."

Father Gregory cleared his throat and inched forward on his seat. "The concept came to me..."

Burke tuned out as Gregory launched into a flowery speech about a homeless children's refuge that didn't exist. While pretending to hinge on every word coming from Father Gregory's mouth, he watched Remy Duvall's face. She listened intently, responding as anticipated to the buzz words Burke had told Gregory to incorporate. Her questions were insightful and intelligent. When Gregory retold the fictitious story of little Jenny, tears came to her eyes.

"It's so tragic."

Because her sadness seemed sincere, it would be easy to start feeling badly about this gross manipulation of her emotions. But then Burke reminded himself of how cozy she'd been with Bardo in the gazebo. Any woman who would willingly consort with Bardo didn't deserve compassion.

He set his cup and saucer on the table at his elbow and abruptly stood up. "Pardon me for interrupting, Father Gregory, but I need to be excused."

Gregory swiveled his head around so fast his neck popped. He looked at Burke with bald panic. They hadn't rehearsed this part. It wasn't in the script. Burke had omitted it intentionally because he hadn't wanted to increase Gregory's anxiety. Since he seemed to be comfortable in his role-playing, Burke felt he could safely leave Gregory alone with Mrs. Duvall for a few minutes, which was all he needed.

"There's a powder room behind the stairs in the entry," she told him.

"Thank you."

"Would you like Errol to show you?"

"No, thanks. I'll find it."

He strolled out of the solarium, but once he'd cleared the doorway, he pulled up short and looked for the bodyguard. He wasn't just outside the room as he'd said he would be. Instead, Burke found him in an adjacent den, watching television. His back was to the door. Apparently he didn't consider Father Gregory and Father Kevin much of a threat.

Burke went into the powder room and closed the door, but only for a moment. Coming out, he took the stairs two at a time, wincing whenever one of the treads creaked.

The first door past the landing opened into another small bathroom. Three seconds max, and he was out.

How many servants were in the house? He had no way of knowing, but a safe guess was several. At any moment, he might bump into a militant housekeeper demanding to know what the holy hell the holy father was doing snooping around Mr. Duvall's house. She would raise a ruckus, which would summon Errol, who would restrain him until Pinkie arrived. By this time tomorrow, his body would be a buffet for carnivorous fish grazing on the bottom of the Gulf.

He opened the second door along the hallway and found what he was looking for—a grand bedroom with separate baths on either side and a wide balcony overlooking the front lawn.

Burke knew nothing about antiques, but each piece of furniture in the room looked like the genuine article. Drug money would go a long way at highbrow auctions. One of the pieces, a cheval glass in the corner that stood at least twelve feet tall, reflected a man wearing unnecessary eyeglasses and the trappings of a priest.

"You're way over the edge on this one, Basile," he muttered.

He peered into what was obviously Pinkie's dressing room, but the maid had been there since the master of the house left that morning. Everything was in order. Nothing was lying out.

In the bedroom, the nightstands were easily distinguishable. Pinkie slept on her left side. On his nightstand were a pair of reading glasses, a copy of *Newsweek,* and a cordless telephone. Burke checked it for a number, but the plastic sleeve that held the label provided by the telephone company was empty. Probably an ultraprivate, unlisted number.

He opened the drawer, hoping to discover a personal telephone directory, a journal, a bankbook. But Pinkie was too smart to have anything in his nightstand drawer except a bottle of Maalox, a leaky ballpoint pen, another pair of glasses, and a notepad on which nothing was written.

On Mrs. Duvall's nightstand was a rosary, a bowl of potpourri, and a crystal carafe of water with the small, inverted glass capping it. In the drawer, nothing except a box of note cards. But there was no address book. Whom did she write to?

How long had he been out of the solarium? Suspiciously long to be taking a leak? What if, during a commercial, Errol poked his head into the solarium and, seeing only one priest, asked where the other one was?

Get on with it.

He crossed into Mrs. Duvall's dressing room. The maid hadn't been here, not since Mrs. Duvall had dressed for her meeting with Father Gregory and Father Kevin. A blouse was lying across the satin vanity stool. Apparently it had been considered, but discarded in favor of the one she was wearing. Burke picked it up, rubbed the fabric between his fingers. Silk. He replaced it across the stool, exactly as it had been.

Noticing the seam in the mirrored wall above the countertop, he depressed it, and a section of mirror swung out, revealing a medicine cabinet. Toothbrush and toothpaste, Visine, Stresstabs, Q-Tips, tampons, aspirin, oral contraceptives. No other prescriptions.

He closed the cabinet and was about to turn away when he noticed that the marble surface of her dressing table was lightly dusted with talcum. The body powder was stored in a round crystal box topped with an ornate silver lid. Beside it was a luxurious lamb's-wool powder puff, which he picked up and sniffed. The fragrance was unmistakably familiar. He brushed his fingertips across the fuzzy surface of the powder puff, conjuring up tantalizing speculations as to the exotic spots it had last visited.

What the fuck are you doing, Basile? Get the hell out of here.

He returned the puff to its place beside the crystal box and left the dressing room as though the devil were at his heels. At the bedroom door he paused to listen. Hearing nothing, he eased open the door and stepped into the hallway.

He was midway down the stairs when Errol appeared in the entry.

Chapter Sixteen

Errol, apparently on his way to use the bathroom, stopped dead in his tracks when he saw Father Kevin loping down the stairs. Burke smiled disarmingly. "If you're going to the can, you might need this." He tossed the bodyguard a roll of toilet tissue.

Errol, still confused, fumbled it before catching it against his chest.

"The powder room was out of paper, so I had to use the one at the top of the stairs."

Errol pushed open the door to the powder room and looked at the toilet tissue spool, from which Burke had removed the roll before going upstairs. He had carried it right back down again, but it appeared that he'd brought it from the other bathroom. "I thought, long as I was up there, I'd replace the roll down here. Never know when someone might need it." He grinned, man to man. "Of course, it depends on what you have to do."

"Yeah," Errol said with uncertainty. "Thanks."

Burke started off in the direction of the solarium before he came back around, as though an idea had just occurred to him. "Say, if Mr. and Mrs. Duvall become involved in Jenny's House, maybe you'd like to participate, too. Helping out with the boys, organizing games, something like that."

"I don't think so. Mr. Duvall keeps me pretty busy."

"Well, it was just a thought." Burke turned away and this time didn't stop until he was back in the solarium, where Gregory was still talking.

"Father Kevin and I think it's essential that the children who stay at Jenny's House are given chores. That will make it seem less like a charitable facility and more like a normal home."

"Excellent idea, Father."

Gregory glanced at Burke with evident relief. "Father Kevin and I agree that giving the children a sense of responsibility, and praising even the smallest achievement, is the first step toward reversing the negative effects they've suffered thus far and building self-esteem."

Mrs. Duvall turned to Burke for confirmation. He nodded in agreement, but at that moment he would have agreed to the theory that the moon was cream cheese. It was damn near impossible to maintain a godly expression so soon after handling her body powder puff. He tried to keep his gaze above the cross hanging from the chain around her neck, but it was a battle royal of wills between his id and his ego.

"God has blessed this visit, Father Kevin." Gregory held up a check for ten thousand dollars made out to Jenny's House.

"You're very generous, Mrs. Duvall. God bless you."

"God bless your mission, Father Kevin."

Burke stood. "We shouldn't take up any more of your time."

"Of course, we wouldn't want to do that." Gregory also came to his feet. "Once I start talking about Jenny's House, there's no stopping me."

"I've enjoyed it," she said. "Can't you stay until my husband gets home? I know he would like to meet you."

"No, no, we've got to run," Gregory said. "More calls to make. Some other time, perhaps."

Burke passed her a business card. "I'm sure you'd like to hear progress reports. Please call anytime."

"Thank you, I will."

"In fact, you might enjoy seeing the facility for yourself."

The suggestion rendered Father Gregory mute. He gaped at Father Kevin with dumbstruck disbelief. Mrs. Duvall, on the other hand, was delighted at the prospect. "Would that be possible?"

"No."

"Of course."

Gregory and Burke answered at the same time, but Burke's reply overrode Gregory's. Sheepishly, he said, "Naturally, whatever Father Kevin wishes. I merely thought we would wait to have a formal open house once the facility is completed. You know, invite all its supporters at once," he added lamely.

"I'm sure Mrs. Duvall would prefer a private tour," Burke said, looking deeply into her eyes.

"I don't expect preferential treatment," she said, "but I would very much like to see the work in progress. Maybe I could help out."

"Your contribution is help enough, I assure you," Father Gregory said, sounding a bit desperate.

"But a favorable report from me might urge my husband to contribute even more."

Burke smiled. "All the more reason for you to make a personal visit. Call whenever you'd like to go. We'll make ourselves available to fit your schedule."

* * *

"'Make ourselves available'? 'Fit your schedule'? Jesus, we're gonna die."

"Will you stop that caterwauling? You're giving me a headache."

"What have you got me into, Basile? I don't like this. I agreed to do you a favor, and I came through, didn't I? Not once, but twice. But this is it. Finis. Applause, applause. Curtain down. Lights out and everybody goes home. No encore. I've performed my last scene with you. You keep changing the dialogue. And where did you go when you left the room?"

"To pee."

"Oh sure, you did. I think you went snooping, is what I think."

"That's one of your main problems, Gregory. You think too much. You'd do better to simply go with the flow."

"If I go with the flow, I'm liable to wind up floating facedown in the Mighty Mississip'. My life is hardly studded with accomplishments, but I'm not ready to die. Consider me out. As of now."

The argument continued all the way to Gregory's townhouse. Burke leaned across the other man and opened the passenger door. "Go in, put your feet up, have a glass or two of wine, and calm down. I'll be in touch."

"I'm out. O-u-t."

"They don't serve Pinot Noir with dinner in prison, Gregory."

"You can't keep threatening me with jail. You've got nothing on me."

"Maybe not today. But give it a week or two. I'll stay on you like a duck on a June bug. Sooner or later, you'll act on those impulses that, by your own admission, you can't control."

"My shrink and I are making progress."

"No, he's making money off what he knows is a hopeless case. You're a psycho sugar tit and he's latched on."

Gregory slumped in his seat. "You're a bastard, Basile."

"We've established that."

"You're stronger willed than I am. I can't win with you. Everybody picks on me."

Burke reached across the car, grabbed Gregory by the hair, and turned his head toward him. "Listen to me, you sniveling, spoiled, little shit. Believe it or not, this might be the best thing that ever happened to you in your whole miserable life. For once, somebody is making you do something you don't want to do. I'm giving you an opportunity to prove that you're better than everybody believes. I'm giving you a chance to be a man."

Gregory swallowed emotionally. "I honestly don't think I can be, Basile. I'd like to be, but as you said, I'm hopeless. I wouldn't count on me if I were you."

"Well," Burke grumbled, releasing his hair, "unfortunately you're all I've got."

Gregory set one foot on the pavement but made no

other move to get out. After a time, he said, "This isn't a police operation, is it?"

"No." Burke looked directly at him. "No, it's not. It's a personal vendetta. It has to do with my friend who got killed last year."

"I figured it was something like that. Thanks for finally being honest with me."

"You're welcome."

Averting his head, Burke gazed through the cloudy windshield of his car. He had to think about it for only a few seconds before saying, "Forget it, Gregory. I shouldn't have dragged you into this. I lied to you and manipulated you every step of the way, and as you said yourself, that's unfair.

"I'm about to do something that's crazy and dangerous. You were right about that, too. In the process, you'd probably panic and screw up and end up dead. I don't need another death on my conscience. I needed your help on the clerical stuff, but I think I can wing it from here. Thanks for your help."

Then, as an afterthought, he added, "I hate to see you screwing up your life, Gregory. If you don't get smart and clean up your act, you'll eventually get busted and sent away for a long time. One of these days your daddy won't be able to buy you out of a serious charge that disgusts not only the general populace but the prison population as well. In there, they'd make your life hell, and might even kill you. Think hard about the consequences the next time you get the urge to whip it out and wag it at somebody, especially a kid."

Smiling wryly, he made the sign of the cross. "Go and sin no more, my son." Then he reached for the gear shift and put it into reverse.

"Wait." Gregory's handsome features were rearranged by indecision. He gnawed the inside of his cheek. "Could I get into trouble? Or hurt?"

"I swear I'd try to prevent that, but there's a risk, yes."

After several long moments of private deliberation, the younger man sighed. "Screw it. I'm in. What else have I got going?"

Chapter Seventeen

W hat do you mean he's disappeared?"

Bardo shrugged. "Just what I said, Pinkie. Nobody's seen him around. When I went back to that shit hole he was living in, he'd moved out. I came down pretty hard on the landlord, but he swore to me that Basile left in the middle of the night. Dropped his rent and key in the mail slot. This isn't the kind of place where you leave a forwarding address. It's like he's vanished. One of our guys in the NOPD has been sniffing around. He says nobody has heard from Basile since he surrendered his badge."

"You should have had someone tailing him."

"Yeah, well, who knew?"

Basile's seeming disappearance made Pinkie uneasy. Basile hadn't declined his job offer with a polite "No, but I'm flattered that you asked." He had refused in a way that left no room for negotiation. This bothered Pinkie for two major reasons.

First, it pissed him off that a nobody ex-cop had insultingly refused a well-meaning offer. This was the first time Pinkie had tried to lure Basile to the other side of the narcotics business, but it wasn't the first time he had considered throwing out some bait to see if Basile would bite. What better way to eliminate an enemy than to enlist him in your camp?

And Basile was an enemy. Within the Narcotics Division, he'd been a constant nuisance, insisting that a post-mortem be conducted on every operation, successful or not. He was a crusader, demanding accountability for mistakes, seeking out the whys and wherefores of every screwup. He was a nagging conscience that kept the department reasonably honest, although not entirely so.

Worse, he appeared to be incorruptible. Pinkie had commissioned purveyors of every conceivable vice to try to find a weak spot in Basile's moral armor. None had been successful—not the bookies, not the drug dealers, not the women. All had tried to compromise him; all had failed.

So for years Basile had plagued Pinkie Duvall's operation. He was a self-appointed general in the war against drugs and he had the ability to rally the troops. When Kev Stuart was killed, the conflict had turned personal. Basile was still bitter over that and, despite the Bardo verdict, was not going to let the matter drop. He wasn't going to rest until he had avenged Stuart's death. Quitting the NOPD had been a smoke screen.

Which brought Pinkie to the second reason he had hoped Basile would sign on with him. He could keep a closer watch on him if he were an employee. As long as Basile was with the police department, his activities were easily monitored. Now he had vanished, and no one seemed to know his whereabouts or his intentions. Pinkie didn't like it.

A man didn't ascend to the powerful position Pinkie held without cultivating a legion of enemies along the way. He couldn't begin to count the threats, real and implied, that he'd received over the years. He paid dearly for protection against people with grudges. He felt secure. Even so, he was smart enough to know that for all the precautions he took, he couldn't be one hundred percent protected, twenty-four hours a day. No one, not even a head of state, was invulnerable.

Burke Basile was out there, a loose cannon with a short fuse, harboring a lot of hatred for Pinkie Duvall. He'd be a fool not to be a little edgy about that.

The system in which Basile had placed his trust had failed him, so he'd thumbed his nose at it and walked away. His actions were no longer governed by the rules and regulations of law enforcement, which made him doubly dangerous.

Of course, Basile couldn't harm him without tarnishing himself, but that was small comfort. Just how crazy was the man? How far was he willing to go to get his revenge? What did he have to lose? Not a career. Not a wife and family. Nothing in the way of material possessions. Not even his integrity or good reputation, which the media had trampled.

That's what disturbed Pinkie most. Experience had taught him that the less a person had to lose, the more of a threat he posed.

"I want him found," he told Bardo emphatically.

"What do I do when I find him?"

Pinkie gave him a pointed look.

Grinning, Bardo nodded. "It'll be a pleasure."

Pinkie's secretary knocked. He beckoned her into his private office. "Pardon the interruption, Mr. Duvall, but you asked for this information as soon as I obtained it."

Having given Bardo his assignment, Pinkie dismissed him and took from his secretary the typed memo regarding Jenny's House. When he had arrived home last evening, Remy was behaving more like her old self. She was excited about the charity, spearheaded by this Father Gregory, who had invited her to visit the facility. Pinkie had promised to think about it. It seemed harmless, especially if it lifted her out of the doldrums she'd been in.

He had questioned Errol at length about the priest's visit and had been surprised to learn that there had actually been two who attended the meeting. One, he was told, was older and more businesslike. The younger one was handsome, but probably gay, according to Errol. It was he, Father Gregory, who'd done most of the talking. Errol said that he had remained in the room for the duration of their visit, and that the two churchmen had discussed nothing except a refuge for kids.

Fingering the business card the priest had given Remy, Pinkie asked his secretary if she had called the number printed on it. "Yes, sir. The phone was answered by a woman."

"How'd she answer?"

"Jenny's House."

"So it's legit?"

"Oh, yes, Mr. Duvall. I asked to speak with Father Gregory. She told me that neither he nor Father Kevin was in, but she would be pleased to give them a message."

The secretary then laughed. "She thought I was calling to make a donation. She gave me much more information about the facility than I asked for. I didn't get it all down verbatim, but as you can see by the memo, I took extensive notes."

* * *

"Very nicely done, Dixie." Burke took the telephone receiver from the girl and hung it up. The pay phone was in the second-story hallway of a flophouse that stank of poor plumbing.

"It was worth forty bucks."

Although he had paid her beforehand, Dixie followed him into the room he was renting by the day under an assumed name. She climbed onto the bed, digging the stiletto heels of her white patent boots into the stained bedspread. When she smiled, he could see her chaw of apple green gum stuck between her molars. "You really think I sounded like a nun type?"

"Could've fooled me. Drink?"

"You bet."

Burke fished a canned soft drink from the Styrofoam ice chest—the room didn't come with a refrigerator—and passed it to her.

"When you said drink, I thought you meant—"

"Nope. You're below legal drinking age."

Finding that very funny, she popped the top on the drink and sipped the fizz that spewed out. "Did you mean what you said?"

"About what?"

"I sounded like a nun? Maybe I missed my calling."

"Maybe."

"But, when you think about it, I'm sorta like a nun."

Burke raised his eyebrows skeptically.

She propped herself up on her elbows, a position that

thrust her breasts almost out of the black-lace demi-bra beneath her open denim jacket. "I'm serious."

"Nuns don't wear red vinyl miniskirts and heavy perfume, Dixie." Her gardenia scent was her trademark. When Vice went looking for her, they sniffed her out, literally. In this small room, where no doubt a thousand sordid transactions had taken place, the sweet fragrance was as thick as a gumbo and slightly nauseating.

"Nuns serve their fellow man. Isn't that what I do?"

"I think the distinction lies in the manner in which you serve."

"Well, sure, if you're going to get technical..." She slurped her drink. "You Catholic, Basile?"

"Raised that way."

"Hard to imagine you praying and stuff."

"It's been a long time," he murmured.

It had been a sure bet that Pinkie would check out Jenny's House, especially if his wife had asked permission to visit it. Working under that hypothesis, Burke had paid a starving artist twenty dollars to sketch a phony logo for the bogus children's refuge. He then went to a self-service print shop and made up a dozen business cards with the logo and the number of the pay telephone across the hall from his room. He'd left one of those cards with Mrs. Duvall.

Earlier today, he'd gone in search of a "secretary" and had bumped into Dixie. She was a good whore and an even better snitch. The former he had no personal knowledge of, but he had bought information from her several times, and it had always proven to be valid. She'd been working the streets since she was thirteen. It was a marvel to Burke that she'd lived to the ripe old age of seventeen.

"You know, I hardly recognized you this morning," she

observed as she rolled the cold can across her heavily rouged lips. "When did you lose the mustache?"

"Few days ago."

"How come?"

"Felt like it."

"You working undercover now?"

"You could say that."

"The bitch on the phone said she was from Pinkie Duvall's office. What gives?"

"You don't need to know."

"Jeez, Basile, you're a hard man to draw out."

"I guess I don't feel like talking, Dixie." He stretched out on the bed beside her and wadded the flat pillow beneath his head.

She rolled toward him and placed her thigh over his. "Fine and dandy with me, honey. We don't have to talk."

Her hand slid down his chest to his belt buckle and began to unfasten it. He covered her hand. "That's not what I meant. You've already earned your forty dollars, and I'm on a tight budget."

She thought about it for a second or two. Then she ran her long fingernail along his recently shaved upper lip. "What the hell, I'll throw it in for free."

"Thanks, but not this time."

"How come? Are you the last remaining faithful married man?"

"Not anymore."

"You're not faithful anymore?"

"I'm not married anymore."

"Then what's the problem? Come on, Basile. I've had other cops. Dozens of them. You're the last holdout, and I've got a reputation to uphold. Can you honestly say you haven't thought about boffing me?"

He smiled at her. "Dixie, you're a knockout. I'm sure boffing you is one of life's greatest pleasures. But I could have a daughter your age."

"What's age got to do with it?"

"Right now, everything. I'm tired and need some sleep."

"It's the middle of the day."

"I was up late last night."

"All the more reason for you to relax and enjoy. I'll do the work." Her hand wandered back to his belt buckle.

Again he stopped her. "Not this time."

She expelled a green-apple-scented breath of disappointment. "Okay," she said grudgingly. "But could I just lie here with you for a while and rest?"

His glance moved from the rosy pout of her lips to the breasts spilling from the lace brassiere cups. "I don't think I'd get much rest."

She grinned impishly. "So I *do* turn you on."

"Scram, Dixie. Let me take a nap in peace."

He gave her an affectionate push, and she scooted off the bed. "Oh well, I gave it my best shot." At the door, she stood with one hand on her hip, the other on the doorknob. "If you're screwing around with Pinkie Duvall, you're asking for trouble."

"I know."

"Good guys like you are few and far between, Basile. Take care of yourself, okay?"

"You too, Dixie."

Just as she opened the door, the pay phone in the hallway rang. Basile came off the bed like a rocket. "Answer it," he told Dixie, pushing her across the hallway ahead of him. "Same as before."

The prostitute sounded like a trained secretary when

she picked up the telephone on the third ring. "Good after-noon. Jenny's House." She listened, then said, "Hold on, please."

Covering the mouthpiece, she whispered. "She wants to speak to Father Gregory."

"She? The same woman as before?"

"No, I don't think so."

"Tell her that Father Gregory is out. Ask if she wishes to speak to Father Kevin."

"And that would be...?"

"Me."

Dixie eyed him suspiciously, but she relayed the message. After a moment, she handed the receiver to Burke. "You're on, padre."

"Hello. This is Father Kevin."

"Hello, Father. It's Remy Duvall."

His eyes closed momentarily. So far, it was working. "Oh, yes. Hello. How are you, Mrs. Duvall?"

"Fine, thanks. Is the invitation to tour Jenny's House still open?"

"Certainly. When are you available?"

"The day after tomorrow? After lunch?"

Day after tomorrow. After lunch. Barely forty-eight hours. Could he make all the arrangements by then?

"That would be fine," he heard himself say. "Three o'clock?"

"Perfect. What's the address?"

"Uh, actually, Mrs. Duvall, it's rather hard to find. In-stead of giving you directions, it would be much simpler if Father Gregory and I picked you up and took you there."

"Oh. I don't know..."

Sensing her hesitation, he said, "Your contribution was a direct answer to our prayers. We used your check to

purchase a much-needed van. We'd like to show it off."
Dixie was giving her chewing gum a vigorous workout
and watching him with amused wonder.

"I'm so pleased you were able to put our donation to
good use," Remy Duvall said.

"So, shall we pick you up?"

"Well, I suppose that would be all right." Then, more
definitely, "Yes, pick us up here."

" 'Us'?"

"My, uh, Errol. He'll be coming along."

"Fine."

"Then I'll see you the day after tomorrow at three."

He agreed to the day and time and hung up but kept his
hands around the receiver. He was standing still, staring
vacantly into near space, but his mind was racing. After
a moment, he realized that Dixie was still there, leaning against the wall with her arms folded, observing him
shrewdly. "What's with you, Basile?"

"What do you mean?"

"You look like a boy who just got a date with the prom
queen, excited and scared at the same time."

"Hardly a date, Dix," he said absently. Then, shaking
himself out of his daze, he thanked her again for her help.
"I couldn't have done it without you."

"What'd you do?"

"Never mind." Impulsively, he began patting down his
pockets in search of something to write on. "Listen, I'm
going to give you an address, and I want you to keep it. If
you ever need a safe place, go there."

He found an old convenience-store receipt in his pants
pocket and scribbled down the address. Dixie barely
glanced at it before tucking it into one of the pockets of
her jacket. "Safe place? Nothing's going to happen to me."

"Don't be stupid. Girls like you have a short life span."
He tapped the pocket where she'd placed the slip of paper.
"Don't forget."

* * *

Burke leaned his head against the headrest of his new car.
Well, hardly new, just different from the Toyota. Although
it was difficult, he resisted closing his eyes. If he did, exhaustion might claim him and he would fall asleep and
miss something.

He hoped that after all the trouble he'd gone to placing
it, the damn bug would work.

Duvall probably had the house swept daily for listening
devices, and, while he wouldn't have known it was Burke
Basile who'd placed the tiny wireless microphone beneath
his nightstand, the two visiting priests would be among
the suspects.

Since state-of-the-art equipment was costly, and
Burke's budget wouldn't stretch that far, he'd called in a
favor from a cop who worked the evidence room. A few
years back, his son had got mixed up with a bad crowd.
One of Basile's squads had busted him for possession.
With the cop's blessing, Basile had come down on the
kid pretty hard, scared him into a more receptive frame
of mind, and turned him around. The family still felt indebted.

The dime-store-caliber rig had been seized in a raid;
nobody would miss it, so the cop had heisted it. He and
Basile had tried it out. It worked, but the quality wasn't
great.

Thus far tonight, he hadn't had an opportunity to test
it. After an hour and a half of surveillance, the master

bedroom had remained dark. He checked his wristwatch. Twelve minutes past eleven. How long could he wait? He was exhausted. Since hearing from Mrs. Duvall earlier today, he'd been busy.

"Father Kevin" had no trouble cashing Duvall's check from the bank he'd written it on. The money had enabled him to pay an individual cash for an inexpensive van advertised in the classified ads. He'd driven the van straight to a cut-rate paint and body shop, where he asked for a rush job. It would be ready by tomorrow afternoon. He then returned to his room and cut out a stencil of cardboard, which he would use to apply the Jenny's House logo to the doors of the freshly painted van.

The limousine glided past.

By the time Burke realized that the approaching car belonged to the Duvalls, he was already looking at its taillights. He held his breath and didn't release it until the limo disappeared through the iron picket security gate at the rear of the property. A short time later lights came on in the master bedroom.

He slipped on the headset and immediately heard voices.

"…in the opera…heard her…and…stunk." That from Pinkie.

Burke readjusted the headset in time to hear Mrs. Duvall say, "…proud of her for making it past the first audition. She's their only daughter."

"Well I was bored stiff. It's hot in here. Turn down the thermostat."

For several minutes Burke heard nothing more and envisioned them in their respective dressing rooms, preparing for bed. The next words were from Mrs. Duvall: "I'll write them a thank-you note tomorrow."

"Whatever. Take that damn thing off."

The light went out. Coming through the earphones were the sounds of rustling bed linens, of bodies readjusting, of Pinkie moving close to his naked wife and caressing the skin dusted with talcum powder from a silver-capped jar.

Burke closed his eyes.

"All the men there tonight were drooling over my beautiful wife."

"Thank you."

Burke told himself not to listen anymore. They weren't going to talk about Duvall's sideline business. He wouldn't learn anything by continuing to eavesdrop on what was obviously a private conversation. But he listened anyway.

"I caught old man Salley looking at your tits. I glared at him. He blushed up to the roots of his toupee." Duvall chuckled. "By dessert, he and every other man around the dinner table was using his napkin to hide a hard-on."

"Don't say that."

"Why not? It's true."

"I don't believe that."

"Believe it, Remy. When a man looks at you, all he can think about is pussy." More rustling, the readjustment of limbs. "See what I mean?"

She murmured something so softly the microphone failed to pick it up.

Whatever she said pleased Duvall because he chuckled with self-congratulations. "You know what to do with it, sweetheart."

A moment later, a satisfied grunt from Duvall.

Burke bowed his head and rubbed his eye sockets hard.

After what seemed like an eternity to Burke, Duvall groaned, "Jesus, baby, that's making me crazy. Come here." Then, "What's the matter with you? How come you're not wet?"

"Let me up, and I'll get something."

"Never mind. Pull your knees...yeah, like that. Like Pinkie taught you."

Burke threw his head back against the headrest. He continued to listen. He listened to Duvall's chant of vulgarities, to his grunts and groans. He listened through it all, until Duvall climaxed, swearing in loud gasps.

Then there was nothing transmitted into the earphones except a faint, electronic hiss. He listened for several more minutes. When his jaw began to ache, Burke realized that his teeth were clenched. His fingers were wrapped so tightly around the steering wheel they were white. Slowly he pried them off. Removing the headset, he irritably tossed it onto the empty seat beside him. He wiped his sleeve across his sweating forehead.

Eventually, he started his car and drove away.

Chapter Eighteen

Burke left the newly painted van parked behind an abandoned warehouse, hoping it would still be there, intact, when he returned for it tomorrow morning. Before rounding the corner, he glanced back at the vehicle, and was pleased with his stencil. From this distance, the Jenny's House logo was barely legible. It looked like an amateur job, which was what he'd wanted.

Lost in thought as he made his way along the banquette, he didn't see Mac McCuen until the man was directly in front of him, blocking his path.

"Burke! Christ, man, I've been looking all over the city for you."

Mentally Burke groaned. The last thing he needed was Mac's distracting chitchat. But he attempted a smile and pretended to be glad to see him. "Hey, Mac. How're you doin'?"

"I almost didn't recognize you. What's with your hair? Where's your mustache?"

"Last time I saw, the bathroom sink."

"That'll take some getting used to." Then, changing pace from reflective to charged, he asked what the hell Burke had been up to.

"Not much. How'd you find me?"

"It wasn't easy. I started asking around a few days ago, but nobody knew where you were at. Either that or nobody was talking. Then I thought of Dixie. She remembered seeing you."

"How much did that cost you?"

"Ten bucks."

"I paid her twenty to forget it."

"Well," Mac said with a philosophic shrug, "you know whores."

Yeah, he knew whores. Some would sell out a friend for ten dollars. Others held out for limousines and mansions.

Knowing that Mac wouldn't be easy to shake, Burke bit the bullet and offered to buy him a beer. To his surprise, Mac declined. "I'm in a hurry now. But the reason I've been looking for you is to invite you to dinner. Tonight. Sort of a retirement party."

Burke couldn't think of an occasion better avoided. "I appreciate the thought, Mac, but no thanks."

"Relax. Dozens of people aren't going to pop out from behind the furniture and yell 'Surprise.' Nothing like that. Just you, me, and Toni. She wants to cook."

"Sounds nice, but—"

Mac, being his irrepressible self, poked his index finger into the center of Burke's chest. "I won't take no for an answer. Five dollars says you've got no other plans for tonight. So be there. Seven o'clock. Know where I live? I wrote the address on the back." He pressed a business card into Burke's reluctant hand.

Even for Mac, who was always overeager and hyper-active, this was strange behavior. As he turned to leave, Burke caught his sleeve. "You've never invited me to din-ner before, Mac. What's up?"

"Your future." Burke tilted his head quizzically. Mac said, "Tonight." Then he pulled his arm free and struck off down the banquette, walking briskly.

Burke turned over the business card and read what Mac had written down. It wasn't his street address.

* * *

Burke had been to the McCuens' house only once, when he'd dropped Mac off after work. Mac's car had been in the garage, and he hadn't wanted to inconvenience his wife, so he had inconvenienced Burke instead.

On that occasion, it had been after dark and Burke hadn't given the neighborhood any particular notice. Now, as he arrived at dusk, he was surprised to see how well the McCuens lived, which was much more affluently than he and Barbara had, or the Stuarts. The houses on Mac's street were spaced far apart, separated by clipped hedgerows and manicured lawns. Cars in driveways were expensive, late models.

Mac opened the front door before Burke reached it. "Glad you're here, Burke. Come meet my wife."

Smiling, shaking hands, and slapping Burke on the back, Mac pulled him into a wide vestibule. There was no trace of mystery in his bearing, none of the nervousness evinced earlier that day. Burke had brought with him a six-pack of imported beer and a bouquet of flowers. He handed Mac the six-pack and presented the bouquet to Toni McCuen when Mac introduced them.

She was a petite blonde who was as good-looking as her proud husband had boasted. She thanked Burke for the flowers in a heavily accented, deep South, sugar-coated voice that was genuine. "I'm so pleased to finally meet you. To hear Mac tell it, Burke Basile is a living legend."

"Hardly. It's a pleasure to meet you, Toni."

"It's nice out tonight. Why don't y'all take your beeah out on the patio. I'll call you when dinner's ready. It shouldn't be too long now."

As they moved outside, Mac showed him where they were planning to install a swimming pool. "I gave Toni a choice—a pool or a baby. She chose the pool." Mac winked. "'Course I'm still doing my best to knock her up. Bet you ten to one she'll be pregnant by the time the swimming pool is in, but what the hell."

The patio furniture wasn't the kind bought cheaply in the hope that it would last at least one summer season. The barbecue setup was the Rolls-Royce of outdoor cooking. By the time Toni called them to dinner, Burke had deduced that either the McCuens were living way beyond their means on credit, or that Toni had brought a sizable dowry into the marriage, or that Mac's gambling was providing a substantial second income.

One thing was certain: They couldn't live this high on the hog on a cop's salary.

After a superb dinner of pork tenderloin with all the trimmings, the charming Toni shooed them out of the dining room so she could clean up.

"Is it too cold for you outside?" Mac asked.

"Not at all."

They returned to the patio with brandies and cigars and, for a while, sat silently enjoying both. Burke waited for Mac to commence the conversation, which he'd obviously orchestrated to take place out of his wife's hearing. Burke had determined not to bring up Mac's obscure reference to his future, or question him about the warning he had scribbled on the back of his business card: *Watch your back. Others are.* This was Mac's party. It was up to him to provide the entertainment.

Out of the darkness, Mac asked, "Why'd you quit, Burke? And don't give me that bullshit about burnout."

"It's not bullshit. After Kev died, my heart just wasn't in it anymore."

"You hated it when I got bumped up to detective sergeant and took over leadership of his squad, didn't you? No, don't say anything," Mac said when he saw that Burke was about to object. "I know you didn't like it. I understood how it was between you and Kev Stuart."

"You make it sound like we were lovers or something."

Mac snuffled a laugh. "I know better than that. But I also know how hard you took it when he died."

Burke couldn't think of a suitable response, so he said nothing. He wasn't going to discuss his innermost feelings with Mac, first because his sentiments were nobody else's business and, second, because he didn't entirely trust Mac.

He had no specific reason to mistrust him. He just had a gut feeling that Mac's flashiness and amiability concealed a darker, more sinister aspect of his personality. Until Burke could identify that character flaw, he would remain wary of Mac.

Mac continued: "What I'm saying is, I don't think that what happened to Stuart is a reason for you to quit."

"That wasn't all of it."

"I know about the split with your wife."

"News travels fast."

"Especially when it's about a legend."

Burke cursed. "That's the second time tonight I've heard that crap. Keep it up and it's going to piss me off. I'm no fucking legend."

Mac chuckled, but his laughter didn't quite ring true. He leaned forward, placing his forearms on his knees and focusing on the fiery tip of his cigar. "Was Kev the one, Burke?"

"The one what?"

Mac lifted his gaze and gave him a direct look. "The leak in our division."

If Mac had offered him the alluring Toni for a night of amorous frolic, he couldn't have been more stunned. Then his shock turned to anger. "Is that what you think?"

"*I* don't think it, no," Mac said. "It's just that people talk."

"What people?"

"You know," he said, lifting his shoulders. "People. Within the division. And I.A. has been asking questions, too."

Internal Affairs was asking questions? Did that mean that the probe he had campaigned for had finally come about? He'd raised the hackles of everybody from Doug Patout right on up to the commissioner by insisting that a covert investigation be conducted within the department until the mole was exposed and eliminated. What an irony it would be if they suspected Kev.

"Some guys, not *me,*" Mac clarified quickly. "But some guys have speculated that maybe you discovered Kev's treachery and, when the opportunity presented itself, you popped him and dropped him. Is that the way it went down?"

"No," Burke said tersely.

"Or..."

When the other man stalled, Burke pressed him. "Come on, Mac. What else are they speculating?"

"That it was you."

Burke showed none of what he was feeling, but Mac must have felt the heat emanating from him and feared an eruption of outrage because he spoke now in a breathless rush: "Well, look at it from their standpoint, Basile. We pulled down a hell of a raid the other night."

"I read about it. Congratulations."

"So it looks—"

"Mighty suspicious that things start turning around in the division's favor the minute I got out."

"It would look a hell of a lot better if you'd come back."

"Not a chance."

"Then tell me they're wrong," Mac said, raising his voice to an argumentative level.

"I never asked to be your goddamn idol, Mac. I didn't ask to be anybody's."

"Who was selling us out?"

"I don't know, and I don't care," Burke lied.

"You may not know, but you care. You care a hell of a lot. I'd stake Toni's ass on that, and I'm very attached to her ass."

"With good reason." He tried to smile, but it didn't quite work, and Mac continued to glare at him, demanding an explanation. "Okay, Mac, I care. I care because the son of a bitch got Kev killed. But the harder I tried to root him out, the more unpopular I became around the NOPD.

"After the business with Sachel, and Ray Hahn turning up dead, I reached a saturation point of disgust, thought 'Screw this,' and got out. I've breathed easier ever since and haven't regretted my decision."

Mac thoughtfully puffed his cigar. "That's your official line. Give it to me unofficially."

"Unofficially? When I find out who was working both sides, I'm going to kill him."

Burke and the younger officer exchanged a long stare. After a moment, some of the tension went out of Mac's broad shoulders. "It makes me feel better to hear you admit it. How can I help?"

"No." Burke adamantly shook his head. "Kev was my key man, and my friend, and he died by my gun. It's my problem."

"Okay, I understand where you're coming from. But I don't think you can do it on your own, and it'll be much harder to do from the outside. Come back to the department and work it from the inside."

"Can't do that."

"The time to resign is when everything is going right," Mac argued. "Not when everything's in the shitcan. Your friend dies bloody. Your marriage collapses. You're under a lot of pressure within the division. Everybody knows you're bummed out. So, if something happens to one of the guys in Narcotics and Vice, who're they going to suspect first?"

Mac's argument had merit, but Basile said, "That's a chance I'll have to take." He narrowed his eyes against the smoke rising from his cigar. "Did Patout put you up to giving me this lecture?"

"No. But if he was here, he'd be telling you the same thing."

"He already has told me the same thing. Just today, in fact."

Burke had had his first appointment with a divorce lawyer early that morning. Barbara hadn't wasted any time in filing, and that was fine with him. It just irked him that he was out the expense of an attorney when he'd already told her she could have her football coach, her divorce, and anything else she wanted.

"Patout called Barbara and got the name of my lawyer. He left a message with him for me to call," he explained to Mac.

"And?"

"He tried to talk me into coming back, just like you're doing. But you're both wasting your breath. I'm out and I'll stay out."

"Okay, fine," Mac said irritably. "But it's not just your reputation that needs protecting, Burke. It's also your hide."

"Ah, the warning on the back of your business card. I thought I'd walked into a detective TV show."

"Maybe I was a little melodramatic, but when you screw with Pinkie Duvall, you'd—"

"Who said I was screwing with Duvall?"

"A lot of people have been asking about you lately. Where are you living? What are your plans? That kind of thing. Most are just curious or genuinely interested. But one of the guys who felt me out is associated with Wayne Bardo. Connect the dots and you've got Duvall. I'm worried that they're planning to move on you, now that you're no longer protected by the department."

"Duvall had plans for me, all right, but it wasn't disposal. He found me and offered me a job."

"A *job*?"

Burke told Mac about the interview.

"A job," Mac repeated thoughtfully. "Well, at least they aren't plotting to kill you. All the same, I don't like it. If I.A. heard that you had dealings of any kind with either Bardo or Duvall, it would look bad for you."

Burke ground out his cigar. "No cause for you to worry, Mac. I've gone on record with my opinion of Duvall." He stood up. "It's getting late. I'd better shove off."

Mac also came to his feet. "Where are you living now?"

"Why?"

"In case I hear something, I need to know how to reach you."

"I haven't found a permanent place yet."

"Let me know when you do."

"Sure."

"What are you going to do?"

"About what?"

"About what we've been talking about," Mac replied impatiently. "Do you have any money? Gossip is that Barbara is cleaning you out."

"I'll manage. In fact, I was thinking about going away for a while."

"When?"

"Soon."

"For how long?"

"I don't know. Long enough to sort things out, make some decisions."

"Where are you going?"

"I haven't decided yet."

"Out of the country?"

"I haven't decided yet," he repeated testily.

If he'd told Mac that he had buried Kev's memory and was going to leave it alone, Mac would have known he was lying. So he had vowed vengeance, which had appealed to Mac's idealism and enhanced his image of Burke Basile the Legend. But this barrage of questions put Burke on guard again. Was Mac's interest as sincere and innocent as he wanted him to believe?

He glanced toward the house, where he could see Mac's young, pretty wife through the windows, moving around in the kitchen. A Playmate of the Month who could cook and clean and obviously liked the role of wife and homemaker. The kid had it all.

Which left Burke to wonder why Mac appeared so hungry all the time. He was like an alley cat, anxious and on the prowl, not like a satisfied cat who had a bowl of cream that never ran empty.

As though sensing Burke's suspicion, Mac smiled his infectious grin and slapped him on the shoulder. "Whatever you decide to do, the odds are definitely in your favor. You'll come out on top. Bet you a hundred to one."

In all seriousness, Burke replied, "That's one gamble you might lose, Mac."

* * *

The temperature began to drop significantly, but Mac sat out on the patio long after Burke had thanked Toni for the dinner and departed.

Burke Basile already had an established reputation when Mac joined the police force. Basile didn't win any popularity contests because he didn't accept graft, but he was respected. He used his brain in preference to his pistol, although anybody who called him a coward was a fool. Basile liked to outsmart the drug dealers, not outshoot them. He considered the most successful operation to be one in which nobody got hurt.

Nevertheless, Mac believed him when he'd said that if he ever uncovered the traitor in their division, he would kill him.

"Mac?" Toni approached on bare feet. "Aren't you cold out here?"

He took her hand and kissed it. "Basile was impressed. Great meal."

"Thank you. Coming in?"

"In a minute."

"Don't forget to lock up." She withdrew, but on the threshold of the patio door, she hesitated. "Is everything okay?"

"Sure, honey. Everything is fine."

"I like Basile."

"So do I."

"He's nicer than I thought he'd be. By the way you described him, I expected him to be sort of scary."

Burke Basile *was* scary. To his enemies he was real scary. Right now, his future was scary.

But no scarier than Mac's.

Chapter Nineteen

We were so fortunate to find this building unoccupied. It's away from the city's corrupting influences, which we consider a real plus."

That was Father Gregory's response to Mrs. Duvall's comment that she hadn't realized Jenny's House was located so far from metro central.

Burke was driving. Gregory, in the captain's seat beside him, droned on about the advantages of the nonexistent facility. The two passengers were seated in back. A portrait of boredom, Errol stared vacantly out the window. Remy Duvall listened with interest and occasionally asked a question.

Burke was more than glad to let Gregory do the talking. While he wasn't much good at small talk, it seemed to be Gregory's special gift. Burke hadn't even got out of the van when they picked up Mrs. Duvall and her bodyguard. "I assume Duvall is at his office," he had said when he parked the van at the curb in front of the mansion. "But on the outside chance he's at home, Father Kevin needs to stay out of sight."

Gregory, looking at peace with God and man, strolled up the front walkway. Errol answered the door and motioned him inside. Burke mentally listed all the reasons he should drive away—now. There were pressing arguments in favor of ending this thing before he committed a serious crime.

But he dismissed them and focused instead on why he must do it: Peter and David Stuart. They were validation enough. Those two boys would grow up deprived of their dad, and Pinkie Duvall was the one ultimately responsible.

The front door opened, and the three came out. Burke looked beyond Errol to the woman, who was smiling over something Gregory had said. The phrase "like a lamb to slaughter" flitted through his mind. But by the time they reached the van, Burke had capped his conscience. When she'd signed on as Mrs. Pinkie Duvall, she'd accepted the risks of being married to a criminal.

Gregory's glib chatter continued mile after mile. He was playing his role well and seemed perfectly at ease. Of course he wouldn't be this composed if he knew how the afternoon was going to end. Not wanting to make him nervous, Burke hadn't discussed the details with him. He assured him only that he wouldn't be harmed and that he wouldn't get into trouble. If all went according to Burke's plan, that promise would be kept.

"Excuse me, Father Gregory," Remy Duvall said, interrupting his ceaseless discourse. "Father Kevin, is that smoke coming from beneath the hood?"

Burke had wondered when someone else was going to notice what he'd been seeing for the last couple of miles.

Father Gregory, who'd been facing the backseat, came around. "Smoke?"

"Steam," Burke said tersely. "I checked everything out before I bought the van, but I must have overlooked a leaky radiator hose."

"What are we going to do?" Father Gregory was rattled. A busted radiator hose wasn't in the script.

Burke smiled at his cohort in as priestly a fashion as he could muster under the circumstances. "We'll make it to our destination."

"How much farther is it?" Mrs. Duvall asked.

"Only a couple more miles."

"I don't think it's gonna make it." This from Errol, who hadn't spoken since leaving the Garden District. Burke could feel his breath on his neck as he leaned forward and peered over his shoulder to assess the situation. "If you keep driving it like this, you're gonna burn up your engine."

Gregory's composure slipped another notch. "Uh, Father Kevin, maybe we should postpone this excursion, try again another day, after the van's been repaired. We don't want to inconvenience Mrs. Duvall."

"Don't worry about inconveniencing me," she said. "I don't want irreparable damage done to your new van."

"Bless you for being so selfless and understanding," Gregory said to her. Then to Burke, "Let's just turn around and go back into town."

"It'll never make it back," Errol said. "Pull into that service station up ahead. You can get this heap fixed, and I'll call Roman to come pick up Mrs. Duvall and me."

Gregory said, "Father Kevin, it seems we have no choice."

The Crossroads was situated in a weed-choked delta of

real estate formed by the convergence of two state roads. The filling station had six gas pumps and two garage bays. The attached café advertised cold beer, boudin sausage, and a variety of crawfish dishes. Flying above the buildings were the American flag, the Louisiana state flag, and the bars and stars of the Confederacy.

Burke pulled the van to a stop and cut the engine. Steam was now billowing from beneath the hood. Hissing water and antifreeze from beneath the chassis splattered onto the pavement. "I'll see if a mechanic is on duty," he said as he got out. "Father Gregory, why don't you take Mrs. Duvall into the café and get her something to drink?"

"That's a very good idea." Gregory looked relieved to have another workable plan already in place.

"I'll call Roman from the café," Errol said. "She doesn't go anywhere without me."

They headed for the entrance to the café; Burke went in search of the auto mechanic. He found him inside the garage. Long, unwashed hair trailed from beneath a grimy dozer cap and lay on his bony shoulders like dirty hemp. He was wearing love beads and sandals with his greasy coveralls.

When he saw Burke, his gaunt face registered astonishment. "When you was here yesterday, I didn't know you was a priest."

"Wonders never cease." Burke pressed a fifty-dollar bill into his hand. "How quickly can you tape up that leak?"

The mechanic gestured to a roll of duct tape. "Soon's it cools down, I'll hop to. Sure you don't want me to replace the hose? Ain't nothing to it. Tape won't hold her for long."

"Taping's fine. How long? Ten minutes?"

He sucked on his stubby, yellow teeth. "Iffy. It's mighty hot."

Burke passed him a twenty. "Wear gloves. The keys are in the van. When you're done, pull it up out front and leave the motor running."

"Will do. Only, I don't get it. How come you rigged your own radiator hose to bust?"

"The Lord moves in mysterious ways."

Burke went into the crowded café and wove his way through the tables to join the party of three already seated. "We ordered you coffee."

"Thank you, Father Gregory."

"Did you speak with a mechanic?" asked Mrs. Duvall.

Sending smiles around the table, he told them confidently that the van would be repaired shortly. A waitress served their coffees. While sipping his, Burke surveyed the room with affected casualness, but mounting concern.

He had checked out the café yesterday afternoon, when he made arrangements with the mechanic, who had told him that puncturing the radiator hose before they set out would guarantee that they wouldn't get far before it started boiling dry.

This place had been perfect for his plan. It was in a rural area, at least four miles from the nearest local police force or sheriff's office. He'd been here just after lunch. With the exception of two tired waitresses, a chain-smoking cashier watching a soap opera on a portable TV, and a handful of desultory diners, the place had been empty. Burke had figured that business might increase around dinnertime when a few locals would come in. Otherwise, it was a quiet, slow, sleepy place that catered to the occasional motorist who grabbed a bite to eat while getting the car filled up.

Unfortunately he'd miscalculated. It was now apparent that the Crossroads was a happy-hour watering hole for blue-collar workers who knocked off early and stopped here for a brew or two on their way home.

The café was far more crowded than he had planned on it being. Cajun music blared from the jukebox that hadn't even been playing when he was here yesterday. Every table and booth was occupied, as well as every stool at the counter. Another problem was the demographics of the clientele. With the exception of the two priests, the babe, and the body-guard, they were testosterone-powered, redneck regulars.

The center of their attention was Pinkie Duvall's wife.

Every man in the place was licking his chops, some lit-erally, some figuratively, but all seemed to be pondering what a crotch-throb like her was doing in the company of two men of God and a meathead.

However, Errol wasn't as stupid as he looked. "Mr. Du-vall isn't gonna like this," he said, glaring back at one of the gawking rednecks. "I called the house. Roman was out on an errand, but he's expected back in about..."—he checked his wristwatch—"twenty more minutes."

"We'll be able to drive the van by then."

Burke's reassurance did nothing to assuage Errol's ap-prehension or to calm Gregory's jitters. Beneath the table his leg was bouncing up and down as rapidly as the motor-ized needle on a Singer. The nervous motion was driving Burke to distraction, and he was on the verge of telling him to cut it out when Gregory scooted his chair back and stood up. "Excuse me." He left the table and headed for the men's room.

"Maybe I ought to call Mr. Duvall?" Errol ventured, putting it to Mrs. Duvall in the form of a question. "He could send Bardo or somebody after us."

"I'd rather not bother him," she said.

"You're worrying for nothing, Errol." Burke's facial muscles strained to smile like a benevolent cleric. "The mechanic promised it wouldn't take more than ten minutes to patch the hose. As soon as Mrs. Duvall finishes that second cup of coffee, we can be on our way. All right?"

"I guess," Errol grumbled. "All I know is, Mr. Duvall isn't going to—"

"*Goddamn faggot!*"

The shout was underscored by shattering glass. Like everyone else in the café, Remy Duvall and Errol turned to see what had caused such an outburst.

Burke shot to his feet. "Shit!"

Gregory lay whimpering on the floor, doused in spilled beer, and cowering from the man who reached down and grabbed him by the nape of his neck and his belt and jerked him to his feet.

In a rough, uncultured, and unmerciful voice, he told the room at large, "There I am, taking a piss, and I look over, and this twisted fuck is *waving* it at me." He planted his boot on Gregory's backside and sent him crashing into another table. "I'm gonna make the little fucker wish he was dead."

The three men into whose table Gregory had careened were now on their feet. They grabbed him in turn, throwing punches and hurling insults. Before long, two others had joined in.

Over his shoulder, Burke said to Errol, "Get her out of here. I'll meet you at the van."

Then he elbowed his way through the homophobic crowd. Everyone was on their feet, some standing in chairs, yelling encouragement to the men who were pummeling Gregory. When Burke reached the epicenter of the

melee, he plunged in and managed to do some damage
to most of the attackers until he came face to face with
the object of Gregory's desire. Love must truly be blind,
Burke thought, because this was one ugly son of a bitch
and every solid, bulky inch of him was bristling with rage.

His fist connected with Burke's chin and sent him flying backward. "You another one?" He bore down on
Burke. "You goddamn perverts that hide behind your
backward collars make me want to puke."

He bent down to pick up Burke and deliver more. But
when his red, temper-congested face was mere inches
away from Burke's, his progress was stopped so abruptly
that inertia almost caused him to pitch forward and land
on top of Burke.

He'd been halted by Burke's pistol, the barrel of which
was digging into the beefy forehead, which Burke used as
leverage as he came to his feet.

"Back off, asshole."

"Wha—"

"Call off your friends, or the next sacrament you receive will be last rites."

By now several of the others had noticed that the priest
was holding their friend at gunpoint. Shock, more than
fear, immobilized them. Within moments, all activity
ceased, and the only sound in the room, except for the
lively music coming from the jukebox, was Gregory's
blubbering.

"Move over there." The redneck obeyed Burke in-
stantly, stumbling over his own big feet, his arms raised.
Speaking calmly to the ring of hostile faces, Burke said,
"Don't anybody do anything stupid." He inched toward
Gregory and nudged him with his foot. "Get up."

Gregory covered his head with his arms and began to

sob even louder. Burke was tempted to lay into the young man himself. Instead he gritted his teeth and said, "So help me God, if you don't get up and move toward the door, I'm going to leave you here for them to do with as they please. Before they're finished you'll be begging to go back to jail."

The warning worked. Still whimpering, Gregory pulled himself to his feet. "I'm sorry. I—"

"Shut up."

"Okay, just don't leave me." He wiped his bleeding face on his sleeve and staggered toward the exit.

Burke, sweeping the room with his extended gun arm, moved backward toward the door. "We're leaving now. We don't want any more trouble. No harm was done. Just go on about your business."

When he reached the door, he shoved Gregory through it, then followed him out. He was relieved to see the van, engine running. "Get in the van," he shouted as he jogged toward the office of the filling station where he could see Errol speaking into the telephone and gesturing broadly.

Burke charged through the door and plucked the telephone receiver from the bodyguard's hand, then knocked him on the temple with it. The blow wouldn't do much damage, but it stunned Errol long enough for Burke to grab Remy Duvall's arm and pull her after him toward the door.

She struggled to free her arm. "What are you doing?"

A woman customer, who'd been paying for her gas, let go an ear-piercing scream. The attendant reached behind the counter for what Burke knew must be a weapon. "Don't!" he shouted. The attendant froze. The aging hippie mechanic, standing in the open doorway that connected the office to the garage, was wiping his hand on a shop rag and saying repeatedly, "Far out."

Burke backed out of the office. Pinkie Duvall's wife was fighting to get free. He wrapped his arm around her waist and hauled her backward toward the van. She dug in her heels and flailed her arms, but she was no match for him, although her high heels connected solidly with his shins several times and caused him to curse in pain. She raked her long fingernails over the back of his hand.

"Stop it!" Tightening his grip around her midriff, he said close to her ear, "You can fight all you want, but it won't do any good. You're coming with me."

"Why are you doing this? Let go of me."

"Not a chance."

"My husband will kill you."

"More than likely. But not today."

He opened the driver's door of the van and boosted her up, then scrambled in behind her. As he pulled the door shut, he shifted into drive and stamped the accelerator to the floor. The tires laid rubber on the pavement as the van lurched forward. Burke took a hard right turn onto one of the state roads and directly into the path of an oncoming tanker. The rig missed the van by a hair.

Gregory was screaming, praying, and cursing in noisy cycles. Burke shouted at him to shut up. "Goddamn it! What were you thinking? You could have gotten us all killed!"

"This is your fault, not mine," Gregory sobbed. "What are you doing with a gun? You didn't say anything about a gun."

"You should be damned glad I had it so I could save your sorry ass. Although why I did, I don't know."

Suddenly Mrs. Duvall, who was still sharing the

driver's seat with Burke, raised the armrest and dove between the two captain's chairs. She lunged for the handle of the sliding-panel door on the right side of the backseat. "Stop her," Burke yelled.

Gregory was in bad shape, but too afraid of Burke not to do as he was told. He plunged between the seats and threw himself on top of Remy, grabbing a handful of her hair. "U'm thorry, U'm thorry." His lips were already grotesquely swollen, and his nose was a bleeding, pulpy mess. "He's mean. I don't want to hurt you. But if I don't do what he says, I'm afraid he'll kill me."

"I understand," she said with amazing composure. "Just please let go of my hair."

Burke addressed her over his shoulder. "Nobody's going to hurt you if you cooperate. Okay?" She gave him a terse nod, but he doubted her sincerity. "At this speed, you'd kill yourself," he said, warning her of the danger if she tried to leap from the van.

"I understand."

"Good. Gregory, let her go and get back in your seat. You," he said to her, "sit here between us on the floor."

Gregory clambered back into his seat. Burke was tense until she was safely between the captain's chairs. "Who are you?" she asked.

Her eyes were teary and wide with fear. Her face had been leached of color. To further emphasize her paleness, there was a trickle of blood in the corner of her lips. Had she bitten them? Or had he accidentally hit her during their scuffle?

Uncomfortable with the thought, Burke returned his eyes to the road, and it was a good thing he did, because in the rearview mirror he saw a pickup truck racing toward them.

"Damn it!" What else could possibly go wrong? Both Gregory and Mrs. Duvall were bleeding, and he had a pickup full of pissed-off rednecks about to climb up the van's exhaust pipe. "Gregory, take the gun."

"Huh? Why?"

"Look behind us."

Gregory glanced at the side mirror on the door and shrieked when he saw the pickup barreling toward them. The man from the restroom was standing up in the bed of the pickup, leaning forward against the cab. He was using the roof of it to support a shotgun, which was aimed at the van. He warbled a blood-curdling yell. Several cronies were riding in the back of the pickup with him, and the cab was packed full of fire-breathing fag-bashers.

"Oh, Jesus. Oh, God," Gregory wailed. "I'm going to die."

"I'm going to kill you myself if you don't pull yourself together," Burke shouted. "Take the gun!" He stretched his arm across Mrs. Duvall and pushed the pistol into Gregory's trembling hands.

"I've never fired a gun before."

"All you have to do is point it and pull the trigger."

Burke was hoping this ridiculous chase wouldn't result in an exchange of gunfire. He was hoping he could stay far enough ahead of the pickup to avoid that. The van was no speed machine, and at any minute the hasty patch job on the radiator hose could become a critical factor. But the pickup was heavy. With its extra load, it wouldn't be performing at maximum capacity, either.

Eventually the angry mob might grow tired of the chase and figure that their time was better spent back at the café drinking another round of beers. Or Burke might be able to elude them once it got dark.

Or they might chase them until they caught them and kill them all.

The pickup continued to gain until it seemed it was riding on their rear bumper. Burke swerved in front of it to keep it from pulling up alongside. Then he swerved to the other side of the road when they approached from that direction. It soon became a contest to see which driver could outmaneuver the other. Burke concentrated on staying ahead of the pickup while keeping the van on the narrow road. One mistake and they would plunge into the foreboding swamp that extended away from the road on either side.

He was concentrating so hard on his driving that he didn't notice Mrs. Duvall's outstretched hand until it was almost too late to stop her from pulling the key from the ignition. His hand shot out and covered hers. She yelped in surprise and pain as the key ring dug into her palm.

"Let it go," Burke ordered. He was now driving with only one hand, and the van veered onto the shoulder, sending up a shower of gravel and almost making him lose control. Gregory screamed in fright.

"You're going to get us killed!" Mrs. Duvall shouted. "Stop the van. I'm sure they'll reason with us."

"Are you crazy, lady? Him and me they'll kill and feed to the alligators. You they won't kill until they've all taken a turn. Now let go of the goddamn key, and we might just stand a—"

A blast from the shotgun shattered the rear window. Gregory screamed again and dove to the floor, although the shot was widely scattered and the high backs on the seats served as protection from flying glass. To Mrs. Duvall's credit, she didn't scream, but she immediately released the ignition key and ducked to the floor.

Burke ground his foot against the accelerator, although it was already on the floor. The van wouldn't go any faster, so it surprised him to see the pickup receding in his mirror. It took a moment for him to realize that it was slowing down. Firing the shotgun had been their last parry. The rednecks were calling it quits.

The truck shrank to a pencil dot in his mirrors, but Burke didn't let up on the accelerator. When he reached his turnoff, he took it on two wheels. His eyes stayed on the mirrors for another few minutes, but when it became apparent that the pursuit was over, he said, "You can get up now. They've decided we're not worth the effort."

Moaning, Gregory pulled himself back into his seat. He hardly resembled the handsome man who'd started out that day impersonating a priest. His bruised features were distorted with swelling and covered with clotted blood.

By contrast, the blood on the back of Mrs. Duvall's jacket was bright red.

Chapter Twenty

Pinkie opened the passenger door of Wayne Bardo's car before it came to a complete stop. A sheriff's unit had already arrived, he noticed, and that was unfortunate but he would deal with it. He spotted Errol standing against an exterior wall with his shoulders hunched, hands deep in his trouser pockets, looking like he might burst into tears at any moment.

He didn't see Remy anywhere about and hoped that meant she had been given refuge in a private office inside the building. That his wife had been even remotely involved in a barroom brawl was unthinkable. The newspapers would have a field day.

As he made his way toward Errol, he ordered Bardo to locate Remy and get her to the car. "The sooner we're out of here, the better."

Bardo angled off in the direction of the filling-station office, where the sheriff was questioning witnesses. Pinkie confronted Errol. "What happened?"

"The...the...the van broke down. I told him to stop here—"

"Told who?"

"Father Kevin. He was the one driving."

Pinkie nodded and urged him to continue. Errol stammered out his story, emphasizing that he never let Mrs. Duvall out of his sight, not even when he used the pay phone to call Roman to come get them.

"You should have called me."

"I suggested it, but Mrs. Duvall said not to bother you. I didn't like it, but she—"

"How'd the fight start?"

Pinkie listened with increasing disbelief. "This is the priest my wife has received in our home?"

"I told you I thought he was a faggot," Errol said in his own defense.

"You didn't tell me he was likely to make a move on a guy in a public toilet. Jesus!"

"I told you like I saw it, boss."

"Okay, what happened next?"

"These guys start knocking Father Gregory around. I hustled Mrs. Duvall toward the door as soon as the fighting broke out. I brought her over here to the filling station. That's where I called your office from. I was explaining to your secretary when—"

"Okay. I can hear the rest later. Let's collect Remy and get the hell out of here."

"Uh, Mr. Duvall..."

"Pinkie!"

Duvall turned toward Bardo's shout. He was running toward him, obviously agitated.

"Your wife's not here. They took her."

"What? Who took her? The sheriff? Where?"

"That's what I . . . I didn't have a chance to explain before, sir."

Pinkie came back around to Errol, who looked like a man facing a firing squad. "By the time I called back to your office, you were already on your way here. And Bardo doesn't have a cellular, so I couldn't call his car. Your secretary said you didn't take your pager. There was no way—"

Pinkie grabbed him by the lapels and shook him hard. "You've got two seconds to produce my wife."

"I can't, Mr. Duvall," he said, starting to cry. "F-F-Father Kevin pulled his gun—"

"His *gun*?"

"Yes, sir. He . . . he hit me over the head and carried Mrs. Duvall off in the van."

Pinkie's world turned red, as though an artery had burst directly behind his eyes and bathed them with blood. He pulled out the .38 he always carried in a holster at the small of his back, and crammed the short, stubby barrel of it into the soft pallet of skin beneath Errol's wobbly chin.

* * *

The jostling of being lifted from the van roused her. Her back and shoulder felt as though they'd been attacked by a thousand vicious bees. She was aware of being carried. She opened her eyes.

It was dark; there were stars overhead. Millions of them. More than she had ever seen. Their brilliance amazed her. Wherever she was, it wasn't near the city. The sky wasn't muddied by manmade lights. The air was cold, but moisture laden.

"Dredd! Dredd!"

She recognized the voice as Father Kevin's. She also heard rapid footfalls on hollow-sounding boards and realized that he was carrying her across what she supposed was a bridge or a pier.

At the end of it was a strange-looking structure, which was actually several buildings that had been seemingly tacked together with no previous planning as to their final form.

Standing behind a screened door was an even stranger-looking man. He was holding a shotgun at waist level, aimed at them.

"Who's that?"

"I need your help, Dredd."

"Jeez Louise." By this time they were within a circle of pale yellow light coming from a fixture mounted high on a pole and illuminating the *galerie*. Apparently the man called Dredd recognized Father Kevin because he set aside the shotgun and pushed open the screened door. "What in tarnation are you doing way out here? What happened to her?"

"Gunshot."

"Dead?"

"No."

"How bad?"

"Bad enough. Where should I put her?"

"I only got one bed, and you know where it's at."

They went past Dredd on their way inside, and she caught a whiff of smoke. His beard seemed to be smoldering. Of course she was hallucinating. She saw animals and reptiles jutting from the walls with fangs bared. Jars of cloudy solutions crowded shelves. Unidentifiable skeletons were frozen in menacing stances. Skins and hides brushed against her. She saw an owl mounted on a perch and didn't realize he was alive until he swiveled his head and fixed his yellow eyes on her, then spread his wings in vexation.

Father Kevin turned sideways in order to pass through a narrow doorway into a small room. A bare bulb dangled from an electrical cord that had been tacked to the rough-plank ceiling. Its meager light cast eerie shadows on the walls, which were covered with yellowing newspaper.

He laid her down in the center of a narrow bed. The bedding smelled musty, like it hadn't been laundered in a long time, if ever. She would have protested if she'd had the strength.

"I hardly recognized you," Dredd said to Father Kevin.

"I hardly recognize myself these days."

"Who's he?"

From the room through which they'd just come, she could hear Father Gregory crying plaintively. "Later," Father Kevin replied.

"He looks like he's been run through a tree shredder."

"If I don't kill him myself, he'll survive. It's her I'm worried about."

"Well, let me take a look-see."

Father Kevin backed away and the strange man approached the bed. Remy was too amazed to scream. His skin was tanned so darkly it hardly looked human and resembled more closely the skins she'd seen in the other room. His face was a network of crisscrossing lines and creases, all deeply etched. He was bare-chested, but half of his torso was covered by a crinkled gray beard that reminded her of Spanish moss.

It was not on fire. He was holding a cigarette in the corner of his lips.

When he extended his callused hands toward her, she

shrank from them. His touch, however, was amazingly gentle. He eased her left shoulder up, until she was almost lying on her side. She groaned with pain and uttered a sharp cry when he probed a spot.

"Sorry, *cher'*," he said gruffly. "I know it hurts now, but Dredd'll fix you up."

Then he tenderly rolled her onto her back again and turned away. "You're in my light," he said crossly, pushing aside Father Kevin, who was crowding close.

"How bad is it? Is she going to be okay? Can you handle this?"

"Oh, so now you ask. After you come barging in here with a woman who's gunshot and only half conscious, and a priest who's busted up 'bout as bad as I've ever seen anybody. After she's bled all over my bed, *now* you ask me can I handle it?"

"Can you?"

"'Course I can. If you'll give me time. Lucky for you it's only bird shot, but she took several pellets."

"What can I do?"

"You can stay out of my way."

Remy closed her eyes. *She'd been shot?*

Then, her mind working backward, she remembered everything—the van breaking down, the café, the fight, the gun-wielding priest.

Her eyes sprang open. He was standing at the edge of the bed, staring down at her with eyes as unflinching as the owl's. His profanity, his fighting skills, and general demeanor belied that the priesthood was this man's chosen profession.

With a detached part of her mind, she wondered how she could have been so naive. Upon close inspection, there was nothing about him that suggested piety. He radiated an intensity that was incongruous with the grace and peace promised to those who walk with the Lord. His mouth wasn't designed for prayer. It was too hard, too cynical, better suited to coarse language. He was passionate, but not in his love of God or mankind. Even though he was standing perfectly still, he seemed to vibrate with an inner heat that frightened her. Not only for herself, but also for him.

The man he called Dredd returned, bringing with him a glass of liquid.

Father Kevin reached for it and sniffed it suspiciously. "What's that?"

"Do I meddle in your business?" Dredd said, snatching the glass back.

"Look, Dredd, she's—"

"She's hurt. I'm trying to make her better. But if you don't trust me, you can take her and that pathetic excuse for a parson out there and leave me be. I didn't ask to get involved in your mess. You forced it on me. Now, what's it gonna be?"

He took Father Kevin's silence for compliance.

"Okay then."

Turning his attention back to her, Dredd leaned down and pressed the glass to her lips. "Drink this." The liquid smelled vile. She tried to turn her head aside, but he laid his hand against her cheek and brought it back around. "Come on, now. This'll make you sleep. You won't feel a thing."

He tipped the glass and she had to either swallow the foul-tasting stuff that filled her mouth, spit it out, or choke. She figured if she spit it out or choked, he'd only come back with a refill. Besides, the promise of oblivion was seductive. She drank it all.

"Good girl. You cold?" He pulled a blanket across her legs. "Now, I'm gonna leave you just long enough to gather my stuff. You'll probably be asleep by the time I get back, but don't you worry. I'll take care of you. When you wake up, you'll feel a whole lot better." He patted her hand and withdrew. On his way out, he said, "You asked for something to do. You can get her undressed and onto her belly."

Then Dredd left the room and she was once again alone with her abductor. He sat down on the edge of the thin mattress and began undoing the buttons on her suit jacket. She was powerless to stop him. Whatever she'd been given to drink was fast-acting and potent. Her fingertips and toes were already tingling. It was becoming increasingly difficult to keep her eyes open.

When he lifted her up to remove her jacket, her head lolled against his shoulder. She seemed to have no connection to the arms he pulled from the sleeves of her jacket. She winced when he pried the blood-soaked cloth away from her skin, but the pain was no longer as fierce as it had been just minutes ago.

She felt her breasts relax against her chest and knew that he had unfastened her bra strap. Ordinarily that would have panicked her. She lacked the energy even to let it matter.

Then he eased her back down and her eyes opened in time to see him wiping sweat from his forehead. The back of his hand, she noticed, bore four bloody scratches where she'd raked him with her nails.

The tip of his little finger touched the corner of her mouth. "Does that hurt?"

"Who are you?"

His eyes connected with hers. After a slight hesitation,

he said, "My name is Burke Basile." He continued to look at her for several seconds, then his hands moved toward her shoulders to slip off the straps of her bra.

"Don't. Please."

He said, "You heard him. I've got to get you out of your clothes and onto your stomach so he can work on your back."

That wasn't what she was protesting. She tried to shake her head but wasn't sure if the command reached her muscles, or if it did, if they could obey it. "Don't do this, Mr. Basile," she whispered. Giving up the struggle to keep her eyes open, she exhaled deeply, then said on a thread of breath, "He will kill you."

Chapter
Twenty-One

So you see, Sheriff," Pinkie said expansively, "Father Kevin used my wife's pistol to protect her. Funny when you think about it—a priest with a handgun."

The sheriff didn't seem to find it all that amusing. "What's your wife doing with a handgun?"

"Over the course of my career, I've made a lot of enemies, which should come as no surprise to you. Even though Mrs. Duvall has a bodyguard, I encourage her to carry a weapon in her purse. Good thing she had it today."

The sheriff massaged his chin. "I don't know, Mr. Duvall. These witnesses claim she was fighting him."

Pinkie chuckled affably. "Sounds like her. My wife is headstrong and doesn't like to be told what to do. Father Kevin was trying to remove her from the scene, but she wanted to stay and defend Father Gregory. She feels a lot of compassion for him because of his... let's be kind and call it a weakness.

"That's the way she is. Always looking out for the underdog and ready to take on a bully. Frankly, I'm grateful to Father Kevin for jumping in the way he did. It was quick thinking on his part to get her out of here. I have a lot to thank him for."

"You're sure they're taking her on back home?"

"Certain." Pinkie stuck out his hand. "I can't say that it's been a pleasure, but it's good to know that over here in Jefferson Parish, y'all know how to respond quickly to a crisis situation."

"Thank you, Mr. Duvall. We try."

"Good night." Pinkie headed for the car.

"Say, one more thing, Mr. Duvall: How come the priest bopped your man there in the head?"

"I'm sure Father Kevin was frustrated with him for letting things get out of hand." He glanced toward the car, then added tightly, "A matter I intend to address immediately." He waved once again as he climbed into the front seat.

"Where to?" Bardo asked.

Pinkie was tempted to strike out in the direction the van had taken, but after dark, without knowing where they were going, they could drive for hours on these back roads and accomplish nothing except to get hopelessly lost. "My office."

Bardo took off in the direction of the city. "What did you tell Barney Fife back there?"

"I made up some bullshit story."

"And he bought it?"

"I didn't give him a choice. If I'd have let him treat this like a kidnapping, he would have called in the FBI."

"Bad for our business."

"Very. Besides, those feds usually can't find their ass with both hands. I'm better off handling this myself."

Bardo glanced over his shoulder into the backseat. "At

least you weren't charged with murder. I stopped you just in time."

Errol was hunkered in a corner of the backseat, still looking shaken from his recent brush with death and a post-traumatic bout of vomiting. Pinkie had been within a blink of pulling the trigger when Bardo stopped him. He'd wrestled the .38 from Pinkie's hand and reasoned with him until his temper was under control.

"Not that I don't want to kill you," he'd shouted to Errol, who was by then heaving into the dead weeds at the side of the building. "The only reason I'm sparing your life is because I need your help to find them."

It was then that the sheriff had approached Pinkie and introduced himself. He shared what his investigating officers had learned. "The clerk was so shaken he could hardly communicate with the nine-one-one operator, so my boys didn't know what the hell they were walking into. Once they got to talking to these folks, they soon realized it was more than a routine disturbance call. Bad as I hate to tell you this, Mr. Duvall, looks like your wife's been kidnapped."

After an hour of debate, Pinkie had finally convinced the sheriff that the witnesses were hysterical and hadn't actually seen what they had claimed. That was one of Duvall's specialties. He'd mastered the technique in hundreds of criminal cases. Witnesses who first swore to one thing recanted their entire testimony after being cross-examined by Pinkie Duvall.

"What about the mechanic?" the sheriff had asked. "He says the priest showed up here yesterday dressed in ordinary clothes and asked how he could rig a hose to bust."

Pinkie drew the sheriff aside and pantomimed smoking a joint. "Get my drift?"

The sheriff did and acknowledged that the testimony

of the mechanic, a reputed pothead, might not be reliable. The woman who'd been paying for her gas when the incident occurred was also adamant about what she'd witnessed, but she, too, eventually wound up doubting her own eyes and ears. The clerk, confused by the alternative possibilities that Pinkie introduced, conceded that the priest had seemed more concerned about getting Mrs. Duvall away from the scene than about harming her. As for the rednecks who had tried to pursue them, they dispersed as soon as they returned and saw the sheriff's car at the Crossroads. Those remaining in the café didn't know nuthin' about nuthin' or nobody.

Pinkie Duvall was a living legend. The first thing the sheriff had said to him was, "A real honor, Mr. Duvall. I've seen you on TV." Having one's face on TV worked powerful voodoo on the minds of common men. He'd taken advantage of the sheriff's awe. The law officer's powers of deductive reasoning and sense of duty were outshone by the radiance of Pinkie Duvall's sun.

Pinkie had achieved the desired result—to prevent an investigation and all-out manhunt—but the exercise had been time-consuming. Consequently, his wife's abductors had a long head start. He turned around to address Errol. "Who were they?"

Errol swallowed hard and raised his meaty shoulders to his earlobes. "They were priests."

"Don't tell me they were priests," Pinkie said, speaking in a voice so soft it was sinister. "Hasn't it penetrated that lump of shit that passes for your brain that these two men weren't who they claimed to be?"

Seemingly impervious to the insult, Errol said, "All I know is, they were the same two men who came to the house a few days ago."

"What do they look like?"

"Pr—" He was about to say *priests* when he saw Pinkie's eyes narrow. "Like I told you before, Mr. Duvall, Father Gregory is young and good-looking. Slender. Dark hair and eyes. Faggy. The guy never shuts up. Father Kevin doesn't talk much, but he's the one in charge. No question."

"What's he like?"

"Smart and shifty. Right off, I didn't trust him. He's the one I caught…uh…"

"What?"

Errol nervously glanced at Bardo. He wet his lips. He rubbed his hands up and down his thighs.

"He's the one you caught doing what?" Pinkie asked, enunciating each word.

"I, uh, was on my way to the bathroom. The one there by the front door? And I…I caught Father Kevin on the stairs. He was coming down."

"He'd been upstairs? He was upstairs at my house and you didn't mention it to me?"

Bardo whistled softly through his teeth.

"He said he used the bathroom up there 'cause the other one was out of toilet paper. I checked. The thinga-majig was empty."

"You're a regular detective," Bardo remarked with a snort. "You and Nancy Drew."

"Shut up," Duvall snapped. "What does this son of a bitch look like? Physically."

Errol described a man who was taller than average height, slim but strong, regular features, no visible scars or distinguishing marks, no facial hair.

"Eyes?"

"Hard to tell. He wears glasses."

"Hair?"

"Dark. Combed straight back."

The description fit a hundred men in Pinkie's wide circle of acquaintances, friends, and enemies. "Whoever he is, he's not going to live long."

Nobody took something belonging to Pinkie Duvall and got away with it. And this bastard had taken his most prized possession. If he touched her...If he laid so much as a finger on her...He relished the thought of killing this unnamed man with his bare hands.

Bardo interrupted Pinkie's murderous fantasy. "Doesn't make sense, two priests, one of them a fag, kidnapping a woman. What do they want with her?"

"It's not Remy they want. It's me."

Pinkie had no proof of that, nor any viable reason on which to base that conclusion. But he knew it with certainty.

* * *

"Push, damn it."

"I am pushing."

Gregory was as useless at ditching a van in a bayou as he was at everything else. Burke admonished him to try harder. The two men attacked it again, putting all their strength into pushing the vehicle across the spongy ground. Finally, it rolled forward several yards. Burke thought they had it licked. But then it became stuck in the silt on the bottom of the muddy creek and rested there only half submerged.

"Now what?"

"We leave it," Burke said curtly. "They'll find it eventually. But by that time, Duvall will know who has his wife."

Burke ignored Gregory's whining as they tramped through the swampy terrain back to Dredd's pickup. He'd driven it to this remote spot, Gregory following in the van. During the drive, Burke had kept a watchful eye on the rearview mirror. Every time he went around a bend in the road, he slowed down until the van's headlights were once again in sight. He expected Gregory to crack at any moment. There was no way to predict what the young man might do when he did.

Docilely enough, he climbed into the pickup for the drive back. Burke followed a winding road, flanked on both sides by swamp. The knees of cypress trees protruded above the surface of the water within a few feet of the road. Overhead was a canopy of low-hanging tree branches hosting Spanish moss. By day they resembled the lace-draped arms of a belle caught in a curtsy. At night they took on the eerie appearance of a zombie's skeletal arms trailing his torn shroud. Occasionally his headlights picked up the glowing eyes of a nocturnal creature that scurried out of their path or slithered back into the swamp.

Burke drove safely but fast. He was worried about the patient.

Dredd had anesthetized her with one of his home-brewed potions concocted of God only knew what. But whatever the ingredients, it had worked. She'd slept through Dredd's careful removal of the shotgun pellets, which had sprayed her back and shoulder on the left side. He'd also removed a few splinters of glass.

The small wounds had bled profusely, but Dredd had cleansed them thoroughly, then treated them with a salve that he claimed would heal them and help considerably with her pain. Burke had hovered close throughout the entire procedure, making Dredd even more irascible than usual.

He had practically pushed Burke from the room, reminding him that if he didn't ditch that van, all of southern Louisiana could be swarming Dredd's Mercantile in the morning. "Nothing hurts a business worse than cop cars parked out front."

So Burke had left, grudgingly, but knowing that his friend was right about the timely disposal of the van. Now that it had been taken care of, he was eager to get back and check on Mrs. Duvall.

"You used me."

"What?" Gregory repeated his petulant statement. Burke replied, "You accepted the terms of the deal, Gregory."

"When you were making that deal, you didn't tell me that the terms involved guns and kidnapping."

"When we picked up Remy Duvall today, what did you think was going to happen?"

"I thought you would get her to contribute a lot of money to this phony charity. I thought that you would swindle Pinkie Duvall, pull a con, like in *The Sting*. I never counted on you doing something like kidnapping his wife."

"It's your fault that you're involved in a kidnapping. If you hadn't flirted with that redneck, you'd have been dumped at the Crossroads. That was my plan, to shake you and Errol there. But no, you went and got romantic. So pout all you want, but don't expect any sympathy from me. It's on account of your perversion that Mrs. Duvall got shot and that all of us barely escaped with our lives."

"I got hurt, too," he sobbed.

"Too bad. If I hadn't been otherwise occupied, for what you did, I would have throttled you myself. Now shut up, or I still might."

"You're mean, Basile. Mean."

Burke uttered a harsh laugh. "Gregory, you haven't seen my mean side yet."

The younger man hiccupped another sob, and Burke felt a twinge of pity. Gregory was in over his head. What at first had seemed like a movie script to him had quickly turned into a living nightmare. Burke planned to have him safely transported back into the city tomorrow. If he kept a low profile for a while, long enough for his face to heal, he would be fine. No one knew his true identity. He would never assume the Father Gregory role again. No one would suspect the third son of a prominent family of taking part in a daring kidnap. Besides, Duvall would be after him, not Gregory. Gregory would be fine.

He continued to sulk and mumble miserably until he fell asleep. Burke shook him awake when they reached Dredd's place. "Want Dredd to do something for your face?"

"Are you serious? I wouldn't let that troll touch me." He glanced toward the structure at the end of the pier and shuddered delicately.

"Suit yourself," Burke said, getting out. "There's a recliner in the front room. I suggest you get some rest."

Gregory was slow getting down from the cab, Burke noticed. Despite his refusal of help, he would ask Dredd to give Gregory something to relieve his discomfort. He found their host still at Mrs. Duvall's bedside.

"How is she?"

"Sleeping like a baby."

Burke winced, the word reminding him of her confession and the baby she lost.

Dredd had turned off the electric light, but a single candle flickered on the unpainted bureau. She was lying on her stomach, one cheek turned up, the other buried in the pillow. Her hair had been smoothed away from her face, positioned on the pillow just so. Dredd was good at what he did.

The wounds had stopped bleeding. For all the pain they'd given her, they were superficial. Burke wondered, though, if they would leave scars. That would be a pity, because her skin was unblemished and looked almost translucent. He thought back to the first night he'd seen her in the gazebo. She didn't look any more real to him now than she had then.

"C'est une belle femme."

"Yes, she is."

"Does this vision have a name?"

Burke turned and looked into Dredd's wizened face. "Mrs. Pinkie Duvall."

There was no outcry regarding Burke's sanity, no exclamation of disbelief, no barrage of questions or demands for an explanation. He merely stared long and hard at Burke, then nodded. "There's a bottle of whiskey in that cabinet. Help yourself." He headed for the door.

"The man out there is in pain."

Dredd waved, indicating he'd heard, but he didn't turn around.

Burke availed himself of Dredd's whiskey, grateful to see that it was a brand name and not rotgut out of a jug. The only chair in the room had rickety wooden legs and a rush seat, which had been snacked on by rodents, but Burke pulled it near the bed and gingerly lowered himself into it.

He hadn't eaten since breakfast almost twenty-four hours earlier. He should forage in Dredd's kitchen for something, but he was so tired he talked himself out of it.

For a time, he just sat there, watching the woman sleep, watching the gentle rise and fall of her back with each breath and feeling like a creep because he was thinking about her breasts mashed flat beneath her.

He'd undressed her with chivalry and reasonable detachment. Reasonable detachment. That didn't mean he didn't notice. God, how could he not? A guy has an opportunity to see the object of his fantasies naked, he's gonna look. He's gonna check out her breasts and note that the nipples are firm but very pale. Who could expect him not to notice thigh-high stockings? Get real. And panties so sheer she might just as well not have bothered?

He drank two shots of whiskey in quick succession. They hit his empty stomach like fireballs.

Her right arm was lying along her side, her hand palm up. He saw the red impressions the key ring had made in her skin when he squeezed her hand around it. He couldn't resist reaching out and tracing the cruel marks with his fingertip. Her fingers responded reflexively and curled in toward her palm. Guiltily, he snatched his hand back.

The third shot went down without burning so badly.

His gaze moved back up to her face. Her eyelids were perfectly still. Her lips were relaxed and slightly parted. Saliva had trickled from one corner of her mouth, and it was tinged pink with blood from the cut on her lip. He touched it as he had before with his little finger, then left the moisture there on the tip of his finger to dry naturally.

He took another swig from the whiskey bottle.

Well, he'd done it. He had committed a felony, a federal offense. His life was irrevocably changed. If he were to return Mrs. Duvall to her husband tomorrow, Burke Basile couldn't resume his life where it had left off. There was no turning back now. All escape hatches were nailed shut.

He supposed he should feel more guilty, ashamed, and scared than he did.

Maybe the whiskey was making him drunk. Maybe he was just too plain stupid to fear the consequences that lay in store for him. But as he fell asleep listening to Remy Duvall's soft breathing, he felt pretty damn good.

Chapter
Twenty-Two

W hat do you mean he's gone?"

After only a few hours of sleep sitting up in Dredd's uncomfortable chair, Burke's neck was stiff, his back felt like an army had marched across it, the whiskey had left him with a dull headache, and daylight had focused the cold light of reality on the fact that he had crossed the line between enforcing the law and breaking it.

"Don't yell at me," Dredd snapped. He used a long fork to turn a piece of meat frying in an iron skillet. "He's your priest, not mine."

"He's not a priest."

"You don't say?"

Burke, massaging his temple, frowned at the other man's sarcasm. "His name is Gregory James and he's an unemployed actor. Among other things."

"Whatever else he is," Dredd grumbled, "he's a god-damn thief. He snuck off in my best pirogue."

Burke lowered his hand. "Are you saying he left by

way of the swamp?" The idea of Gregory James poling through the hostile environment of the swamp was unthinkable. "The closest he'd ever come to the swamp was last night when we tried to sink the van. He'll never survive out there alone."

"Probably not," Dredd said with a shake of his long gray ponytail.

Impervious to the season, he was wearing ragged denim cutoffs. No shirt and no shoes. His callused feet looked as tough as hooves as they shuffled across the buckled linoleum floor. He would have turned heads on a downtown city boulevard, but his odd appearance suited the environment he had created for himself. A ragged, faded Union Jack served as a window curtain. The unvented cook stove stood at the end of the counter where he rang up sales for tobacco, beer, and live bait, and within sight of where he did his taxidermy. It was a health inspector's worst nightmare, but Dredd's limited clientele wouldn't be fussy about such things.

He was philosophical about Gregory's chances for survival. "I just hope that when the food chain catches up with him, my boat will drift back. You ready for breakfast?"

"What is it?"

"Are you hungry or particular?"

"Hungry," Burke replied reluctantly.

Dredd dished up the fried meat and ladled over it a gravy he had made with the meat drippings, a handful of flour, and a little milk. He served it with plain white bread and strong New Orleans–style coffee with chicory.

"While you were washing up, I checked on Remy," Dredd mumbled through a mouthful.

Burke stopped eating and looked at him quizzically.

"She told me her name."

"She's awake?"

"In and out."

Burke mopped up the last of the gravy with a crust of bread, actually surprised to see that his plate was empty. The unidentifiable meat had been incredibly tasty, but then Dredd was as good with seasonings as he was with the roots and herbs that went into his home remedies. Scooting his empty plate aside, he reached for his coffee. "I don't think she stirred all night."

"The effects of the sedative began to wear off while I was applying more salve to her wounds. I dosed her up again. She should sleep through most of the day."

"When can I move her?"

Dredd had finished his own meal by now and went in search of cigarettes. He found a pack, lit one, took a drag, and held the smoke in his lungs for an extended time. "Not that it's any of my business, but what the hell are you doing with Pinkie Duvall's wife?"

"I kidnapped her."

Dredd harrumphed, took several more drags on his cigarette, and picked bread crumbs from his beard. At least Burke hoped they were bread crumbs. "Any particular reason why?"

"Vengeance." Burke related his story, beginning with the night Wayne Bardo tricked him into shooting Kev Stuart, and ending with their hair-raising escape from a mob of angry men. "When I saw she was hurt, I thought of you first. I didn't know where the nearest hospital was, and we were only a few miles away from here. I know how you value your privacy. I hate like hell involving you, Dredd."

"Forget it."

"The thing is, I know I can trust you."

"You trust me, huh? Do you trust me enough to tell you like it is?"

Burke knew what was coming, but he motioned for Dredd to speak his mind.

"You must've gone plumb crazy, Basile. The authorities could throw the book at you, but that threat's nothing compared to Duvall. Do you know who you're up against?"

"Better than you."

"So it doesn't bother you that Pinkie Duvall will gut you like a hog and leave your carcass for the buzzards?"

Burke grinned wryly. "Ouch."

Dredd, however, didn't find any humor in the remark. He shook his head with annoyance as he lit another un-filtered smoke. "Before this is over, somebody will be dead."

"I'm aware of that," Burke said, no longer smiling. "I'd rather it not be me, but if it is..." He raised one shoulder eloquently.

"You've got nothing to live for anyway. Is that what you're trying to tell me? You killed your own man, your career is over, your marriage went to hell, so what's to live for? Does that about sum up your view of things?"

"Something like that."

"Bull...shit." He divided the expletive into two distinct words as he spat a flake of tobacco off his tongue. "Every-body's got something to live for, if it's nothing except to see another sunrise." He leaned across the table and shook the cigarette at Burke's face as though it were a mother's remonstrative finger. "You killed Stuart *accidentally*. You quit the NOPD, it didn't quit you. You had a miserable marriage. It was past time you got shed of that woman. I never did like her."

SANDRA BROWN

238

SANDRA BROWN

"I didn't confide the details of my personal life with you so you could throw them back at me now."

"Well, tough tittie. I'm overstepping my bounds. I earned the privilege when you came busting in here last night and dumped a bleeding woman on me. Besides," he added grumpily, "I sorta like you, and I'd hate to see you get yourself killed."

His reproving expression turned softer, although compassion contrasted with his ogreish appearance. "I know what I'm talking about, Basile. Believe me. Things can get fucked up real bad, but life is life, and dead is dead. Forever. It's not too late to cut bait and back out of this thing."

Dredd was one of the few men Burke truly respected, and he knew that his respect was reciprocated. "Valid advice, Dredd. And I know you're well intentioned. But, whatever the consequences, I have to punish Wayne Bardo and Pinkie Duvall, or die trying."

"I don't get it. Why?"

"I told you why. For revenge."

Dredd stared hard at him. "I ain't buying it."

"Sorry." Burke picked up his coffee mug and sipped, with that gesture closing the topic to further discussion.

Apparently Dredd saw the futility of arguing. Anchoring his cigarette in the corner of his lips, he stood and cleared their dishes off the table, tossing them into a metal sink. "What're you going to do with her?"

"Nothing. I swear. It's my fault that she got hurt, and I hate like hell that it happened. I never intended to lay a hand on her. I wouldn't do that. For chrissake, I wouldn't."

Dredd turned his fuzzy head and shot Burke a pointed look.

"What?"

"You're protesting an awful lot to an innocent question."

Burke looked away from Dredd's twinkling eyes. "This isn't about her, it's about him."

"Okay, okay, I believe you," Dredd said. "All I meant was, where do you figure on stowing her while you're baiting Duvall? I'm guessing, of course. You are using her to bait a trap, right?"

"More or less. I'm going to keep her in the fishing cabin."

Burke used the cabin only once or twice a year, if he was lucky enough to get away for a few days. Whenever he did, he always stopped at Dredd's Mercantile to buy his food, beer, and bait.

Dredd's shop was off the beaten path, but to fishermen and hunters who knew their way through the labyrinth of bayous, it was a well-known spot and a point of reference. Only one gravel road led to it. The primary form of transportation to and from it was by boat.

Dredd didn't make a lot of money, but he didn't need much. Most of his income was earned during alligator season. He hunted them, then sold the skins. He also did some taxidermy as a sideline.

"Who else knows about your cabin?" Dredd asked.

"Only Barbara, but she doesn't know where it is. She never went there with me, because she hated even the idea of it."

"Anybody else?"

"My brother, Joe, met me there a couple of times for a weekend of fishing. Not in a couple of years, though."

"You trust him?"

Burke laughed. "My *brother*? Of course I trust him."

"If you say so. What about that Gregory character?"

"He's harmless."

"And you're a damn fool," Dredd said harshly. "Supposing he gets lucky and finds his way out of the swamp before a cottonmouth gets him. Supposing he starts to thinking about what Pinkie Duvall would do to him if he catches him. Supposing he figures he'll go to Duvall first and sell out your hide to save his."

"I'm not worried about that."

"Why not?"

"Because Gregory is a coward."

"He was brave enough to steal my pirogue and go into the swamp."

"Only because he's more frightened of me than he is of the elements. He thinks I still might kill him for what he did at the Crossroads. I threatened to enough times; maybe he thinks I meant it. Anyway, he'll survive. He's lived a charmed life. When the swamp spits him back, he'll run as far and fast as he can. He won't go to Duvall."

"How do you plan to contact him?"

"Who, Duvall? You got it all wrong, Dredd. He'll contact me."

"How's he going to do that?"

"That's for him to figure out. In the meantime, I'm endangering you by staying here. So back to my original question: When can I safely move her?"

* * *

Doug Patout slowly lowered his feet from the corner of his desk and set them on the floor. At his elbow, his mug of coffee began to cool. He reread the story three times.

It was an insignificant insert, the text using up no more than six inches of the *Times Picayune*'s page twenty. It was a brief account of a fight that had broken out in a roadside café in Jefferson Parish. Involved were two Catholic priests, the wife of a famed New Orleans attorney, and her bodyguard. According to a sheriff's office spokesman, the incident was resolved without any arrests being made.

Two aspects of this seemingly innocuous story attracted Patout's attention: How many famed New Orleans attorneys' wives had bodyguards? Second, witnesses noted that one of the unidentified priests had a quirky habit of flexing his right hand.

Patout depressed a button on his intercom. "Can you come in here a minute?"

In under sixty seconds, Mac McCuen strolled in with his characteristic jauntiness. "What's up?"

"Read this."

Patout pushed the newspaper across the desk and pointed out the story. After reading it, Mac looked up. "So?"

"So, do you know someone with a quirky habit of flexing his right hand?"

Mac lowered himself into the chair facing his superior's desk. He scanned the story again. "Yeah, but he for damn sure isn't a priest."

"When was the last time you saw him?"

"I told you about it, remember? A couple nights ago, he came to my house for dinner."

"How did he seem?"

"The same old Basile."

"The same old Basile carrying the same old grudge against Pinkie Duvall?"

McCuen glanced down at the newspaper. "Oh shit."

"Yeah." Patout rubbed the top of his head as though

worried about his spreading bald spot. "Did Burke drop any hints about what he's been doing since he resigned?"

"He didn't say much. But, hey, he never did. Always played his hand close to his vest. All he said was that he planned to go away for a while and do some thinking."

"Alone?"

"That's what he said."

"Where?"

"Said he didn't know yet."

"Do you know how to contact him?"

"No." McCuen laughed nervously. "Look, Patout, this is crazy. The guy with the funny hand action was a priest. And it doesn't specifically identify the woman as Duvall's wife. It couldn't be her. Bodyguard or not, Duvall wouldn't let her within fifty yards of Burke Basile."

"True. They're sworn enemies."

"Even if they weren't. From what I've heard, she's a dish and a lot younger than Duvall."

Patout raised his eyebrows, signaling McCuen to complete his thought.

"Well, Burke's the strong, silent type that women go nuts for. He's no Brad Pitt pretty-boy, but Toni thinks he's attractive. I always figured it was his mustache that gave him sex appeal, but obviously he's got more than that going for him. Something that only broads—"

"He shaved off his mustache?" Patout's stomach did a nosedive.

"Didn't I mention that?"

Patout stood and reached for his suit jacket hanging on the coat tree.

McCuen was nonplussed. "What's the deal? Where are you going?"

"Jefferson Parish," Patout answered over his shoulder as he rushed through the door.

* * *

Dirty gutter water soiled the tires of Bardo's car as he pulled up to the crumbling curb. "This is it."

Pinkie looked at the building with distaste. It was the same caliber neighborhood, the same caliber flophouse in which he'd found Remy living with her mother and infant sister. "Squalid" was an inadequate adjective.

He had been brainstorming all night, trying to identify the two kidnappers who'd masqueraded as priests. His underground network was humming with news of the abduction. He had offered a sizable reward to anyone who came forward with information.

During one of his repeated recounts of the incident, Errol remembered something previously forgotten. "The guy calling himself Father Kevin was ready to hammer the other one himself. I heard him say something about jail."

"Jail?"

"Yeah. I can't remember his exact words on account of I was busy doing my duty and getting Mrs. Duvall out of there. Whatever he said made me think Father Gregory had been in jail for doing something like that before."

The bodyguard was so desperate to win back his favor that Pinkie wondered how reliable this information was. It was feasible that an ex-con with a grudge was trying to avenge a long-forgotten slight, but it was just as feasible that Errol was making it up in order to get his ass off the firing line. But Pinkie couldn't discount any clue, so he had one of his snitches in the NOPD working up a list of repeat sex offenders.

A telephone company employee, who was working off a legal fee, was tracking the number on the business card bearing the Jenny's House logo, which Pinkie now knew was a fake. His secretary had checked it out, but apparently she'd been tricked by some very clever individuals.

Less than half an hour ago, when they received word that the number on the business card belonged to a pay phone in this building, Bardo had hastily assembled a team of four men, who had followed them here in another car.

Pinkie had insisted on riding along with Bardo. When these audacious priests died, Pinkie wanted to be looking them in the eye. Flushed with adrenaline and indignation, he alighted onto the littered banquette. Bardo stationed two of the men at the front door and signaled the other two to go around to the back of the building in case the kidnappers tried to hustle Remy out a rear exit.

Pinkie and Bardo stepped over a wino sleeping in the recessed doorway and went inside. Pinkie had the odd feeling that he was being led, that he was doing exactly what the kidnapper wanted him to do. Tracking the phone number had been too easy. For having planned such an elaborate kidnapping, the perpetrator shouldn't have overlooked something so elementary. It left Pinkie wondering if the oversight had been intentional.

On the other hand, he knew from experience that even the cleverest crooks got trapped by the stupidest mistakes.

To the left of the entrance was a reception desk, but no one was attending it. Bardo moved across the seedy lobby to the public telephone mounted on the wall and checked the number. He shook his head. Pinkie motioned him upstairs.

They trod softly. When they reached the second-floor

landing, they saw the telephone about halfway down a narrow hallway decorated with graffiti. The lighting was so dim that Bardo had to hold his cigarette lighter up to the cloudy plastic sleeve on the front of the telephone to read the number. He gave Pinkie the thumbs-up.

Pinkie's blood pressure soared. He hitched his chin toward the door at the end of the hallway. When Bardo's low command to open the door met with no response, he kicked it open. Inside was a man sprawled across a bed, deep in a drunken stupor. No Remy. They determined from his condition and the number of empty rye bottles surrounding him that he wasn't their culprit. Furthermore, he was pudgy, pink, and sixtyish, and didn't fit the description of either priest.

The second room was empty, and bore no signs of recent occupation. In the third, a woman cowered from them in terror and began a lament in loud, rapid Spanish. Bardo backhanded her across the mouth. "Shut up, bitch," he ordered in a nasty whisper. She shut up and clutched several hungry-looking children against her to keep them from crying.

The fourth and last room was also unoccupied. But on the bed a white envelope was propped against the pillows, and on that envelope was printed Pinkie Duvall's name.

He snatched it up and ripped it open. A single sheet of paper drifted from it onto the grimy rug. He retrieved the paper and read the typewritten message.

Then he uttered a roar of rage that shook the windowpanes.

Bardo took the note from him. He cursed when he read the message. "They wouldn't dare."

Pinkie rushed from the room and bounded down the stairs, Bardo on his heels. Bardo's men were ordered to

follow. They piled into the second car and raced to catch
up as he sped away.

Pinkie could barely contain his fury. His eyes were hot
and murderous. "I'm going to kill them. They are dead
men. Dead."

"But who are they?" Bardo asked, as he swerved to
avoid hitting a delivery truck. "Who would do that to
Remy?"

Remy. *His* Remy. His property. Snatched from him.
Whoever these motherfuckers were, they had nerve, he'd
give them that. Too bad such courage was squandered on
someone who was going to die so soon. And they would
die. Slowly. Painfully. Begging for mercy, then pleading
for death. For taking from him what was his, what he had
created, they would die.

When they reached Lafayette Cemetery, the two cars
screeched to a halt and disgorged six men. Duvall and
Bardo were in the lead as they entered through the tall
iron gates. Pinkie didn't wait for Bardo or the other men.
He went in search of the row specified in the note, weaving his way through the avenues of tombs until he reached
the one he was looking for. He ran along the path, the
crushed-shell gravel crunching beneath his shoes, his
breath fogging in front of him.

What he would find he couldn't guess. Remy's remains
zipped into a body bag and dumped here? A recently
opened tomb, her blood sprinkled on an altar of stones? A
shoe box with ashes inside? A voodoo sacrifice?

Once he'd ordered Bardo to cut off a woman's face and
deliver it in a pizza box to her husband who had ignored
previous, more subtle warnings. Pinkie expected this message to him to be just as jolting.

No longer would he underestimate this unnamed enemy. The man was smart, devious, and he knew Pinkie Duvall well enough to know the right buttons to push. He'd sent Pinkie on this macabre treasure hunt that would end with his finding—*what?*

His feet skidded in the gravel as he came to a sudden stop, recognizing it the instant he spotted it.

It wasn't a body or blood he found, but the message was just as bold. Temples throbbing, hands balling into fists, he read the name engraved on the tomb. It was the resting place of *Kevin Michael Stuart.*

Chapter
Twenty-Three

Is he going to kill me?"

Dredd spooned soup into Remy's mouth and, when he dribbled some, made a fuss of blotting her lips with a paper napkin. He muttered self-deprecations about his clumsiness, but he didn't respond to her question.

"Stop pretending you didn't hear me, Dredd," she said, stilling his hand when he tried to ladle another spoonful of soup from the bowl. "I won't panic. I'd just like to know. Is he going to kill me?"

"No."

Reading nothing in his expression to cause doubt, she relaxed once again against the cushions he'd placed behind her back so he could feed her more easily. She had claimed she could feed herself, but he'd insisted on doing it, and now she was glad she had consented. The wounds on her back weren't as painful as before, but her head was muzzy from her long, drugged sleep. She would have lacked the energy to lift more than a few spoonfuls to her mouth, and she was surprisingly hungry. The soup, *court-bouillon* according to Dredd, had been made with a fish stock to which tomatoes, onions, and rice had been added. It was hot and flavorful.

"Is it ransom he's after?"

"No, *cher'*. Basile doesn't care overmuch for worldly goods." He glanced around the room, which had been furnished and decorated out of a junkyard. Winking at her, he added, "He and I are alike that way."

"Then why?"

"You know about Basile's friend, Wayne Bardo's trial, all that?"

"Revenge?"

The old man answered in Cajun French, but his eloquent shrug spoke volumes.

"My husband will kill him."

"He knows that."

She looked at him inquisitively.

"Basile doesn't care if he dies, so long as he takes Duvall with him. I tried to talk sense into him this morning, but he wouldn't listen. Devils are driving him."

Hoping that she might enlist Dredd's help, she reached for his hand and clutched it tightly. "Please call the authorities. Do this, Dredd, not just for me, but for Mr. Basile. It's not too late for him to turn himself in. Or forget the authorities. Call my husband. Basile can disappear before Pinkie gets here. I'll persuade Pinkie not to press charges against him. Please, Dredd."

"I'd purely love to help you, Remy, but Burke Basile is my friend. I would never betray his trust."

"Even if it was for his own good?"

"He wouldn't see it that way, *cher'*." Gently, he pulled his hand free. "To Basile this is a...a mission. He made a covenant with himself to avenge Kev Stuart's death. Nobody could talk him out of it now."

"You know him very well."

"As well as anybody, I guess. He's not an easy man to know."

"What kind of man is he?"

Dredd thoughtfully scratched his chin through his dense gray beard. "This ol' boy up in N'awlins used to beat his wife and three kids. I mean, he really worked them over whenever he was drunk, which was most of the time. But his white-trash family and friends finagled him out of jail every time he was arrested.

"One night, nine-one-one gets a domestic disturbance call from a neighbor, says he must be killing them all this time because you could hear the kids screaming all over the neighborhood. The first cop on the scene doesn't wait for backup, because the kids're in danger, and besides, he doesn't figure he'll need help containing one mean drunk. He goes in alone.

"Well, when all the shouting is over, the wife-beater is dead on his kitchen floor, and his wife and kids are enjoying the first peace they've ever known. But the officer who shot the son of a bitch is being investigated by Internal Affairs.

"See, some of the desk jockeys in the department wondered if maybe that cop was so sick and tired of this turkey using his wife and kids as punching bags that he popped him when he had a chance, and only claimed it was self-defense.

"The drunk came at the cop with a butcher knife long as his arm, but the facts didn't matter to I.A. It's bad p.r. when a suspect is killed by an arresting officer. NOPD gets nailed in the press. Everybody gets on this kick about police brutality. Anyhow, nobody sided with the cop.

"Nobody except Basile. Basile stood by him when no one else would even speak to him. The other cops didn't want to be seen associating with an officer under investigation, you see, but Basile made a point of befriending him when he needed a friend most and none were to be had."

Having finished his story, Dredd removed the tray from her lap and carried it to a bureau across the room. "What happened to the officer?" Remy asked.

"He resigned under pressure."

"And established Dredd's Mercantile?"

He turned around to face her. "That was eight years ago. Haven't shaved since." His beard split to show a brief grin.

"Was it self-defense?"

"Yes, but that's not the point. The point is that Basile gave Officer Dredd Michoud the benefit of the doubt. Basile had no rank, but he sided with me and made no secret of it, even though it was the unpopular and unpolitick thing to do."

When he returned to her bedside, he brought with him a cobalt blue bottle. Uncorking it, he poured a drop of the substance into a cup of tea, which had been steeping on the shipping crate that served as a nightstand.

"Here, now, drink this, *cher'*. I've worn you out with all this jabbering. It's time you went back to sleep."

"What are you giving me?" she asked.

"I think it's Bayer dissolved in water." Remy glanced up to see the topic of their conversation standing in the open doorway. He added drolly, "But the mysterious-looking bottle is a nice touch, Dredd. Makes you look like a genuine alchemist."

Dredd scowled. "Shows how much you know. A shot

of this would knock you on your smart ass and keep you there for about a week."

The room was already crowded with Dredd's junk collection, but it seemed to shrink even smaller when Basile wedged himself between the bureau and the foot of the bed.

"How is she?"

"Why don't you ask her?"

Actually Remy was glad Basile hadn't spoken directly to her. She'd rather ignore him. "Where did you learn your nursing skills, Dredd?"

"From my grandmother. Ever hear of a *traiteur*?"

"A treater?"

"You know French?"

That from Basile, who sounded surprised. "And Spanish," she replied evenly, then addressed Dredd again. "The Cajun dialect is different from classroom French, isn't it?"

"You could say so," he cackled. "When we're talking among ourselves, other folks can't tell a word we're saying. And that's the way we like it."

"What was your grandmother like?"

"Scary as all get-out. She was already old when I was born to her youngest son. For some reason I never could figure, the old lady took a shine to me. Used to take me with her into the swamp where she'd gather the natural ingredients for her potions. She had dozens of them. People would come to her to cure everything from jaundice to jealousy."

"She sounds like a fascinating woman."

He nodded his grizzly head. "Treaters have been around for as long as there've been Cajuns. Some think of them as witches practicing black magic. Actually they're women with a special healing touch and a knowledge of herbs."

"Women?"

"For the most part. I'm rare," he said, almost as a boast. "I didn't learn all that Granny Michoud knew, not by a long shot, but once I moved out here, I started mixing up some of her less complicated elixirs."

Basile said, "One of these days you're going to poison somebody."

"Well, not tonight," Dredd retorted. Then, making a point of snubbing Basile, he pressed the cup of tea to Remy's lips. "Drink up, *cher'*."

Basile could be right. The tea could be toxic and she would sleep so deeply she would never wake up. But she felt an instinctual trust for Dredd, so she drank until the cup was empty. He added it to the supper tray and carried it as far as the door, where he paused and growled to Basile, "Don't bother her."

Once they were alone, Remy avoided looking at him. He seemed more menacing than the alligator skull atop the bureau behind him, or the six-foot snake skin tacked to the newspapered wall. Actually she favored being alone with Dredd's macabre decorations to being alone with Basile. A welcome drowsiness was already stealing over her, but she felt vulnerable lying there with her eyes closed while he stared at her. Above the hem of the dingy sheet, her shoulders were bare. She didn't remember how she had come to be undressed. She didn't want to remember.

"If I really thought he could poison you, I wouldn't have brought you to him."

He spoke quietly, but in the small room his voice seemed unnaturally loud, the sound waves palpable. More likely, Dredd's homemade sleeping potion had dulled her mind but sharpened her senses.

She fought the impulse to look at him, but her eyes

were inexorably drawn to the foot of the bed. His hands were folded around the iron railing of the footboard. He appeared to have a very tight grip on it, and he was leaning into it, bearing down, as though he feared it might begin to levitate.

"If you hadn't brought me here, Mr. Basile, what would you have done with me? Dumped me on the side of the road?"

"I never intended for you to get hurt."

"Well I did." He remained stubbornly silent, but it didn't surprise her that no apology was forthcoming. "Your disguise was very good."

"Thanks."

"Is Father Gregory genuine?"

"No. He's an actor I bullied into helping me pull this off. It's his fault you got hurt. You and I were supposed to leave the Crossroads alone."

"What have you done with him?"

"I haven't done anything with him," he snapped. "When I woke up this morning, he was gone. He took off sometime before dawn."

She didn't know whether or not to believe him, but she supposed that if he had wanted to dispose of Father Gregory permanently, he would have done so yesterday when he was so angry with him. "You'll never get away with this, Mr. Basile."

"I don't expect to."

"Then what do you hope to gain?"

"Peace of mind."

"That's all?"

"That's a lot."

She gave him a long look, but his expression was unreadable. "What about me?"

"You'll live to tell about it."

"Pinkie will kill you."

He stepped around the footboard and moved to the side of the bed. His hand, still bearing the four vicious scratches her nails had made, reached toward her.

"No!" she cried. Despite her lassitude, she grabbed his wrist.

"Let go."

"What are you going to do? Don't hurt me."

"Let go," he repeated.

She dropped her hand, because she didn't have the strength to fight him. Her eyes fearfully followed his hand as it moved to the side of her head. His fingers touched her hair.

Then he pulled his hand back and she saw it, being twirled between his thumb and finger, a feather—white, downy, curling upon itself, an escapee from Dredd's musty-smelling pillow.

"Are you frightened of me?"

Her eyes were fixed on the slowly swirling feather as though it were a hypnotic talisman. Slowly, she looked away from it and up at him. "Yes."

He assimilated that, but didn't hasten to assure her that she had no reason to fear him. "Are you in pain?"

As though reminded that she'd been sedated, her eyes closed. "No."

"Anywhere?"

"No."

"Does your mouth hurt where you bit your lip?"

"Did I?"

"It was bleeding last night."

"Oh. I remember now. No, it doesn't hurt."

"Did Dredd's medicine make you sick to your stomach?"

"Not at all."

"I've been thinking that maybe you shouldn't be drinking that stuff. It might not be good for... What I mean is, should I tell him about the baby you lost?"

"If I was still pregnant, maybe, but..." She was jolted into sudden awareness, but her eyes were slow to open, and even then it was a struggle to bring Burke Basile into focus.

He was still standing at the bedside, unmovable except for his right hand, which was flexing, his stare unflinching and seemingly able to read her mind and see into her soul.

"How did *you* know about my baby?"

* * *

When Doug Patout returned to his office, he wasn't surprised to see Pinkie Duvall waiting for him. Before he was completely inside, Duvall launched his offense. "Where have you been all day?"

Patout, reading his guest's mood and knowing the reason for it, dispensed with customary pleasantries. He shrugged off his coat and hung it up, then sat down behind his desk. "Jefferson Parish. Curiously enough, it's become a hot spot during the last twenty-four hours. As I understand it, you were over that way yourself last evening."

"So you know."

"Yeah, I know. What I don't know is why you put on that dog-and-pony show for the sheriff. Why didn't you let the authorities take over while the trail was still hot?"

"I handle my problems my way."

"This is significantly more than a problem, Duvall."

"You were out of your jurisdiction, Patout. Where did you leave it with those hicks?"

"The same place you left it, but I spent a couple hours in the sheriff's office. Out of professional courtesy, they let me read the statements of the eyewitnesses. I talked to the deputies who were first on the scene. Although you convinced them that the incident was nothing more than a bizarre sequence of misinterpreted events, it appears to me that your wife has been kidnapped." He finished by asking testily, "Don't you think the FBI should know about it?"

"No. Because when I catch Burke Basile, I'm going to kill him myself."

His arrogance appalled and angered Doug Patout. "You've got your goddamn nerve, coming into my office and announcing that." He yanked open his bottom drawer and took out a bottle of Jack Daniel's. He poured the oily dregs of his forgotten morning coffee into the plastic liner of his trash can, then refilled the cup with whiskey. "There's an extra cup around here somewhere."

"No thanks. I don't drink with cops."

"Arrogance *and* insults." Patout raised his cup to Duvall, fortified himself with a shot of whiskey, poured another, drank it, then addressed himself to the most powerful attorney in the city who had just boldly declared that he was going to kill a cop—former cop—for kidnapping his wife.

"How'd Mrs. Duvall become involved with these so-called priests?"

Duvall told him everything he knew about the Jenny's House scam, and admitted to his own detective work earlier that day, which had led him to the flophouse. When Patout heard about the cemetery, he smiled wryly. "That sounds like Basile. That also explains his motive for doing this." Shaking his head with remorse, he muttered, "Jesus, he must be crazy."

"No, he isn't crazy," Duvall said. "If he were crazy, I might feel sorry for him and kill him quickly. But since he's a devious bastard who knows precisely what he's doing, I'm going to tear out his fucking heart while it's still beating."

"I advise you to watch yourself, Duvall. Remember where you are."

"I know where I am, and I don't care. Nothing I say will go beyond this desk. You don't want that lamebrained sheriff or the feds in on this any more than I do, because you want to protect the reputation of the NOPD and your friend Basile."

"Who quit. He's no longer affiliated with the department, and therefore, no longer my responsibility."

"No, not officially. But if he's gone this far 'round the bend so soon after his resignation, people are going to start wondering how come somebody didn't read the signs before he cracked. Why wasn't psychological counseling mandated after he shot Stuart? Why wasn't the head of his division aware of his emotional decline? You see what I'm getting at, Patout? If I don't get to Basile before the authorities do, you'll end up with a pile of shit on your head."

"Stop shouting threats at me, Duvall."

"I'm just telling you like it is."

"If Burke has broken the law, he'll be punished accordingly."

"You're damn right he will be."

Doug wished Burke were here. He would enjoy seeing Pinkie Duvall reduced to a common man's temper tantrum. It sure as hell was gratifying to Doug to see Duvall this unhinged. Mentally, he saluted his friend for bringing it about.

"Killing Basile might not be as easy as you think," he said. "Do you realize the kind of individual you're up against? He's got integrity coming out the kazoo. Honor is his middle name."

"Really?" Duvall snorted with contempt. "Apparently you don't know him as well as you think you do."

"Maybe not," Patout admitted. "I never thought he'd go for broke and do something this dramatic, but he has, which makes the situation even more perilous for you. Basile doesn't expect this to end peaceably. He won't harm your wife. I'm not afraid for her safety. But I am for yours."

"I'm not scared of this burnout who goes around masquerading as a priest, for chrissake."

"You should be. Basile is smart. A whole lot smarter than me, and maybe even smarter than you, Duvall, although I know you don't believe that's possible. And he's motivated by revenge. That's strong stuff. You'd be a fool not to fear him."

Duvall glared at him, but he didn't challenge either the insult or the character reference he'd given Basile. "Who's this other fellow?"

"The second priest? I don't know."

"Where do I start looking for Basile?"

"I don't know that either. But he won't get far in that van. From the description, it can't be hard to spot."

"The van has been found."

That news startled Patout. "Where? Who found it?"

"I had some people looking. It was found two hours ago, abandoned and half-submerged in six feet of water in a bayou between here and Houma."

"Where is it now?"

"You'll never know."

"Duvall, I insist that it be turned over to the authorities as evidence."

"You insist?" he taunted. "Forget it, Patout. Even if you *insist*, the van's history by now."

Patout gaped at Duvall, shaking his head in bafflement. "You're as nuts as Burke is. I can't let this unravel any further." He reached for his telephone, but Duvall knocked the receiver from his hand.

Patout shot to his feet and angrily confronted the lawyer. "This has already gone too far, Duvall, even for you. You've got to notify the FBI."

"Pinkie Duvall doesn't need the FBI."

"Doesn't need, or doesn't want?" Patout poked Duvall in the chest with his index finger. "You don't want the FBI involved because you've got too much to hide. If they started investigating your affairs, they might forget all about the kidnapping of your wife and go after something *really* big."

Although Patout realized that he was gazing into the eyes of a monster without a conscience, the monster was grinning. Duvall's voice was cool, silky, and sinister. "Careful, Patout. You don't want me to get upset, do you?"

He pushed aside Patout's hand. "I know how well you like your present position with the NOPD. I also know you have your heart set on a deputy superintendent's position. Therefore, I suggest that you start looking for your boy Basile immediately, and that you not stop looking until he's found, or your career prospects end here."

Patout's world revolved around his career. He'd decided early on that his aspirations were incompatible with a successful home life, so he had sacrificed having a marriage and children to living singly and devoting himself wholeheartedly to his work. With no regrets, he'd made his career the center of his life. He sure as hell didn't want to lose it.

Knowing how well connected Duvall was, he couldn't laugh off his threats. He also knew that for every threat Duvall uttered, there were a dozen more implied, and it was those unspoken warnings that worried him most.

"If I can find them," Patout said slowly, "and if Basile agrees to end this insane vendetta here and now, you've got to give me your word that you won't touch him."

Duvall thought about it for a moment, then reached across the desk and shook Patout's hand, as though they had struck a bargain. But he said, "No fucking way, Patout. The bastard took my wife. He dies."

Chapter
Twenty-Four

Everything's ready," Burke said, ignoring the silent reproach of his two companions. Remy Duvall was sitting in
a rusty metal lawn chair on the *galerie*. The exterior wall
behind her was armored with ancient license plates.

Dredd was baiting a fishing pole, a cigarette anchored
in the corner of his mouth. The smoke curling from it min-
gled with the mist rising off the surface of the swamp. "If
you go through with this, you're a damn fool," he mumbled as he skewered a live crawfish onto his fishhook.

"So you've told me about a thousand times." Burke
motioned Remy out onto the pier and toward the small
boat, which he had loaded with supplies from Dredd's
store.

"Can't you see she's weak as a kitten?" Dredd dropped
his fishing apparatus and went over to her, placing his
knotty hand beneath her arm and assisting her to her feet.
He guided her around the white porcelain commode that
served as a planter in the summertime but which now was

used as a receptacle for trash and cigarette butts. Together they made their way along the pier to the piling where the boat was tied up.

Burke got into the boat first and offered his hand up to her. He noticed that she hesitated before placing her hand in his, but she did, and gingerly stepped into the wobbly craft. Burke steadied her as she lowered herself onto the rough plank that spanned the shallow metal hull to form a crude, uncomfortable seat. She placed her hands on either side of her hips and gripped the board hard while staring into the swirling mist and the murky water beneath it.

"In a day or two, I'll come around for more supplies," Burke told Dredd as he unwound the line from the short piling.

"You're sure you won't get lost?"

"I'm sure."

"If you do—"

"I won't."

"Okay, okay." Looking down at Remy, Dredd said, "See that he takes care of you, *cher'*. If he doesn't, he'll have me to answer to."

"You've been very kind, Dredd. Thank you."

The softness of her voice made Burke feel like he was the fifth wheel in a very tender tableau.

Dredd said to him, "If any of her wounds open up—"

"You already told me what to do," he interrupted impatiently.

The older man muttered something beneath his breath that Burke didn't catch, and he figured it was just as well that he hadn't. He'd heard it all, chapter and verse, until he could recite Dredd's sermon by memory.

Dredd was practically a recluse. He didn't form attachments to anyone. But he had developed a dimwitted devotion to Remy Duvall that Burke would have considered amusing if it wasn't so damned irritating. She seemed to have an effect on every man she met, a different effect for each man, but an effect that was similar in degree.

However, not wanting to leave Dredd on bad terms, he called up to him, "Thanks for everything, Dredd."

The old man spat into the water, missing Burke by mere inches. "Keep your hands inside the boat. It's a little early for 'em yet, but they'll be good and hungry in a week or two."

Burke had heard of the two old alligators that Dredd was too fond of to kill and which he in fact treated like pets. Whether it was fact or fiction created by Dredd to keep intruders away, Burke wasn't sure, but he waved acknowledgment of the warning as he shoved off.

Giving the trolling motor more gas, he angled the rudder and the craft cut through the fog. Just before rounding a bend in the bayou, he glanced back. Dredd was seated on the edge of the pier, fishing, his gray braid reposing in the groove of his spine, bare feet dangling above the water invisible in the fog, the mist swirling around his calves.

"Doesn't he get cold?" Remy Duvall was also looking back at the old man.

"His skin's too tough. Since he moved out here, that's all the clothes I've seen him in. Are you cold?"

"No."

"Let me know. I'll get you a blanket." Swaddled as she was in some of Dredd's castoffs and draped in a vinyl poncho, he didn't see how she could be cold, but something was wrong with her. She sat as rigid as a post, gripping the board beneath her as though her life depended on it.

"You'll get splinters."

"Pardon?"

"If you keep holding on to that board like that, you might get splinters in your hands. You can relax. We've reached top speed. You don't need a high-performance boat to navigate these bayous."

"I wouldn't know the difference. This is the first time I've ever been in one."

"In a swamp?"

"In a boat."

He laughed with misapprehension. "You live in a city that practically floats and you've never been in a *boat*?"

"No," she shot back. "I've never been in a boat. How much clearer can I say it?"

Her sharp retort caused a pelican to take flight. It left its roost with a great, noisy flapping of wings that caused Mrs. Duvall to start.

"Steady," Burke said.

The large bird skimmed the surface of the water only yards from them but apparently decided there might be better hunting elsewhere. He rose up out of the mist like the symbolic specter from a myth and disappeared above the treetops.

Depending on one's point of view, the swamp could be either a temple or a terror. Burke was respectful of its dangers, but he loved it. He'd been introduced to it during college when he and his fraternity brothers spent beer-blurred weekends exploring its matchless miles of bayous and bogs. Looking back, he realized they'd been reckless and stupid on these adventures, but somehow they had survived with no more serious repercussions than hang-overs, sunburns, and insect bites.

He had promised himself that if he ever scraped to-gether enough cash, he'd buy a getaway place. As it turned out, his brother had split the cost of the fishing camp with him. Joe enjoyed the weekends they spent there together, but he had never acquired Burke's worshipful regard for the swamp's primitive mystique.

This morning, it looked particularly foreboding, a surreal, monochromatic landscape of water, mist, and stark, moss-laden trees, their gnarled, bare branches raised in imploring attitudes toward glowering clouds of gunmetal gray.

Through the eyes of someone who'd never been exposed to its peculiar beauty, the swamp must seem like the landscape of a nightmare. Especially if that initiate were alone with someone she mistrusted and feared.

He glanced at her and was disconcerted to catch her staring at him. "How did you know about my baby?"

Last night he'd been able to avoid answering. She had gazed at him for only a few wordless moments before Dredd's potion worked its magic. Then her eyes closed, she wilted into the pillows, and fell instantly into a deep slumber.

Sometime yesterday, it had occurred to him that maybe she shouldn't be medicated so soon after a miscarriage. Could Dredd's elixirs cause cramping, more spontaneous bleeding? The possibilities were alarming. What happened to a woman when she lost a child? How long did it take to recover, and what was involved? Damned if he knew.

Since his first consummated sexual experience at sixteen, he had charted the terrain of the female body many times. He knew his way around it very well. Certainly years of marriage had increased his knowledge. By osmosis he had acquired, and had a fair understanding of, the vocabulary. He had a rudimentary knowledge of cycles and tubal ligations and estrogen and D and Cs and hysterectomies.

He didn't want to know more. Beyond medical professionals, did any man really want to know and understand the intricacies of a woman's body? The mysteries confined within that relatively small space had tantalized and fascinated Man since Creation. The countless galaxies hadn't inspired as much speculation, or wonder, or awe.

The secrecy was intrinsic to the allure. At least to Burke Basile it was. He didn't want his illusions dispelled. He didn't want to tamper with the poetic imagery that femininity aroused in him.

Nevertheless, he'd had to ask about her miscarriage last night. For his own peace of mind, he had to know that Dredd's remedies wouldn't harm her.

"Answer me," she demanded now. "How did you know about my baby? No one knew, except my doctor. I didn't tell a single soul."

"You told someone."

He watched her face while she puzzled through it, and knew the instant she arrived at the answer. Her lips parted on a silent gasp. Then, looking at him as though he were the Antichrist, her eyes filled with tears. One slipped over her eyelid and rolled down her cheek. He remembered the blood trickling from the corner of her mouth. This single tear was more poignant.

"You heard my confession?"

He averted his head, unable to look at her.

"How is that possible?"

"Does that matter now?"

"No. I guess it doesn't matter how you did it; you did it." After a moment, she added, "You're evil, Mr. Basile."

He didn't feel very proud of himself about it. But his guilty conscience only made him want to lash out. "Casting stones, Mrs. Duvall? That's funny. Coming from a woman who whored herself into marrying a rich man."

"What do you know about it? What do you know about me? Nothing!"

"Shh!" Burke held up his hand for quiet.

"I don't know what you think about me. I don't care—"

"Shut up," he barked. He quickly turned off the boat's motor and listened.

The sound of an approaching chopper was unmistakable. Cursing, he restarted the motor and, opening up the throttle, headed for the thickest grove of bald cypresses. The hull bumped against the knobby roots of the trees, which broke the surface like stalagmites.

Placing his hand on Remy's head, he pushed it forward and down toward her lap so she wouldn't be struck by the low branches. As soon as they were beneath the limbs, he stopped the engine again and caught hold of one of the cypress knees to keep the craft from drifting. Luckily the mist camouflaged their wake.

Remy strained against his hand, trying to raise her head.

"Be still."

He kept his palm firmly in place on the back of her head, his eyes on the sky. As he'd guessed, a helicopter appeared above the treetops, flying low. It was too small to be one of the choppers that transported oil workers to offshore rigs, and not distinctive enough to be a police helicopter. If it was a traffic helicopter, the pilot was lost because there wasn't a car for miles. It could be an instructor giving his student a bird's-eye view of the swamp, but on a foggy day what was the likelihood of that?

A closer guess was that it was a rogue outfit hired by Pinkie Duvall to look for his wife and her captor.

Reaching above her head, Mrs. Duvall tried to dislodge his hand. "It's gone now. Let me up." She made herself heard even though her voice was muffled by the fabric of the shapeless clothes Dredd had given her.

"Stay put." He strained his ears to hear if the chopper was retreating, or if it might be coming back for a second pass.

"I can't breathe." She began to struggle in earnest.

"I said stay put. Just for—"

"Let me up."

Sensing her panic, Burke released her. She tried to stand but bumped her head on a tree limb and fell back. The boat rocked dangerously, which only caused her to grab for the sides and increase the danger. Burke took her by the shoulders. "Be still, damn it. Unless you want to capsize. And I don't think you do."

He pointed his chin and she turned. A gator was gliding past not ten yards from the boat, cleaving the mist silently and malevolently, only the reptilian slits of his eyes visible above the surface.

She stopped struggling but sucked in short, rapid gasps. "I couldn't breathe."

"I'm sorry."

"Let go of my arms."

Watching her warily, Burke gradually withdrew. She stacked her hands on her chest as though trying to contain its rapid rise and fall. "Do...do anything else to me, but don't smother me."

"I wasn't trying to smother you. Only to keep you from hitting your head on a branch."

She looked at him retiringly. "You were trying to keep me from signaling the helicopter. I'm not stupid, Mr. Basile."

"Okay, true. I pushed your head down to keep you from signaling the chopper. But don't fight me like that again. You nearly caused this damn thing to capsize. Next time we might not be so lucky."

"The last thing I want to do is wind up in the water. I can't swim."

He snorted skeptically. "I'm not stupid either, Mrs. Duvall."

* * *

"That's him! That's the one. Father Gregory." Smiling triumphantly, Errol tapped his finger against the mug shot of Gregory James. For hours, he had been looking through the illegally obtained files of the NOPD.

Pinkie was still skeptical, believing that Errol might have invented that part of the story to reinstate himself. "Gregory James," he read from the file. "No aliases. A history of arrests for public indecency. One plea bargain and one probation." He turned to an idle gofer. "Find out what his status is now."

"He's with Burke Basile and Mrs. Duvall," Errol said when the clerk left to do Pinkie's bidding.

"You didn't recognize Basile from the Bardo trial. Why should I think you can identify Father Gregory?"

"I'd only seen Basile from a distance. And anyway, he looked different as Father Kevin. I'm positive that's Father Gregory. He even used his own name."

Pinkie remained noncommittal. "We'll see."

Errol sweated buckets before the gofer returned. "It checks out, Mr. Duvall. Gregory James served some jail time a few months ago. He's on probation."

"Well, I guess I owe you an apology, Errol. Thanks to

you, it seems that Father Gregory's identity is no longer a mystery."

Errol cast smiles all around. Pinkie dismissed him, but asked him to hang around in case he was needed. Errol practically bowed on his way out of the inner office, just as Bardo came in. "Del Ray is driving everybody nuts. He's been here for an hour. Says he's got some vital information, but he'll only talk to you directly. Can you see him now?"

Unenthusiastically, Pinkie told Bardo to send him in.

Del Ray Jones was a crook of all trades, but his main gig was loan-sharking. With the advent of riverboat gambling in New Orleans, his business had boomed, elevating an ego that was already disproportionate to the man's worth.

He was a vicious, mean, weaselly little bastard who was very handy with a knife. One night he'd gotten a little carried away with one of his clients who was late on a payment and had slit his throat. That was his first and, to date, only murder. Scared spitless, he'd run to his lawyer for advice.

Pinkie had told him to keep out of sight for a few weeks, assuring him that the disappearance of one small-time gambler would create hardly a ripple in New Orleans' underworld. He'd been right. The crime remained unsolved. Meanwhile, Pinkie knew where the body was buried. Literally.

Now that Pinkie's life was in upheaval, Del Ray was eager to return the favor and to demonstrate his loyalty and usefulness. Bardo escorted him in. Cutting to the chase, Pinkie said, "You'd better not be wasting my time."

Del Ray licked his small, sharp teeth. "No, sir, Mr. Duvall. You're gonna love this."

Pinkie doubted that. Del Ray was a self-serving hustler, a slick operator, a Sachel without the panache. He would pimp for his mother if there was a dollar to be made.

But surprisingly, Pinkie's interest mounted as he listened to Del Ray's story, related in an ingratiating, high-pitched voice. When he concluded, Pinkie glanced at Bardo, who said, "Sounds good."

"It is good, Mr. Duvall," said Del Ray.

"Get on it then."

"Yes, sir." Smiling like a happy rat, Del Ray scuttled from the room. Bardo followed him out.

Left alone, Pinkie got up and stretched his aching lower back. Early this morning, he'd showered in his office bathroom. Roman had brought him a change of clothes from home. He was refreshed but far from rested. His eyes were gritty from lack of sleep.

He poured himself a drink. Scorching the palate he'd cultivated for vintage wines, he quaffed some of Scotland's best export, straight up. He sipped the second drink while thoughtfully pacing his office.

What had he overlooked? What else could he do? What favor could he call in that might expedite finding Remy and killing the son of a bitch who'd taken her?

He had utilized every available resource. He had galvanized a considerable number of men. Working with the precision of stealthy, well-trained commandos, they were combing the city and surrounding parishes, asking questions, listening to gossip. None had turned up a single clue as to his wife's whereabouts. Others were working solely on gathering information about Burke Basile, his interests, strengths, weaknesses. A helicopter had been chartered to fly low over the swamps in search of them, but so far all that had turned up was the abandoned van.

With blood in it.

Gregory James's? Probably. According to witnesses who would talk, the rednecks had hammered him good. But the van's rear window had also been shattered. Bird shot had been found imbedded in the upholstery. It was possible Remy's blood had been shed, too. But Pinkie couldn't risk the investigation it would require to determine that. To prevent the authorities, federal and local, from becoming involved, he'd had the van destroyed.

If Remy was alive but hurt, if she was in the swamp, she would be terrified.

Or would she?

Another possibility had insidiously wormed its way into Pinkie's consciousness. At first it had been nothing more than a tickle of a thought, like the first twinges of a discomfort that couldn't be identified or localized, merely a vague uneasiness that all was not right, and a premonition that it was going to get worse before it got better. As the hours passed without yielding any information about Remy or her kidnapper, without receiving a call or a ransom note, the idea had begun to eat at him slowly like a cancer.

What if Remy hadn't been kidnapped? What if she had run away with Basile?

It was an absurd idea. He was appalled that his subconscious could have produced such a bizarre alternative to what seemed obvious. There was no basis for it. None whatsoever. She had no cause to leave him. He doted on her. He'd given her everything she wanted.

No, that wasn't entirely true.

She had wanted to be married in the Church by a priest, and he had refused. Marriage was a sacrament, a big deal to someone as religious as Remy. Pinkie had declared that was nonsense, as was most Catholicism. Religion was for women and weak men. So they'd been married in a judge's chambers without any folderol.

To this day, in Remy's mind, they were living in sin.

Also, she'd wanted a child. Pinkie frowned with distaste at the thought of her ballooned up like a blimp. At the end of nine miserable months of puking every morning, assorted disfigurements, and lousy sex, what did you have? A baby. Jesus.

It was bad enough he had to share Remy with her kid sister. Their mutual affection was a constant source of annoyance and inconvenience. He felt about family much as he did about religion. No self-reliant man needed it.

But the sisters' devotion to each other also worked to his advantage. He used it like a rudder to redirect Remy whenever she veered off the course he'd set for her.

As soon as he had returned from Jefferson Parish, where his wife was last seen, he checked with the faculty at Blessed Heart. Without mentioning Remy's kidnapping, he inquired after Flarra and had been relieved to learn that his young sister-in-law was within the cloistered walls.

Remy wouldn't have left without taking Flarra. Which shot to hell the theory that she had run away with Basile. After all, where would she have met him? When and how could they have hatched this elaborate plan? Pinkie shook his head in firm denial of his own misgivings. She hadn't run away; she'd been taken by force and against her will.

By Burke Basile. The son of a bitch who had laughed in his face when he'd offered him the chance of a lifetime now had his wife. That much he knew. What he didn't know was what Basile would do with her.

But he could imagine.

Inflamed by the thought, he hurled his glass across the room, where it shattered against the wall, spattering it with expensive scotch. Errol barged through the door to check on his safety. "Get out!" Cowed, Errol withdrew, pulling the door closed as he backed out of it.

Pinkie prowled the room as though seeking an outlet for his anger. Since the day he'd bartered with Angel for her daughter, Remy had been his. He'd placed her in Blessed Heart to assure she would remain pure. Her scholastic courses were necessary, but, in Pinkie's mind, secondary in importance to the other education he had insisted upon. He demanded that she receive instruction on proper speech and etiquette, that her manners be polished, so that when he did allow her out in public she would be a glowing tribute to him.

After their marriage, he had taught her all a woman really needed to know, and that was how to please a man. He selected her clothes, her shoes, her jewelry. He had tailored her for himself, created her for his exclusive use.

The wife of Pinkie Duvall must be as perfect as his orchids, or his wine, or his career. That's why he was so angry. Remy was ruined for him now. He could never enjoy her again.

Even if Basile didn't lay a hand on her...

But of course he would.

But even if he didn't, everyone would assume he had, which was just as bad.

How could he endure everyone assuming that his enemy had fucked his wife? He couldn't. He wouldn't. He would be a laughingstock.

No, the moment Remy was taken, she became tainted and tarnished and, as such, unacceptable.

Consequently, along with Basile, she must die.

Chapter
Twenty-Five

The cabin stood on stilts, forming an island of weather-beaten wood surrounded by water the color and viscosity of pea soup. "It's not the Ritz," Basile remarked as he brought the boat alongside one of the old tires attached to a piling. He climbed onto the pier, tied the boat to a post, then helped her out.

"There's a pier connecting the cabin to that peninsula," he explained, motioning off to his right, "but during the winter when the water level is higher, it's submerged. It's near collapse anyway."

She looked across the channel and saw a tangled forest thick with underbrush and lined with saw grass. From where she stood, no dry ground was visible. It appeared that all the vegetation, even the trees, was growing out of water.

"How deep is the water?"

"Deep enough," he said curtly, passing up to her a brown paper bag filled with groceries. "Door's unlocked. Take this in as you go."

Remy left him unloading the boat and stacking supplies onto the pier, which was about three feet above the water. Her footsteps made hollow thuds against the weathered planks as she walked toward the structure he had referred to as a cabin but which could more appropriately be called a shack.

Lifting the latch, she pushed open the door. The interior was dim because all the shutters were closed. It smelled of mildew. Even in the finest homes in southern Louisiana, it was a challenge to stay ahead of the corrosive effects of living at sea level. The shack, apparently, had surrendered to them long ago.

"I warned you that it wasn't luxurious." Basile came up behind her and nudged her across the threshold. "Put that sack on the table for the time being. I'll have to check for roaches before we unload."

Remy did as she was told, then gave the shack's interior a closer inspection. Basically, it was one room, although there was a door onto which someone had painted a quarter moon, designating it as the toilet.

"It flushes—most of the time—into a septic tank over on the peninsula," he told her. "And there's running water, but I suggest you drink only bottled water. To wash up, there's a cistern outside against the west wall. I don't recommend the bayou for bathing or swimming."

She shot him a dirty look over her shoulder as she went to a window and opened the louvers of the shutters. The day was still gray, so the light was meager, but it alleviated the gloom somewhat.

Along one wall was an upholstered sofa that looked like a Goodwill reject. In the center of the room stood a fifties-vintage kitchen table with a laminated top and rusted chrome legs. The legs of the matching three chairs were in a similar state of corrosion, but they had bright blue vinyl seat cushions. There was a butane stove with two burners, no refrigerator.

"There's no electricity," he said, as though reading her mind. "But we've got a heater fueled on butane and I brought a full tank from Dredd's. Are you cold?"

"Chilled."

He began tampering with the heater; she continued to get her bearings. Beyond one chest of drawers and a few random shelves and tables, the only other significant piece of furniture was a double bed. Its exposed springs were rusty. The mattress was covered in blue-and-white ticking that was hopelessly stained. Above the bed hung a wad of mosquito netting.

Even as she was looking at the bed, a stuffed pillowcase landed in the middle of it. "I brought along some clean sheets," Basile told her. "While I'm fumigating for bugs and putting this stuff away, you can make up the bed."

Grateful for the distracting chore, she shook the contents of the pillowcase onto the bed and was relieved to see that along with plain white linens, he had also included a quilted mattress cover. "How long will we be here?"

"For as long as it takes your husband to find us."

"He will."

"I'm counting on it."

"Perhaps you should also count on him killing you."

He had been efficiently transferring canned foods from the brown paper sack to the crude shelving. Now he paused, placed one of the cans on the lower shelf, positioned it precisely, then slowly turned toward her.

"I think it's only fair that you know this. A few weeks ago, I held my pistol in my hand and considered blowing my brains out. The only reason I didn't is because I'm going to kill the men responsible for my friend's death. After that, I couldn't care less what happens to me."

"I think you're wrong, Mr. Basile. When it comes right down to a choice between living and dying, you'll choose to live."

"Have it your way," he said indifferently and went back to his task.

"What about your family?"

"Don't have one."

"No wife?"

"Not anymore."

"I see."

"No, you don't." He balled up the empty paper sack. "I didn't tell you all that to stimulate conversation. I only told you so you would spare me and yourself any scare tactics you're planning to use. They won't work. I already know what a big bad boy your husband is. Nothing he does will stop me from avenging Kev Stuart's death."

He tossed the sack into the corner, then walked out and returned to the boat to unload more gear. The heater was putting out a sufficient amount of warmth. Remy slipped off Dredd's plaid wool, moth-eaten jacket and finished making the bed. Spotting a quilt folded up in a box beneath it, she pulled out the box and removed the quilt. She sniffed it experimentally and decided that it was basically clean but could use shaking out.

She got as far as the open doorway, where she met Basile coming in, carrying a duffel bag. "Where are you going?"

"To shake out the quilt."

He slung the duffel bag off his shoulder onto the pier. "I'll shake it out."

He held it over the edge of the pier and shook it hard. When he was satisfied that no varmints or bugs had nested in it, he brought it back to her. "It's free of vermin."

"Thank you."

When she turned away, she heard him curse beneath his breath. "Put the quilt down."

"Why, what's wrong?"

"Just do it."

Without waiting for her to comply, he took the quilt from her, tossed it onto the bed, and, in the same motion, turned her around so that her back was to him. He tugged the tail of her flannel shirt from the waistband of the pants Dredd had loaned her and, before she could protest, raised it to her shoulders, leaving her back bare.

"What are you doing?"

"The back of your shirt is spotted with blood. Some of the sores have opened up. Dredd'll have my ass if they get infected. Sit down." He pulled out one of the chrome dining chairs and, pressing her shoulder, tried to push her into the seat. She resisted. "What's the matter?"

"I've been kidnapped by a man who's just stated his intention to kill several people. If I'm a little jumpy, that could be why."

He swore. "I'm not going to hurt you. Okay? You can stop flinching every time I come near you. Now sit down and turn around."

She did but perched on the very edge of the seat.

Dredd had packed everything he needed in a canvas bag, which he brought to the table. Then he rolled the back of her shirt up tightly around her neck so it would be out of his way. Remy held it in place in front by folding her arms across her chest. He dabbed the bleeding spots with a cotton ball soaked in antiseptic.

"Sting?"

"No," she lied. It stung like crazy, but she endured it stoically.

He worked methodically and in silence, first cleansing the wounds before applying Dredd's medicinal salve to each one. His movements were untrained and unsure; he didn't have Dredd's finesse or healing touch, nor did he keep up a stream of soothing chatter. The silence was more uncomfortable than the stinging.

"How often do you come here?"

"Not so often than anybody will look for me here. In case you were thinking that a friend might drop by."

"I wasn't."

"Whatever."

"Do you generally come alone?"

"Sometimes with my brother."

"It's an awfully small cabin for two men."

"We toss to see who gets the bed."

"The loser sleeps on the sofa?"

"Hmm." He snapped shut the lid on the tin of salve to signal that he was finished. "The sores must've opened up when you made the bed. Better take it easy for the rest of the day."

"What about me?"

"What about you?"

"Will I be tossing you for the bed?"

When he didn't answer right away, she turned her head. Her arms were still folded across her chest, but the back of her shirt remained tucked up around her neck. As she looked at him over her bare shoulder, she realized too late that her questions must have sounded to him like a provocative proposition.

"How would the wager go, Mrs. Duvall? Tails I lose

and get the couch? Heads I win and get the bed, and you?" He made a scornful sound. "I guess I should be flattered, since you sell it to Duvall for much more. But just the same, no thanks."

* * *

"Mrs. Duvall?"

Del Ray Jones thrust his face within inches of his client's. "Did I stutter?"

"No, but you have a real bad habit of spraying people with your spit, Del Ray. Your mama should've put you in braces when you were little. That overbite of yours is as good as a shower head."

Del Ray's beady eyes shrank even smaller. "I'm sure if you put your mind to it and think real hard, you'll come up with some information about Mrs. Duvall."

"Mrs. *Pinkie* Duvall?"

"See, you already know more than you thought you did."

"Lucky guess," the other man said, making a motion with his shoulders as though to loosen them. "If it's Pinkie's old lady you're referring to, I've never laid eyes on her, and don't know what the hell you're talking about."

The loan shark tilted his head and grinned in a goading way. "Aw, now, come on. Don't be lying to ol' Del Ray. We've been friends for too long."

"Friends, my ass. You're not my friend. You're a pestilence."

"I'm wounded," Del Ray said, placing his hand over his heart. "Do you promise you don't know anything about Mr. Duvall's wife?"

"I promise."

"You haven't heard that she's missing?"

"Missing?"

"Good, good. That was real good. Real sincere. If I didn't know better, I might actually believe that you were surprised by that piece of news."

The other man's shoulders were still tense. He fessed up. "Okay, I've heard some rumors, but I don't know any facts. Now, get out of my face. We have an appointment on Friday. I don't want to see your ugly self until then."

As his client turned away, Del Ray's hand shot out. In it was a switchblade. He pressed the tip of it against the other man's cheek. No longer smiling—not even his evil grin—Del Ray said, "You could go for your gun, but your face would get fucked up before you could shoot me."

"You gave me till Friday," the man said, barely moving his lips. "You'll get your money then."

"You've lied to me before."

"Not this time. I've already got the cash lined up."

"No shit?"

"Swear to God."

"Tell you what." Del Ray withdrew the blade and tapped the flat edge of it against his palm as though mulling over a fresh thought. "If you come with me now, I might persuade someone to pay your debt for you."

"Pay my debt for me?"

"And you said I wasn't your friend. Ain't you ashamed?" The loan shark motioned his client toward a Cadillac parked at the curb. "Mr. Duvall wants to talk to you."

"Pinkie Duvall wants to talk to me?"

"Yeah. And weren't it nice of him to invite you, personal like?"

* * *

"I'm glad you could make it on such short notice, Mr. McCuen."

Mac stepped into Pinkie Duvall's high-rent inner sanctum. Del Ray Jones and Wayne Bardo followed at his heels. If this wasn't the lion's den, he didn't know what was. And guess who was Daniel. The odds were definitely with the house.

Trying to appear nonchalant, he sat down in the chair indicated. Bardo and Del Ray took up posts at each of his shoulders. He looked the attorney squarely in the eye. "Well, here I am, Duvall. What do you want?"

"I want my wife back."

"Back?" Mac forced a laugh. "You've lost her? Huh? Well, I don't have her, but you're welcome to frisk me."

He could tell Duvall didn't appreciate his sense of humor. "It's no laughing matter, McCuen. She's been kidnapped."

"The hell you say?" he exclaimed. He swiveled his head up and around, looking first at Del Ray, then at Bardo, raising his eyebrows to show how impressed he was by the importance of this meeting. Coming back around to Duvall, he said, "Kidnapping's a federal rap. What do you want me to do about it?"

"It's not a mystery to be solved. I know who kidnapped her. Burke Basile."

Even though Mac had seen it coming, had braced himself for it, even had foretold it himself, hearing it straight from Duvall made it official.

Doug Patout had been edgy since he read the newspaper account of the strange incident at the Crossroads. He practically had snapped Mac's head off when he asked what Patout had learned in Jefferson Parish. Mac had plied him with questions, but Patout had refused to elaborate, insisting that it had turned out not to be a police matter. Maybe not an *official* police matter, but there was no mystery now why Patout had been upset—his fear of Basile's involvement had been confirmed.

Basile had a good reason to get revenge on Duvall. But he'd gone about it in a damned dramatic way. Was revenge his only motive, Mac wondered? It was disturbing to think there might be more to it than what was obvious. But he reasoned that the best way to get information from Duvall was to continue playing dumb.

"What makes you think Basile's got your wife? What would he want with her? Ah," he said, feigning sudden enlightenment. "Revenge for Kev Stuart, I bet."

Duvall looked up at Bardo and shrugged in a way that made Mac nervous. The gesture implied, *I've tried to be a nice guy and it's not working.* "McCuen, I'm tired, worried, and angry. So I'm going to come straight to the point."

"Fine. I've got better things to do, too."

"Despite your lucrative sideline, you owe Del Ray in the vicinity of fifty thousand dollars, isn't that right?"

Mac had found himself in a bind when the bankcard companies threatened to cut off his credit if the outstanding balances weren't paid. He couldn't tell Toni that he'd been gambling away his income instead of taking care of their debts. Nor could he tell her to stop using the overextended credit cards.

Desperate for cash, he'd sought help, which had manifested itself in the revolting form of Del Ray Jones. Del Ray had lent him some money, which he'd lost on the Super Bowl. Since he couldn't pay back the first loan, Del Ray had lent him more. Then more.

He pledged now that if he left this building under his

own power, with all his limbs intact, he would never gamble again as long as he lived. He wouldn't bet the ponies or the major sporting events. He would swear off blackjack, craps, and poker. He'd quit cold turkey. Hell, he wouldn't even toss a coin.

Since Duvall obviously knew about his debt already, he might just as well own up to it. "It's more like thirty-five thousand."

"After tonight it goes up to fifty," Duvall informed him. "And tomorrow it'll be more. Or..." Here he paused to make sure Mac was listening. "Or your debt could be canceled. Paid in full. It's your choice."

Knowing how Duvall operated, he knew the offer was too good to be true. His heart didn't even pitter-patter with glee. "In exchange for what?"

"Basile."

Mac laughed with incredulity. "I don't know where he is!"

"You must have some idea."

"He didn't confide in me when we worked together," Mac said, hearing his own voice grow thin with nervousness. "He sure as hell doesn't now."

"He had dinner at your house the night before he kidnapped my wife."

Mac swallowed. Jesus, the man knew everything. "It was a gesture on my part, a goodbye dinner. That's all."

"He didn't outline his kidnap plan to you?"

"Hell, no! Look, Mr. Duvall, Basile confides in nobody. Especially since Stuart died, he's a goddamn clam. Nobody's close to him. Not even Patout, really. Basile's a loner."

"Yes," Duvall snarled. "And right now he's alone with my wife."

"Well, I don't know anything about it. You've wasted your time." Mac stood and turned to leave but came face to face with Del Ray. "You could have saved yourself a trip uptown, asshole. I told you I didn't know anything about this. You'll get your money on Friday, just like I said." He shoved the loan shark aside and headed for the door.

Behind him, Duvall said, "Sleep on it, McCuen. Search your memory. Perhaps Basile dropped a clue you don't readily remember."

Mac seized the doorknob and pulled the door open. "I don't know where Basile is. Don't bother me about it anymore."

"Mr. McCuen?"

"What?" Mac was angry and scared. How the *hell* was he going to come up with fifty thousand dollars? By Friday, no less. Even if he could talk Del Ray into an extension, Duvall was another matter entirely. He turned and faced the attorney with a cockiness he didn't feel. "What is it, Duvall?"

"Give my regards to your wife."

Mac's heart nearly leaped from his chest. "My wife?" he rasped in a voice as dry as a husk.

"Toni is such a lovely girl."

Mac shifted his gaze to Bardo, who made an obscene smacking sound with his lips and tongue that caused Del Ray to giggle.

When Mac slowly closed the door to Pinkie Duvall's office, he was still on the inside.

Chapter Twenty-Six

For a moment Gregory thought that he was onstage again, although the spotlight was dim and its beam diffused. He heard applause. It seemed different from a normal ovation, but it was sustained and that was gratifying.

But when he blinked the spotlight into focus, he discovered that it wasn't a theater light shining down on him after all; it was a watery moon. What he'd mistaken for applause was actually the rhythmic thumping of the boat as it rocked against a solid object in the water. That obstruction could be a submerged tree trunk or the body of a leviathan. Gregory didn't know and was close to not caring. Paradoxically, terror had dulled his fear.

The swamp had a timeless quality, particularly on overcast days, when the light was the same from dawn till dusk and the only subtle variance was the degree of the grayness. He estimated that thirty-six hours had transpired since he'd sneaked out of Dredd's Mercantile, leaving the bearded proprietor of that macabre place snoring in his BarcaLounger.

Basile had been in the back room, sleeping at Mrs. Duvall's bedside sitting upright in a chair, his chin resting on his chest. Gregory had seen him through a window as he crept past on his way to the end of the pier. He feared Basile even when he was sleeping, and justifiably so. In Basile's relaxed right hand was the pistol he'd used during the kidnapping.

Swallowing a whimper of distress, Gregory had tiptoed to the end of the pier and stepped down into the boat, which he'd spotted earlier tied to one of the slimy piles. He hadn't realized how small the boat was until he unwound the rope and pushed the craft away from the pier. In a moment of panic, he realized that he didn't even know if the damn thing would float. He wouldn't put it past Basile to go to the extreme of European explorers to new worlds. To prevent their frightened and superstitious crews from fleeing, they'd destroyed their own ships.

He considered turning back at least a hundred times during those first few anxious minutes in the water. Ultimately, however, he feared Basile more than he feared the swamp. He'd chosen an unknown terror in which he might perish over Basile, whom he knew for certain was capable of killing him.

After about a half hour, he allowed himself to believe that Basile hadn't punched holes in the boat and that he wasn't going to sink into the miasma. The boat had no motor, so he propelled it through the water with an oar until his shoulder and back muscles burned. Every strange sound spooked him. Each moving shadow struck terror in him. He wanted to surrender to tears and despair, but he kept rowing, blindly pushing the boat through the alien waterways, without destination or direction, telling himself that he would become oriented as soon as dawn broke.

But sunrise only heightened his anxiety. Daylight revealed all the hazards kindly concealed by darkness. Each ripple in the water caused him to envision poisonous serpents and malevolent alligators watching him from beneath the surface. Birds with monstrous wingspans swooped low, squawking in vexation.

And the constancy of the terrain was enough to drive one mad. He moved forward in the hope that just beyond the near horizon he would find an alteration in the infernal sameness. But he put what seemed like miles behind him, and saw no change in the landscape, only slight shifts of light and shadow.

By noon the first day, he acknowledged that he was hopelessly lost. He was exhausted from not having slept the night before. He felt the effects of the beating more than right after it had happened. One of his eyes was swollen almost shut. His breath whistled through displaced nostrils that every once in a while dripped fresh blood. A tentative exploration of his lips with his fingertips assured him that they were grotesquely swollen.

Bruised inside and out, he would have given a million dollars for an aspirin tablet, but even if he'd had one, he would have had to swallow it dry. Thinking that within an hour or two he would find a place to go ashore where he could revive himself with food and drink and then hire transportation back to New Orleans, he hadn't brought along any provisions, including water.

Nor did he have any food, although that seemed of little consequence when compared to the misery of knowing that he was going to die alone and unloved in the wilderness. What an ignoble end for a boy who'd grown up with every advantage America afforded its rich and beautiful.

Even when he happened upon what appeared to be solid ground, he never even considered disembarking. The most horrible time of his life—prior to this past week— had been a summer camp he'd been forced to attend to toughen him up. He had failed to master even the most elementary camping skills. After two weeks, the frustrated camp faculty called his parents and promised to rebate the tuition if they would come and get him.

Even seasoned hunters and fishermen had become victims of the swamp, killed either by the hostile terrain or the beasts that inhabited it. He'd read accounts of appalling deaths. Some luckless souls had disappeared without their families ever knowing exactly what brutal fate had befallen them. If Gregory James couldn't hack it at summer camp, he certainly wasn't equipped emotionally, mentally, or physically to survive the swamp, and it would be suicidal to attempt slogging through it on foot.

As long as he remained in the boat, he might stand a chance. It wasn't much of a craft, but it served as a floating island of relative safety. It protected him from direct contact with the elements, and carnivores, and poisonous fangs.

But as the hours stretched out, his chances for survival became slimmer and his meager hopes faded. He didn't remember at what point he surrendered, set the oar aside, and lay down in the foul-smelling hull of the boat to wait for Death. It might have been yesterday, because he vaguely remembered passing another night. Had the low clouds finally produced rain today or was that the day before? He'd lost track.

Now it was night again. The weak moon was trying to penetrate the clouds. That was nice. A valorous moon contributed a touch of romance to his demise. If he went back to sleep, maybe he would dream again that he was in the spotlight, starring in the hottest new play on Broadway, performing to rave reviews before audiences that adored him and gave him hour-long standing ovations.

Suddenly Gregory's dreamy doze was shattered by a light so bright it seemed to pierce his skull. Reflexively, he threw up a hand to shade his eyes. Words were hurled down at him, but he didn't understand them. He tried to speak but discovered he had no voice.

Huge hands reached from beyond the glare of light and caught him beneath his arms, hauling him up and out of the boat, then unceremoniously dumping him onto spongy, wet earth. The mud felt blessedly soft. He wanted to lie in the mud, pillow his cheek against it, and return to his dream.

But he was rolled onto his back and yanked to a sitting position. An object was thrust against his lips, and he cried out in fear and pain. Then a trickle of water filled his mouth and slid down his throat. Greedily, he began drinking, until he choked.

When his coughs subsided, he tried again to speak. "Th…thank you." His lips felt large and rubbery, like he'd spent the day in a dentist's chair. He ran his tongue over them and tasted blood.

The light that had awakened him had thankfully been extinguished, but there was enough natural light for him to see that his good Samaritans wore mud-caked boots that came to their knees. The legs of their pants had been stuffed into them. Nonsensically it occurred to him that he'd never worn his pants tucked into boots of any kind.

He worked the difficult equation in his head: Four boots equals two men.

They were talking together in low voices, but Gregory still couldn't distinguish the words. He angled his head back, wishing to thank them again for saving him, but when he saw their faces, the words died on his swollen lips and he fainted.

* * *

"What time is it?"

At the sound of her voice, Burke turned from the stove. She was sitting on the edge of the bed, rubbing sleep from her eyes.

"Going on six."

"I've been asleep that long?"

"Some of Dredd's medicine is still in your system."

She went into the toilet. When she came out, she poured herself a glass of water and drank from it slowly. After a moment, she said, "Your grease is too hot."

Admittedly, he was no master chef, but he'd fried fish before, and it had been edible. "Who made you a cook?" he asked peevishly.

"I'm self-taught."

He harrumphed.

"I'm a little rusty. I don't have many occasions to cook anymore, but I certainly know how, and if you don't turn down that flame, the breading is going to burn before the fish is done. I'd be glad to take over for you."

"I'm sure you would. And I'd wind up with a face full of hot grease."

"Actually, Mr. Basile, I'm hungry. I'd like something to eat before I stage my daring escape attempt. Besides, I doubt I could lift that iron pot using both hands."

Inside the sizzling grease, two fillets of fish were becoming way too crisp, way too fast. He glanced down at her and reasoned that she probably did lack the strength to disable him without also disabling herself. So he moved aside and motioned for her to take his place.

"Did you catch the fish?"

"This afternoon."

"If you don't mind, I'll start over. Would you please take the pot off the burner?" He did as she asked; she turned down the flame. Using a wire spatula, she removed the charred fillets from the smoking grease. While it was cooling, she sifted his flour and cornmeal breading mixture through her fingers. "Did you add salt?"

"Uh, no."

"Any seasonings at all?"

He shook his head.

Several tins of spices were lined up on a narrow shelf behind the stove. She reached for the cayenne pepper. Burke took a hasty step backward, which caused her to laugh. "City cop succumbs to cayenne," she said as she shook the pepper into the breading mixture. "I can see the headlines now."

"I'm not a cop anymore."

"No, you've gone over to the other side and started committing crimes."

"I've committed only one. So far."

"Isn't kidnapping a little ambitious for your criminal debut?"

"Are you teasing me, Mrs. Duvall? You think this is funny?" Startled by his tone, she turned to him. "Do you find it amusing that Wayne Bardo has already killed two people since your husband got him acquitted? Two that we know about, that is. That's a real hoot, isn't it?

"And how's this for grins? When Kevin Stuart died,

he left two young sons who'll grow up not knowing what a great guy their dad was. The next time you feel like a chuckle, think about that."

"It's Pinkie's job to get his clients acquitted. That's what defense attorneys do."

"Well I see he's got you well indoctrinated. But then you're a smart cookie, aren't you? Even at an early age, you had learned enough about whoring from your mother to snare yourself a rich and powerful man."

"You don't have the slightest idea of what you're talking about."

"Wrong, Mrs. Duvall. I do. I know all about Angel, about her regular job as a topless dancer, as well as her lucrative sideline as a whore that supported her drug habit."

That evoked a reaction, but he couldn't categorize it. Was she surprised that he knew so much? Angry that he had dredged up a past she wished to forget? Was she embarrassed or mad? He wasn't sure. Whichever, she lashed back.

"If you know all that, how can you blame me for wanting to get away from her and that life? If I hadn't met Pinkie, Flarra and I—"

"Flarra?"

"My sister."

Sister? How had he missed that part? Then he remembered her going to the ritzy girls' school. "How old is she?"

"Sixteen. But she was only a baby when Pinkie took us away from our mother."

"Angel just let you go?"

"Not exactly."

"Then what? Exactly."

She averted her head, but he moved in front of her

and forced her to look at him. "How'd you link up with Duvall?"

"I thought you knew all about it, Mr. Basile," she mocked.

"I think I can fill in the blanks."

"Be my guest."

"Angel dances in one of his clubs, but he pays her for more than dancing. He's one of her clients. One day, he notices you, and you look better to him than mama. Angel tells you to put into practice something of what she's taught you, promising that if you do, you'll snag yourself a rich man. Is that about it?"

Her head dropped forward in what appeared to be defeat and remorse, but it lasted only a moment. When she defiantly threw back her head, her eyes were bright with angry tears.

"Angel taught me, all right, Mr. Basile. By age six I could shoplift cigarettes for her without getting caught. By the time I was eight, I had worked my way up to stealing food so I would have some supper. But stealing cans and boxes got cumbersome, so Angel had one of her clients coach me on how to pick pockets. He said I had a natural talent for it. My fingers got limber. I practiced until I was better than my coach. Which was good, because when Flarra came along, the money I made picking pockets came in handy to buy her milk and other necessities."

She paused to wipe a tear off her cheek. "Except there never seemed to be enough money for everything, and sometimes Angel took it from me to buy drugs before I could spend it on the baby. So I had to get bolder, steal more often.

"One day, outside Antoine's, I picked the wrong

pocket. Pinkie Duvall chased me all the way home, ready to have me arrested. But then he saw how we lived and changed his mind."

"He made Angel an offer. He'd forget the theft in exchange for you."

"In exchange for both Flarra and me. Mother agreed to make him our guardian."

"I bet she did. She saw where Duvall was coming from. She watched his lights go on when he looked at her ripe, young daughter."

"That's not the way it was," she insisted with a hard shake of her head.

"Pinkie Duvall became your guardian out of the goodness of his heart, out of Christian charity?" Burke laughed. "Even you don't believe that. What makes you think I would?"

"He didn't have to assume responsibility for Flarra, too."

"He did if he wanted to make it all nice and legal. A judge might not swallow his wanting to become the guardian of a nubile girl, but two abused and impoverished sisters went down much smoother."

Maybe it was the reminder of Kev's family who had rejected his friendship, or maybe it was because he felt a tinge of pity for little Remy and baby sister Flarra, or perhaps it was his own guilty conscience fueling his anger and urging him on. He felt a dark meanness rising within himself. He wanted to bludgeon Remy Duvall with cruel insults, so that somebody else on the planet would know what real heartache felt like. It was like having barbed wire wound around your heart. He thought it was time that someone else experience what he'd been living with since the night he killed his own man.

He moved several steps closer, until she was backed up as far as she could go and he could see himself reflected in the obsidian mirrors of her pupils.

"You've whitewashed it in your mind, but you knew then and you know now what Duvall wanted. He wanted a young whore who had learned from an old pro."

"Why do you hate me?"

"I bet your virginity was guaranteed, wasn't it? Duvall could return you if you weren't as pure as Angel claimed."

"I won't let you talk to me this way."

"Did he wait a day or two, or did he try you on for size that very first night?"

She flung the wire spatula at him and bolted.

Hot grease splashed in his eye. Holding a hand to it, he staggered across the room and through the door. The instant he cleared the opening, something hard landed against the back of his head and knocked him to his knees. Then again, his head was struck from behind.

By the time he collapsed face-first onto the pier, he was unconscious.

* * *

"Nanci?"

Nanci Stuart was shooing her rambunctious sons into the backseat of her car. When she heard her name, she came around and exclaimed in surprise, "Doug! What on earth are you doing here?"

Patout said, "I got here in time to see some of the practice. You're raising two major leaguers there."

"Personally I think it's too cold for baseball, but the coaches like to get a running start on the season."

"Got a minute?"

"Well," she hedged, "we're on our way to a team pizza party."

"Hmm." He looked around and then down, and shifted around some gravel with the toe of his shoe. "I apologize for ambushing you like this, but I need your input on something that shouldn't be discussed over the telephone."

Worry settled on her pretty features. "What's going on?"

"It's about Basile. He's flown the coop. I need to find him."

The boys began complaining about the delay. Nanci opened the car door and motioned them out. "Go ride with the Haileys. Tell Mrs. Hailey that I'm coming along right behind you. And settle down!"

Disregarding that last instruction, they ran pell-mell across the parking lot toward a van being loaded with rowdy little boys. The other mom ushered the Stuarts aboard, then waved at Nanci to acknowledge receipt of her message.

Turning back to Patout, Nanci said, "The boys miss Burke. They ask about him constantly. I didn't want them to overhear this conversation."

"They miss him?" he asked, confused. "I thought he was a regular fixture at your house."

"He was, until I asked him not to come anymore."

Patout listened as she explained her reasons for asking Basile to stop visiting. "I know I hurt him, Doug, but seeing him so frequently was hurting me. Each visit was a painful reminder of Kev and how he died. I was trying to make it part of my past. Burke was keeping it in the present."

Patout asked when that last visit had taken place, and when she told him, he frowned. "That's about the time he resigned."

"Resigned? He's left the department?" He told her about Basile's gradual but steady decline. Dismayed, she said, "I didn't even know about his and Barbara's breakup. He didn't say a word to me about it."

"He didn't take it nearly as hard as he did Kev's death. That's still eating him up. Even I didn't realize how much until... this."

"What's happened, Doug? What did you mean when you said he'd flown the coop? Do you mean he's disappeared?"

"Looks like it."

She raised shaking fingers to her lips. "You don't think he'd harm himself?"

"No. It's not that, but anything else I say would be unfair to Burke because the details are still sketchy."

"Details of what? Has he... done something?"

Patout hedged. "I'd rather not discuss it, Nanci. There was an incident, but it isn't a matter of record yet because the other involved party wishes to keep it contained. But it's a volatile situation. If I'm very lucky and locate Basile soon, I might be able to prevent a real disaster. If not, for all practical purposes, his life will be over."

Wringing her hands, she groaned. "This is my fault."

"No, no it isn't. He was close to the edge and would have gone over even if you hadn't stopped his visits."

Far from convinced, she offered to do whatever she could to help.

"Tell me where he might have gone," Patout said. "Did he ever mention a getaway to you? Some special place?"

"I don't know. A fishing cabin maybe, but..." She massaged her forehead as though to stimulate her memory. "If he ever said where it was, I don't remember. Barbara would know."

Patout's expression turned sour. "I'd been trying to reach her at home, when I gave up and called the school where she teaches. She and her boyfriend took some personal days and went to Jamaica. They were already out of town before Basile disappeared. I'm sure she knows nothing about it."

Nanci looked forlorn. "I wish I could help. I love Burke. He was a dear friend to Kev and to me. It tore me apart to ask him to stop coming around. But you understand my reasoning, don't you?"

"Yes, I do. And I'm sure he understood, too." He touched her hand in farewell and apologized for keeping her from the pizza party. Moving away, he said, "If you think of anything, call me."

"Have you spoken with his brother?"

Patout stopped. "Brother?"

Chapter
Twenty-Seven

Burke was unconscious for only a couple of minutes, but in that brief amount of time Remy Duvall had managed to row the boat twenty or thirty yards out. She was struggling to start the motor.

He crawled to the end of the pier and called her name. Rockets of pain exploded behind his eyeballs, and he wondered what she had hit him with, and how a woman that slender could have put that much power behind the blow.

She was headed toward land in the direction that he'd indicated to her earlier, when actually the old pier was on the opposite side. He had deliberately told her wrong. "Mrs. Duvall, even if you make it to solid ground, you'll die out there. You'll get lost and never find your way out."

Giving up on the motor, she retrieved the oar and began to row again. Burke considered jumping in and going after her. In some parts of the swamp the water was no more than knee deep. But here it was at least over his head.

Ordinarily that wouldn't pose a problem. Swimming, he could cover the distance to the boat in seconds. But he was dizzy and nauseous and unsure he could remain conscious if he tried to swim. He might drown. Then both of them would perish, because, damn it, he'd meant it when he warned her of the dangers awaiting a person alone and lost in the swamp.

There was only one choice left to him, and it was a bitch.

But, seeing no other way to stop her, he forced himself to stand. He swayed on his feet and had to close his eyes for a moment while the horizon rocked itself back into its rightful position. When the worst of the dizziness passed, he stumbled toward the cabin in a listing gait that he thought must look like a poor imitation of John Wayne.

The pistol was where he'd hidden it.

Moving as quickly as his distressed equilibrium permitted, he returned to the end of the pier, cupped the pistol in both hands, and aimed it at the small boat. "Turn around and come back, Mrs. Duvall." She ignored him. "If you don't, I'm going to shoot holes in the boat and sink it."

She looked back at him and saw the gun, but it didn't faze her. "No you won't, Mr. Basile."

"Why not?"

"Because gunshots would alert someone that we're here, and you don't want that."

"Ever hear of silencers?"

That got her attention. She dropped the oar. "You're no murderer. If you sink the boat, I'll drown."

"Pick up the oar and start rowing back."

She did neither. "Remember, I told you I can't swim."

"And remember I told you that I'm not stupid."

He fired the pistol, deliberately missing her, but lining

up a row of perfect holes in the side of the boat an inch below the waterline.

Later, it occurred to him that she didn't scream as one might expect. Or if she did, he didn't hear it above the squawking of birds that had already roosted for the evening in their nests in the upper branches of surrounding trees. They staged a noisy protest. Even with the silencer, the spitting sounds of the gun had seemed loud in the cottony silence of descending night.

The water leaking into the craft panicked her immediately. She tried to stop the flooding by pressing her hands against the bullet holes, but, of course, to no avail.

"You might just as well jump on in and swim back, Mrs. Duvall. Tow the boat back while you're at it."

"I can't."

"Sure you can. Just take hold of the rope and pull it behind you."

She was becoming increasingly more frantic, which looked convincing from a distance. Burke suspected a trick. She looked about as dangerous and cunning as a butterfly, but she'd fooled him too many times—lunging for the side door of the van during the high-speed chase, trying to pull the key from the ignition, throwing a spatula dripping hot grease at him, and damn near braining him with a club when he came through the door of the cabin. He wasn't going to be taken in by her fragile and guileless facade anymore.

He had to admit, though, that this was her best performance yet. She seemed in the throes of panic when she stood up, dangerously rocking the boat. "Please, Mr. Basile. I'll drown."

"You're not going to drown."

"Please!"

It happened when she stretched out her arm as though to grasp his hand from that distance. The boat tipped, then flipped over, spilling her into the viscous water. She splashed crazily, but sank. And stayed under. Burke couldn't see her. Holding his breath, he anxiously scanned the water until he saw her head break the surface.

He exhaled. Another of her tricks.

But she was visible only for a second before disappearing again, gasping and thrashing on her way down. This time she didn't reappear.

"Shit," Burke whispered. Then louder: *"Shit!"*

Forgetting about his burning eyes, disregarding the possible concussion he'd sustained, taking no time to tug off his shoes, he dropped his pistol onto the pier and dove into the water.

It was like trying to swim through a bowl of breakfast grits. Like in a nightmare, the longer his strokes and the stronger his kicks, the less progress he seemed to make. By the time he reached the capsized boat, his muscles and lungs were on fire. Throwing his arms across the upended hull, he sucked in several huge breaths, then let go and slid beneath the surface.

He swam in widening circles, groping blindly, until he had to come up for air. When he did, he saw air bubbles breaking the surface about ten yards away. Fortifying himself with another deep breath, he lunged in that direction.

He felt her hair brush his arm like silky seaweed, but when he reached for her, his fist closed around nothing except water. His hands searched wildly until they found her. Lungs near to bursting, he wrapped his arms around her and used the slippery bottom of the bayou to give himself a push-off. The water wasn't that deep, but it was dense, and it seemed that he would never reach the surface.

When he did, he gulped air, but long before he regained his breath, he began swimming for the pier, pulling Remy Duvall behind him. She hadn't moved or resisted his life-saving attempts as people on the verge of drowning customarily do. He was afraid to learn why. Forcing himself to look, he glanced down at her face. It was as still and white as death, covered with filth.

When he reached the pier, he was presented with another problem: how to climb up onto the pier while holding on to her. Haste was a priority. She lay limply across his bent left arm. How long since she'd been without oxygen?

Urgency gave him the strength to reach up and grip one of the cleats with his right hand. He tried twice, unsuccessfully, to chin himself up far enough to get his right leg onto the pier. On the third try, when he swung his leg up, his heel struck the plank and he dug it in, then hung there for several seconds, trying to summon strength and convince his muscles that they could do what he was about to demand of them.

With Herculean effort, he worked his right foot along the pier until it, too, could be used as leverage. Eventually, using his right hand and elbow, right foot and knee, he pulled himself up. When his belly touched the planks, he expelled a near-laugh of relief.

He pulled Remy Duvall up and stretched her out on the pier. Strands of hair clung to her lips. These he pushed aside and began immediately to administer CPR. Push push push, rest. One two three, rest. Close the nostrils, breathe into the mouth. Push push push, rest.

How long had it been? She had been under no more than twenty seconds when he jumped in. Okay, maybe thirty. Add the forty-five seconds, maybe more, for him to swim to the boat. One minute beneath the surface. That added up to, how long?

Push push push, rest. Push push—

She coughed up water. Laying his hand along her cheek, he turned her head to the side so she wouldn't choke as she heaved up the water she'd swallowed. It took several minutes for her breathing to return to normal and the bluish tint on her lips to fade.

When she opened her eyes, he was in her direct line of vision. There was no way she could avoid looking at him, no way he could avoid the accusation in her gaze. "I'm sorry. I didn't believe you. I thought it was a trick." He couldn't think of anything else to say, so he repeated, "I'm sorry."

Wearily, he pushed himself to his feet and looked across the dark water. Because it had capsized, the boat was still afloat. If it wasn't retrieved, they'd be in trouble. He had to do something now, before total exhaustion set in and he was incapable of moving. For the second time, he dove into the water.

* * *

The milk of human kindness wasn't exactly flowing through every vein, but at least they hadn't killed him. Yet.

Gregory made every attempt to appear harmless, which wasn't difficult, because he wasn't only harmless; he was utterly helpless. Besides, he doubted Old Nick himself could have intimidated these folks. They might slit his throat for entertainment, but not because they felt threatened.

As for himself, his bowels were quaking with terror. They could probably smell his fear over the tantalizing aroma of the gumbo that bubbled in a pot on the cook stove. The woman of the house brought him a bowl of it, ungraciously setting the crockery down on the table with a decisive *thunk*.

She was no friendlier than the menfolks—her husband and teenage son, Gregory surmised—who'd virtually dragged him through the woods to this house where the woman and two younger girls had subjected him to suspicious scrutiny. He supposed he should be grateful that he'd been rescued before he became gator chow, or succumbed to hunger, thirst, or exposure.

They'd saved him from the perils of the swamp, but their hospitality left much to be desired. At any moment their misgivings could give rise to menace. These were the kind of people you did not mess with. The movie *Deliverance* came to mind.

Trying to establish a friendlier mood, he smiled up at his hostess. "This looks delicious. Thank you, ma'am."

She practically snarled, revealing a gap where several teeth should have been. She said something to her husband in Cajun French. He grunted a surly response. The children were as taciturn as their parents. They stood by silently and watched Gregory spoon the gumbo into his mouth.

He was ravenous, but after a couple of bites, he realized that he should have given the gumbo a trial run before gobbling. It was dark and thick with various shellfish, onion, tomatoes, okra, and rice, but the cook had been liberal with spices that seared his esophagus.

After taking a long drink of water, he ate more slowly. His stomach had shrunk over the last couple of days, so he got full quickly and finished only half the portion. "Thank you very much," he said, patting his tummy. "It was delicious, but I'm full."

Without comment, the woman removed the bowl and his utensils but left his glass of water. The man sat down across from him. He was a hairy cuss. Coarse black hair sprouted from his nostrils and ears and knuckles. The hair on his head had been plastered down by his dozer cap, but his chin was obscured by a thick beard that extended all the way down his neck to meld with the pelt that filled the V of his collar.

"What's your name?"

Gregory, upon hearing him speak English for the first time, stammered, "Uh, Gregory."

"Father Gregory?"

Momentarily taken aback, Gregory then remembered that he was still wearing the reversed collar. "Uh, yes. Yes. *Father* Gregory." A priest might be treated with deference. For instance, his death might be quick and painless as opposed to slow and torturous.

His lie evoked the hoped-for response. Impressed to have a man of God in their midst, they began talking excitedly among themselves. Eventually the head of the house whistled shrilly and the others fell immediately silent.

He eyed Gregory with blatant distrust. "What happened to your face?"

"Tree branch."

Two eyebrows that looked like caterpillars glued to his forehead came together to form a suspicious furry frown.

"See, I got lost," Gregory said. Their expressions remained immutable. He elaborated. "I, uh, a friend and I were camping. He went on ahead in the car with our supplies. I was supposed to take the boat and meet him at a designated spot. But I got lost. Wasn't watching where I was going and plowed right into a tree. Knocked myself silly. I drifted for I don't know how long until the boat got caught up where you found me." He formed the sign of the cross between them. "Bless you, my friend." Then, to cap off the monologue, he added, "My fellow priest is probably worried sick by now. He's probably organized a search party."

The hirsute man looked up at his wife and grunted non-committally; she sucked the empty space where an incisor should have been.

Gregory took their rejection hard. He felt like crying. He'd reached rock bottom, leaving him only one viable option—throwing himself on the mercy of his parents. They'd washed their hands of him a dozen times, but they always came through when the situation was desperate, and he couldn't imagine a situation more desperate than this.

Surely he could think of something to tell them that would strike a chord of parental concern, or, short of that, obligation. After all, they'd spawned him. They would gladly finance a trip. Maybe to Europe or the Orient. They would send him far, far away just to get rid of him and avoid any embarrassment his presence in New Orleans might cause them.

He would leave tomorrow. His daddy could make it happen. In a matter of hours, he would be safely away from Burke Basile and Pinkie Duvall and the whole damnable mess. He rued the day he had become involved, but now he'd seen the light and salvation was only a telephone call away.

"You've been awfully kind. Now, if I could please use your phone—"

"No phone," the man said brusquely.

"Oh, okay." There was a telephone in plain sight not ten feet away on the kitchen wall, but Gregory thought it prudent not to point that out, especially since another heated family discussion was underway. He knew a smattering of French, but none he'd studied sounded like this, so he was unable to follow the debate that continued until, again, the father motioned for silence.

"You'll marry that boy there."

Gregory stared at him with misapprehension. "I beg your pardon?"

He pointed to the stocky youth who had assisted in the rescue. "He wants to get married. You'll marry him, *oui*?"

The gumbo was bubbling again, this time in Gregory's stomach. He'd eaten too much after days of fasting. He was sweating as profusely as the lady of the house, who kept mopping her upper lip with the dish towel slung over her shoulder.

This situation was becoming trickier by the minute. To get out of it alive would require all his acting skills. The boy looked about eighteen and promised to be as hairy as his father in a few years. Gregory smiled at him benevolently. "You want to get married, my son?"

The boy glanced at his father to answer for him.

The bearded man startled Gregory by barking an order in Cajun French.

A door off the main room opened and an impossibly young girl emerged. That is, impossibly young to have her belly swollen by an advanced pregnancy.

"Oh, Jesus," Gregory groaned, and not in prayer.

Chapter
Twenty-Eight

Burke towed the boat back to the pier, swimming about as agilely as a man with an anvil tied to his neck. His head felt like it had been pounded with a meat mallet. When he reached the pier, it cost him reserve amounts of energy to pull the boat from the water. He retrieved the pistol he'd emptied into the hull, but he didn't immediately assess the damage. Right now he was less concerned about Dredd's boat than Duvall's wife.

She was where he'd left her, but she had turned onto her side and drawn her knees up to her chest, probably for warmth. When he leaned over her, his clothes dripped water onto her face. She didn't move. He pushed his hand into her shirt and touched her throat to assure himself there was a pulse.

"Why didn't you make it easy on yourself and let me drown?" Only after she had spoken did she open her eyes.

"You're no good to me dead," he said in a husky voice.

Now, having had time to think about how close she'd come to dying, he was weak with relief.

"Wouldn't my death have been your revenge?"

"I don't want Duvall to mourn you. I want him to come after you."

Then she did the last thing he expected—she laughed.

Angrily, he withdrew his hand and left her to her joviality, figuring that if she felt well enough to laugh, her dunking in the bayou hadn't had any serious effects. He was a sap to get all emotional about it.

His shoes squished on the planks as he stepped over a crowbar—no doubt her weapon—and made his way to the far side of the shack, where he ignored the cold and stripped to the skin.

He washed himself vigorously with water from the rain barrel and a bar of no-nonsense soap. He scrubbed his hair with shampoo and rooted into his ear canal with a soapy cloth, hoping to discourage any microorganisms from moving in permanently. When he felt sufficiently clean, he went into the cabin to dry himself in front of the heater before dressing.

The shampooing had aggravated the goose egg on the back of his head. It hurt like a son of a bitch, but neither his vision nor his memory was impaired, so he didn't think he'd suffered a concussion. He took a few aspirin to dull the pain, then went back outside.

Mrs. Duvall's case of the giggles had subsided. In fact, she appeared to have fallen asleep. "Hey." He nudged her knee with his toe. "You've got to get cleaned up."

Groaning, she drew her knees closer to her chest.

"That water's got all sorts of creepy-crawlers in it. I don't want you dying on me of some parasite."

He tried to take her hand and pull her up, but she didn't

cooperate. Swearing beneath his breath, he bent down and forced her to sit up. "I'm tired, too, lady. You brought this on yourself. If you hadn't done such a damn stupid thing, you wouldn't be feeling so bad."

He made her stand, then half led, half carried her to the side of the shack and the cistern. He refilled the bucket with fresh water and slapped the bar of soap into her palm.

"Wash all over," he instructed. "Ears, nose, everything. Scrub hard. You should be as pink as a baby's butt when you're done. After you're finished, I'll tend to the wounds on your back." He was concerned about infection. Open wounds were extremely vulnerable to bacteria, and the swamp was a hatchery for unicellular killers.

He left her to wash and went back into the cabin, where their uneaten fish supper was beginning to stink. He gathered up both the cooked and uncooked portions and wrapped them tightly in a plastic bag. He placed the lid on the cooking pot, deciding that he would dispose of the grease later. He no longer had an appetite and doubted she did. But maybe he should ask her.

On his way out, he grabbed an extra couple of towels and pulled the quilt off the bed. Taking these with him, he moved to the corner of the shack. "Mrs. Duvall?" he called. She didn't respond. He listened for the sound of splashing water, but heard nothing. He didn't detect any sound or movement at all. "Mrs. Duvall?"

When she failed to answer a second time, he looked around the corner, but he needn't have worried about being a Peeping Tom. She was still dressed, sitting on a low stool against the wall, her head bowed, her hands lying listlessly in her lap. The bar of soap, Burke noticed, was still in her right hand.

"What's the matter?" He approached warily. Her seeming disassociation with her surroundings could be another trick. When he got closer, he saw that she was shivering. "I know it's cold out here, but you really should be washing that stuff off you. The sooner the better."

"I wanted to die."

"What?"

"I wanted to—"

"I heard what you said," he said testily. "It's just a hell of a way to go, drowning in that shit."

"No," she said, shaking her head, which was still tangled and wet and matted with duckweed. "When I was a little girl, I prayed every night before I went to sleep that angels would come down and carry me to heaven before I woke up."

He realized now that her laughter on the pier had been a symptom of hysteria. This was phase two of it. She'd been terrified of the swamp, of drowning, maybe of him. Should he shake her, slap her, or humor her? He decided on the last. "At one time or another, all kids pray that. Usually when they're pissed off at their parents and want to teach them a lesson for being so strict."

"I was ashamed."

"Of wanting to die?"

"No, of the things Angel did and made me do."

If this was an act designed to spark pity, it was a damn good performance. She spoke in a faraway voice, sounding very much as she must have as a child, curled up beneath the covers, imploring angels to come down for her.

"I think that's why God took my baby. To punish me for praying for the wrong things."

Burke had heard enough. "Come on, stand up."

He pulled her to her feet and began undoing her belt

buckle. If the fabric had been dry, the oversized pants would have dropped the moment the belt was loosened. Instead the heavy material clung wetly to her thighs.

He dropped to his knees and pulled the pants down her legs. "Listen, it doesn't work that way." Taking hold of one ankle, he guided her foot from the pants leg. He did the same with the other foot. "God's too busy running the planet to keep scorecards on everybody."

He tossed the pants aside and went for the buttons on Dredd's old shirt, undoing the bottom one first and working his way up. He talked to distract himself from the smooth belly he was addressing. "All that guilt shit, it'll eat you up. Believe me, I know. So you've got to stop thinking that you're to blame for losing your kid, or you'll get as crazy as me. It was biology. That's all."

"You don't have to do that."

He raised his head and looked hard into her eyes and saw that she was lucid. Her malaise had passed. He came to his feet, but his hands remained resting lightly on her waist. "You were losing it."

"I'm okay now."

"Are you sure?"

"Are you afraid to leave me alone after what I said about wanting to die?"

"Maybe."

"If I still wanted to die, I could have let myself drown. I didn't want to."

"I didn't want you to either. If you had, it would have been my fault for not believing you when you told me you couldn't swim."

"And your conscience is overloaded as it is?"

"Something like that."

He lost track of the seconds that ticked by, because

he had her undivided attention—at least her gaze didn't waver from his—and he was acutely aware of her skin warming beneath his palms.

Apparently she became aware of it too, because she glanced down at his hands, and, when she did, he released her and stepped back.

"That muck is beginning to dry," he said. "It'll be hard to get off. Lean over the railing and I'll help you wash your hair."

She looked hesitant, uneasy with that idea. A little vexed over her diffidence, he added, "A bucket of water is heavy, especially if you're trying to pour it over your head. Okay?"

Without any more discussion, she moved to the edge of the pier and leaned across the railing. Burke emptied half a bucket of clean water over her head, then worked shampoo into a good lather, scrubbing her hair from roots to ends. He rinsed out the worst of the filth, then shampooed a second time.

Soap suds foamed over his hands as his fingers slid up through her hair to massage her scalp. Lava flows of bubbles ran down her nape and into the valleys behind her ears. A strand of soapy pearls slid down her throat, over the gold chain of her cross, and beyond, into the collar of Dredd's ugly flannel shirt and onto what Burke knew were beautiful breasts.

He didn't stop shampooing until the lather completely gave out, and then reluctantly. He filled the water bucket again. Dialogue seemed inappropriate, somehow, so he reached around and cupped her chin in his hand and tipped it down. Slowly he poured the rainwater over her head, moving it first to one side, then the other, guiding it by applying the slightest pressure to her chin.

Finally the last drops trickled from the bucket.

Burke backed away. For a moment, he just stood there, staring at the back of her bowed head, then he filled the bucket again and set it on the pier near her feet. "There's a towel behind you there on the stool. You'll be cold when you finish. Might want to wrap up in the quilt." Then he left her.

Inside the cabin, he stood in the center of the room, breathing hard and pressing the heels of his hands into his eye sockets. His headache had migrated from the knot on his head to the backs of his eyeballs, where it pulsed like a gangsta rap beat. He was sweating like it was July instead of February.

Clumsily, he assembled the first-aid items on the table. He was repositioning the table and one of the chairs nearer the heater when she appeared in the doorway wrapped Indian-fashion in the quilt, a towel turban around her head. "I left my clothes soaking in the bucket. I'll rinse them out in the morning."

He motioned for her to sit down. "We might just as well do this before you get dressed."

"All right."

When she was seated with her back to him, he pushed the quilt off her shoulders, exposing her back. He examined the wounds and was relieved to see that all looked closed and none showed signs of recent bleeding. With as much detachment as possible, he dabbed each one with antiseptic, then reapplied the salve.

They didn't speak. Nor was there any white noise to fill the claustrophobic silence—no radio or TV or traffic sounds. Nothing alleviated the absolute quiet except their breathing.

When he was finished, he awkwardly raised the quilt

to cover her shoulders and patted it into place. "Warm enough?"

"Yes."

"I, uh, brought some stuff along. Things I thought you might need while we're here. You'll find them in a totebag in the bathroom." He'd known to pack for a few days when he left New Orleans for the tour of Jenny's House. She hadn't.

"Thank you."

"Sure."

She went into the bathroom and closed the door. Burke uncapped a bottle of water and drank nearly all of it. His arms and legs felt shaky; he was still slightly dizzy and his ears were ringing. He blamed his light-headedness on taking aspirin on an empty stomach, on the exertion of saving his hostage from drowning and a boat from sinking, on the blow to his head. He attributed it to everything except the actual cause.

When she came out of the bathroom, the towel around her head was gone, but her hair was still wet, tucked behind her ears. She was wearing a gray sweat suit. It was one he had bought for her before leaving New Orleans. "I would've given you that to wear this morning," he said, "but Dredd already had you up and dressed. He wasn't in any mood for me to undo something he'd done."

She was looking directly at him, but he got the impression that his words weren't registering. At first he thought she might have lapsed into another semicatatonic state, but he understood her speechless dismay when he glanced down at her outstretched hand.

The box of body powder wasn't crystal and it didn't have a silver lid. It wasn't nearly as fancy as the one he'd seen on her dressing table, but it was the same fragrance, the scent he'd detected on her in the French Market and in the confessional.

Reading the question in her eyes, he shrugged slightly and said, "The day Father Gregory and I came calling, I snooped around."

She set the box of powder on the table and continued to stare down at it while tracing the familiar embossed logo on the lid with the tip of her finger. "How did I ever mistake you for a priest?"

Was he supposed to answer that? He didn't know, so he said nothing.

Still staring at the box, she said, "That day in the confessional..."

"Umm?"

She made a small motion of dismissal with her shoulder. "Nothing."

"What?"

"Never mind."

"Go ahead. What?"

"Did you..." She paused to take a deep breath. "Did you touch my hand?"

It seemed to take a long time for her eyes to reach his. In fact, time slowed to a standstill. Her last word hung in the air for several seconds, like the final vibrating note from a violin. When it finally died, the silence was palpable and sweetly oppressive.

Burke's heart was beating hard and fast. Something delicate was hanging in the balance, but he didn't dare define it. The distance between them had miraculously dwindled, although he couldn't remember stepping closer to her. Nor had she moved. Her hand was still on the lid of the powder box, while the other remained motionless at her side.

It was that hand that the back of his brushed against. Barely. Withdrew. Hesitated. Touched again, and this time stayed. Hands turned simultaneously. Palms slid against each other. Held. Held, then pressed. Fingers slowly interlaced.

Burke bent his elbow, raising his right hand, her left. Then he rotated his wrist, bringing her hand topside. He looked down at it, marveling over the delicacy of her skin, the slenderness of her fingers. Her third finger in particular.

"Your wedding ring is gone," he remarked.

"It slipped off in the water."

Her wedding ring was gone. But she was still another man's wife. Not just *any* man's wife, but his bitterest enemy's. If Duvall felt like kissing her neck where a vein pulsed against the slender gold chain, then he was entitled to do so. If he wanted to see and touch and fuck her, he could do that, too. And that pissed Burke off, so he took it out on her.

"You can buy yourself another diamond. With Duvall's life insurance settlement."

"That's a horrible thing to say," she cried, jerking her hand free.

"If I really wanted to get horrible, you know what I'd do."

To her credit, she didn't recoil in fear. Rather, she tilted her chin defiantly. "Am I supposed to thank you for not raping me?"

"You're not supposed to do anything. This isn't about you. It's between Duvall and me. All you are is bait to draw him out."

"You're doomed to fail, Mr. Basile." She shook her head and gave him a sad smile. "I understand the reasoning behind your plan, but you've miscalculated my husband. He won't take the bait. He won't come for me. After I've spent several days and nights alone with you, my husband won't want me back."

He laughed shortly. "Nice try." Reaching into his back pocket with one hand, he took hers with the other.

"What are you doing?"

"Handcuffing you." He locked the manacles around her wrist with a decisive click.

"To what?"

"To me."

Chapter
Twenty-Nine

Pinkie left the remainder of his muffuletta sandwich on his desk and moved to the window of his office. Through the slats of the blinds, he looked out across the nighttime skyline. "Why in hell can't somebody find them? They couldn't have simply vanished."

"Looks like they did," Bardo mumbled around a mouthful of his carryout dinner.

Since the discovery of the abandoned van, there'd been no further development in locating Basile and Remy. People monitoring public transportation into and out of New Orleans had seen nothing. The helicopter pilot had spotted nothing worth investigating. None of Duvall's informants anywhere in southern Louisiana had anything to report.

"You're sure that whore was straight with you? She didn't know anything?"

Bardo belched behind his hand. "Dixie? When I found out she'd helped Basile, I worked her over pretty good." Pinkie turned and gave him a pointed look. Bardo grinned.

"No, I didn't go that far. She's probably back on the street by now. But I did a good enough job on her, if she'd've known something, she would've told."

Pinkie went back to staring out the window. The city lights were diffused by fog and mist, but he didn't really see them anyway. He was wholly given over to his dilemma. The moment Errol called him from the Crossroads, his perfect, structured life had toppled. His clients had been put on hold. Judges had granted him postponements because of an "illness in his family." His calendar had been cleared of all appointments and social engagements. Telephone calls went unreturned unless they related specifically to the crisis.

Goddamn Burke Basile for reducing his well-programmed life to chaos.

The bastard was going to pay, and pay huge. But where in hell was he? Pinkie had put the fear of God into Doug Patout, but his only contribution so far had been to report that Burke Basile's wife was out of the country with her boyfriend, and Pinkie's people had already determined that.

His built-in lie detector indicated that Doug Patout was telling the truth when he said he didn't know where Basile was. Even so, Pinkie might suspect Patout of abetting Basile, except for one thing: Patout's love for his position transcended the high regard he had for each man in his division, and that included his favorite, Basile. Patout wanted to advance into the upper echelons of the NOPD. He was no milk toast, but he wasn't stupid, either. He recognized the hazards of making Pinkie Duvall unhappy.

After the scare they'd given Mac McCuen, Pinkie predicted he would play on their team. But, who knew? He might turn out to be as loyal and trustworthy a friend to Basile as Basile had been to Kev Stuart.

"Fucking cops," he muttered.

"Come again?" Bardo asked.

"Never mind."

After a moment, Bardo said, "You know, I've been thinking."

"About what?"

"About how much Mrs. Duvall knows about our business."

Pinkie came around slowly. "Meaning?"

"Meaning that Basile could probably be a persuasive guy if he set his mind to it. Especially with a woman."

Unwittingly, Wayne Bardo had tapped into the mother lode of Pinkie's concern. He had never discussed the details of his various sidelines with Remy, but she could have picked up threads of information, which, woven together, could form the rope that would hang him. She probably knew even more than she realized. Even an offhanded comment could prove useful to someone like Basile, whose police training had honed his innate deductive skills. If he threatened Remy's life, God knows how much she would suddenly remember about her husband's enterprises and compromising connections. All the more reason why she needed to be found and silenced.

"If Basile sweet-talked her, blew in her ear some, she might spill her guts," Bardo surmised. "What do you think?"

"What I think," Duvall said evenly, "is that if you talk like that about my wife again, I'm going to tear out your tongue." It was all right for him to speculate on Remy's allegiance; it wasn't all right for someone else to.

"Jeez, Pinkie, don't get sore. All I meant was—"

"I need to get out of this room," he said abruptly.

"Where're you going?"

"Out."

"I'll come, too."

"You'll stay here. You have work to do. Remember?"

Pinkie angrily yanked open the door, then strode through the lobby of his law office. Errol, who'd been sleeping in a chair, groggily raised his head, then jerked to attention. "Where to, Mr. Duvall?"

"I'm going for a walk. Alone."

He took the elevator to the first floor of the building, passed the security guard without a glance, and pushed through the glass doors, which the guard unlocked electronically from the reception desk.

Pinkie walked two blocks before he hailed one of New Orleans's notoriously expensive taxis. When he gave the female driver the address, she shot him a droll look in the rearview mirror.

* * *

Mardi Gras celebrants were keeping the girls at Ruby Bouchereaux's place busy. From now until midnight on Fat Tuesday when Lent began, the gentlemen were limited to one hour, unless they were willing to pay exorbitantly. Ruby had reminded her girls that the more frequent the turnover, the more profit for everybody.

The week of Mardi Gras was always an enormous moneymaker. Nightly, the house was packed with regular clients seeking additional fun without their wives after the grand balls and parties, and out-of-towners who flocked to the city for the celebration. Men ranging from eighteen to eighty sought fun and frolic in the best whorehouse in the best party town in the country.

Most evenings Ruby could be found on the gallery

above the main salon. From this excellent vantage point, she could observe the activity going on below, while letting her excellent personnel handle the general operation. Puffing a cigar and sipping brandy, she mentally tabulated what this night's profits would be, and smiled complacently at the estimate.

Her smile deflated when she saw Pinkie Duvall.

Speaking to no one, he made his way to the bar and ordered a drink, which he drank quickly and ordered another. To Ruby, the most amusing of his pretensions was that of being a wine connoisseur. Belying that image, he was tossing back shots of hard liquor as rapidly as a sailor on shore leave after six months at sea.

Catching the eye of one of her hostesses, she signaled her toward Pinkie. The svelte blonde was one of Ruby's classiest girls. A United States diplomat's daughter, she had traveled extensively with her parents and attended the most prestigious schools in the world. She spoke several languages fluently and was conversant on a wide variety of topics. She could hold her own with a stuffy intellectual, or be quite the coquette. No fantasy was too bizarre if it meant pleasing a client, although she drew the line at abuse and pain. Having absolutely no shame or inhibitions, she approached sex as an art form, practicing the exotic methods she had learned abroad while executing her own idea of foreign relations.

A nasty incident in Burma—when it was still Burma— involving her and a high government official had resulted in her father's dismissal from foreign service. He, in turn, had renounced her. Penniless and scandalized, she had made a natural career choice and had never regretted it. Clients paid dearly for her. Even after Ruby's percentage, she was getting rich, and because she looked younger than her years, she could probably work well into her thirties. She went by the name of Isobel.

Pinkie was an easy sell tonight. The transaction at the bar took less than a minute. He followed the beauty up the wide staircase. Ruby left her cigar smoldering in a crystal ashtray and intercepted them on the landing.

"Good evening, Pinkie." Although she'd rather have spit on him, she gave him her most disarming smile.

He was no happier to see her than she was to see him, and was probably annoyed that she had forced him to speak to her. "Ruby."

"I haven't seen you since Bardo carved up my girl. How good of you to grace us with your presence."

He ignored the barb. "Your business is thriving. But then whoring has always been profitable."

Ruby's smile turned brittle at the corners, and her eyes glinted with malice. "Because there've always been men who can't get it without paying for it. Which brings me to wonder why you're here tonight. Wasn't your wife in the mood? Remy, isn't it? Did Remy refuse your attentions tonight?"

She was rewarded by seeing the blood vessels in his temples expand. With a brusque gesture, he motioned Isobel up the stairs. Ruby thoughtfully watched them go.

During his bachelor days, Pinkie had come around several times a week. Since his marriage, his patronage had slacked off considerably, although he wasn't entirely a stranger to the bedrooms upstairs. Sometimes he came for recreation, other times to work off steam, but Ruby had never seen him as agitated as he was tonight. Interesting.

"Miss Ruby?"

She turned. One of the maids, who'd worked in the

house even while Ruby was growing up in it, spoke to her softly in her melodious West Indies accent. "You said for me to come get you when that poor little lamb woke up."

They moved along the gallery, then made a right turn down a hallway that led to the rear of the house and a room that was tucked under the eaves. "How is she?" Ruby asked as they approached the closed door.

"Mostly, she's scared."

The chamber was comfortably furnished, although it was too small to use for business. Usually it was given over to a girl who was sick and needed to be kept quarantined from the others while she was contagious, or to a new girl who needed a place to sleep while she was being trained and taught the policies of the house.

Ruby approached the bed and leaned over the girl with the attention of a loving mother. "How are you feeling?"

Dixie experimentally touched the tip of her tongue to the corner of her mouth, where blood had coagulated over a nasty abrasion. "That bastard busted me up good, didn't he?"

"The doctor said none of the bones in your face were broken."

"The way he was hitting me, I don't know why not." Tears filled her eyes. "Do I look like something a goat puked up?"

"You've looked better," Ruby said, laying a gentle hand on her arm. "And you will again. Don't fret. The doctor left some pain medication. You can rest here for as long as it takes to heal. I'd guess two weeks, maybe three."

"Two or three weeks?" Dixie tried to laugh, but the effort made her wince with pain. Moving only her eyes, she took in the room, Ruby, and the hovering maid. "If I don't work, I don't eat. How am I supposed to pay you?"

"When you arrived, you said Burke Basile had sent you. Is he a client of yours?"

"You mean a john? Don't I wish," Dixie mumbled. "He's paid me, but for information only. Nothing else. Last time I saw him, he told me that if I got into trouble, I should come here. You a friend of his?"

"Let's just say that he and I share a mutual respect and a common goal."

"Hmm. Well, if he has to pay for this, it'll serve him right. It's on account of him that Bardo—"

"Wayne Bardo?" Ruby's soft expression hardened. "He did this to you?"

Dixie nodded. "Made me suck him off. Then, when I wouldn't tell him anything about Basile, he started beating the crap out of my face."

Ruby sat down on the edge of the bed and studied the girl with an experienced eye. Her face was a mess, but she had excellent bone structure, and, when they'd undressed her, Ruby had taken note of her alluring figure. Ruby usually disparaged girls who worked the streets, but obviously Basile considered this one a notch above the rest, or he wouldn't have recommended she come here.

She needed refining. Her name would be changed to something more unusual and intriguing. Her days of bathing in cheap gardenia scent were over. The silver nail polish and red vinyl skirt would have to go.

She needed a complete makeover, but the girl definitely had potential.

Ruby smoothed the hair off her forehead where Bardo's fists had left bruises. "Why was Bardo inquiring about Mr. Basile?"

"He was looking for him."

"Did he say why?"

"No. Only I think it has something to do with—Wait, maybe I'm not supposed to tell. Basile paid me to keep my mouth shut."

"But he wouldn't mind your telling me. He sent you here, remember."

"Yeah, I guess. Okay. I think it has something to do with Pinkie Duvall's wife."

"Really?" With affected indifference, Ruby listened to Dixie's very interesting story. "A priest?"

Dixie snorted. "Can you imagine that? If Basile was a priest, every woman in the church would be getting off during Mass. Say, listen, if this isn't going to cost me, could I maybe have a drink?"

"Certainly." Ruby turned to the maid and asked her to fetch a cup of tea.

"It wasn't exactly tea I had in mind," Dixie remarked as the maid withdrew.

Ruby smiled indulgently. "You'll drink your tea, take your medicine, and rest. If you do everything I tell you, this beating could be the best thing that's ever happened to you. But we'll talk about all that later when you're feeling better."

Ruby left Dixie under the maid's care and resumed her place on the gallery to ruminate on what the girl had told her. Could it be that Burke Basile was responsible for Pinkie's foul mood? Did his vendetta against Duvall involve his young and beautiful wife? Was that why he'd been so interested to hear everything Ruby knew about her?

"How very clever of you, Mr. Basile." Ruby chuckled deep in her throat and raised her snifter of brandy in a silent toast to the former narcotics officer.

How unfortunate, though, that he wouldn't live very long.

Not if he'd laid a finger on Pinkie Duvall's wife.

* * *

Mac left for work earlier than usual, telling Toni that he had paperwork to catch up on. He thought he was leaving well before rush hour, but traffic on I-10 was already sluggish because of the weather. A low-pressure system from the Gulf had moved into the area overnight, bringing with it heavy rains.

When he reached headquarters, he parked but didn't enter the building. Instead, he wrestled with an umbrella and walked several blocks to a café, where he ordered only a cup of coffee. He burned his tongue by drinking it before it had time to cool. Then he got change from the cashier, went to the pay phone, and placed a call to the number he'd taken from Burke Basile's retired files the evening before.

"Hello?"

"Joe Basile?"

"Yes."

Mac silently mouthed a thank-you to the god of lucky breaks. It had been years since Burke had designated his brother in Shreveport the person to call, other than his spouse, in case of an emergency. Since then, brother Joe could have moved or changed his number. Mac felt damn lucky to have hit on the first strike.

"My name is Mac McCuen." He kept his voice friendly, upbeat, and conversational. "I work with your brother. Or did. Until he recently resigned."

"In the Narcotics Division?"

"That's right. Has Burke mentioned me to you?"

"You headed one of the squads after Kev Stuart got killed."

"Right again." He wondered in what context Basile had mentioned him. In complaint? In praise of? He didn't have the guts to ask. "I learned a lot by working with your brother and hated like hell that he quit so suddenly."

"He was bummed out. At least that's the excuse he gave me. He swore off police work forever, but it wouldn't surprise me if he went back to it. Maybe not in New Orleans, but somewhere."

"The world would sure be better off if he did." Then, not wanting to lay it on too thick and arouse suspicion, Mac said, "Burke was over at the house the other night and mentioned that he was going away for a while. My wife's old lady is coming to visit," he ad-libbed. "So I thought to myself, why not take a few days off and leave the house to them? Why not join Burke? Hang out, drink beer, talk over old times. You know."

"Hmm," brother Joe said, very noncommittally.

"Only I don't know how to contact him."

"What makes you think he wants to be contacted?"

Shrewdness was a Basile family trait. Brother Joe wasn't a cop, but he was no mental midget either. "Before he left, he said it was too bad I couldn't go with him, something to that effect. Now that I can, I figure he'd welcome the company."

During the long silence that ensued, Mac gnawed on his lower lip. His eyes darted about the café, trying to detect any early morning diner who might be spying on behalf of Pinkie Duvall or Del Ray Jones. None seemed the least bit interested in the nervous man hunched over the public telephone.

Finally Joe Basile said, "I'm afraid I can't help you, Mr. McCuen. When I last spoke to Burke, he sounded pretty down in the dumps. He mentioned getting away to me, too, and, frankly, I got the impression that he wanted to be left alone."

Forgetting his recent prayers, Mac mouthed a few obscenities. "I see."

"Tell you what, though. If Burke calls me, I'll pass along your message. Then if he wants to invite you to join him, he can. Okay? That's the best I can do."

Mac considered telling Joe that his older brother had committed a federal crime. That might make him more cooperative. But he rejected the idea almost as soon as it occurred to him. Duvall didn't want it broadcast that his wife had been abducted. If the news got out and the leak was traced back to Mac McCuen, he'd be dead sooner than later.

"Look, Mr. McCuen, I've got to go," Joe Basile said. "It was nice talking to you. If I hear from Burke, I'll tell him you're available to join him. Have a nice day."

He hung up, leaving Mac holding a dead phone. He replaced the receiver and trudged back to the counter, where he asked for a coffee refill, then stared into it morosely.

Jesus, how had things gotten so bad, so fast?

A couple of weeks ago he'd been feeling pretty damn good about his life. He'd been in debt to Del Ray Jones, but he'd been in debt before. One could always get some money, big money, if he knew how to go about it. Sure, the numbers were higher than ever before, but wasn't that just a matter of zeros? True, he'd been a fool to get involved with Del Ray—that scumbag gave loan sharks everywhere a bad name—but it was a temporary crisis, and a solution was waiting right around the corner. He'd been confident that everything would work out.

Now all hell had broken loose. Basile had up and quit, tossing the whole Narcotics Division on its ear. Internal Affairs had decided it was time for another probe, which put everybody, including Mac, in a very bad mood. Patout was disconsolate and distracted by Basile's resignation and involvement in what seemed a kidnapping. Del Ray Jones had reared his ugly head, and he had Pinkie Duvall behind his threats, making them much more viable.

Mac's only hope of salvation was to find Basile for Duvall, and his only hope of finding Basile had just told him to have a nice day.

"Not fucking likely," he mumbled as he fished a couple of bills from his pants pocket and left them on the counter.

Pinkie had given him twenty-four hours. By nightfall he had to know where Basile was holed up with the lawyer's wife—or else. The odds were lousy.

* * *

Joe Basile thoughtfully hung up the telephone in the den and pondered the strange call from Mac McCuen. But he couldn't dwell on it long because there was a guest seated at the dining table in the kitchen drinking coffee with Linda. His wife hadn't planned on being a hostess early this morning. Pulled from bed by the ringing doorbell, she was in her oldest, warmest robe. Her eyes were still puffy from sleep.

She looked at him as he reentered the kitchen. "Who was on the phone?"

"Somebody from the office, asking what time I'd be in."

She gave him an odd look, but said nothing, and offered to cook their guest some breakfast.

"No thanks, Mrs. Basile," Doug Patout replied. "I grabbed something at Denny's before coming over. I apologize for showing up at your front door this early in the morning."

"No problem."

"You drove up from New Orleans last night?" Joe asked him.

"Yeah, I got in late, and I'm heading straight back as soon as I leave here. I knew it would be a quick-turn-around trip."

"Why didn't you just call?"

"I could have, but I thought we should talk in person."

"It's that important?"

"I believe so. Over the course of your brother's career, he's cultivated a number of enemies, not only among criminals, but inside the police department. I thought it best if we not discuss this matter over the telephone."

"You're scaring us, Mr. Patout," Linda said. "Has something happened to Burke?"

"That's what I don't know but want to find out. He resigned from the department, then a few days later disappeared under mysterious circumstances."

"He called and told me he was going away for a while to sort things out," Joe offered. "In light of his and Barbara's split, and his sudden retirement, I don't consider those circumstances mysterious."

"You're unaware of other factors involved."

"Such as?"

"I'm sorry, Joe, but I can't discuss them. It's classified police information." Placing his folded hands on the table, he appealed to them. "Please. If you have any idea where Burke might have gone, tell me. It's essential that I locate

him before anyone else does. I can't impress upon you
how important this is."

"Are you saying his life is at risk?" Linda asked.

"Possibly."

Meaning yes, Joe thought. He felt the weight of his
predicament. He and his older brother saw each other only
once or twice a year, but they were closer than those infre-
quent visits indicated. He would go so far as to say they
loved each other.

If Burke was in some sort of jam, he would move
heaven and earth to help him out of it. His dilemma arose
from not knowing what to do, because he didn't know
whether or not Burke wanted to be found. By anybody.
McCuen. Or Doug Patout.

Joe had a gut feeling that if Burke had left without
telling anyone where he was going, then he wished to be
left alone. Having quit the police force, wouldn't he have
washed his hands of "classified police information"? And
why were McCuen and Patout looking for him separately?
Neither had mentioned the other. If the situation was as
critical as they independently claimed, why hadn't they
made locating Burke a team effort?

"I'm sorry, Mr. Patout, I can't help you," Joe said, repeating what he'd already told McCuen. "Burke didn't tell
me where he was going."

"Any ideas?"

"No."

"If you knew, would you tell me?"

He answered honestly. "No, I wouldn't."

Patout sighed. He looked at Linda and determined instantly that she supported her husband's decision. He
smiled crookedly. "You're very much like your brother,
Joe."

"Thank you. I consider that a compliment."

Patout laid his business card on the table and stood. "If you change your mind, contact me at any hour. Mrs. Basile, again I apologize for barging in without calling beforehand. Thank you for the coffee."

The Basiles watched from the front door as he got into his car and drove away. Linda turned to Joe. "Your office never calls to ask what time you're coming in."

"It was Mac McCuen, another cop. Guess what he wanted?"

"To know where Burke is?"

"Exactly. And Patout drove all the way to Shreveport to see us this morning."

"What does it mean? What is going on, Joe?"

"Damned if I know. But I'm going to find out."

He returned to the kitchen and thumbed through their personal telephone directory until he found the number for Dredd's Mercantile.

* * *

Dredd, unmindful of the rain, had already been out to check his trotlines. He was squatting at the end of the pier, gutting fish, tossing the entrails back into the water, when he heard the telephone ringing.

Cursing the interruption, he jogged toward the building in his bowlegged gait, his flat bare feet slapping against the wet planks of the pier.

"Hold on, I'm coming," he said out loud as he opened the screen door. Winded from the exercise, he grabbed the receiver and gasped, "Hello?"

Nothing but a dial tone. He slammed down the receiver. "Damn it to tarnation!"

He hated telephones and didn't really mind missing the call. If it was that important, the caller would call back.

What irked him was that as he'd reached for the phone, he'd glanced outside in time to see a pelican making breakfast of his catch.

* * *

Despite the rain, tourists queued up for the paddle-wheel *Creole Queen* excursion upriver to view the antebellum plantation homes. They juggled brochures, umbrellas, plastic rain bonnets, cameras, and camcorders as they traipsed up the loading plank to the boat.

The embarkation was delayed by the inclement weather and by a group of senior citizens, some of whom needed special assistance getting onboard.

The embarkation was stopped altogether by a blood-curdling scream.

It came from a woman, who slumped against her astonished husband and aimed a shaking finger down toward the muddy water of the Mississippi River, into which she'd been absently gazing while inching along in line.

Others crowded close to the railing in order to look down and see what had caused the woman's distress. Some gasped and turned away in repugnance. Some placed their hands over their mouths to keep from retching. Those with stronger stomachs took pictures or shot videos. A few prayers were whispered.

Attracting much more attention dead than he ever had alive, Errol, floating on his back, stared up through the water with eyes already turning milky.

Chapter Thirty

Burke was standing in the open doorway of the shack, sipping a cup of coffee and watching the rain when he heard her come up behind him. He glanced over his shoulder, almost expecting to see her raising an iron pot or some other blunt instrument with which to brain him.

Last night she hadn't taken too well to being handcuffed to him and had put up quite a struggle, which he had trouble quelling without hurting her. "This wouldn't be necessary if you hadn't tried to escape," he had told her. "I can't run the risk of you knocking me out or killing me while I'm asleep."

"That never even occurred to me."

"Well, it occurred to me." He had stretched out on the bed, dragging her down with him. "It's been a long, tiring day for me. I'm going to sleep. I suggest you do the same."

She refused to lie down and sat on the edge of the bed, seething with resentment. He closed his eyes and ignored her. Eventually she surrendered to exhaustion, lay down, and was asleep long before he was. This morning, he'd unlocked the handcuffs and gotten up without waking her. Clearly she was still miffed, but she wasn't trying to sneak up on him with a weapon.

"Coffee's on the stove," he told her.

Nonchalantly, he resumed his contemplation of the weather. The swamp was curtained by a heavy rain that showed no signs of letting up anytime soon. It was a good thing he'd brought enough supplies to last a couple of days. He wouldn't be going to Dredd's today. Not that he could get there anyway since the boat now had bullet holes in it.

The weather was keeping them inside the cabin. Didn't it stand to reason that it would also keep everyone else out? How close was Duvall to locating them? When would he show up? Within the next ten minutes? Or would it take another week?

Burke hoped it was sooner rather than later. The shack seemed to be shrinking around them. He was beginning to feel the squeeze, and the pressure was getting to him. Lying beside her last night, he'd been aware of each breath she took. Every time she moved, he knew about it. His sleep had been constantly interrupted by her sighs. Now, even though his back was to her, he knew exactly where she was standing and what she was doing.

In New Orleans, she had worn clothing that blatantly advertised her as a sex object. Her wardrobe was expensive, but bordered on trashy.

Now, dressed in the gray Wal-Mart sweat suit, she looked softer and sexier even than she had that night in the gazebo in the low-cut black dress. Without makeup, her cheeks rosy from sleep, her hair tousled, she looked as warm and snuggly and innocent as a kitten. And as erotic as hell.

It was becoming impossible for him to ignore the desire she aroused in him, and had since the first time he laid eyes on her. That night, he'd experienced a surge of lust that hadn't abated even when he discovered that the ethereal goddess in the gazebo was the wife of Pinkie Duvall.

When he realized who she was, why hadn't he had the good sense to find some nice obliging woman and spend the night with her, just to take the edge off? The last few months of his marriage, he and Barbara hadn't been intimate, so he'd had lots of time to build up a full head of steam. He should have taken Dixie up on her offer of a freebie. Or Ruby Bouchereaux. An hour with one of her talented girls would have done him a world of good. But he'd said no thanks. What was he, nuts?

Although he feared that even an experienced whore using every carnal trick in the book wouldn't have put out this particular fire.

Where the devil was Duvall?

Was the power he reputedly wielded just so much hype, part of a promotional campaign to inspire fear in his enemies? Was his army of mercenaries fictitious? If they were in fact real, were they a bunch of incompetents? Or was Burke Basile a kidnapper without equal? Did he have a knack for it, unrealized until now?

For whatever reason, the bottom line was that he was now entering the fourth day with his hostage, and it was getting harder, not easier, to remain objective about the outcome of this situation.

He tossed the dregs of his coffee out into the rain. "Are you hungry?"

"Yes. We never got around to eating dinner last night."

He shot her a look that said, *And whose fault is that?*
But what he actually said was "I'll see what we have."

Burke inventoried their stock of canned goods taken
from the shelves of Dredd's Mercantile. "Along with
bread and crackers we have sardines, beer nuts, tuna fish,
mustard greens, chili, tomato soup, potted meat, beans,
Beefaroni, pineapple, more beans, and peanut butter."

"Mustard greens?"

"I guess even outdoorsmen need roughage."

"I'll have a peanut butter sandwich and some pineapple."

While they were eating, he asked about the wounds on
her back. "I checked them in the mirror over the basin in
the bathroom," she told him. "I think they're healing. Do
you think it's necessary to treat them again?"

"Dredd'll never let me hear the end of it if they get infected. Better let me see to them, at least through today."

"Maybe I could do it myself."

Having reached for her empty paper plate, he dropped
it back onto the table. "Oh, I get it. It's not the medication
you object to, it's having me touch you."

"I didn't say—"

"My hands are as clean as Bardo's, and you didn't
seem to mind having him paw you, so don't pull this shit
on me."

"Bardo?" she exclaimed.

"Yeah, I saw you in action with him in the gazebo the
night he was acquitted. Duvall hosted the party, but you
and Bardo were having quite a celebration of your own."

"I don't know what you thought you saw, Mr. Basile,
but you're wrong."

"I saw enough. I left before it got really embarrassing."
He scraped his chair back and stood up quickly. "And

don't think I haven't noticed how you cross your arms over your chest like I'm going to steal a peek at your tits. I've seen them about to fall out of your dress, so I know this sudden rash of modesty is a goddamn act. It isn't going to make me feel any kinder toward you, Mrs. Duvall. In fact, it pisses me off."

Concluding his speech there, he marched from the shack.

Rain or shine, he had to get that damn boat back into service.

* * *

Before opening his eyes, Gregory tried convincing himself that he'd been having one hell of a wild dream. He'd drunk too much the night before, or smoked some strong Panama red, or done *something* that had caused his subconscious to invent a bizarre adventure involving Burke Basile, Pinkie Duvall, a hermit who lived in the swamp and skinned alligators, a beautiful woman, and, to round out this weird ensemble of characters, he himself had played the role of a priest.

Thank God the nightmare was over.

But when he opened his eyes, they weren't greeted by the louvered shutters on the windows overlooking the courtyard behind his townhouse. Instead he saw a pair of ugly curtains hanging unevenly from an oxidized brass rod. Meager gray light leaked through the faded calico. Raindrops as heavy as sinkers dripped from the eaves of the house in which he'd spent the night.

He had blessed his rescuers for saving him. He had thanked them profusely for their hospitality. They, in turn, had asked his blessing on their son and his pregnant second cousin. Father Gregory, having no alternative that he could see, had agreed to perform a wedding ceremony.

It was planned for today. He hoped he remembered all the words. Seminary seemed eons ago. But then so did all his life prior to the night Basile had arrested him in that men's room in City Park. Gregory cursed his rotten luck. What had compelled him to cruise the park that evening? Why hadn't he gone to the movies instead?

It wouldn't have mattered, he thought dismally as he pulled on his soiled clothes. Sooner or later Basile would have conscripted him to fight in his private war against Pinkie Duvall. Basile had needed someone with Gregory's unique combination of qualifications. If Basile hadn't accosted him in the park, it would have been somewhere else.

After checking his appearance in the cloudy mirror, he left the bedroom. The family were gathered in the large room where the kitchen was separated from the living area by a bar. The groom was sitting at it slurping up Lucky Charms, the bride putting curlers in her hair.

Preparations for the wedding were in full swing. A cup of coffee was pushed into his hand as he was introduced to the grandmas, aunts, and nieces who had already arrived, volunteers pitching in to get everything ready in time for the guests' arrival. The rain was good-naturedly cursed; he was asked to intercede and ask God for sunshine later in the day. Smiling sickly, he promised to pass along the request.

Delicious cooking aromas emanated from the cook stove. Cases of beer were carried in on the shoulders of burly male relatives. Being as unobtrusive as possible, Gregory moved from window to window, looking through the rain in search of an avenue of escape. Last night it had seemed that the house was built on an island. He was relieved to see that it was actually situated on the tip of a peninsula with a crushed-shell road about fifty yards long, leading from solid ground along that narrow finger of land to the house.

By noon the house had begun to fill up with friends and relatives, all bearing food—gumbos and crawfish, andouille and boudin sausages, shrimp creole, red beans and rice, smoked pork, even a multitiered white coconut cake with a plastic bride and groom on top.

Gregory understood only a few words of their lively conversation. It was obvious they were a closely knit group, and that he was definitely the sole outsider. Each new arrival regarded him with suspicion. He tried to dispel their distrust with a beatific smile, although he wasn't sure it was convincing since his face still looked like it had been trampled by a horde of linebackers. None of the family or wedding guests asked why he was willing to perform the ceremony when other priests had declined on moral grounds. When he signed the marriage license, the father mumbled thanks.

Although they didn't embrace the stranger in their midst, they thoroughly enjoyed being around each other. The walls of the house seemed to expand and recede with the racket they generated, especially when the musicians began tuning their instruments.

At two o'clock in the afternoon, the bride sheepishly entered the large room. She was wearing a long, flowered dress Gregory had seen one of the grandmas hastily altering earlier, presumably to accommodate her distended stomach. The menfolk shoved the stumbling, half-drunk groom forward to take his place at the side of his blushing bride.

Together they faced Father Gregory, who began the ceremony by invoking God's blessing on this wonderful gathering of family and friends. If he boggled the sacrament, they weren't sober enough to notice.

In under five minutes, the happy couple turned to one another to seal with a kiss a marriage that was entirely fraudulent. Father Gregory didn't give a flying you-know-what. He just wanted to get the hell out of there before he was exposed as an imposter.

He ate with them. He drank one beer. They showed no such restraint and consumed seemingly endless quantities of it. The more they drank, the louder the music became and the more energetic the dancing. Two fistfights erupted but were settled with a minimum of bloodshed. As dusk fell, the interior of the house grew steamy from the simmering food, sweating people, and the passion that seemed to fuel everything they did. Someone opened the doors to help ventilate the house.

And it was through one of those doors that Father Gregory sneaked out, wearing one of the male cousins' wool jacket and cap.

Rain pelted him, but as soon as he cleared the doorway, he made a mad dash for the shed that sheltered the boat that had conveyed them there the night before. He didn't even consider getting back into the boat he'd stolen from Dredd and which was now moored beside the family's craft. No more swamp, thank you very much. From now on, he'd take his chances on land. It was rife with potential hazards, but at least they weren't quite as alien.

Looking back toward the house, he saw no sign that anyone had noticed his escape. He ducked his head against the rain and ran from the shed. Moving along in a crouch, he ran as hard as he'd ever run in his life, exerting himself to the maximum of his limited capacity, racing until he thought his lungs would burst. He sobbed with unrestrained joy when he reached the end of the lane.

The intersecting road was a paved two-lane state highway. Bracing his hands on his knees, he sucked in huge draughts of air, then struck off walking briskly in what he hoped was the direction of the nearest town.

He couldn't go far on foot. His only hope was for a car to come along before someone at the party noticed that Father Gregory was no longer among them and came looking for him. Now that he had sanctified the sinners, he was dispensable.

When he saw headlights coming up behind him, his heart lurched. It could be someone from the party, sent to find him and bring him back. Or it could be one of several law enforcement agencies searching for Mrs. Duvall's kidnappers. Or it could be someone on Pinkie Duvall's payroll who'd been offered a huge reward to find her abductors.

Or it could be his ride back to civilization.

Please, God, he prayed as he did an about-face and stuck out his thumb. The pickup slowed, the driver looked him over, then passed him and showered him with muddy rainwater. Gregory was so disconsolate he sobbed. He was still crying five minutes later when the next vehicle came along. He must have looked so wretched that he evoked pity from the driver because after passing him, the car stopped.

He jogged toward it. A teenage girl was in the passenger seat. One even younger was behind the wheel. They regarded him with interest. The passenger asked, "Where's your car, mister?"

"I dumped it in the swamp after impersonating a priest in order to kidnap the wife of a rich and famous man."

They giggled, assuming he'd just told them a whopper. "Cool," the passenger said. She nodded toward the backseat. "Get in."

"Where are you headed?" he asked cautiously.

"N'awlins," the passenger told him. "We're going to party."

"Cool," he said, repeating her word as he got in.

The driver floored the accelerator; the car fishtailed on the rain-slick pavement, then shot off into the wet darkness.

No more than fifteen, if that, they were dressed in a manner that would have made Madonna blush. See-through blouses and push-up lace brassieres. Their ears, noses, and lips pierced. Dramatic makeup accented their eyes and lips.

When they reached the French Quarter, he asked them to drop him off, but they tried to wheedle him into sticking with them. "We could show you a good time," one said.

"Don't think we don't know how," boasted the other.

"That's just it," he said, flashing his most engaging grin. "You girls are too experienced for me."

The flattery worked. They pulled to a stop at an intersection and Gregory got out. They blew him kisses as they drove away. He was astounded by their stupid recklessness. Hadn't their parents warned them against picking up hitchhikers? Didn't they watch the nightly news? For all they knew he was a pervert.

Then, glumly, he reminded himself that he *was* a pervert.

Dodging the crowds who'd defied the weather to start the Mardi Gras celebration, making eye contact with no one, he walked the few remaining blocks. His mood lifted when he reached his street. He jogged the final twenty yards to his townhouse. The latchkey was still hidden where he'd left it the morning he'd joined Basile to pick up Mrs. Duvall for an excursion to Jenny's House.

"Speaking of somebody being stupid and reckless," he muttered in self-deprecation.

His picture was probably being circulated throughout FBI offices all over the country and abroad. He was a wanted man. There was a price on his head for kidnapping and God only knew what other crimes. This was going to send his father's blood pressure off the charts. Gregory would be disowned and disinherited.

So, what to do? First order of business: a cold bottle of wine and a long, hot shower. He would stay here tonight. Pack in the morning. Then get the hell out of Dodge tomorrow.

He was a little hazy on exactly how he would finance a trip without his father's help. Should he throw himself on the mean old bastard's mercy one last time? Maybe if he spoke to his mother first, he could appeal to her maternal instinct, if Batlady had one.

Deciding to sleep on it, he flipped on the light switch.

"Hello, Gregory."

He screamed. Two policemen were lounging on his living room sofa. Like giant spiders, they'd been sitting in the dark waiting for him.

In fact, one admitted it. "'Bout time you showed up. For two days we've been waiting for you. Jesus," he said, scrutinizing Gregory's face up close. "You look like shit. They can't call you Pretty Boy anymore."

The other said, "Life as a fugitive just ain't what it's cracked up to be, huh? Well, your escapade is over. Your criminal career has been cut short, Gregory. Nipped in the bud, so to speak. Like that." He snapped his fingers an inch from Gregory's lumpy nose.

He slumped backward against the wall, closed his eyes, and, moaning, rolled his head from side to side. The nightmare continued.

Chapter Thirty-One

The rain had slacked off, but dark, sulky clouds formed a low ceiling over the bayou. Remy stood in the open doorway of the shack and watched Basile lower the boat, bow first, into the water.

He'd patched the bullet holes with materials stored in a deep wooden box that stood against an exterior wall. From what she could tell, he had used a pitch-like substance and duct tape. The crude repair job also had required extensive crude swearing, but obviously it had worked because the boat remained afloat. He tethered it to the pier.

"Is it watertight?" she asked as he approached the shack.

"I might get there without sinking."

"Where?"

"Dredd's."

"When?"

"In the morning. If the rain clears out. Could you fetch

me a towel? If I go in like this I'll track water all over the floor."

He'd worked stubbornly and steadily throughout the day in a drenching rain without any protective gear. His jeans and shirt were soaked through. He took the towel from her with a laconic "Thanks," then retreated around the corner to wash up. When he reappeared a few minutes later, the towel was wrapped around his waist. Saying nothing, he took a change of clothing with him into the bathroom.

His shoulders, she noticed, were sprinkled with freckles.

When he came out of the bathroom, he motioned toward the table. "What's that?"

"Supper." Using what was available, she had laid out two place settings. She'd even found a candle in one of the drawers where cooking utensils were stored. It was standing in a pool of its own wax on a cracked saucer, but it softened the rusticity of the shack. "It's just chili and beans, but I thought you'd be hungry since you didn't eat lunch."

"Yeah. Fine."

He sat down and she served the meal. A box of crackers and bottled water rounded out their menu. They ate in silence for several minutes. He was the first to speak. "Not quite what you're used to."

She lowered her spoon to her bowl and gazed around the single room. It was furnished with mismatched castoffs, warmed by a space heater, lighted by a Coleman lantern, but it was snug and dry, a sanctuary from the hostile terrain. "No, it's not what I'm used to, but I like it. Maybe because it's so different from anything I've seen before."

"Didn't a Cajun beau ever take you to his fishing camp on a date?"

"I never went on a date, and I didn't have any beaux." She nibbled the corner off a saltine, then laid it on the rim of her bowl and reached for her glass of water. Catching his eye, she wondered at his astonishment. "What?"

"You never went on a date?"

"Not unless you count Pinkie. I went straight from life with my mother, to Blessed Heart, to Pinkie's house. Not much opportunity for boyfriends. I didn't even attend the school-sponsored dances."

"How come?"

"I lived with Angel in a one-room apartment," she said quietly. "My impression of men wasn't very favorable. I had no desire to go to dances. Even if I had, Pinkie wouldn't have permitted it."

They lapsed into another silence, broken only by their spoons clinking against the crockery bowls. Finally he said, "Did you ever consider becoming a nun?"

The question amused her; she laughed softly. "No. Pinkie had other plans."

"The payback."

"I guess you could call it that. He married me the night after I graduated."

"No college?"

"I wanted to go, but Pinkie wouldn't allow it."

"Pinkie wouldn't have permitted it. Pinkie had other plans. Pinkie wouldn't allow it."

Taking umbrage at his tone, she said, "You don't understand."

"No, I don't."

"I'm not ignorant. I took every college course by correspondence that was offered."

"I don't think you're ignorant."

"Yes you do. Your low opinion of me is all too obvious, Mr. Basile."

Looking ready to argue, he changed his mind, shrugged, and said, "It's none of my business. I just can't understand how a person, man or woman, turns their life over to someone else and says, 'Here, run this for me, will you?' Didn't you ever make an independent decision?"

"Yes. I once defied Pinkie's wishes and secretly applied for a job in an art gallery. I had studied art, I loved it, and during my interview I conveyed my appreciation and knowledge to the owner of the gallery. He hired me. It lasted two days."

"What happened?"

"The gallery was burned to the ground. The building and everything in it was completely destroyed." She looked at him meaningfully. "They never caught the arsonist, but I never applied for another job, either."

No longer eating, he sat with his elbows on the table, clasped hands covering his mouth, staring at her over the ridge of his knuckles. There was a sprinkling of freckles across his cheekbones, too, she noticed. His eyes weren't brown, as she'd previously thought, but green, so deeply green they appeared brown unless one looked very closely.

"Would you like some more?"

At first he seemed not to understand the question, then he glanced down at his empty bowl. "Uh, please."

He ate his second portion in silence.

When he was finished, she began clearing the table. He offered to wash the dishes and she let him. She dried.

"I've never met anyone like you," he said. "This morning you practically begged me to return you to your husband,

when it sounds to me like Duvall defines emotional abuse.
You're like a prisoner in your own home. You make none of
the decisions. Your opinion doesn't count even where your
own future is concerned. You're nothing except Duvall's possession, something he shows off."

"Like his orchids."

"Orchids?"

"He spends hours in his greenhouse cultivating orchids."

"You're kidding."

"No. But that's irrelevant. Please, finish your thought."

"My thought? I guess it doesn't bother you to be no
more than a possession when you think of all you get
in return. Fancy clothes. Jewelry. A limousine and driver.
Like mother, like daughter. You just charge more than Angel."

If he had slapped her, it couldn't have stung more.
Throwing down the dish towel, she turned away, but one
of his wet hands shot out and caught her by the wrist.

"Let go of me."

"You sold yourself body and soul to Pinkie Duvall, and
you feel that because your mother was a drug-addicted
whore your decision was justified. Well, it doesn't wash,
Mrs. Duvall. Kids can't choose their parents or the circumstances of their upbringing, but as adults, we have
choices."

"Do we?"

"You disagree?"

"Maybe your choices were more clear-cut than mine,
Mr. Basile."

"Oh, I think your choice was very easy. If I was a beautiful and desirable young woman, I might peddle myself
to the highest bidder, too."

"Do you think so?"

"I might."

"No, I mean do you think I'm beautiful and desirable?"

Looking like he'd taken a clip on the chin, he released her wrist. But even though they were no longer touching, he held her with his stare. After a time, he said, "Yeah, I do. Furthermore, you know I do. You use your sexuality like currency, and every man you meet wants to cash in, from a crusty old curmudgeon like Dredd to that stammering guy in the French Market who sold you the oranges."

Her lips parted in wordless surprise.

"That was me in the baseball cap, running after you with a goddamn sack of oranges," he said, sounding angry. "I was spying on you then, and I was spying the night you had your little tryst with Bardo in the gazebo."

"I did not have a tryst with Bardo. Not that night or any other time. He makes my skin crawl."

"That's not what it looked like to me."

"You're so self-righteous and quick to judge, which I find surprising since you of all people should know that things aren't always what they appear. You should know how extenuating circumstances can shade a situation."

He advanced on her a step. "The hell you talking about?"

"You killed your partner. You fired the gun that caused his death. Technically that's what happened. But judgments based on that fact alone would be unfair to you. Because there were contributing factors. When taken into account, those factors exonerate you."

"Okay. So?"

"So, until you know all the circumstances of my life, how dare you preach to me about choices?"

"Mrs. Duvall?" he said calmly.

"What?"

"Have you ever yelled at your husband like this?" The unexpected question, and the calm manner in which he posed it, took her off guard. His eyebrows went up. "No? Well, maybe you should. Maybe he'd stop burning down buildings if you ever said 'How dare you' to him and threatened to leave."

"Leave?" she exclaimed on a bitter laugh. "What a brilliant idea, Mr. Basile! Why didn't I think of that? Why didn't I—"

"Shh!" He stepped up to her, placed one arm around her waist and the other hand over her mouth. She tried to wiggle free, but he increased the pressure of his arm, squeezing her waist tighter. "Shh!"

Then she heard the noise that he had picked up seconds earlier. It sounded like a trolling motor.

"Since you don't know who it is," he said in a low voice, "I advise you to keep quiet."

Remembering the men who had chased them from the Crossroads, she nodded in understanding. He released her. "Get the candle." She blew it out as he reached for the lantern, turning it down to barely a glow. "Stay out of sight."

Placing his hand on the top of her head, as he had done in the boat when the helicopter flew over, he pushed her down and motioned her under the table. She crawled beneath it.

As nimble as a shadow, he moved to the cabinet and she watched him take the pistol from behind the top shelf. That was about the only place she hadn't searched for the gun today while he was busy with the boat. He tucked the pistol into the waistband of his jeans at the small of his back, then went to stand on the pier just outside the door.

The sound of the motor grew louder. Soon a light appeared, flickering through the moss-draped branches and casting a faint apron of light on the rippling surface of the water in advance of the approaching boat. She could see enough to discern that it was approximately the size of the craft Basile had repaired that day.

A man called out to him in Cajun French. He responded with a laconic "Evening, y'all."

Remy felt the vibration when the boat pulled up alongside the pier and bumped into one of the rubber-tire buffers on the piles. On hands and knees she crawled from beneath the table and across the room to the window that afforded her a better view. She raised her head only far enough for her eyes to clear the windowsill. There were three men huddled in the boat.

She didn't know whether to reveal herself and alert them that she was a captive, or to remain hidden. She desperately needed to return to New Orleans, but would these men provide her safe passage? Or was she safer with Basile?

While debating what to do, Basile asked them if the fish were biting. So they weren't lawmen. Or was Basile tricking her into thinking they weren't?

She took another clandestine peek. The men were barely distinguishable in the pale light, but there was nothing in their rough appearance to distinguish them as law enforcement officers, nor were there any official insignias on their boat.

In English, the spokesman of the group told Burke that they weren't on a fishing expedition. "We're looking for someone. A priest."

"Just any ol' priest or one in particular?" Basile kept his tone light, but Remy knew the friendliness was counterfeit.

"This priest, Father Gregory, we think maybe he was in trouble. Who knows?" She detected the Gallic shrug behind the Cajun's words. "If he has enemies, we don't want any trouble from them."

"What made you think he might have enemies?"

Basile listened to the man's tale without comment. When he finished, Basile said, "Lost in the swamp? Poor fool. In any event, nobody's been by this way since I got here several days ago."

The three men in the boat held a whispered consultation, then the spokesman thanked Burke, bade him good night, and they pushed off. Turning the boat around, they started back the way they'd come.

Remy considered charging through the door and calling out to them but decided against it. What about them had frightened Father Gregory more than the perils of the swamp? He must have had a compelling reason not to trust them.

Or had he feared only that they would turn him over to the authorities?

She stood up and ran toward the door, but Basile was there to block her. "You can scream and they'll come back," he said in a low, urgent voice, "but you have no guarantee that they won't hurt you."

"What guarantee do I have that you won't?"

"Have I so far?"

She couldn't see his eyes, but she felt their intensity, and she knew he was right. Her safety was reduced to choosing the devil she knew.

Sensing her decision, he crossed the room and extinguished the lantern, plunging the shack into total darkness. "Just in case they're around the bend watching," he said.

"What do you think happened to Father Gregory after he sneaked away from the wedding?" she whispered.

"God knows. But at least I know he made it that far."

* * *

Gregory had resigned himself to dying soon.

He wouldn't receive the death penalty for the role he'd played in the kidnapping, but he wouldn't last long in prison. Guys like him were prey, and they were outnumbered by predators. In a cell block, his life span might be a couple of months. But after even that amount of time, death would be a welcome release.

He cowered in the backseat of the unmarked police car, his heart tripping crazily. But, surprisingly, they weren't heading toward the Vieux Carré station. "Are you taking me uptown?" The arresting officers ignored him and continued their conversation about their upcoming Mardi Gras party plans.

When they passed police headquarters without even slowing down, Gregory's terror went into overdrive. "Where are you taking me?"

The man in the passenger seat turned to him. "Will you shut up? We're trying to talk here."

"Are you guys feds?"

They laughed and the driver said, "Yeah, that's us. Feds."

Disliking the sound of their snickers, Gregory began to whimper. "I was forced to be an accomplice. Basile, he's meaner than hell. He threatened to kill me if I didn't help him. I didn't even know what he was going to do. I...I didn't know anything about the kidnapping until it was a done deal."

Since his avowals of innocence didn't seem to faze them, he took another tack. "My daddy's rich. If you take me to his house, he'll pay you a lot of money, no questions asked. Just tell him what you want, and you'll get it. He's wealthy, I swear."

"We know all about you, Gregory," said the one in the passenger seat. "Now shut the fuck up, or I'm liable to get mad."

Gregory swallowed his next earnest entreaty and began to cry quietly. It was obvious to him now that he wasn't in the custody of law officers, and all doubt of that was removed when they drove into the underground parking garage of an office building. At this time of night, the garage was empty save for only a few other cars.

A parking garage had been the setting for countless movie murders, and those grisly scenes kaleidoscoped through his mind. He figured that this was where they would have him face the concrete wall and shoot him in the back of the head. His faceless body would be discovered tomorrow morning by an office clerk arriving early for work.

"Please," he blubbered, recoiling against the seat when they opened the car's rear doors. "Please don't."

But the man he'd mistaken for a cop reached into the backseat, grabbed him by the front of his shirt, and hauled him out. He sank to his knees and began to beg for his life, but they pulled him to his feet and prodded him toward the elevator.

Okay, so they weren't going to shoot him in the parking garage. Probably didn't want to get blood on their clothes. They were going to take him up to the roof of the building and throw him off, making his execution look like a suicide. For being an accomplice in a kidnapping, Gregory James had gone over the edge. Literally.

However, before reaching the roof, the elevator stopped on another floor. When he was dragged from the cubicle, Gregory was surprised to find himself in a carpeted corridor, lined on either side by mahogany doors. At the end of the austere hallway was a set of double doors bearing an engraved plaque.

When he read the name etched into the brass, Gregory's knees buckled, and he collapsed to the floor.

"Get up," one of his escorts said.

"Come on, don't be an asshole."

Gregory assumed the fetal position and whimpered miserably.

The double doors opened, and he heard a voice thundering down the hallway. "What's going on?"

"He won't get up. What do you want us to do with him, Mr. Duvall?"

Hearing the name spoken aloud was worse than reading it on the brass nameplate. Gregory covered his ears. But he watched a pair of shiny reptile loafers coming nearer, making size-eleven impressions in the plush forest green carpet. When the shoes were within a few inches of his head, they came to a stop.

From above him, Pinkie Duvall said, "It's not what we're going to do with him, gentlemen. From this point, Mr. James's fate is entirely up to him."

Chapter Thirty-Two

M r. Duvall? Sir, pardon the interruption. It's Miss Flarra on the telephone. She's in a state."

"Thank you, Roman. I'll take the call." As soon as the butler withdrew from his study at home, Duvall picked up the extension. "Flarra? How are you, sweetheart?"

"I'm worried sick is how I am! What's going on? I had to beg Roman to let me speak to you. He said he'd been instructed to hold all calls. Where's Remy? Why hasn't she come to see me? I haven't heard a word from her in days. Something terrible has happened, I know it."

"Calm down. Nothing terrible has happened."

"Then what's going on? Remy hasn't been here all week, and she never misses. Every time I call the house, I'm given the runaround."

"Your sister's had a bout with strep throat."

Evidently alarmed, she said, "Is she okay?"

"A few days, more rest and she'll be fine."

"Why wasn't I told?"

"Remy didn't want you to worry unnecessarily, so she asked the staff not to mention it to you. She's on antibiotics and is doing much better, although her throat is still very sore. It's hard for her to talk. I've been distracted by a case that is demanding all my time. I apologize for not calling. It's unforgivable of me."

Pinkie listened to the silence coming from the other end as Flarra assimilated his lie. If he had told her the truth, he would have a hysterical woman on his hands, and that would only compound his problem. Flarra was impulsive and unpredictable; he didn't need the additional worry of how she might react to her sister's abduction. Soon he would be faced with informing her of Remy's demise, but he'd cross that bridge when he came to it.

"Can I come see her tomorrow?" she asked.

"I'm afraid not, sweetheart. She's contagious. The last thing she'd want is for you to catch the infection. Sister Beatrice would never forgive us if we started an epidemic of strep throat at the school."

"Did Dr. Caruth prescribe Remy's medication?"

"What difference does it make?"

"I don't know, Pinkie, it's...Remy's been so run down lately."

"So?"

"Well, I was just thinking that maybe—I'm guessing, of course—but could she be, you know, pregnant?"

Pinkie's eyes focused on the Steuben crystal paperweight on his desk, but he didn't really see it. Nothing registered except his young sister-in-law's absurd suggestion, which suddenly didn't seem so absurd.

Unaware of his reaction, Flarra continued. "If she is, should she be taking antibiotics?"

"She's not pregnant."

"Are you sure?"

"If my wife was pregnant, don't you think I would know it?" he snapped.

"Well you don't have to bite my head off. I don't mean to pry, Pinkie. It's just that I think Remy secretly yearns for a baby and regrets that she's never been able to conceive. I was hoping that might be the reason she's been so puny lately. I even asked her."

"What did she say?"

"She said no."

"So there you have it. Why would she lie?"

"I guess you're right," Flarra said. "It was just a thought." Then she asked if he would hold the phone up to Remy's ear. "Just so I can say hi to her. I won't make her talk."

"She's asleep."

"Oh, well, I guess you shouldn't wake her," she said, obviously downcast.

"She's been told about your calls and appreciates your concern."

"One reason I was so worried," she said as an afterthought, "Remy must be awfully upset over Errol."

"You heard about that?"

"I read about it in the newspaper. Remy must have freaked out."

"Actually she doesn't know yet. She's been so ill I haven't had the heart to give her the bad news."

"Do the police have any leads?"

"None that I know of. I'm afraid it was one of those random acts of violence, a crime that will remain unsolved."

"Errol was strong as an ox," Flarra mused aloud. "How could an ordinary mugger get the jump on him?"

"I don't wish to speak unkindly of the dead, but Errol's physical strength far exceeded his mental fortitude. He should have known better than to go for a stroll along the levee alone in the middle of the night."

"I guess, but it seems strange that—"

Tiring of the conversation, Pinkie interrupted. "Flarra, sweetheart, you must excuse me."

"Have you given Fat Tuesday any thought? You know, about me coming to your party?"

"I've given it some thought, yes. But I haven't yet reached a decision, and I really can't talk about it now. Another call has just come in, and it pertains to my case. I'll give Remy your love."

"Okay," she replied with a marked lack of enthusiasm. "Tell her to call me as soon as she feels up to it. Bye-bye."

As soon as he hung up, Pinkie asked Roman to summon Bardo. When the man arrived and entered the study, Pinkie handed him a Rolodex card. "Put one of your best guys on this. Have him be discreet, but I want to know what she eats for breakfast." Bardo nodded and pocketed the card. Pinkie asked him, "Has our pseudopriest decided to cooperate?"

Bardo grinned evilly. "We're giving him a little longer to think it over."

"What about McCuen? Heard from him yet?"

The policeman had failed to keep his appointment with Bardo earlier that evening. Men were sent to check his house. They reported that no one was at home and that the place was in total disarray, as though it had been abandoned in a hurry.

"I've got guys looking for him. He'll turn up," Bardo said with his customary cockiness. Then, less sure, he asked, "What if neither the fag or McCuen comes across?"

Pinkie glanced down at the telephone and recalled his most recent conversation. Stroking the receiver with his finger, he smiled like a gambler with a winning ace up his sleeve. "I'll try something else."

* * *

"Lord, who could that be?"

Joe Basile figured his wife had every reason to sound grumpy. Her day had got off to a bad start at dawn with Doug Patout's unannounced visit. Now she'd been awakened by the telephone in the wee hours. He groped for the receiver and answered on the fifth ring.

"Mr. Basile, this is Mac McCuen again. Please don't hang up on me until you hear me out."

"What is it, Mr. McCuen?" he said impatiently.

"I lied to you this morning."

Joe levered himself into a sitting position on the side of the bed. "How so?"

"I told you Basile had invited me to join him on a getaway. He didn't. But I must get in touch with him. I lied because I didn't want to involve you in this. Unfortunately I've run out of options."

"Involve me in what?"

"Your brother is in a shitload of trouble."

Although more crudely put, his statement was consistent with Patout's. "By trouble, do you mean that he's in danger?"

"Grave danger. If you know where he is, you've got to tell me. I must reach him before anyone else does."

That, too, was almost verbatim what Patout had said. After calling Dredd's Mercantile twice and receiving no answer, Joe hadn't tried again. Now he wished he had.

If Burke had gone on a retreat, he was most likely at their fishing cabin. If Burke was anywhere in that vicinity, Dredd would know.

Personally, the grizzled taxidermist and his spooky dwelling gave Joe the willies, but there was a strong bond between Dredd and Burke. Joe reasoned he could rely on Dredd to tell him the truth, if he knew it. Unfortunately he hadn't been able to reach him.

"Mr. Basile, Joe, please tell me," McCuen implored. "Do you know where Burke is?"

"I told you this morning that I didn't."

"That's what you told me, but do you?"

His tone didn't sit well with Joe Basile. "Forgive me, Mr. McCuen, but you're the one who sounds desperate and in trouble, not Burke."

After a long pause, McCuen said, "I apologize for insinuating that you're lying. In your place, I'd lie, too. I respect your loyalty to Basile. But you've got to believe me when I tell you that you're doing him harm by not telling me how I can reach him."

"At the risk of sounding repetitive, I don't know where he is," Joe said, enunciating each word.

"You must have some idea," McCuen argued. Joe hesitated for only a millisecond, but McCuen seized upon it. "What can I say that'll convince you to help me find him? What can I *say*?"

* * *

Characteristically, Burke was a light sleeper. That's why it surprised him that he didn't come awake until she began thrashing her arms. She was trying to raise her right hand, and couldn't because it was shackled to his left. It was the sharp tugging on his wrist and the bite of the handcuffs that roused him from a deep sleep.

At first he misunderstood the reason for her agitation. "Hey! Cut it out."

But as he came more fully awake, he realized she wasn't struggling to free herself from him. The mosquito netting hanging from the ceiling had fallen and landed directly over her face; she was frantically trying to extricate herself from it.

Her attempts had resulted in the fabric becoming wrapped around her left arm. The harder she tried to shake it off, the more entangled she became. She opened her mouth to scream, but her inhalation sucked the fabric into her mouth, increasing her panic.

"Relax. I'll get it off."

Her eyes were open, but either she was in the throes of a nightmare or panic had pushed her beyond reason, because when Burke moved his hand toward her face and tried to help pull the gauzy material away, she began fighting him. She flung her head from side to side. When she tried to raise her head, that only drew the netting tighter across her face. She slapped at Burke with her left hand and continued to yank her right hand against the unyielding metal cuff. He threw his right leg over hers to protect himself from her vicious kicks. Again she tried to scream, but the cloth was in her mouth and the only sound she made was a harsh gasp.

"Be still, for God's sake," he said. "I'm trying to help you."

Finally, he managed to get hold of the netting and pulled at it so hard that it ripped, relieving the tension across her face. But the torn sections drifted weblike over her. She brushed at them with her left hand until they were no longer touching her. Her breathing was labored and loud and rapid.

"You're all right," he said, speaking in a low, soothing voice. "It's gone now. You're fine."

He reached up to smooth away strands of hair, but her left hand struck his hard. "Don't touch me!"

"Calm down," he said, patting the air between them. "The mosquito netting fell over you. That's all it was." She stared at him dazedly while her breathing gradually slowed down. "Could you use a drink of water?"

She nodded. Earlier she had set a glass of water on the rickety three-legged table that acted as a nightstand. Burke reached across her for it. "Can you sit up?" Propping herself on her elbows, she drank from the glass he held for her.

Rain was still pattering monotonously on the shack's corrugated tin roof. Even so, a muddy gray moonlight shone through the windows. Tense and watchful, he had stood at the door for at least half an hour after the men in the fishing boat departed. He hadn't sensed any menace from them, merely curiosity over the priest whom they had rescued from certain disaster, only to have him vanish during a wedding celebration. But preferring to err on the side of caution, Burke had refrained from relighting the lantern and had stood vigil until he was satisfied that they posed no threat.

Finally, he had suggested that he and his hostage turn in. He had handcuffed her to him again, which had sparked another argument, which he had won by citing that she had a possible means of escape now that the boat had been repaired. In light of her nightmare, he felt pretty rotten about keeping her shackled, especially since it wasn't entirely for safety's sake that he wanted to lie beside her.

She drank from the glass so greedily that water dribbled from the corners of her mouth. When she had drunk it all, he returned the empty glass to the table. "Better now?"

Again, she didn't speak, but only nodded.

His eyes touched on her brow, cheekbone, nose, and mouth. After only a moment's hesitation, he whisked the pad of his thumb across her chin and lower lip, and it came back wet.

"I'm not going to kick you, Basile."

Something, desire maybe, had made him muddle-headed. "What?"

She shifted uncomfortably, and he realized that his leg was still lying across hers, trapping them against the mattress. His foot, his calf, even the inside of his thigh—touching her as a lover might. His crotch was pressed snugly against her hip. His eyes lowered to her lips again. He had touched them with his thumb. They were wet. And incredibly soft.

"Don't, Basile. Please."

Chapter
Thirty-Three

The words were whispered, but they couldn't have been clearer. Her plea for him to desist covered about six transgressions that sprang immediately to mind. With more self-restraint than a man should have to exercise in a lifetime, he withdrew his leg and lay back down. For a time, he was absorbed with his own misery. But he became aware of her massaging her right wrist with her left hand.

"Does it hurt?" he asked.

"A little."

"You were yanking on it hard. That's what woke me up. Do you need something for it?"

Now, wasn't he being a good Boy Scout? Not only was he keeping his hands off her at her request, he was also offering to render aid. Either he deserved a medal of commendation or the Pussy of the Year award.

"If you're so concerned about my wrist, you could remove the handcuffs."

"Not a chance."

"Please."

"No. Don't ask me anymore." *Screw Boy Scouting.*

They were close enough for him to feel every breath she took, and desire wasn't something that retreated upon command. But there were barriers between them more impenetrable than a steel bolster. Not the least of which was that she had said "Don't, Basile," and, although he was a kidnapper, he wasn't a rapist.

Second, she was another man's wife. True, adultery was a popular, acceptable sin. If public stoning were still the punishment for extramarital fun and games, the planet would have been depleted of rocks a long time ago. As sins go, adultery was a huge yawn.

Religious aspects aside, there was the moral implication. He would like to think himself a notch above Barbara and her football coach. And, anyway, the lady candidate had said no, so it wasn't going to happen no matter what, so he ordered himself to stop thinking about it and go to sleep.

He lay there for a long time, wide awake and about as relaxed as a two-by-four. He sensed she was finding it equally difficult to fall asleep again. He wasn't particularly in the mood for a chat, but he feared if he didn't break the strained silence, his jawbone was going to crack. "Was it a nightmare?"

"Not exactly," she replied. "More like a... Yes, I guess you could call it a nightmare."

"Associated with your fear of suffocation?"

He felt her nod.

One didn't have to think about it too long and hard to figure it out. "What happened to you?"

She took so long to answer he thought she was going to ignore the question. But then she did begin to speak, haltingly. "I was twelve. He was one of Angel's regulars.

I had learned at a very early age that when a man was in the house I was to keep still and quiet. Not to cry. Not to whine. Not to ask for anything or draw attention to myself. I tried to make myself as small as possible, first to avoid punishment, then later to avoid being noticed. I wished to be invisible so they wouldn't look at me.

"But this one wouldn't let me ignore him. He always placed himself in my path, teased me, made remarks to Angel about me that I didn't understand at first, then came to understand too well.

"One night she brought him home with her after work. It was very late, and I was already asleep, but their laughter woke me up. They were high, of course, and continued their party without paying any attention to me. Eventually they passed out in Angel's bed, and I went back to sleep.

"I'm not sure how much time passed. If I'd come awake sooner, I could have fought him off and run out of the apartment. But when I woke up, he was already on me, holding my arms above my head. I was wearing a T-shirt and panties. He had pushed my shirt up and covered my face with it."

Burke closed his eyes and lay perfectly still.

Several moments elapsed before she continued in a faraway voice, "I had just begun to develop. My breasts were tender. He...he was whispering...horrible things. His breath smelled bad, and his fingers pinched, and I couldn't breathe. He pushed his hand inside my underwear and...Well, he was hurting me. I tried to call out, but my face was covered and I couldn't breathe."

Gasping again, she laid her left hand on her chest. Gradually, her rising panic subsided. "Angel woke up and saw what he was doing. She raised a ruckus and threw him out."

"Did she report him, have him arrested?"

Simultaneously they turned their heads toward each other. Remy gave him a strange look. "Angel wasn't angry at him. She was angry at me. I got a lashing for luring her boyfriend into my bed."

"Jesus Christ."

"I was lucky she woke up before he could do more than fondle me. Actually the episode gave her the idea of putting me to work. I guess she saw more earning potential from a child prostitute than a child pickpocket. She never actually shared the idea with me, but I knew what she was thinking. I'd catch her watching me with a thoughtful, speculative expression.

"After that night, I began sleeping with a butcher knife. I cut two of her friends and threatened several more. But I knew that it was only a matter of time before one of them raped me.

"Then Angel got pregnant. She was furious because she didn't realize she was pregnant until too late to have an abortion. As her pregnancy progressed, she dealt more drugs to make up for the lost income from dancing and...the other. When Flarra was born, she put me in charge of the baby so she could go back to work. She never got around to implementing her plans for me. I was lucky."

"Wasn't any of this ever reported? Where were the child-protection people?"

"An agent from social services came around regularly." Wryly, she added, "She bought drugs from Angel until the agency found out and fired her. They never assigned a replacement."

Burke covered his eyes with his right forearm. A good part of his childhood he'd been without a father, but, as he recalled, the main challenges facing him had been to get his homework turned in on time and to keep his half of the room he shared with Joe reasonably straight to avoid a lecture from their mother, who was affectionate and attentive even though she had to work very hard to support them.

Remy had faced daily challenges just to survive. The creep who'd fondled her when she was twelve years old had left her with a legacy of nightmares, a pathological fear of suffocation, and self-consciousness. The story explained why she frequently crossed her arms over her breasts.

But that didn't gel. She wore low-cut dresses and outfits that emphasized her bosom.

Lowering his arm, he sat up and looked down at her. "Why'd you tell me that story? Did you make it up so I'd feel sorry for you?"

"It's the truth, but I don't care whether or not you believe a word of it."

"So long as it kept me off you, right?"

"Go to hell," she said angrily.

That was the first time he'd ever heard her use even a mild curse, and it stunned him into a more rational frame of mind. He believed her story. Three times he'd seen her panic when her breathing was hampered. Besides, who could have invented such a tale? It was too horrific not to be true.

Slightly mollified, he asked, "Okay, why'd you tell me?"

"Because you're the man who has me handcuffed," she shot back. "I've been a victim. I didn't like it. I refuse to be *your* victim, Mr. Basile."

"Have I harmed you?"

"Harmed me?" she repeated on an incredulous laugh. "You don't understand anything, do you? For a street-savvy narcotics officer, you're not very smart. No, you haven't beat me, or raped me, or starved me, or physically hurt me. But, after this, do you really think a man as fastidious as Pinkie will have me back?"

"Why in hell would you want to go back?" he asked, angry in his own right. "He's got you locked into a relationship that's goddamn medieval. I didn't know such a thing existed in the free world. Why in God's name do you stay with the son of a bitch?"

"Don't you think I've tried to leave?" she cried. "I did. Once. I saved enough money to buy a bus ticket—that's right, Mr. Basile. I don't have any money of my own. I get an allowance. Spending money. I can afford to buy oranges in the market, but not much more than that.

"It took me months to scrape together enough to buy that ticket, and I did so by stealing money from Pinkie's wallet a few dollars at a time so he wouldn't notice. My bodyguard at the time was a man named Lute Duskie. I slipped away from him inside Maison Blanche.

"I got all the way to Galveston, Texas, where I got a job watering plants in a nursery. I found an inexpensive boarding house that rented rooms by the week. I took long walks on the beach, relishing my freedom and making plans on how I would send for Flarra and we'd start a new life. I was on my own for four whole days.

"On the fifth day, I glanced up to see Pinkie walking toward me down the aisle of the greenhouse where I was watering flats of begonias. I'll never forget the expression on his face. He was smiling. He congratulated me on my cleverness. It wasn't often that someone put something over on him, he said. I should feel very proud of myself.

"Naturally, I was flabbergasted. I expected him to be furious. Instead, he said if I no longer wished to be married to him, he had no intention of holding me. If I'd only asked, he would have let me go with no hard feelings. If I wanted my freedom, I could have it."

"There was a catch."

"Yes. There was a catch," she said, her voice hoarse with emotion. "He asked me to walk back to the car with him. I only had to look beyond the tinted windows in the backseat of the limousine to know the price I must pay for my freedom. Flarra.

"He'd brought her with him. She was about the age I was when my mother's johns began to notice me. I was free to go my own way, Pinkie said, but Flarra would remain with him." Finding his eyes with hers, she said, "You talk of choices, Mr. Basile. Tell me, what choice did I have?"

He expelled an expletive. "She would replace you."

"That's the best I could hope for her."

"The *best*?"

"From the day Pinkie became my guardian, he coddled me because, in his mind, he loves me. He has no such feeling for Flarra. He's generous and kind to her. But his kindness is extended only to pacify me and has nothing to do with an emotional attachment to her.

"Pinkie knows I love my sister more than anything in the world. If I ever left him, he would use her to punish me. And I'm afraid that for getting myself kidnapped, that's what he'll do.

"Oh, one more thing. On our return trip home from Galveston, we stopped for something to eat. Pinkie took Flarra inside the café, but asked that I remain behind and lend a hand to Errol, Lute Duskie's replacement. What

Errol did was take several heavy plastic bags from the trunk of the limo and throw them into a Dumpster behind the restaurant. I never saw or heard of Mr. Duskie again." She paused and looked at him puissantly. "I think, Mr. Basile, that the best you can hope for is to die quickly."

This was a night for firsts. She began to cry. Throughout the ordeal, she hadn't shed a single tear. He'd seen tears well up in her eyes, but she'd never actually wept.

He almost touched her, caught himself just in time, and withdrew his hand. But then he saw tears leaking from the outside corners of her eyes and rolling down her temples into her hairline. He moved his hand nearer, until his knuckles barely touched the side of her face and brushed the tears away. She didn't recoil, so he wiped the tears from the other side of her face as well.

"I can't let Flarra be damaged on my account," she said in an urgent whisper. "I love her. From the day she was born I've loved her and tried to protect her. She's all that is mine on this earth. Even my baby was taken from me."

Burke suddenly understood that, when he'd seen her in the gazebo, what he'd mistaken for a display of her sensuality had actually been an expression of unbearable loss. She repeated the gesture now, splaying her left hand over her lower abdomen.

Reacting impulsively, not stopping to think about it first, he covered her hand with his. Stunned by the intimacy, she stopped crying instantly. Burke was rather astonished himself. He stared at their stacked hands to confirm that what he was feeling was real.

A stillness settled over them. Each was aware of the other's suspended breath, of heartbeats, chaotic but oddly in sync, of spreading heat beneath their skin, of the pressure of his hand covering hers.

He raised his head and looked at her. The darkness was split by their searching gazes, eager to connect.

"Did you love your wife?"

Her whisper was so faint, he could barely hear it above his pounding heart. "Barbara?"

"Did you love her?"

Barbara had made more of an impact on him than any woman he'd met up to that point. She had excited and stimulated him. He had felt better when with her than without. But through courtship and years of togetherness, all the times they'd had sex before and after marriage, through every bitter quarrel as well as the good times, he had never felt what he was feeling now. It was a total, complete, saturating, all-encompassing passion for another human being.

"I thought I did," he answered, baffled by the misconception he had lived under. "Maybe not."

Slowly, he repositioned himself until his face hovered above hers, until their hands, those handcuffed together and those not, were clasped on either side of her face, and he could feel her breasts rising and falling beneath him, and taste her breath on his lips.

He laid his cheek along hers, rubbed his nose against her earlobe, inhaled her scent. For one forbidden moment, he imagined his mouth being intimate with hers, his hands exploring, that demanding part of himself being enveloped by her body.

The images were so real, he moaned with longing. But he pulled back. When he did, she opened her eyes. Tears still glazed them. They also reflected her confusion. "Basile?"

"God knows I want you," he said raspily. "But I won't take you. I won't give you a reason to hate me."

Chapter Thirty-Four

Dredd saw him coming and was standing at the edge of his pier. "'Bout time you showed up. I gave you up for a thirty."

"Nobody's killed me yet," Burke said, responding to the policeman's term for a murder victim. "The rain kept me away."

Noticing Burke's primitive repairs, he asked, "What happened to my boat?"

"It got me here, didn't it?" Burke snapped, immediately defensive.

He was in the worst of moods, and the sooner his friend understood that, the better. Ground rules for any dialogue should be laid now, so there wouldn't be hard feelings later.

His malcontent stemmed from the night he'd spent lying next to Remy while upholding his resolve not to touch her. What he'd told her last night was only partially true. If he made love to her, she would hate him. He would be like all the other men, including her husband, who had exploited her.

The flip side to that coin was that if he made love to her, he would hate himself.

Five days ago, he'd been contemptuous of her for maintaining a relationship, *any* relationship, with a bastard like Pinkie Duvall. His contempt had shielded him from his own attraction. But now, knowing what he did about her life before and after Pinkie entered it, his opinion of her had changed. Drastically. Disturbingly. He could no longer rely on his contempt to keep him honorable.

"How's it going?"

As the boat drifted toward the pier, Burke tossed the rope up to Dredd. "Don't ask."

Dredd maneuvered his cigarette to the opposite corner of his mouth. "Hmm. I'd ask, 'What's up?' but I think I can pretty well guess that. The *pichouette* is getting to you, is she?"

As Burke climbed onto the pier, he shot his friend a sour look. "What makes you say that?"

"I weren't born yesterday, that's what makes me say that. If she'd been a butt-ugly ol' gal, this still would have been a bad idea. But seeing as she's—"

"I get your point," Burke said testily.

Dredd wheezed his chain-smoker's laugh. "I'd gauge by *Father Kevin's* scowl that he hasn't broken his vows of chastity, but he's sure as hell been tempted to."

Burke ignored his teasing and strode along the pier toward the building. "Have you got any coffee?"

"Do gators shit in the water?"

"I don't know. Do they?"

"Where's Remy at?"

"I left her in the cabin."

"Alone?"

"She'll be okay."

Dredd's dubious look made Burke feel even more uneasy about a decision that had made him uneasy in the first place.

"How long will you be gone?" she'd asked before he left.

"As long as it takes me to get to Dredd's place, pick up some supplies, and get back."

"Hours."

"You'll be fine."

"Take me with you."

"Bad idea."

"Why?"

"Because I don't know what I'll find when I get there. I might have to be ... flexible, and I can't be if I'm worried about you getting hurt."

"I could get hurt here."

"If a boat comes by, stay out of sight. I'll get back as soon as I can."

"What if they arrest you, and I'm stranded here?"

"I'll tell them where you are."

"What if you're killed, and I'm stranded here?"

"Dredd knows where to find you."

The argument continued for another half hour, but he had remained resolute. Now, as he sipped Dredd's strong coffee, he was still haunted by her little-girl-lost expression as she stood in the doorway of the shack and watched him leave. He wouldn't draw an easy breath until he got back and found her safe. He hadn't forgotten about the men who'd happened by early last evening looking for Father Gregory.

He mentioned Gregory to Dredd now. "Did he by chance come back here?"

"After stealing my boat? Not bloody likely. I'd've shot him on sight."

Burke related the story he'd heard from the search party. "I'll be goddamn," Dredd cackled. "A wedding?"

"That's what they said." Burke gestured toward the vintage black-and-white TV set. Dredd disdained communication with the outside world and turned on the TV only if there was a hurricane brewing in the Gulf. But Burke had asked him to monitor the local news. "Anything about us?"

"Nary a word."

"As I thought. Duvall doesn't want anyone to know his wife's been abducted. Bad publicity."

"It appears that way. But how long can his wife be gone before somebody else notices?"

"There are servants in the house, but they'll keep quiet if Duvall tells them to. However, Remy's got a sister. She'll begin to wonder if she hasn't already."

"Oh, it's 'Remy' now, is it?"

Ignoring the gibe, Burke took a slip of paper from the pocket of his jeans and slapped it onto the counter. "Here's my shopping list. Do you have anything fresh?"

"Like what?"

"Vegetables. Fruit. She likes oranges."

"Likes oranges," Dredd repeated as he took a final drag on his cigarette before grinding it out in the hollow belly of a ceramic alligator. "Burke, if I was a younger, stronger man, if I didn't like you so much, I'd wrestle you down and hog-tie you to keep you from going through with this business. But I am old, and not as strong as I used to be, and I do like you. So all I've got to fight you with is a few words of caution. I don't like messing in any other man's business, but—"

"Here goes."

"Yeah. Here goes." Dredd blew out a cloud of smoke that he'd been savoring in his lungs. "Why don't you take that pretty lady on out of here? If you like her, and she feels the same, why don't you two just disappear? Get out while you can. Leave this business behind and go off someplace together?"

"She wouldn't run away with me, Dredd. And even if she would, I wouldn't leave this business, as you call it, unfinished."

"How's it going to wind up? Where's it going?"

"I don't know."

"But you know where it *ain't* going," Dredd said, emphasizing his statement by jabbing a horny finger at Burke. "It ain't going nowhere nice."

"No, it's not."

Dredd tugged on his beard in exasperation. "You've got your revenge on Duvall," he said, raising his voice. "You took his wife. Whether or not you've screwed her, you've made your point with him. End it, Burke."

"It'll end when Duvall is dead."

"Why are you doing this? Why?"

"Because I have to!" he shouted. Then, ameliorating his tone, he said irritably, "Just get the stuff so I can get out of here, okay?"

Grumbling beneath his breath, Dredd snatched up the list and began gathering the items from his shelves and angrily tossing them into a paper bag. Burke walked over to the pay phone, fed it coins, and placed a call.

It was answered on the second ring. "Good morning, Duvall," he said. "I thought I might catch you up early."

"Basile."

Coming from Pinkie Duvall's lips, his name sounded like an epithet. Good. He hoped to God he had become the lawyer's nemesis.

"You have made one huge mistake, Basile, a larger, more suicidal mistake than Stuart made when he ran into that warehouse."

"Kevin didn't know what he was up against. I do."

"Then you know that I'm going to kill you."

"Kill me? You've got to find me first, you mother-fucker."

Burke hung up, but for several moments he stared thoughtfully into near space. The man's wife had been kidnapped. She'd been missing for several days, in the custody of a man who'd sworn vengeance. Yet Duvall hadn't made a single inquiry about her well-being.

Burke repeated, this time with real feeling, "You mother-fucker."

* * *

The dial tone filled Pinkie's ear. "It wasn't long enough to trace, Mr. Duvall," said an assistant from the adjoining office. "Sorry. We can have our man over at central trace it, but it'll take a while."

"It doesn't matter."

To the assistant's dismay, Duvall began to laugh, softly at first, then with a sinister gusto. Looking across at Wayne Bardo, who was also smiling, he said, "Basile sounded so goddamn complacent. The son of a bitch doesn't know we already have him."

Bardo, sharing Duvall's good humor, dropped a manila folder onto his desk. "This will make your morning."

Pinkie read the label on the envelope as he dumped the contents onto his desk. "So soon? I'm impressed."

He thumbed through the black-and-white photos. They were grainy, the quality hampered by distance, but the subjects in them were clearly identifiable. Pinkie *tsk*ed. "Shame, shame, Dr. Caruth." Then to Bardo: "Get the new guy to bring the car around. I'm going to make a house call."

* * *

Dredd had placed the staples in the boat by the time Burke rejoined him on the pier. "Found a couple of oranges," he muttered grumpily.

"Thanks."

"You got enough there to last you several days."

Burke nodded, but he was distracted by other concerns. "Dredd, I fanned Duvall's fire just now, so watch yourself. First sign of trouble, you head for the swamp and lose yourself."

"I can take care of myself, thank you, sonny. I may be old and gray, but I'm not helpless."

"Listen to me," Burke said, making sure he had Dredd's undivided attention. "Anybody on Duvall's payroll you *do not* fuck around with. Promise me you'll make yourself scarce if anyone suspicious comes around. Be on guard."

"Okay, okay—Aw, hell, there's the phone."

"I'll see you in a couple of days if not before."

Dredd headed back toward the shack, cursing either the ringing telephone or Burke's admonition, Burke wasn't sure which. He was fond of the older man. If anything happened to Dredd, he would never forgive himself for involving him.

"Burke!"

He'd covered only about twenty yards when he heard Dredd's shout above the boat motor. He turned and looked; Dredd was signaling him back. He brought the boat around, shouting, "What is it?"

"Telephone for you."

His heart lurched. Had he miscalculated his timing? Had Duvall traced the call that quickly? Was he on his way here now? Adrenaline kicked in. He leaped onto the pier before the boat came to a full stop. "Who is it?"

"Your brother."

Burke drew up short. "Joe?"

"How many you got?"

"What's he want? How'd he know to reach me here?"

"Shouldn't you be asking him?"

Burke jogged back to the shop and was breathing hard when he reached the telephone. "Joe?"

"Hey. Can't believe I'm actually speaking to you. I was calling to leave a message with Dredd for you to phone me if you showed up at his place."

"You okay?"

"Hell, big brother, I'm fine. You're the one who's supposed to be in trouble. At least everyone seems to think so."

"What are you talking about?"

"For starters, Doug Patout shows up here yesterday morning just after daylight. He'd been driving most of the night and was about as glum as anybody I've ever met."

"Over what?"

"Your mysterious disappearance. He hem-hawed around before coming right out and saying that you were in a jam. Asked me did I know where you had gone."

"To which you told him..."

"The truth. I didn't know. I told him I might have a hunch, but family loyalty being what it is, I wouldn't share my speculations."

"Good. Thanks, Joe."

"Hold it. There's more. While Linda was entertaining him in the kitchen, I took a phone call in the den. It was Mac McCuen."

"Jeez. What did he want?"

"Same thing. His hints were a little more exaggerated—"

"That's Mac."

"But I told him exactly what I told Doug Patout—that I couldn't help him. After Patout left, I tried twice to reach Dredd on the outside chance you were at the fishing camp and the two of you had been in touch. Neither of those calls was answered. I got sorta spooked, and thought maybe you *were* in danger."

"I'm not."

"Then why are Patout and this guy McCuen convinced you are? McCuen doesn't take no for an answer."

"How well I know."

"He called again in the middle of the night, sounding even more strung out than before. I told him to fuck off."

"Good."

"But, Burke, he called again this morning. By now, Linda's freaking out, thinking you're dead or something. McCuen's begging, swearing he means you well, vowing that if I didn't tell him what he needed to know, we'd be planning a funeral. He said that if I didn't shed light on your whereabouts, you were as good as dead. So I did."

"Did what?"

"Shed light."

Burke backed into the wall, thumping it hard with his head.

"What's going on, Burke? Did I do the right thing?"

Burke couldn't fault his brother for divulging information to McCuen. Mac was persistent and persuasive. Joe's heart had been in the right place. "Don't worry about it."

"What's up? Is there something I can do? Patout said it was a confidential police matter."

"Something like that."

"Burke, if you're in trouble..."

"Listen, Joe, I'm sorry, but I haven't got much time." His mind was clicking along at a furious pace. Now he began speaking just as rapidly. "Don't interrupt, please. Just do what I'm telling you. Get out of town for a few days. Take the family. Go by car, pay in cash. No credit cards, no public transportation."

"What the hell—"

"Do it!" Burke shouted. "I love you, Linda, the kids. Do it."

After a moment, Joe reluctantly agreed. "Okay. For how long?"

"I'll call your office and leave a message on voice mail. Get a new retrieval code. Don't let anyone know where you're going. Clear?"

"Clear."

"And, Joe, call Nanci Stuart."

"Kev's widow?"

"Right. Tell her to take the boys and go somewhere. Same instructions. Same urgency. Got it?"

"Yes."

"Thanks, Joe. What time did Mac call this morning?"

"Less than an hour ago."

"From New Orleans?"

"I suppose, yeah."

"Did you give him directions to Dredd's?"

"No. He wanted to bypass Dredd's and go straight to our cabin."

Shit! "Now I've really got to go. Take care, Joe."

He hung up and raced for the door. Dredd was on the *galerie,* blocking his path. Burke dodged him with the alacrity of an NFL running back and continued running down the pier without breaking his stride. "Joe gave Mac McCuen directions to our cabin," he called over his shoulder.

"Damn. What side is McCuen's bread buttered on?"

"I don't know. That's what worries me."

"Will somebody be with him?"

"Wouldn't surprise me. In any case, I've got to head him off."

"Want me to come along?"

"This is my problem, Dredd. Untie that line, please," he said as he jumped into the boat.

"I had a problem once. You helped me."

"You've already helped. And I'll be eternally grateful." He started the motor. "By the way, you'll be glad to know your medicines worked. Remy's wounds have healed. If something happens to me, be sure and tell her...Just... Tell her I'm sorry for everything."

Chapter Thirty-Five

Mac McCuen mentally calculated the odds of his getting lost and figured them very good.

He had rented the boat from a guy with more warts than teeth who claimed never to have heard of the Basile brothers or their fishing camp. McCuen suspected him of lying and was glad he had Joe Basile's directions written down. The locals seemed to regard the swamp as their terrain and resented the intrusion of others.

As far as he was concerned, they could keep this godforsaken country to themselves. He couldn't fathom why some rhapsodized the natural beauty of the bayous and swamps of his native state. They were infested with insects, snakes, alligators, bobcats, boars, and other wildlife, and he wanted no part of any of it. Even as a kid he hadn't liked the great outdoors. A horse-racing track was about the closest he wanted to get to it. That and his own backyard.

Thoughts of home brought Toni to mind. God, what must she be thinking? Last night, about the time he was supposed to be meeting Del Ray Jones and Wayne Bardo, he'd been packing his young, beautiful wife off to her mama in Jackson, Mississippi. When he began slinging her belongings into suitcases, naturally she had become a trifle upset and demanded to know what in hell was going on.

He'd improvised a cock-and-bull story about a drug dealer they'd busted, who'd threatened the narcs involved in the sting with reprisals against their families. "It's probably just so much talk, but Patout advised us to take the necessary precautions."

She'd bought the lie. But even if she hadn't, he wasn't giving her a choice. She was getting safely out of town, period, end of argument. Duvall's deadline had expired and that wasn't going to go unnoticed. They would come looking for him with the hunting instinct and determination of bloodhounds.

Duvall's subtle remarks about Toni had got his attention just as the attorney knew they would. Mac knew what Wayne Bardo was capable of doing to a woman. He'd seen the eight-by-tens of murder scenes where Bardo was implicated but never indicted.

So Toni had been shuttled out of town, and she would remain in Jackson until this mess between Burke Basile and Pinkie Duvall was resolved one way or another.

Goddamn, how had he gotten himself caught in the cross fire?

Of course he knew how. Gambling. His addiction was responsible for all the wrong choices he'd made, and he'd made plenty. Every misdeed he'd ever committed harkened back to supporting his habit. It was common knowledge that he placed a bet or two here and there, but no one was aware of the lengths to which he'd gone to cover debts—not his folks, or his wife, or the people he worked with. No one. But *he* knew. And his conscience ate at him.

He swore to God that if he and Toni got out of this situation unscathed, he would never make another wager as long as he lived. But in the next breath, he bet himself a hundred to one that he would break that vow.

Suddenly, there was the cabin.

Mac almost laughed out loud. When he'd set out in the boat, he didn't believe he had a prayer of actually finding the place, but he had followed Joe Basile's directions to a T, and, lo and behold, there it was, just as Basile had described it, right down to the retreads attached to the pier.

It was too late for approaching with caution. In the desolate silence, Basile had surely heard the boat's motor well before it came into view. Right now, he was probably watching from one of the screened windows. Mac's heart was knocking inside his chest as though it knew it was in the crosshairs of a rifle's scope.

He killed the motor and let the small craft drift alongside the pier. He called out, "I'm alone, Basile, and I've got to talk to you." With both hands, he reached for one of the posts and held on, then clumsily climbed out of the boat and secured the rope.

Although the day was cool, his pores were leaking nervous sweat. He sensed hungry, hostile eyes watching him from myriad hiding places along the banks of the bayou, but none so menacing as Basile's.

His footsteps echoed loudly as he walked along the pier toward the crude dwelling. He was trained to spot signs of impending danger, but all his policeman's training deserted him. He had embarked on new territory, as remote and alien to him as Neptune. He felt incompetent and clumsy, and that was no way for a law officer to approach a problem, especially one on the scale of Burke Basile.

When he reached the screened door, he swallowed dryly. "Burke, this is no good, man. Let me come inside and talk to you. Okay?"

Keeping his hands in sight, he pulled open the screened door. The wooden door behind it was unlocked. Mac pushed it open, hesitated a moment, then stepped inside.

Eyes darting about, he gave the single room a quick survey.

"Son of a bitch!"

He felt like a fool, and was exceedingly frustrated, because the shack was deserted, and it was immediately obvious that it hadn't been occupied for a long time. Not by humans anyway. A varmint had chewed up part of the seat cushion in one of the armchairs. Roaches headed for cover. A spider ignored him as he continued to weave his web around the lantern hanging on a peg. Water dripped ponderously from the faucet over the stained kitchen sink.

Joe Basile had been wrong. Either that, or he was as wily as his older brother and, sensing danger for Burke, had deliberately sent his gullible colleague on a wild goose chase.

Now what? Now what was he fucking going to do? He couldn't go back without Basile. Without Basile...He didn't even want to think about it, but suffice it to say that the stinking, scary swamp was nothing compared to the hell awaiting him back in New Orleans if he didn't produce Basile.

Disgusted, Mac turned. He drew up short and sucked in a quick breath when he saw the silhouette outlined in the screened door.

* * *

Dredd was baiting a trotline when a car appeared in the gravel lane leading from the main road. He watched it approach, brake to a crawl, then come to a stop. The driver alighted. Seeing Dredd, he waved.

"Hi, Dredd." Gregory James came along the pier cautiously, smiling sickly. "How's it going?"

"You peckerwood," Dredd snarled. "Where's my boat? I ought to open you up and use your guts as bait." He brandished the knife he'd been using to cut up his bait.

Gregory held up his hands in surrender. "I'm sorry about your boat. I'll pay for it. My daddy's rich."

"What are you doing here? Too bad you weren't here earlier. You just missed your friend Burke Basile."

"Where is he?"

"Wouldn't you like to know?"

"Can we go inside and talk?"

Dredd turned away. "I got better things to do."

"Dredd, please. Look at me."

Dredd stopped what he was doing and looked more closely at the younger man's face. Parts of it were still swollen and rearranged. It was badly bruised. But between the bruises, his skin was pale, and his features were pinched and tense.

Mumbling self-deprecations to his softheartedness, Dredd motioned for Gregory to follow him into the store. As soon as they got inside, Gregory began babbling. "I only have ten minutes."

"Till what?"

"Till they come here after you. They're going to hold you at gunpoint if they have to, torture you, I don't know. But they're not going home without Remy Duvall and

Burke Basile, and you're going to take them to their hiding place."

"The hell I am."

"Then they'll kill you."

"Who's *they*?"

"Men who work for Duvall."

"Bardo?"

He shook his head. "Bardo stayed in the city. These are two other guys, guys who were waiting for me at my house when I got home."

"I'm still listening."

"I made a deal with Duvall last night. I could either go to jail with the assurance of being locked up with bull queers who'd have their way with me until my bowels ruptured and I bled to death, or I could lead these hit men to the place where I last saw Basile and Duvall's wife."

Dredd snorted with contempt. "Sounds like you made yourself a sweet deal, you chickenshit faggot."

"If I had really accepted the deal, would I be warning you?" Gregory said, his voice squeaky with desperation. "Besides, after I've expended my usefulness, they'll exterminate me, too."

"So that's why you're warning me? So I'll protect you?"

"Probably. But, I don't know..." He tugged on his lower lip, drawing blood from a cut still there. "I felt bad about screwing up Basile's plan. It's on account of me that Mrs. Duvall got shot. Or maybe it's because I've always taken the coward's way out and this is a way to redeem myself."

"Save it for confession," Dredd said scornfully. "Ash Wednesday's still two days away. You can make atonement then."

"Okay, I don't blame you for mistrusting my motives. But we're down to seven minutes. They're waiting at the main road. If I'm not back to report that there are no other customers in the store, they're going to come in, pretending to be fishermen, and take you off guard."

Dredd thoughtfully scratched his chin through his beard. "If you're being straight with me, why'd you lead them here?"

"So I would at least have a fighting chance of getting out of this alive."

"How do I know you're not setting me up? How do I know that you're not betraying me by pretending to betray Duvall?"

"Do you think I'm that clever?"

Dredd gave him a long, calculating look. "Good point."

"So you believe me?"

"Call me a damn fool," Dredd muttered, "but I think I do."

"What are we going to do?"

"I don't know yet. But you need to sit down before you fall down. You're as nervous as a whore in church. Thirsty? I'll get you a Dr Pepper."

Gregory gratefully took a chair at the table Dredd indicated. From the corner of his eye Dredd saw him recoil from the baby alligator heads. A dozen of them had been shellacked and left to dry on the table.

"Here." Dredd passed him an opened can of the cold drink. Gregory clutched it with a shaking hand and gulped it.

"What's our plan?" he asked between drinks.

"I'll be on the pier, fishing."

"Okay," Gregory agreed. "Where will I be?"

Dredd peered deeply into the younger man's eyes. "Hmm?"

"I shaid...I shaid...Wha'thu hell?"

Going out like a light, Gregory fell forward, his head thumping on the tabletop an inch from one of the gators' gleaming, open maws.

"The boy just can't hold his Dr Pepper."

Dredd moved behind Gregory, caught him beneath the arms, and dragged his limp form into the bedroom, where he placed him on the far side of the bed between it and the wall. It wasn't an ideal hiding place, but it would be temporary.

Gregory would wake up with a slight headache from banging his head on the table, but he would suffer no aftereffects from the sleeping potion that Dredd had added to his soft drink. It was a small dosage, just enough to knock him unconscious and keep him out of the way while Dredd dealt with Duvall's goons.

The adrenaline rush he was experiencing was better than any drug Mother Nature or Man had devised. He didn't miss the bullshit politics of his former job, the rules and regulations, the confinement, but he did miss the excitement. Until now, he hadn't realized how badly he'd missed it. He was looking forward to the next several minutes.

If Gregory was telling the truth, and if his calculations were correct, Dredd figured he had four minutes at the outside until the "fishermen" showed up. Between now and then, he had a lot to do.

* * *

"Hey, Mac. What brings you out this way?"

"You scared the shit out of me."

Burke pulled open the screened door and stepped into the cabin. "Who were you expecting?"

"Nobody. I mean, I was expecting you to be inside here with Mrs. Duvall."

"Really?"

"Yeah, your brother—"

"I know all about it. I spoke to Joe this morning. He told me about your frantic phone calls. I don't appreciate the fright tactic you used on him, Mac."

"I had no choice."

"So what's the crisis?"

"Goddamn it, Burke, cut the crap," Mac exclaimed. "You've gone 'round the bend. You've kidnapped Pinkie Duvall's wife and you're hiding her here in your fishing cabin."

"That's only partially true," Burke said blandly. "I have gone 'round the bend, and I did kidnap Mrs. Duvall, but I had the good sense not to bring her here."

Dredd had warned him against taking Remy to his fishing cabin, where it was possible someone eventually would come looking for them. Instead, he had suggested that Burke use a shack he owned and sometimes leased out. It was similarly equipped, but located in a more remote spot on a hard-to-find slough off a seldom-navigated bayou. Because he had heeded Dredd's advice, the hideaway was still a secret known only to him and Dredd.

"If you're looking for Mrs. Duvall here, you're cold, Mac. Very cold. You're also trespassing. Clear out."

"Burke, listen to me, please. I know you've never thought too highly of me. Fine. I know I got on your nerves, and you probably think I'm a lousy cop. That's okay, too. Think what you want, but give me credit for knowing what I'm talking about this one time. He's going to kill you."

"I assume you're referring to Duvall."

"He won't dirty his hands, but he'll have your head on a plate, or he'll die trying."

"That's what I'm counting on. That he'll die trying."

"And you'll spend the rest of your life in prison."

"I'm familiar with the criminal statutes for the state of Louisiana, but thanks all the same for the brush-up course and for your advice. Now, I'm busy. See ya, Mac."

Mac stepped around Burke, placing himself between Burke and the open door. "Is she all right?"

"Hell, yes, she's all right," Burke answered angrily. "Do you think I would hurt a woman?"

"No, but I didn't think you'd kidnap one either!" Mac shouted. Then, getting a grip on his temper, he used a more reasonable tone. "I'm trying to keep you from ruining your life. You're up to your hairline in shit, but it's not too late to reverse the situation. Return Mrs. Duvall to her husband. Then, with my help, maybe this thing can be worked out."

Burke laughed. "Duvall's not going to forgive and forget that I took his wife, Mac. What dreamworld are you living in?"

"Okay then, let me take her off your hands and return her home. You disappear. End of story."

"The end of the story doesn't come until Duvall's heart stops beating and Bardo is dead. Before they die, I'm going to have them identify the cop who's been selling out our division, and then I'm going to kill him, too."

"You're turning murderer?"

"Executioner for crimes committed."

"That's not up to you."

"Apparently it is."

"Leave it to Internal Affairs."

Burke laughed again, more bitterly than before. "They're as corrupt as the rest. Even if they sniffed out the traitor, do you think they'd turn him over to the D.A.? Hell, no. Nobody in the NOPD is going to do a goddamn thing except heap cover-up onto cover-up and line their own pockets in the process."

"There are some honest cops, too, Basile. One fewer now that you resigned."

"Those few can't change things."

"Will more killing bring Kev Stuart back?"

It occurred to Burke that he'd never seen his young partner this earnest about anything. He was desperate, and so jittery he'd almost developed a facial tick.

"What are you doing here, Mac?"

"I told you."

"What you told me was bullshit. You didn't stick your neck out for me because you admire me. It's not like we were blood brothers. There's something wrong with this picture. What is it?"

Mac's eyes shifted away from Burke's for several seconds before reconnecting. "I'm into a loan shark for fifty grand."

"I see," Burke said, putting the pieces together. "It's starting to make sense now. Duvall found out about your debt and offered to pay it off if you delivered me and his wife to him. That explains your desperation."

"What could I do, Burke? They threatened to hurt Toni."

Burke grabbed him by the front of his shirt. "Did you lead them here?"

"No, hell no." Mac wrestled himself free. "I was supposed to meet them last night, but I failed to show. I hoped to find you before they found me. They don't know where I am."

"Well, they'll find out. See you, Mac. Good luck."

Burke tried to move past him, but McCuen blocked him again. "Basile, I swear, I wouldn't risk coming through that goddamn swamp to find you if this was just about money. My parents-in-law would cover my debt if I asked them to. There's much more to this than you know."

"Yeah, and I'm sure it makes for interesting conversation, but right now I'm a little pressed for time." Burke was worried about Remy being alone in the shack. He'd been away much longer than he'd anticipated.

Besides, nothing Mac said would sway him. The guy was untrustworthy. What guarantee did he have that Mac hadn't led Bardo and a team of assassins straight to him? He would retrieve the boat where he'd hidden it on the bank, then return to Dredd's shack with dispatch. He wasn't worried about Mac tracking him. He would be easy to shake in the labyrinth of bayous.

Mac grabbed his arm. "I can help you, Basile. We can help each other."

"You're only interested in helping yourself. Now get the hell out of my way."

"I can't let you go through with this."

"You can't stop me."

When Burke tried to shove him aside, Mac reached toward the small of his back.

"Jesus, Mac, no!"

But he needn't have worried about Mac shooting him. Before Mac could get a grip on his weapon, Burke heard a gunshot. Mac looked at Burke with stunned surprise, then his eyes went blank and he pitched forward.

Chapter Thirty-Six

Dredd heard the car's approach. "Haven't had more than three customers this week," he said to himself. "This morning, I'm doing a land-office business."

According to Gregory's schedule, Duvall's men were right on time. Maybe the boy was seeking redemption after all.

Two car doors were heard opening and shutting, then footsteps crunched through gravel. "Good morning," a voice called out.

"Same to you, asshole," Dredd said beneath his breath, not loud enough for his visitors to hear.

"They biting this morning?"

That from a second voice. Dredd didn't respond to it either. He had arranged it so that Duvall's heavies saw an old man sitting with his back to them on the end of the pier, feet dangling above the water, fishing pole in his hand. His plan was for them to figure that the geezer was hard of hearing.

They didn't venture into the store, where they doubtless thought Gregory was cowering, waiting for the action to unfold. Instead, they came toward him along the pier. One, Dredd discerned by his footsteps, was significantly heavier than the other.

"You must be Dredd."

Dredd didn't move.

"What are you using for bait?"

He estimated they were ten feet away from the end of the pier now. Close, but not close enough.

"Is he deaf or what?" he heard one ask the other in an undertone.

"Hey, old man," the first voice said. "We're going fishing. We need to buy some supplies."

Still Dredd waited, motionless and silent.

"Son of a bitch must be deaf."

"Or else he's ignoring us just to be ornery. Hey, old man! I'm talking to you."

During his police career, Dredd had frequently relied on human nature to assist him in doing his job. Homo sapiens acted on ancient impulses, which made them predictable. Dredd was counting on bullies being unable to resist a chance to bully.

"Maybe he needs a little prodding," suggested one.

"Yeah," the heavier one chuckled. "Maybe he needs prodding."

With the toe of his boot, he nudged the old, deaf fisherman in the spine just below his ponytail. It wasn't a hard kick, but to his consternation, the fisherman toppled into the water.

His fishing hat fell off. And so did the gray wig. The Spanish-moss beard floated away. A Halloween mask stared up at him, except that the slits for the eyes were empty.

Leaning down for a closer look, he exclaimed, "What the—"

Dredd reached from beneath the pier where he'd been hiding and grabbed the guy by the ankle. Unbalanced, he grabbed at air, but fell into the water. Dredd's knife cut a clean arc beneath his chin. He was dead before he got completely wet.

Dredd's outlook was that some people just weren't fit to live among decent folk. He'd had his fill of the chronic wife beater that night he answered the domestic violence call. He saw on the guy's wife and kids the bloody evidence of his violent temper. The bastard hadn't kept his repeated promises to reform. He was an expensive drain on the system that routinely jailed him and then released him to abuse his family again. He was an emotional and physical blight on society and everyone around him.

Do everybody a favor and pop this son of a bitch now had been Dredd's thought when he pulled his weapon. For all the grief the incident had caused him, he didn't regret snuffing the guy. Given the same set of circumstances, he would do it again.

This guy, now lying limp in his arms, had killed before, and he would have killed him and Gregory after they had served their purpose. Dredd had no compunction against striking first. It wouldn't cost him a second's sleep tonight.

If he lived until tonight.

Taking a deep breath, he dragged the body beneath the surface of the water with him and secured it to one of the pilings with a grappling hook. He resurfaced only far enough to breathe through his nose.

"Charlie? Charlie?"

That's right, dimwit, give away your position with your

voice. Dredd stealthily moved through the water beneath the pier toward the voice.

"Charlie?" Then, "Oh, Jesus."

Dredd didn't have to guess what had caused the assassin's switch in tone from mystification to horror. Dredd had been around them long enough to sense their movements even when they were submerged and unseen. He'd studied their patterns, observed them in their natural habitat. Hell, he shared their natural habitat.

Gators.

His pets had spent the winter in semicatatonia, out of sight, not eating, not doing much of anything except waiting around for the first day that was sunny enough and warm enough to get their systems jump-started after months of lethargy. Today was the day. He sensed them moving with predatory intent through the water toward Charlie's fresh blood.

Dredd didn't panic. He waited. Waited. Waited.

"Charlie?"

Sheer panic was in the man's voice now. Dredd could read his mind. He wanted to bolt, to get the fuck out of this spooky place and to hell with Duvall and finding his wife. But he and Charlie had worked together for a long time. Next to himself, Charlie was the meanest sumbitch he knew. And ol' Charlie had practically disappeared before his very eyes. It was human nature to want to know what had happened to his buddy. Human nature.

When the guy leaned over to inspect the underside of the pier, Dredd put all his strength behind a scissors kick that launched him out of the water with the impetus of a sea monster. The guy outweighed him by seventy pounds, but surprise gave Dredd a huge advantage. He hooked his hand around the back of the guy's neck and pulled him into the water. As he fell forward, Dredd's knife pierced his Adam's apple.

* * *

When Gregory regained consciousness, he was lying eyeball to eyeball with a twelve-foot alligator.

Screaming, he scrambled to his feet, banging his head on the iron bed frame. Pulse pounding, gasping for breath, in a near state of cardiac arrest, he crawled across the bed on which Dredd had nursed Remy Duvall only a few days ago.

Once he was on the far side of the room, he peeped beneath the bed to make certain that the gator he'd seen was a stuffed model and not a living specimen. He wouldn't put anything past Dredd, even to keeping a live alligator beneath his bed.

But the menacing eyes were glass. Moderately calmed, Gregory hastily made his way through the macabre chambers of Dredd's Mercantile. The table on which Dredd ate his meals was littered with alligator heads sealed in shiny shellac, and they brought back a disturbing memory, although it didn't crystallize. Outside, the old man was washing down the pier with a garden hose.

When he heard Gregory's footfalls on the planks, he turned. His beard was wet, as were his denim cutoffs. "Get your nap out?" he asked pleasantly.

"What happened? Why was I on the floor behind the bed? I can't remember . . . No, wait. I do remember."

The fog inside Gregory's head gradually began to lift. "You gave me a Dr Pepper. Did you drug me?" Then his memory slammed into him full force. He spun around and saw the second car parked beside his. "They're here?" he squealed in panic. "Where are they? What did you tell them? Why'd you knock me out?"

"Relax, sonny. You didn't miss much. They're gone."

"How'd you get rid of them? What did you tell them?"

"Actually, I didn't have the pleasure of a meeting. Any dialogue they had, they had with my friend there."

Gregory turned in the direction Dredd indicated, and was startled to see an effigy of Dredd sitting in a dilapidated rocking chair on the *galerie,* wet fishing hat and wig slightly askew atop a Halloween mask from which hung a Spanish-moss beard.

"I made him a couple years ago to bait a thief," Dredd explained. "This asshole kept coming in and raiding my store every time I went out to fish or hunt.

"So I rigged up the dummy and set him adrift in one of my boats. Caught the guy red-handed and beat him within an inch of his life. Never came back." He chuckled. "I got sorta attached to my friend and decided to keep him around. He listens when I want some company. Damned ugly son of a bitch, but no uglier than me, I reckon. He sure came in handy this morning."

Gregory came around slowly. He looked at the recently scrubbed pier, looked into the water below it with repugnance, looked at the two monstrous gators sunning themselves on the far bank, looked at Dredd, who stared back at him with satisfaction and calm defiance.

It was easy to guess the fate of the two men who had accompanied him here. Gregory swallowed his revulsion, but he supposed he owed Dredd his life. However, remembering Pinkie Duvall's determination, he knew the reprieve would be temporary. "Duvall will send somebody else."

"Most likely," Dredd replied with a philosophical shrug. "That's why you'd best be on your way."

"What about their car?"

"I'll take care of it."

He didn't elaborate on how he planned to take care of it, but Gregory was confident that the vehicle was about to disappear permanently.

"I . . . Thanks, Dredd."

Dredd expelled a gust of cigarette smoke. "You did good, boy. When I see Basile, I'll be sure and tell him that you made up for your past mistakes."

Gregory was touched by the old man's commendation, to an embarrassing degree. Tears came to his eyes, and Dredd must have noticed them because he, too, became embarrassed, and that made him cantankerous. "Well, don't just stand there. After surviving what you've been through already, Basile would be pissed if I let you get dead or hurt or locked behind bars. So go on now. Git."

* * *

Reflexively Burke reached for Mac McCuen as he fell. "Mac!"

But Mac wasn't going to answer; he was dead. Even knowing that, Burke continued repeating his name as he lowered him to the floor.

Hearing approaching footsteps, he looked up to see Doug Patout running along the pier toward the shack. "Is he dead?"

"Goddamn it, Doug," Burke said angrily. "He didn't have a prayer."

"You wouldn't have either if he'd shot you in the chest from point-blank range."

Patout knelt down and felt Mac's carotid artery. After a moment, he stood, moving as though he carried a thousand-pound burden on his back. He swore softly and dragged his hand down his haggard features. Then he placed a hand on Burke's shoulder and looked at him with concern. "Are you okay?"

"Okay? Jesus, Doug. No, I'm not okay. I just had another of my men shot before my eyes."

"Mac was going for his gun. It was him or you."

Indeed, Mac had fumbled his handgun from the holster at the small of his back. It was lying inches from his supine right hand. Despite this evidence to the contrary, it was hard for Burke to believe that McCuen would have shot him in cold blood.

Patout said, "He was dirty. He'd made a deal with Duvall."

"He admitted that much."

"Did he tell you the terms?"

"The cancellation of a fifty-thousand-dollar debt in exchange for me."

"That's partially right. Actually the deal was the cancellation of his debt *plus* a larger share of the profit if he killed you."

"Profit?"

Patout nodded down at Mac. "That's the guy you've wanted. We've got indisputable proof that McCuen has been working for Duvall."

Burke looked at Patout with disbelief. "Mac's a joker, a nuisance, a screwup."

"Part of the act. He was smarter than he let on. He made himself likable, he performed his duties reasonably well, but he didn't excel. He persisted until he was assigned to Narcotics and Vice. All part of their plan. He's been Duvall's inside man since he signed on."

"There was always something a little off," Burke

mused out loud. "A cop's salary didn't jibe with Mac's standard of living. I had decided he was either a damn good gambler or the luckiest bastard I ever met."

"His luck ran out today."

"You say you've got proof of his connection to Du-vall's operation?"

"For months Internal Affairs has been conducting a covert investigation. I'm the only one in the division who knew about it. I knew you were frustrated by the seeming lack of interest to ferret out the traitor, but I was sworn to secrecy and couldn't tell you. Although," he added, "I was tempted to so you wouldn't quit on me.

"Anyway, after months of exhaustive investigation, I.A. traced the thwarted busts back to McCuen." Softly, he added, "Including the one that went south the night Kev was killed."

Burke looked at him sharply.

Patout nodded. "That's right. You've wanted the guy who tipped the dealers of the raid that night and got Kev killed. There's your culprit."

Mistrusting what he'd heard, Burke stared hard into Patout's eyes. When the words finally sank in, his knees went weak and he leaned against the wall, then slowly slid down it until he was crouching.

Patout gave him a moment to reflect. Finally, he asked, "You all right?"

"Yeah. Fine." Burke had to clear his throat before he could continue. "I thought...I thought I would feel different when I found out who it was."

"How do you feel?"

"Empty."

They were quiet for a time. Burke noticed that the pool of blood that had formed beneath Mac's body had stag-

nated. Soon it would congeal. So much blood. From Mac.
From Kevin.

After a time, he looked up at Patout. "If the information
Mac supplied to Duvall kept his drug trade thriving,
wasn't he too valuable to squander by sending after me?"

"Apparently getting you superseded everything else in
Duvall's life. Mac was close to you, someone you might
trust to be bringing a message of goodwill. And Mac was
dispensable."

"Because Duvall's resources are unlimited. He's probably already got another cop to replace Mac."

Patout nodded grimly. "You're probably right."

Burke stared down into Mac's death mask and thought
about the young man's annoying habits but undeniable
charm, thought about his pretty young wife, thought about
the waste of it all. It made him want to hit something very
hard.

He asked Patout, "How'd you know Mac was coming
here this morning?"

"We've been closing in on him, watching his every
move. We recently learned he was in debt to a loan shark
named Del Ray Jones."

"I know who he is."

"When Del Ray took Mac to a meeting with Duvall
night before last, it was easy to deduce what was going
on."

Burke came to his feet. "That's pretty flimsy evidence,
Doug. How do you know Mac wasn't coming here to warn
me, or to deliver a message from Duvall? That's what he
told me he was doing."

"He was going for his gun, remember? Would you have
rather I waited to see if he shot you first?"

Burke conceded the point.

"Anyhow," Patout continued, "I knew what Mac had been sent out here to do, because I spoke to Duvall. I called him this morning and told him that Mac was blown. Using that cryptic lawyer language that's inadmissible in court, he implied what Mac's errand would accomplish. Then he boasted that whether Mac got you or not, he had a backup plan."

"He was bluffing. I spoke to him this morning myself. He's still hungry for a taste of me. Whenever he comes, whatever form his backup plan takes, I'll be ready for him."

"Jesus, will you listen to yourself?" Patout shouted. "You and Duvall are in a pissing contest like a couple of junior-high boys. Wake up, Burke, and put this thing into perspective. One man's already dead over this mess, and I take that hard because I had to kill him. Whether he was dirty or not, Mac was one of my own men."

Changing tones, he said, "I'm begging you to give this up. Now. You've got who you were ultimately after, and that's the cop that got Kev killed. So let's pick up Mrs. Duvall, wherever you're keeping her, and see her safely home."

"Not until I see the whites of Duvall's eyes."

"Okay, say you succeed in killing Duvall and Bardo, but you wind up in prison on death row. Who have you spited?"

"I'm not taking her back."

"Worst-case scenario. What if Duvall survives and you go to prison? Do you think he'll let it drop? Never. He'll hurt you any way he can. Remember Sachel and his son? Duvall is ruthless. What's to keep him from turning Nanci Stuart over to Bardo? He'll use the people you care for to torture you. I've met your brother. He's a nice guy. You won't be able to protect them, Burke. Not from a cell in Angola."

"All the more reason for me to make sure that neither one survives."

"Damn it, Burke, listen to me."

"No, you listen to *me,*" Burke shouted back. "I started this and I'm going to finish it."

"I'll arrest you."

"For what?"

"Kidnapping."

"Have I written a ransom note? What evidence do you have that I took Mrs. Duvall by force? Maybe she and I cooked this up together so she could escape that tyrannical son of a bitch."

Patout shot him a retiring look. "It's not too late to turn this thing around. Duvall approached me shortly after the abduction and warned me then that he was going to kill you. If you persist, you'll be on your own. But if you come in with me now, you'll have the protection of the department behind you."

"No thanks. The department—"

Before he could react, Patout's pistol was coming down hard on his temple. He staggered toward the door, pyrotechnics exploding behind his eyes. The pier beyond the screened door seemed to stretch for miles, as though he were looking at it through reversed binoculars. The tunnel of vision continued to shrink as blackness closed in around it. Then it disappeared altogether.

His last conscious thought was of Remy. She was alone, waiting for his return.

Chapter
Thirty-Seven

Burke came awake to the sound of voices, although the words were indecipherable. Total awareness was slow in coming, but gradually he discerned that he was indoors, lying on his side, that his hands were shackled behind him, and that he had a bitch of a headache.

Wherever he was, there was a lot of activity going on beyond the walls. He didn't actually see the emergency vehicle lights, but he felt their pulsing against his closed eyelids. Until he knew more, he decided to keep his eyes shut and pretend to be unconscious.

One of the voices finally distinguished itself.

Dredd was saying, "Been like Grand Central Station out here today," he remarked grumpily. "With all the coming and going, the fish won't bite for a week."

"Like who?" Doug Patout asked.

"Like who what?"

Even though he was still half-addled, Burke realized

that Dredd was playing dumb. He wondered if Patout was aware of it.

"Who was out here today coming and going?" Patout asked.

"Oh, well, to start, two guys came by this morning, asking for Burke Basile."

"What two guys?"

"Didn't know them, but I'll tell you this, I don't care if they ever come back. They were bad news."

"How do you know? What did they do?"

"Nothing in particular. It was just a feeling I got, you know? It's been years since I was a cop, Patout, but the instinct hasn't left me." Burke sensed that Dredd was pausing to take a draw off his cigarette. "They were dressed like fishermen, but if those two ever caught a fish in their lives, I'll eat those gators over there."

"You did eat those gators over there."

Dredd chuckled. "Right you are, Patout, but you know what I mean. Anyhow, I rang up their six-packs of Bud in a hurry, and was glad to see the last of them."

"What'd you tell them about Burke?"

"There wasn't any more to tell them than what I've told you. Burke was by here several days ago."

"What day?"

"Can't recall exactly. I don't pay much attention to the calendar anymore, although I did notice that tomorrow's Mardi Gras. Guess the city's gearing up to—"

"About Burke..."

"Oh, right. Basile shot the breeze with me for a time, but he isn't what you'd call talkative, you know. He bought a few things, then was off."

"And the woman was with him?"

"Woman is an understatement. Whooee!" In an undertone, Dredd added, "I jerked off twice after they left. Who'd you say she is?"

Patout gave him the capsulated facts, which, of course, Dredd already knew. When Patout finished, Dredd said, "Hmm. I'd never have figured her for Basile's hostage. Didn't look to me like he was forcing her into anything. She got right into the car with him."

"They left here by car?"

Dredd launched into an elaborate lie about the make, color, and model of the nonexistent car. If the circumstances hadn't been so grave, Burke would have laughed out loud. "Since you can't see the main road from here, I don't know which way they headed."

Patout asked if there had been another man with them, possibly a priest. Dredd laughed and said no, that he avoided contact with clergymen, and Basile didn't strike him as a religious sort either. After a pause, he added, "I can't figure Basile for a kidnapper."

"Nor can I, but it appears he is."

"Tell me again, Patout, who's this fellow you popped?"

"Detective Sergeant Mac McCuen."

"One of your own."

"Yeah," Patout said bitterly. "He made a deal with Pinkie Duvall to return with Burke and his wife. I followed Mac out here, and it's a good thing I did. He was sent to assassinate Burke." He briefed Dredd on Mac's dirty dealings within the department.

"You ever killed a man before, Patout?"

"Once. In the line of duty. It's not something you get over easily."

"Guess it all depends on how bad the guy needs killing," the retired policeman said. Burke could imagine him raising one of his sunburned shoulders in a shrug.

"You rid the department of a real dirty cop, this McCuen. Sounds to me like you saved everybody a lot of time and trouble."

"I hate it that anybody had to die. All along I hoped to end this thing peaceably. At least I spared Basile from making a mistake that he would be paying for the rest of his life. Whether he thinks so or not, I've done him a favor."

Dredd snorted his skepticism. "Somehow I doubt he'll look upon being knocked out and handcuffed as a favor. You'll have your hands full when he wakes up."

"He's going to be pissed," Patout agreed, "but what I did, I did for his own good. Damn his stubborn hide." Then he said, "There's the ambulance."

Burke heard chairs scraping backward, the sound of shuffling feet. "I'd better go supervise the transport of Mac's body and clear up the paperwork with the parish officials. Soon as I get the ambulance underway, I'll come back for Basile."

"What about Duvall's wife?"

"That's the first thing I'm going to ask Basile about when he comes around. The lady must be taken home immediately."

Burke waited until Patout's footsteps could no longer be heard, then opened his eyes. As he'd already guessed, he confirmed that he was lying on a sofa in Dredd's main room.

"How long you been awake?" Dredd asked in a whisper. He wasn't facing Burke at all, but was standing at a window, calmly smoking, and watching the commotion outside through the cloudy glass. Burke wondered, not for the first time, if the *traiteur* was indeed a warlock with supernatural powers. Beyond his healing abilities, did he have eyes in the back of his head?

"Long enough to overhear Patout's recap of the situation."

"Was it like he said?"

"Exactly. I reached the cabin a few minutes before McCuen got there and hid my boat in the saw grass. When he and I came face to face, he admitted to striking a deal with Duvall. He thought we could negotiate with him and work it all out."

"Fuck that."

"My reaction exactly. Mac's future was at stake, so he wouldn't take my no for an answer. He went for his gun. Patout had him under surveillance and had followed him there. He must have had a bead on him. The bullet went straight through his back to his heart. Now Patout's hellbent on playing the rest out by the book."

"He's only half your problem. Duvall is pulling out all the stops. He's after you, son."

While appearing to do nothing except watch the loading of Mac's body into the ambulance, Dredd told Burke about Gregory's coming to the store and warning him of the gunmen who'd accompanied him.

"So what you told Patout about the two phony fishermen was true."

"Most of it," Dredd said. "They were here, but they didn't leave."

The words had an ominous ring that halted any further questioning. Burke thought he was better off not knowing the fate of the two men. "What about Gregory?"

"There's hope for the boy. He could've screwed us over good, but he came through. I told him to hightail it, and he took my advice."

"Good." He pulled against the handcuffs. "Get me out of these damn things."

Dredd turned away from the window. "The body is loaded and Patout is conferring with the sheriff. We've got maybe ninety seconds to get you away from here."

"Where's my gun?"

"Patout's got it. But you can borrow one of mine."

Dredd took a Magnum .357 from a drawer, checked to see that all the chambers were loaded, scooped up a box of bullets, then assisted Burke to his feet. His legs were wobbly and his head felt like a watermelon precariously balanced on his shoulders as he followed Dredd through the misshapen assortment of rooms and out a back door.

In a toolshed, which seemed to contain every implement invented since the Iron Age, Dredd located a pair of bolt cutters and snipped off the handcuffs. He gave Burke the pistol and the bullets, then pulled a boat from beneath the pier.

"You're using up my boats like a horny kid with a box of rubbers. At the rate you're disposing of them, I'll soon be out of business."

"I'll make it up to you, Dredd."

"Yeah, yeah, just try and not get yourself killed before you do. The boat's gassed up, but don't start the motor until you've gone at least half a mile. You up to rowing that far?"

"I've got no choice. Remy's out there alone."

"Basile? You like that girl?"

The two men exchanged a long look, but all Burke said was, "Thanks again, Dredd."

"Don't mention it. Good luck and . . . oh, shit. I hate this part."

Burke slammed his fist into Dredd's chin, and even his bushy beard couldn't cushion the blow. Then as he fell backward, Burke clouted him once more on the side of the head, regrettably having to make it look like he'd over-powered him. However, he didn't hit him hard enough to cause the older man too much residual pain.

Then he jumped into the boat and pushed away from the pier.

As he reached for the oar, a shout went up and he heard running footsteps.

To hell with rowing; he started the outboard and gunned it.

*   *   *

As early as noon, Remy began watching for him. She had even held off eating lunch in anticipation of his being hungry when he got back and of them eating together. But noon came and went with no sign of him.

During the long afternoon, she ventured outside and tried to enjoy the first sunny day she had experienced in the swamp, but she couldn't totally relax and take in its exotic beauty because her mind was preoccupied with Basile and what could be keeping him away so long.

Sunset increased her anxiety. Like a sentinel at his post, she paced every inch of the pier. She listened to catch the sound of the trolling motor above night sounds of the swamp, which originally had frightened her, but which she now found familiar and somewhat comforting.

When dusk gave way to night, she went back inside. For added safety, she didn't light the lantern, so her vigil was continued in complete darkness. She hadn't eaten since breakfast, but she wasn't hungry.

What had happened when Basile returned to Dredd's Mercantile?

What if, somewhere along the way, he'd been ambushed by the three men who'd come to the shack last night, ostensibly searching for Father Gregory?

What if Pinkie had men waiting to attack him when he returned to Dredd's?

What if he and Dredd had been killed and no one knew where she was?

The grim possibilities marched relentlessly through her mind. Finally exhaustion forced her to lie down and close her eyes. In her turbulent state of mind, she had thought sleep was impossible, so when she was abruptly awakened, her first reaction was surprise that she'd fallen asleep.

Her second reaction was to wonder what had awakened her. As when she had been awakened by Angel and one of her countless men, Remy lay perfectly still, heart pounding.

What had startled her out of sleep? A sound? A menacing movement in the darkness? A premonition of danger?

She strained to hear a sound, but there was nothing. Had she been awakened by the vibration of a boat bumping into one of the pilings supporting the pier?

Was she just going to lie here and pretend to be invisible as she had in her corner of Angel's sordid world? She was no longer a child. She had declared to Basile that she would never be a victim again. What or who could be more threatening than the man she'd lived with for twelve years? She had withstood Pinkie's cruel psychological abuse; she could withstand anything.

Slipping out of bed, she crept across the room and located a kitchen knife. It was dull, but it was the closest thing she had to a weapon since Basile had taken his pistol. As an afterthought, she also grabbed the lantern and a matchbook, then she moved to the nearest window and peeped out.

She saw a form, nothing more than a darker shadow among shadows, tiptoeing along the pier. Once, he paused as though listening, then continued moving silently toward the shack.

Remy sank to the floor and gripped the knife. She wondered exactly how one went about using a Coleman lantern as a weapon.

When the door's rusty hinges creaked, the intruder hesitated before pulling it open only wide enough for him to slip inside. He eased it closed behind him.

"Remy?"

Her heart nearly burst with relief. "Burke?"

She shot to her feet and ran toward him, but drew up short when she saw the gun in his hand.

* * *

Burke was so relieved to see her unharmed; he was on the verge of grabbing her and clutching her to him when he spotted a knife in one hand and the lantern in the other.

He hadn't used the boat motor for the last mile or so, knowing how far sound carries over water. He hadn't wanted to lead the people looking for him into this hidden slough. Struggling like hell to get back, it hadn't occurred to him that Remy herself might pose a threat.

But the knife clattered to the floor and she set the lantern and a book of matches on the table.

He engaged the safety on the pistol and set it beside the lantern.

Then they faced each other. He spoke first. "Are you all right?"

She nodded vigorously. "Frightened."

"Of what?"

"I didn't know who you were at first."

"I was afraid you might not be here."

"Where would I go? Why were you sneaking up—"

"To avoid being captured."

"Captured?"

"There's a manhunt on for me."

"Why?"

"It's a long story."

"You're sweating."

"I've been rowing."

"Oh."

Again they just stood there looking at each other across the darkness.

Then she said, "You were away so long."

"I know. I'm sorry. I couldn't get back."

"It's okay, I just—"

"It couldn't be helped. If—"

"What happened?"

"Did anyone come here?"

"No."

"Have you seen anyone?"

"Not all day. I've been frantic."

"With fear?"

"Worry."

"Worry?"

"That something had happened to you."

The space separating them narrowed. Later, he didn't recall consciously reaching for her. He didn't remember placing his arms around her. It happened without forethought. One second he was longing to hold her, and the next he was.

He clutched her tightly. She felt incredibly small and soft against him. He buried his face in her neck beneath her hair. His hand cupped her head and pressed her face against his throat.

Her lips moving against his skin, she said, "I was afraid you wouldn't come back for me."

"Nothing could have stopped me from coming back."

"I didn't know."

"You knew, Remy."

"How was I to know?"

"Because I promised you I would."

With that, his lips searched blindly for hers. He kissed her hard, crushing her mouth first at one angle, then another, and yet another. He was awkward, clumsy even. But ravenous men eat gracelessly. He kissed her hungrily, not with finesse. Tasting her for the first time, a low moan rose out of his chest, partially from gratification, partially from heightened want.

Eventually, he pulled back, pushed his fingers through her hair, tilted her head back, and looked down into her face to see if he had mistaken her response. But in her expression he read the same wonder and confusion he was feeling.

Shyly, she reached up and touched his mouth with her fingertips.

Burke closed his eyes and swayed toward her. He dipped his knees slightly, fitting himself into the notch of her thighs. His hands moved to her hips and held her firmly against him. Her hand, now resting lightly on his hair, guided his head down to her and they kissed again with more passion and less restraint than before.

He stumbled backward toward the bed, dragging her with him, until the backs of his legs touched the mattress.

He sat down, spread his knees, and pulled her between them. Impatiently he peeled the sweatshirt over her head. The sweatpants were pushed to the floor for her to step out of. First his eyes, then his hands moved over her—shoulders, breasts, waist, hips, thighs—touching as much of her as he could as quickly as he could.

Then he rested his hot cheek against her belly, and her arms enfolded his head. He caressed the backs of her calves and thighs. He squeezed her ass. He kissed her V through her panties, then nuzzled her with chin and nose and brow in a rubbing motion that felt like loving.

He placed her on the bed, stretched out beside her, and slipped his hand inside the front of her underpants. Springy hair curled around his fingers. He parted the swollen lips. The center of her sex was very wet. He sent his fingers deep, then withdrew them and used the ball of his middle finger to lightly massage that most sensitive spot.

Her soft gasping of his name he took as permission. Within seconds, his jeans were open, and he was positioned above her. When he entered her, he almost sobbed from the pleasure of it. He didn't want it to be rushed, but the sensations were so intense, so long anticipated and frequently fantasized, that they overtook him, and he could no longer hold back.

The climax passed too quickly. He raised his head, an apology on his lips. But her features were soft and slack. Beads of sweat dotted her upper lip; her eyes were closed. Beneath him, her chest rose and fell. Her nipples were tight. He feathered them with his thumb. He felt her belly quicken against his an instant before she caught her lower lip between her teeth.

He rocked forward slightly and stayed inside her to

share each rippling, pulsing pressure. When it subsided, he rolled to his side and drew her close to him, pressing her head to his chest and stroking her back. They lay like that for a long time, and he could have stayed that way forever. But he felt compelled to say something.

"I know how religious you are. You probably regard adultery as a mortal sin. So, you can say I forced you if you want to. Just...just don't feel bad about it, okay, Remy? I don't want you to feel bad about this. About me."

She worked her head free so that she could look into his face. She laid her palm against his cheek and searched his eyes. "You don't have to worry about that. I'm not really married."

Chapter
Thirty-Eight

From the window of his office, Pinkie watched the revelers on the street below. The Orpheus parade was over, but the crowds were still out in full force, sinning with a vengeance before the start of Lent, almost twenty-four hours away.

Hearing the door open and close behind him, he turned. Bardo slunk in, looking uncharacteristically subdued. "My men won't go near the place. Said it's still crawling with heat in all its forms. Cops, sheriff's deputies, state police, coroner. You name it."

"It's been confirmed that McCuen is dead?"

"As a doornail. Story is, Patout whacked him to protect Basile."

"What about Basile?" Pinkie asked.

"You aren't gonna believe it. Patout had him in custody, but he got away."

Duvall swore viciously.

"Basile overpowered the old codger who runs the bait shop."

"Overpowered my ass," Duvall roared. "Did Patout buy that?"

"I don't know."

"Didn't that Gregory character tell us that Basile and Dredd what's-his-name are thick as thieves? The way you describe the heat around the place, even Saint Basile couldn't have escaped that compound unassisted. And what the hell happened to Gregory and the men I sent with him? Any news?"

Bardo shook his head. "Nothing."

"I don't think they ever made it to Dredd's Mercantile. Obviously they double-crossed us."

"They're two of my most dependable guys," Bardo argued. "I tell them what to do, and they do it, no questions asked."

"Gregory James's family has a lot of money. He bribed them to let him go. By now they're probably in Vegas banging whores two at a time."

"They couldn't be bribed," Bardo said stubbornly.

"Then explain to me where they are."

Bardo shrugged, and Pinkie cursed.

He didn't remember ever feeling this confounded or incompetent. He'd had two excellent chances to trap Basile, and both had failed. McCuen had apparently planned to bypass Del Ray Jones and act independently. Duvall didn't have a problem with that. In fact he admired McCuen's initiative. Except that it had backfired and McCuen had got himself killed. *Thank you, Doug Patout,* Pinkie thought. He must be dealt with later.

In the meantime, Gregory James had vanished and taken two expert hit men with him. How the hell had that sniveling queer coward managed that? Wherever Basile was, he was probably laughing his ass off at these bungled attempts on his life. Just thinking of that caused Pinkie's blood pressure to skyrocket.

Bardo interrupted his thoughts. "Don't get steamed at me for saying this."

Pinkie turned, but Bardo went on, undaunted by the lawyer's glare. "Basile could have popped Mrs. Duvall and dumped her body in the swamp same day he took her. She could be dead already. Or..."

"Well? Or what?"

"Or, hell, Pinkie, think about it. If she's been shacking up with Basile for almost a week, maybe she's...you know...She could be making it so *interesting* for him, he doesn't care about revenge anymore. Either that or he's getting his revenge in another way."

Pinkie's eyes went dangerously cold and blank. "So your theory is that either my wife is dead, or she's fucking her brains out with Basile?"

Bardo spread his arms eloquently. "You know broads. They're kinda like dogs. Long as you feed them, and pet them once in a while, they love you. Why do you think they're called bitches?"

"I've never thought about it."

Bardo didn't seem to notice that his boss was holding his temper under rigid control. Unwisely, he continued. "I've got a real bad feeling about this. It's been bad business from the beginning. Everything has worked against us."

"You're beating around the bush. What's on your mind?"

Bardo slipped his hand into his pocket, jingled change. Rolled his shoulders arrogantly. "I'm out, Pinkie."

"Like hell you are."

"Look, I'm not getting myself killed, especially over a piece of ass I never even got to have."

Pinkie, seeing red, lunged forward and grabbed Bardo by his two-thousand-dollar lapels. Remy probably deserved the insult, but he sure as hell didn't. No one resigned from his service simply because he wanted to. Where did Wayne Bardo get the unmitigated gall to think he could?

"You'll do what I tell you to, or I'll put a bug in Littrell's ear about the life and times of Wayne Bardo."

"You're my lawyer. You can't tell the D.A. shit without having yourself disbarred."

"True," Pinkie conceded in the soft voice he used in the courtroom to ask a question he knew was going to discredit a witness. One local journalist, an admirer, had dubbed it the velvet hammer.

"I can't betray privileged information, but I can get someone else to do it for me. Any number of someones would grant me that favor in a heartbeat. Before you could blink. And if that happens, you'll go down, Wayne. No pussy where they'd stick you. They'll strip you of your jewelry, your nice car, and all your pretty clothes. They'll lock you away so deep, you'll be doing good to get a shit, a shave, and a shower once a month."

Without giving Bardo time to make a rebuttal, he stepped closer, thrusting his nose inches from Bardo's. "This bad business, as you call it, won't be finished until Basile is dead. Are we clear on that?"

He decided to keep his plans for Remy to himself. Bardo certainly wasn't squeamish when it came to killing women, but Pinkie didn't want to whet his appetite too soon.

"In the meantime, I've got another chore for you." Pinkie released him, smoothed down the lapels, then slapped Bardo's cheek affectionately. "But you're going to relish this one."

* * *

"Pinkie refused to marry me in the Church. If the Church doesn't recognize our marriage, neither can I." In a whisper, Remy added, "Which I suppose makes me the whore you accused me of being."

Basile stroked her cheek. "You're not a whore."

They held each other tightly, a tinge of desperation in their passion. He had released her only long enough to get up and remove his clothes. She rubbed her cheek against his hairy bare chest. "What's going to happen to us, Basile?"

His name came naturally to her lips, and that made him smile. But her question was sobering. He sighed. "I don't know."

"You must let me go. I have to go back."

He shook his head.

"But—"

Angling his head back, he looked down at her. "No." Then he kissed her possessively.

When they finally broke apart, she asked him about his marriage to Barbara. "What caused it to break up?"

"I couldn't make her happy."

"Did she make you happy?"

"No, she didn't," he said, realizing for the first time that their unhappiness hadn't been entirely a failure on his part. Barbara hadn't gone out of her way to fulfill him, either. "We settled for a workable relationship. I guess most people do."

"But they shouldn't have to."

"No, they shouldn't have to." He studied her closely for a moment, touching the individual features of her face. "If you could do or be anything, what would it be?"

"You mean if Pinkie's charity hadn't had any strings attached?" He nodded. "I'd work in an art gallery," she said without hesitation. "I've studied the masters and I know a lot about contemporary artists. I'd be very good."

"I'm sure you would," he said, meaning it.

She stacked her hands beneath her cheek on the pillow, her expression and voice wistful. "What would have happened if we'd met in another time and place, under ordinary circumstances? Let's pretend I was working in one of the upscale galleries on Royal Street, and you wandered in and saw me."

"In the first place, I couldn't afford to even darken the door of any of the galleries on Royal Street."

"This is make-believe, Basile. Anything can happen."

"Okay. I walk in and see you, right?" She nodded. "Well, after tripping over my tongue, I probably would try and work up enough courage to speak to you."

She laughed. "You would engage me in conversation. That's good. Then what?"

"Then nothing. You'd see right off that I was a hopeless ignoramus."

"Why?"

"I could probably point out the *Mona Lisa* in a lineup, but that's about the extent of my knowledge of art. You'd run me out of the joint."

"I doubt that." She smiled shyly, confessing softly, "Father Kevin certainly left a lasting impression on me."

"That dour priest?" he scoffed.

"He was rather intense, yes, but I thought about him a lot."

"What did you think when you thought about him?"

"Wicked things."

"Naw."

"Um-huh. I thought that he would be a temptation to every woman in his parish."

"Come on."

"It's true," she averred. "I thought that he was far too attractive to be holy."

"I'm not holy."

"But I didn't know that at the time. I thought he had incredible sex appeal."

"Really?"

"Yes. And that was before I knew he had freckles on his shoulders."

He laughed, enjoying her attention, her flirting. "No I don't."

Laughing with him, she said, "Yes you do."

They spent the next several hours nuzzling and kissing and exploring each other's bodies with the sweet curiosity reserved for new lovers, delighting over each discovery.

They bought into the fantasy that they had met at another time and place, and that they were free to laugh and indulge themselves for the sheer pleasure of it. They teased lavishly, but there were also long stretches of time when they did nothing except gaze at each other.

"You're so beautiful," he said at one point. "I can't believe I'm with you like this."

"I like your face," she whispered back. "It's very honest, but..."

"But what?"

"It's very dark behind your eyes, Basile." She stared

into them. "What do you keep hidden back there in the dark?"

"All my sins and shortcomings."

"There can't be that many."

"You'd be surprised. Or maybe you wouldn't," he added with a soft laugh.

She traced his lips with her fingertip. "You smile here, but not with your eyes. Why is that? What's made you so unhappy?"

It was unnerving that she could read him so well, but at the same time he was touched by her ability to do so, and by her desire to know the whole man. He wanted to tell her how much her caring meant to him.

"Remy..." He searched her face, the depths of her eyes, and words failed him. So he kissed her instead, and held her close and reluctantly told her that they probably should try to get some sleep.

He turned her to face away from him, but placed his arm across her waist and drew her against him, fitting her butt into the curve of his belly. He had honestly thought that that intimacy would be sufficient. But it took very little for him to become inflamed again.

Soon his erection was probing her cleft. He reached for her breast and stroked the nipple to full hardness. Kissing the back of her neck, he pushed his hips forward, found her soft and open, pressed, and murmured her name when her wet heat surrounded him again.

He began to thrust into her, and was almost lost in the rhythm when a small sound from her yanked him from the erotic daze.

He disengaged himself and turned her onto her back. She was crying. He wiped the tears off her cheeks. "I'm sorry, Remy. I'll stop. It's okay."

"I didn't want you to stop."

He swallowed hard. "Then what?"

She took his face between her hands. "You know what my life with Pinkie has been like. You know why he took me for his own, and what he made of me, and what I've been to him all these years."

There was no mistaking her meaning. He nodded somberly.

"I've performed for him on command," she said, insistent that he understand.

"I know that."

She drew in a shuddering breath. "And you still want me?"

"Want you?" he repeated with dismay. "*Want* you?"

He covered her and entered her again, all in one fluid motion. Sliding his fingers up through her hair, he held her head in place while speaking to her in a low, urgent voice.

"I may die before this thing is finished. Or I may spend the rest of my life behind bars. In either case, it's okay."

Subtly he pressed himself deeper inside her. "But I couldn't stand you going back to him. Anything but that I deserve and I'm willing to accept." He squeezed his eyes tightly shut and pressed his forehead against hers. "But you can't go back to Duvall. You can't. Anything, anything but that."

Chapter
Thirty-Nine

Mr. Duvall?"

"Who's this?"

"Doug Patout. Your wife's been found."

Roman had brought the cordless telephone to Pinkie, who was having breakfast at the dining table. "Where?" he asked brusquely.

"Dredd's Mercantile. Deputy sheriffs are with her. I'm on my way there now."

"What about Basile?"

He sensed Patout's reluctance to tell him. "He dropped Mrs. Duvall there and took off."

"How is she?"

"According to Mr. Michoud, she's fine. Eager to get home."

"I want Basile found, Patout. I want every goddamn inch of Louisiana searched until he's found and brought to justice."

"I seriously doubt it's justice you're seeking," Patout

said with infuriating placidity. "You never considered it a kidnapping, or you would have had the director of the FBI himself down here searching for your wife. But, if you insist, I'll call the feds in now to question Mrs. Duvall."

Pinkie was gripping the telephone so tightly his knuckles were white. The diamond ring was digging painful rims into his small finger. But he couldn't counter Patout's statements, and he was certain Patout was aware of that.

"May I be frank?" Without waiting for permission, Patout continued: "All indications are that this is a domestic matter. The solution to it doesn't rest with law enforcement authorities, but with you and your wife. And perhaps Basile. I suggest you work it out among yourselves."

Later, Pinkie wasn't sure how he'd managed to control his temper, but it had taken tremendous restraint. Patout's sanctimonious remarks tested it to the limit.

"Thank you for the advice, Patout, but I don't need any lessons from you on how to handle my *wife*. You'd like to think the matter is closed, wouldn't you? You'd like to tie it up in a neat bow and consider it over and done with. Because through this whole ordeal, you've protected your boy, Basile, and you'd be relieved if he came through it without too many dents and dings."

Constantly paranoid that his telephones were bugged, Pinkie was too smart to outline his plans for Basile via fiber optics. He'd already told Patout, perhaps ill-advisedly, that he planned to eliminate the former narc. He saw no reason to reiterate those plans now.

He did, however, want Patout to know that his attitude and lack of cooperation would be remembered. "You can kiss goodbye your ambitions for the number-one spot in the NOPD, Patout. From this minute forward, enemies are going to be charging you from all sides. You can count on it."

To Patout's credit, he kept his cool. "I've dispatched a police helicopter to take me to Jefferson Parish. I'll personally escort Mrs. Duvall home. We should arrive in a couple of hours." Then the cordless phone went dead in Pinkie's hand.

Roman approached, asking tentatively, "Is Mrs. Duvall returning home today, sir?"

"That's right, Roman."

"Praise Jesus."

"Hmm. Yes." Deep in thought, Pinkie rapidly drummed his fingers on the tablecloth. After a moment, he looked up at the butler and smiled. "I think this calls for a blowout celebration, don't you?"

"Then you haven't forgotten, sir, that today is Mardi Gras? Our last day to party for a while."

"No, Roman, I hadn't forgotten. I've just been preoccupied. I had every intention of hosting a party. Here. Tonight. Will you see to it that preparations are made?"

"Already done, sir."

Roman rushed out to share the happy news with the rest of the staff. Pinkie punched in Bardo's telephone number. "Remy's been found."

"Where?"

"I'll give you the details later. Patout is delivering her."

"Basile?"

"Presently unaccounted for."

"So what do you want me to do now?"

"What we discussed last night."

"Even though Mrs. Duvall is coming home?"

Pinkie stared at the empty dining chair in which Remy

usually sat. "Especially since Mrs. Duvall is coming home."

* * *

Sister Beatrice's lips were pursed with stern disapproval. "This is highly irregular."

"Yeah, well, it might be irregular, but that's what Mr. Duvall wants." Wayne Bardo's arrogance communicated that he wasn't impressed either by her nun's habit or her reverent base of operation. Far as he was concerned, she was just another broad giving him a hassle. He could go over, around, or through her, but she wasn't going to keep him from doing what Duvall was paying him to do.

"I'm calling Mr. Duvall and speaking with him personally."

"Fine. You do that, Sister."

Bardo slid her telephone across her desk toward her, then, with a notable lack of respect, sat down without an invitation to do so and propped his ankle on his opposite knee. He whistled tunelessly through his teeth as she placed a call to the Duvall residence.

"Mr. Duvall, please. This is Sister Beatrice at the Blessed Heart Academy. It's imperative that I speak with him."

Smirking, Wayne Bardo listened to her side of the conversation as she verified that Duvall had sent him to the school to pick up his sister-in-law.

"And Mrs. Duvall approves of these arrangements?" she asked. After a moment, she murmured, "I see. Very well, Mr. Duvall. Forgive me for troubling you, but please understand that I'm concerned for Flarra's safety." At that, she glared at Bardo, who flashed her his most beguiling smile.

When she hung up, he said, "Everything cool?"

"Yes, everything's cool."

She was so cool she was downright icy as she stood and rounded her desk, her traditional habit rustling and her rosary beads clacking. "I'll notify Flarra to gather her things. She'll be with you shortly."

"Shortly" turned out to be twenty minutes. By that time, the place was beginning to get on Bardo's nerves, what with the painting of a bloody, crucified Christ staring at him with soulful eyes that seemed to follow him as he meandered around her office. Saints and angels floating around on pink clouds condemned him from their ornate gilt frames. He could swear the statue of some soldier saint standing in the corner raised his righteous sword against him. All that religious shit was enough to give anybody the creeps.

By the time the office door opened behind him, he was a bundle of jitters. Spinning around, he exclaimed, "Jeez Louise!"

The mild profanity caused Sister What's-her-name's lips to pucker up even tighter, but Bardo couldn't help himself. Pinkie had promised that, in addition to being well compensated for this assignment, he was going to enjoy it.

What an understatement! He was fucking going to love it! In a nanosecond, he thought of a dozen different depravities to ply on baby sister Flarra.

Her cheeks were flushed with excitement as she came across the room toward him, her right hand extended. "Hello, Mr. Bardo. A pleasure."

"Likewise, Miss Lambeth." It was probably the first

time in his life he'd ever shaken hands with a woman, but he welcomed the opportunity to touch this creature who was almost too hot to be believed.

"Is it true what Sister Beatrice told me? Am I really getting to attend the Mardi Gras party tonight?"

"True as can be. Mr. Duvall thinks you've been cooped up in here long enough. No offense, Sister," he said, addressing the nun over Flarra's shoulder. "Your brother-in-law wants you to live it up tonight. He said he considered this your coming-out party."

"And Remy's okay with it?"

"Yeah. She wants you to be there tonight. In fact, she personally picked out your costume."

Placing a hand on her chest, from which jutted two pert tits, she gasped giddily. "They're really letting me go! I can't believe it!"

Bardo picked up her suitcase and offered her his arm. "Believe it, sweetheart."

* * *

Pinkie was waiting for them at the front door. He opened it before Patout rang the bell. Even at this point in time, there was a sliver of a chance that he would reverse the plans he had already in place, and that he and Remy would carry on as though nothing had happened.

But even that slim possibility died the instant he looked into her eyes. Because, although she gave him a weak smile and spoke his name in a tremulous voice as she came into his arms, he knew that Basile had had her.

The son of a bitch might just as well have poisoned his prizewinning orchids, or pissed into a bottle of Château Lafite Rothschild. Remy had been defiled. The glorious girl he'd cultivated into a perfect courtesan was ruined for him now.

Hiding his repugnance, he pulled her against him. "My darling, thank God you're back. When I think of what you've been through..." He stopped, pretending to choke up with emotion. "Were you harmed in any way?"

He listened as she described the bird shot she'd taken in the back when they fled the Crossroads. "But those wounds have begun to heal. I'm just very tired."

"Basile didn't..."

Lying, she shook her head. "He wanted to make his point with you, Pinkie. That's all. He didn't mistreat me."

Doug Patout, who'd been standing in the background so as not to interfere with their reunion, now stepped forward. "Mrs. Duvall was reluctant to discuss her ordeal on the way here. But now I'd like to hear her version of what happened and ask her some pertinent questions, if you don't mind."

"I do mind," Pinkie said curtly. "You reminded me earlier today that this is a private matter. I believe you're right." He closed the door in Patout's face.

"Mr. Patout is afraid that you're planning a reprisal against Basile," Remy said as he motioned her upstairs. "You're not, are you, Pinkie?"

He merely smiled and patted her arm solicitously. Upstairs in their bedroom, Roman brought her a plate of food, but she left it on the tray, untouched. When they were again alone, Pinkie asked her more specific questions about her abduction.

"I'd like to see this fishing shack where he kept you. Could you lead me to it?"

"I'm afraid not. All parts of the swamp look the same to me."

"Why'd he let you go?"

"I don't know," she said thickly. "He got me up very early this morning and announced that he was releasing me. All along, he said he was using me as bait to draw you out, and that he didn't care how long it took.

"He offered no explanation for his sudden change of heart, except it had something to do with a policeman who was killed yesterday. And Dredd. He didn't want Dredd, or Patout, or any of his former colleagues affected by his criminal actions. He said it was time to call it off, before anyone else got hurt or killed."

"He should have thought of that before he started this. It's too late now."

"What do you mean?"

"Never mind. Did you ever try and escape?"

"Of course!" she exclaimed. She told him about her near-drowning experience. "After that, he kept me handcuffed." Raising those incredibly expressive eyes to his, she laid her hand on his arm, gripping it hard. "But I'm safely back with you and that's all that matters. I look upon it as a bad dream that'll soon be forgotten."

She slipped her arms around his neck. "Pinkie, please listen to what Mr. Patout says. Don't perpetuate this feud with Basile. It would be pointless. He only wanted to shake you up, and now that he has, that's the last we'll see or hear of him. If Basile can walk away from it, we should be able to. Hmm? Let it go."

He stopped her pleas for her lover's life with a hard kiss, which he ended abruptly. He could tell she was surprised that he ended it. Did the bitch actually expect him to take her to bed? He felt like laughing out loud, in her face, but it wasn't yet time to spring the surprises she had in store.

"Get some sleep," he told her, patting her cheek. "I want you to look your best tonight."

"Tonight?"

"At our party."

"Party?"

"Remy, is that echoing speech pattern something you acquired from Basile?"

"I'm sorry. What party?"

"A Mardi Gras party. Have you forgotten that today is Fat Tuesday? Tomorrow we must atone for our sins, but tonight we can be self-indulgent. I certainly intend to satisfy—"

"I can't attend a party tonight."

"That's another tiresome habit you've picked up," he said, frowning. "Interrupting me while I'm speaking."

She bit back another interruption. After a moment, she said with that soft tremor in her voice, "It's just that I'm flabbergasted that you expect me to host a party on my first night back."

"What better time to celebrate your safe return?"

"I'd rather we celebrate alone."

"That's sweet, my dear, but I'm afraid I can't call off the festivities now. Too many people would be disappointed." He tweaked her cheek. "Including Flarra. I've invited her to participate."

Her face drained of color. She swallowed convulsively, as though to hold back nausea. "Really?" she said with transparently faked excitement. "What made you decide to include her? You never have before."

"I've reconsidered the points you made during our last discussion about her. I think they're valid. It's time we cut her some slack. She is, after all, no longer a child, but a young woman."

"Actually, I was wrong, Pinkie. You were right. You're always right about these things."

He frowned. "Your turnabout comes too late, Remy. I can't disappoint Flarra now that she's already been invited. You wouldn't want me to do that. That would be cruel. Now, you take a nap," he said, coming to his feet. "Maybe it'll put some color back into your cheeks. Forgive me for saying so, but you look a little worse for wear."

"I realize how frightful I must look. My hair and nails are a wreck. I'll arrange to have them done before tonight."

"You can take care of the beauty treatments yourself after your rest." He moved toward the door. "Oh, by the way, I removed the telephone so you wouldn't be disturbed."

She glanced toward the nightstand, and he delighted in the frantic expression that appeared on her face. "I'd like to call Flarra. It's been over a week since I spoke to her, and I'm sure she's wondering why."

"Not to worry. I told her a little white lie about your having strep throat. By now she's been told that you've recovered and that you're looking forward to seeing her this evening."

"But I need to speak with her."

"Tonight will be soon enough. I've instructed the staff to leave you in absolute privacy. I alone will be checking on you throughout the day." He blew her a kiss, then made certain that she saw him locking the door from the outside before he pulled it closed.

* * *

Remy rushed to the door and gripped the knob with both hands. She tried moving it up and down, and from side to side, but it didn't budge. With a sob of frustration, she slumped against the door.

She had trusted in the paradox that she must return to Pinkie before she could successfully escape him. She had known it would take all her acting skills to convince him that she was devastated by her capture, and anxious to put the unpleasant episode behind her and resume her life as it had been. She was willing to continue the charade for as along as it took to get Flarra safely out of Pinkie's grasp, even going so far—God help her—as to share his bed, although she hadn't told Basile that.

But Pinkie hadn't immediately hustled her up to bed, which was uncustomary, and because it was, it was also alarming. There was only one reason he would abstain: if he suspected her of being intimate with Basile. And if he suspected that, then her life, as well as Basile's and Flarra's, was in peril.

Pinkie must have guessed as soon as he kissed her, or even before, that she was coming home to him different than when she left. It must have been instantly obvious to him that she was radically changed. If he could spot a minute imperfection on a blossom of one of his orchids, or detect that the wine was served a degree too warm or too cool, he could sense something as profound as the change she had undergone in the swamp, where she had come to love Burke Basile, in addition to coming to love herself again.

If she lived to be a hundred, or died today, she would be grateful for those days of isolation in that exotic and primal place. She'd been forced to take a good hard look at herself and acknowledge that she had become just what Basile had called her—a whore. She had prostituted herself for the best of reasons, and that was to protect her sister. But everything had been sacrificed to that end—her pride, her self-esteem, her soul. Having wholly given up herself, what good was she to Flarra or to anyone?

She now despised Mrs. Pinkie Duvall, who was passive and afraid, whose only means of survival was through feminine wiles and manipulation. But she had developed a growing respect for Remy Lambeth, whose opinions had merit, who was strong and courageous, who was a survivor, who warranted the love of a man with humanity and integrity.

Basile! He must be alerted that their strategy had backfired. But before she could even place a telephone call, she must get out of this room. She pitched herself into finding a way.

Her mother's john had taught her how to pick most standard locks. But technology in door locks had advanced along with everything else, and Pinkie insisted on having state-of-the-art everything. When the house was renovated a few years earlier, the master bedroom had been made into a safe room, a place to take refuge should intruders penetrate the other security system. On the outside doorjamb was a numerical keypad. One had to know the sequence of numbers in order to unlock it. A key would dismantle it from the inside, but Remy's exhaustive search of the suite, including Pinkie's dressing room, didn't produce it. In desperation she tried manicure scissors, a nail file, a hairpin, but, as she suspected, the lock was too sophisticated for an amateur with makeshift tools.

She considered the windows next. Drawing open the drapes and shutters, she was dismayed to see that the exterior shutters had been closed. Only once before, when there had been warnings of an approaching tropical storm, had they been closed. But now they'd been battened down. Daylight was struggling to leak through.

Not that it mattered. The locks on the windows were ordinary, but the alarm system wasn't. Even if she unlocked a window and opened it, the security alarm would beep intermittently to alert the staff of an interruption in the circuit. Someone would report it to Pinkie.

Dismissing the windows as a means of escape, she paced the rooms, racking her brain for another possible outlet.

Through the air-conditioning ducts? She removed the grill over an air-intake vent. Too small.

Up through the fireplace chimney? Hardly.

She couldn't walk through walls or seep beneath doorways like smoke.

Smoke!

The house was equipped not only with an anti-intrusion security system, but also with smoke and heat sensors, which were linked to the alarm company's monitoring service as well as to the local fire department. Once an alarm went off, fire trucks were dispatched. It was an irrevocable signal; none were considered false alarms. Under no circumstances could the fire trucks be recalled until every sensor in the house was checked by an official.

There was a smoke detector above the door leading into her dressing area. She removed the drawers from the night table, set the lamp on the floor, and dragged the piece of furniture into position.

She lit a scented candle, kicked off her shoes, and scrambled onto the nightstand. Stretching her arm up, she managed to bring the flame to within inches of the detector.

"It won't work, Remy."

Startled, she dropped the lighted candle, which immediately singed a hole in the carpet. Pinkie crossed the floor and stamped out the candle, then looked up at her with censure and amusement.

"You look rather silly, Remy, but I must say I'm impressed by your ingenuity. You've exhibited more sagacity in the last half hour than in all the years I've known you."

In a courtly manner, he extended her his hand to help her down. When she disdainfully ignored it and climbed down from the nightstand on her own, he chuckled. "I wouldn't have overlooked something as elementary as the smoke and fire alarms, my dear, although I confess to being pleasantly surprised that you were clever enough to think of them yourself."

"I've always been smarter than you gave me credit for, Pinkie."

"You were smart enough to conceal a pregnancy and miscarriage from me, I'll concede that. Surprised, Remy? Dr. Caruth was more than willing to confide everything when I presented her with some rather compromising snapshots of her and her lover, who, coincidentally, is her nurse. Her female nurse.

"While I'm tolerant of the sexual preferences of others," he continued mildly, "I think it's safe to assume that the society mavens who smugly tout Dr. Caruth over any of her male colleagues would be aghast to learn about her private life. Even if they suspect such, they would rather their suspicions not be confirmed, which would, of course, necessitate their boycotting her.

"Now, what were we talking about? Oh, yes, your IQ. Intelligence is wasted on women like you, Remy. I'd venture to say that even Basile agrees. I seriously doubt that he engaged you in stimulating conversation before he fucked you. And he did fuck you, didn't he?"

"He made love to me," she said defiantly. "For the first time in my life, I made love with a man."

He backhanded her across the face, her cheekbone catching most of the thrust. She reeled from the impact and the blinding pain. Her knees buckled. She went down.

"You're a cunt, Remy. That's all you ever were, and that's all you'll ever be because that's what spawned you. You may have romanticized the time you spent alone with Basile, cozy in your little cabin, just the two of you in the wilderness. But don't delude yourself. Basile is a man, and all men recognize you exactly for what you are. He fucked you, but only to insult me. Now, where is he?"

"I don't know."

He kicked her in the kidney. She almost fainted from the pain, but she clung to consciousness and staved off the waves of nausea.

"Where is he?"

"He dropped me off at Dredd's. Then he left."

"By boat or car?"

"Boat." Her tears were genuine as she recalled those last few moments they'd been together, both wishing there were another way out of their dilemma. "I didn't want to be left behind, but—"

Pinkie's snicker interrupted her. "Just as I told you, Remy. Basile had got what he wanted from you, while you, poor dear, wound up with a broken heart."

She glared up at him. "You can't keep me locked in this room indefinitely, Pinkie. Sooner or later, some way or another, I'll get out."

"Remy, by the time this night is over, you won't care

whether or not you leave this room. You'll be totally indifferent to what happens to you."

"What do you intend to do, keep hitting me until I'd just as soon die as go on living?" She raised her head to a proud angle. "You can try, Pinkie. But you'll be surprised by how resilient I've become. You no longer have the power to hurt me. I'm not what you say I am. I know that now. Your insults are wasted on me. I'm immune to them."

"Love has made you strong?" he taunted.

"That's right."

"Really? Brave talk, Remy. But let's see how courageous you are after something that you value is tainted by someone whom you detest."

Remy's chest seemed to crack around the sob that rose out of it. "Don't touch her."

"Ah, so you've guessed. Sweet Flarra." He kissed his fingertips. "So ripe, so eager to experience life."

Remy gripped the edge of the nightstand and pulled herself to her feet, then she lunged at him, her fingers going for his eyes. He knocked her away, slinging her down onto the bed.

"The girl is practically bursting with vitality, isn't she?" he said pleasantly, as though they were discussing the merits of a race horse. "She blatantly declares her sexuality. It crackles around her like electricity. She's got more potential for pleasing a man than even you, Remy. How exciting it'll be for the man who takes her for the first time."

Remy slid off the bed. On her knees, she walked toward him and threw her arms around his thighs, begging him hoarsely, "Please, Pinkie, don't hurt her. I beg you. I'll do anything you say. Anything."

She clutched him tighter, using his clothing for hand-holds as she climbed him, pulling herself to her feet. Then she kissed him and caressed him through his trousers. "Do anything with me, but don't harm her."

He avoided her kisses and pushed her hands away. "Stop it, Remy."

"Please, Pinkie," she sobbed. "Please, don't touch her."

"I don't intend to, darling. Are you under the misconception that I'll replace you in my bed with Flarra? Not at all." He reached out and stroked her cheek. "I've given her as a present. To Bardo."

For several seconds after he left, relocking the door from the outside, Remy stood as though nailed to the floor, swaying slightly from his last verbal blow. *Bardo. With Flarra.*

She crossed her arms over her stomach, and bent forward. She stifled a keening sound by biting her lower lip. Then she whispered an earnest prayer of thanksgiving to God for giving her one last chance to save the situation.

Uncurling her fingers, she stared at the key lying in her palm—the key she'd picked from Pinkie's pocket while pretending to beg his mercy.

Chapter Forty

don't get it. Why aren't I going straight to Remy's house?"

The girl's naïveté was as much a turn-on as mental visions of her out of the school uniform. Seductive, sweet-smelling Flarra was going to be the best time he'd had in a long while. It was all he could do to keep from licking his chops in anticipation of things to come.

"The house is in an uproar," Bardo said by way of explanation. "They're decorating for the party. Workers so thick you can't stir them with a stick. So your sister asked me to bring you here, where you can get dressed in peace and quiet."

"That seems an odd thing for Remy to do, especially when it's been more than a week since I've seen her. Maybe I should call her."

Bardo sensed her wariness as he led her down the breezeway of the motel toward the room in which he was already registered. He'd thought about reserving a room in a swank hotel but changed his mind. Why waste the money on amenities like room service and scented soap when the outcome of this afternoon was a foregone conclusion?

Besides, if Flarra created a ruckus, it was more likely to be ignored in a place where, with no questions asked, you could sign in as Mickey Mouse so long as you paid cash in advance.

Hoping to allay her apprehension at least until he got her inside the room, he sighed. "I wasn't supposed to tell you, but you leave me no choice."

"Tell me what?"

"They're planning a big surprise for you. Something real special. That's why they told me to keep you away from the house till they're ready."

"Really?" she squealed, flashing him a thousand-watt smile. "What could it be, I wonder."

"I know, but I'm sworn to secrecy."

"Give me a hint. Please, Mr. Bardo?"

"Nothing doing. Both the boss and Mrs. Duvall would skin me alive if I gave away their surprise. I've told you too much already. You've got to promise to act surprised."

"I promise."

He unlocked the door of the room and ushered her inside. The box containing her costume was tucked under his arm. Leave it to Pinkie not to overlook a single detail. As soon as they got to the car, Flarra had lifted the top of the box and taken a peek inside, but had refrained from tearing off the lid and plowing through the tissue paper. When he asked what she was waiting for, she had told him she wanted to savor the anticipation.

But as soon as they were inside the room, she grabbed the box and set it on the bed. "I can't wait any longer!"

She tossed the lid aside and separated the folds of pastel tissue, then a long, rapturous "ahhhh" escaped her as she gazed down at the shimmery, sheer fabric studded with sparkling stones and colored crystals. She even folded her hands beneath her chin like a little girl saying grace at suppertime.

"It's almost too beautiful to touch. What is it?"

"Take it out and see."

She lifted the two garments from the box as though handling holy relics, although there was certainly nothing sacred about the costume. The brassiere was two stone-studded, glittering cones held together by flesh-colored strings. The bottom half was a pair of harem pants with a similarly jeweled bikini. The legs were sheer and banded at the ankles with rows of stones. Also in the box were a pillbox hat with veil attached, and a pair of gold leather slippers with bells on the toes.

Her reaction was a wide-eyed mix of delight and dubiety. "Are you sure this is for me? Maybe you picked up the wrong box."

"Don't you like it?"

"Oh, yes. Very much. It's gorgeous," she said in a gush of breath. "It's just sort of skimpy."

"You think so? Why don't you try it on? Then if you don't like it, you'll have time to exchange it for something else." He looked her up and down critically, drawing his brows into a steep frown. "You know, you may be right. It does seem a little too risqué for a girl your age."

The reverse psychology worked like abra-ca-fucking-dabra. Nose in the air, she snatched up the costume and headed for the bathroom, closing the door firmly behind her and locking it. Bardo chuckled. Women were so damned predictable; was it any wonder men had to invent new ways to amuse themselves with them? Old, young, beautiful, ugly, skinny, fat, white, black, or any other color, what woman, having been insulted, even mildly, wouldn't want to prove him wrong? Now Flarra couldn't wait to show him how mature and sophisticated and daring she was.

He drew the drapes on the window and checked to see that the door was latched and the chain lock secure. Then he sat down on the edge of the bed to wait and to savor his own anticipation.

But when she didn't reappear after a full ten minutes, his patience began to wear thin. "Flarra? Need any help? Is everything all right?"

"No. I mean, no I don't need any help. And, yes, everything's all right. I guess."

"Doesn't it fit?"

"Hmm."

"Well, let's see it."

After a few moments' hesitation, the bathroom door opened. Bardo's gut clenched with expectancy, but even a connoisseur of women like him wasn't prepared for the living fantasy that stepped across the threshold in slippers that jingled when she moved. The veil covering her nose and mouth only emphasized the charming modesty with which she gazed back at him. Her breasts were barely contained within the small cups of the bra.

"I don't think my sister realized how brief it is," she said, self-consciously moving her hand down her exposed belly. One less sequin and he could have seen pubic hair. "Do you think it's okay?"

"Oh, yeah." It seemed his tongue was stuck to the roof of his mouth. "I think you look great."

"Honest?"

He stood and walked toward her. "Honest. In fact, you look good enough to eat."

His smile must not have been very trustworthy because she laughed nervously and took a step backward. "Thanks." She turned away. "I think I'll change back into my clothes until it's time to dress for the party."

He caught her hand and brought her back around. "It's time, sweetheart. *This* is the party."

He ripped off the hat and veil, then stamped his mouth over her lips, which had parted with alarm. Pushing his tongue into her mouth, he curved his arm around her bare waist and pulled her against him, grinding his pelvis into hers. She struggled, which only tantalized him. She even struck his face, which provided him an excuse to hold her tighter and to wrestle with her until he had her arm behind her and pressed up between her shoulder blades.

"What are you doing? Stop!" she cried. "That hurts."

Lowering his head, he bit her breast where it swelled out of the bra cup. She screamed.

"Shut up." He squeezed her jaw painfully between his fingers and thumb. "You do that again, and I really will hurt you, understand?" She began to cry, and her tears only intensified his lust. He loved it when they cried either out of fear or pain.

"If you hurt me, Pinkie will kill you."

He laughed. "Yeah, sure he will, sweetheart."

"What are you going to do?"

"Now what do you think?" he purred, sliding his hand between her thighs and squeezing.

She shuddered in what he knew to be revulsion. To him, it was as good as a shiver of ecstasy.

"Th-they know you have me," she stammered. "They'll come looking for me."

"Haven't you caught on yet, honey? Your brother-in-law arranged this little party."

"You're lying. Pinkie would never—"

"But he has. You'll have him to thank for all the fun we're going to have together."

"My sister—"

"Has problems of her own. She won't be worrying about you."

The reality of her situation finally seemed to sink in. She cried even harder. Bardo licked the tears off her face. "Relax, sweetheart. Do everything I tell you, and, who knows, you might become as good a whore as your mama. Yeah, I know all about Angel. You were born to it. You've got the potential to become a terrific whore."

"Please don't," she sobbed, trying to wriggle free.

He took a switchblade from his pants pocket. It sprang open with a vicious click, which caused her to scream again. He placed the tip of the blade against her lower lip.

"You use it, you lose it. Got that? One more scream and off it comes. And that would be a damn shame because I got ideas about what you're going to do with that sweet mouth of yours."

He slid the blade beneath the shoulder strap of the bra and cut it. With the tension released, the cup fell forward, revealing her breast. She whimpered and her lower lip quivered uncontrollably, but she didn't scream again. He cut the second strap in the same brutal manner. "Look at what we have here," he cooed. This time he pressed the tip of the blade against her nipple. He tapped it lightly and it tightened.

"Shame, shame," he taunted. "A nice Catholic school-girl like you. What would Sister What's-her-name say?"

Behind Bardo the door crashed open. "Drop the knife and get away from her!"

* * *

Burke Basile was in a crouched stance, both hands wrapped around a Beretta. The next millisecond passed in a blur. His ears rang with the girl's scream. He fired at Bardo, but the lucky bastard ducked the shot. The bullet missed his head and decimated a patch of ugly floral wallpaper behind him. Burke didn't fire again out of fear of hitting the girl. He shouted, "You're under arrest, Bardo."

"And you're real funny, Basile," Bardo yelled back as he threw his knife.

"Har-dee-har-har, asshole," said the sharpshooter who materialized behind Basile.

Bardo had an instant to look stupefied before a bullet cut a neat trench between his eyes. He dropped without a whimper. The handle of his switchblade was still vibrating in the doorjamb, having missed Basile by a hair.

Tactical officers eddied around Basile as they rushed into the room. Basile rushed over to the girl, who was staring in horror at the bloody mush that had been Bardo's head only a few seconds before. Basile removed his coat and placed it around her shoulders. "Are you all right?" She regarded him with the same stupefaction as she did the corpse. He had to repeat the question before she nodded with uncertainty.

One of the men detached himself from the others. "We'll handle it from here, Basile."

Basile shook hands with him. "Thanks. Your men did good, from the surveillance to that," he said, indicating Bardo's body.

The officer saluted him.

Basile grabbed the girl's hand and pulled her through the doorway and along the breezeway. When they reached the parking lot, which was filling up with official vehicles, Basile pushed her into the passenger seat of an unmarked car, then jogged around the hood and got behind the wheel. Tires squealed as he sped past an arriving ambulance.

They'd only covered half a block when the girl swore. "Jesus H.! What took you so fucking long? That son of a bitch was creepy as hell. And how dare he tell me I had the potential of being a terrific whore!"

Vexed, Ruby Bouchereaux's most talented girl, Isobel, reached up and pulled off the curly black wig.

Chapter Forty-One

Looking younger than her years, Isobel was also smart, and she possessed a spirit of adventure. Her specialty at Ruby's house was acting out fantasies for the clients who could afford it. The combination of those qualities had made her a perfect choice to portray Flarra Lambeth in Burke Basile's setup.

Of course, she'd also been paid very well for her time and trouble. After presenting her with a sizable check, Basile and the prostitute parted company at the door of Ruby's office. He was in a hurry, but it would have been rude to decline the madam's offer of a drink after she had been instrumental in trapping Bardo.

"So, everything went according to plan?" Ruby asked, extending Burke a glass of whiskey.

"Perfect." He slammed back the drink. "I listened from Sister Beatrice's outer office. Even I was convinced that Isobel was an innocent schoolgirl."

"And so she was, way back when," Ruby said, laughing

softly. "But I'm pleased that the ruse worked. You know your enemies well, Mr. Basile."

He watched the whiskey tumbling from decanter to waiting glass as Ruby poured him a refill. "Remy was positive that Pinkie would try and get to her through her sister, and she was right, although we weren't relying entirely on her gut instinct. Bardo had been under surveillance. His conversation with Duvall was intercepted this morning, so we knew he was picking up Flarra and for what purpose."

"The man needed to die."

"I couldn't agree with you more," Burke said grimly. "Isobel and I arrived at Blessed Heart no more than half an hour ahead of him. When she and Bardo left the academy, the van followed them to the motel. It went off without a hitch, although Isobel blistered my ears for letting it go so long before stopping it."

"Where is Flarra now?"

"Under police protection. *Incorruptible* police protection."

"And Bardo is dead?"

"Definitely," Burke said quietly, then downed his second drink.

"Too bad you didn't bring me his ear, or some other appendage. I would have liked a souvenir." The madam raised her glass to Basile, then drank her shot.

"Thank you for lending us Isobel," he told her. "Once again, I'm indebted to you."

"Nonsense. Bardo's death evened our score. Besides, I owe you for another favor. You sent me Dixie, who I think will be a profitable addition to the house."

He smiled. "I figured the two of you would hit it off, but I hate that she waited until Bardo beat her up before coming here."

"She's making a nice recovery." She offered him another round, but he shook his head. "You've earned my gratitude, Mr. Basile, as well as the hospitality of the house whenever you wish to use it."

"Thank you, but I doubt I'll ever cash in that marker."

The madam practically purred. "You and Mrs. Duvall?"

"Remy," he corrected.

The hardest thing he'd ever had to do was leave her that morning. They had talked long into the night, holding each other, making love, and assessing what had seemed a hopeless situation.

With morning came the ugly realization that, for a time, she must be returned to Duvall. She was easier with the plan than Burke, who had vowed that she would never darken the doorway of Duvall's house again. "I won't let you go back. Not for an afternoon. Not for an hour."

But even as he said that, he knew it was their only viable option.

"I don't look forward to it, but I'll handle it," she had told him. "Maybe I couldn't have or wouldn't have a week ago. But now I can and will. Just see to Flarra, and please, please, take care of yourself."

They had continued to cling to one another until Dredd intervened, warning them that timing was critical to Basile's plan, and that they were liable to blow it if they didn't get a move on. So Burke had placed her in Dredd's safekeeping until Patout arrived.

Burke had figured District Attorney Littrell for a basically honest man who was up against overwhelming odds to keep the NOPD from living up to its national reputation as one of the most corrupt law enforcement agencies in the country.

Littrell held a lower opinion of Lieutenant Burke Basile because it had been colored by negative publicity, hearsay, and malicious gossip. So when Burke barged unannounced into his office, the D.A. was at first taken aback and threatened to have Burke evicted from the building.

But Burke's fast talking soon got Littrell's attention. He listened with mounting dismay to everything Burke told him. With a politician's characteristic caution, however, he made no promises other than to look into the matter and get back to Burke in due course.

At which point Burke had picked up the telephone on the D.A.'s desk and brandished it like an evangelist with the Holy Bible. "Either you call the A.G., or I'm going to call him myself. Either way, doesn't matter to me. This is merely a courtesy call on you, Mr. Littrell. I'm giving you a chance to prove which side of this corruption you're on."

Littrell had placed a call to the state attorney general. With his sanction, things had come together with headspinning haste. As a result of quick action, coordination, and luck, Bardo was dead.

Burke stood and shook hands with Ruby Bouchereaux. "Thank you for the drink, and forgive me for rushing off, but I'm hoping to be in on Duvall's arrest."

"Tonight? Oh, I seriously doubt he'll be arrested tonight, Mr. Basile."

"Why?"

"It's Mardi Gras."

"So?"

"So, the only news coming from Duvall headquarters is about the costume party he's hosting. In fact, a few of the gentlemen who've joined our party here came straight from Pinkie's house, where the party is already in full swing. From what they've said, it's quite a blowout."

Burke stared at her as the frightening implications of this development began to sink in. He checked his pager. It was on; no indication of a low battery. Remy hadn't called it, which was to be his signal that something had gone terribly wrong.

He asked permission to use Ruby's phone. "This is Basile," he said as soon as his call was answered. "Do we have Duvall yet?"

He was patched through to three different desks until one brave soul finally broke the shattering news to him. "Arresting a celebrity citizen like Duvall is a tricky undertaking, especially if you're trying to maintain secrecy. There are miles of red tape involved. We want to do it by the book so it doesn't result in a mistrial. It might take days—"

"Days!" Burke shouted. "Are you fucking crazy?"

"We're doing the best we can, Mr. Basile. And shouting obscenities at me—"

"Lives are in danger, you idiot."

"We might be able to pull it off tonight, but—"

"Stay on it, you hear me. You get that warrant issued and served tonight, or I'll have Littrell and the A.G. on your ass, and then I'll personally come down there and stamp the shit out of you."

He slammed the receiver down. "I gotta get over there." *Days*. Remy couldn't stay with Duvall for days while the bureaucrats sorted through the paperwork. As soon as he heard about Bardo, Duvall would go on red alert. He thought Bardo was locked away in a motel, deflowering his sister-in-law. When he learned differently, he would start piecing it together and eventually come around to Remy.

"Mr. Basile," the madam said, catching his sleeve as he rushed past her on his way out, "you'll be very conspicuous gate-crashing Pinkie Duvall's party dressed like that. Would you care to borrow a costume?"

Burke didn't have a moment to waste, but he saw the advisability of taking the time for her to locate him a costume. He paced her office, cursing the system that had once again let him down, and at the same time thanking it.

The delay uptown gave him an opportunity to do one better than arrest Duvall.

It gave him a chance to kill the bastard.

* * *

The pain in Remy's back had receded to a dull ache. A bruise was beginning to appear on her cheekbone, but the swelling was minimal. These aches and pains she could tolerate. What she couldn't abide was the thought of her sister being abused by Bardo.

Burke had sworn to see to Flarra's safety first, even before arresting Pinkie. He would keep that promise if he could. But what if, in spite of his valiant attempts, he'd failed? She had. Pinkie had readily seen through her pretense. Maybe Burke had had no better success than she. Maybe he'd been unable to persuade the district attorney and the attorney general to act swiftly.

Because she didn't know otherwise, she had to assume that he'd failed, which meant that saving Flarra still rested with her. A telephone. That's all she needed. She had met the first challenge of figuring a way out of the master bedroom—she now had a key. The next step was finding an available telephone.

As soon as she felt it was safe to try the key, she did

so. The lock slid open with hardly a click. She paused, waiting, her heart pounding in her ears, but when nothing happened, she pulled open the door.

The hallway was clear. She immediately checked the foyer table at the top of the stairs where there was usually a telephone, but, of course, her husband hadn't overlooked that detail.

She crept along the corridor until she reached the top of the stairs. Before stepping onto the landing, she paused to consider what she would do if she were confronted by one of the house staff. Their loyalty lay with Pinkie, not her, because all of them were former clients whom Pinkie had saved from years of incarceration, if not death row. None would grant a request from her without clearing it with him first.

Errol? What if she met her bodyguard? Could she persuade or trick him into assisting her? He wasn't terribly bright. Maybe she could manipulate him into sneaking her out. She hadn't forgotten what happened to Lute Duskie, the bodyguard who'd allowed her to escape to Galveston. The thought of duping Errol wasn't very appetizing, but she would do what she had to and try to protect him later.

Bolstering all her courage, she stepped onto the landing.

But that's as far as she got. There was a man posted at the foot of the staircase, but it wasn't Errol.

She ducked back out of sight before he noticed her. Where was Errol? Why had he been replaced? And then, of course, she realized why. He had been derelict in his duties at the Crossroads. Had he paid for that mistake with his life?

Whether he had or not was irrelevant to her present problem. Could the new man be cajoled into helping her, or was he steadfastly loyal to Pinkie? She favored the latter. He was new. He would be eager to impress his boss.

The only advantage she had was in their not knowing that she now could leave the bedroom. And how much longer would she have that luxury? When would Pinkie discover the key missing from his coat pocket? Before he did, she must come up with another plan. Trying not to let this setback defeat her, she tiptoed back to the master suite and locked herself in.

How long had Burke needed to set into motion the juggernaut he claimed would crumble Pinkie's empire? How long before he was arrested? And what was going on with Flarra in the meantime?

If only she knew that Flarra was safe... but she didn't. So she continued to fret until she heard approaching footsteps. She quickly lay down on the bed, drawing her knees to her chest. She stared vacantly into near space, as though she had lost all hope.

Pinkie rushed into the room, and drew up short when he saw her lying there lethargically. Had he missed the key? Had he expected to find her gone? Apparently so, because when he saw her, the wrinkles of worry on his forehead smoothed out and he smiled.

He moved to the bedside and gazed down at her. "Guess who I heard from this afternoon?" Remy didn't respond or even react as though she'd heard him. "Sister Beatrice," he continued in that same pleasant voice. "She called from the academy where Bardo picked up Flarra, ostensibly to escort her to our party. By this time, he has introduced your beloved baby sister to the pleasures of the flesh. By morning, who knows? Sometimes Bardo's passion gets out of hand."

She drew her knees up closer to her body and buried

her face in the pillow. Laughing softly, Pinkie went into his dressing room and locked the door behind himself. Twenty minutes later he came out dressed as Henry VIII.

"You don't seem to be in a very festive mood, Remy. I'll make your excuses to our guests."

He paused on the threshold. "Oh, by the way, it's only a matter of time before we track down your lover, but I've given strict instructions that he's not to be killed until it can be done in your presence, and only then after he's watched you being fucked by all the personnel of the NOPD on my payroll, which, I assure you, is no small number of men and women. That should be quite an evening."

He was obviously deranged. He had lost all touch with reality, believing himself unstoppable and untouchable, the common downfall of egomaniacs, men who gorge on their own power until it, paradoxically, consumes them.

But Remy didn't point this out to him, or argue against his insane delusions, or warn him of the impending collapse of his world. Instead she remained seemingly unaffected by his chilling plans for her and Basile.

But as soon as she heard the door lock behind him, she scrambled off the bed. Inadvertently, Pinkie had given her another idea.

* * *

Bozo the Clown wended his way through the merry-makers.

He declined the glass of champagne offered to him by a masked waiter dressed in cowboy hat, boots, and chaps. On one cheek of the wrangler's bare butt was tattooed a red heart.

No one could touch Pinkie Duvall when it came to hosting a party. There was enough food and liquor to stock an oceangoing vessel for a long cruise. The decorated rooms of his home teemed with merriment and resounded with music and laughter. Masked men and women cavorted with bacchanalian abandon as the clock ticked toward midnight and the end of Fat Tuesday.

King Henry VIII was flirting with a mermaid with gold glitter on her nipples when Bozo spotted him. He moved in their direction and reached the king's side in time to hear him say, "Wiggle your tail for me."

The mermaid playfully swatted his groping hand with her jeweled scepter, then undulated away.

Bozo said, "Great party, Your Royal Highness."

"Thank you," Duvall replied absently, still watching the mermaid.

"I understand you're looking for Burke Basile."

Suddenly the king's eyes connected with the clown's. He peered past the makeup. "Jesus," he hissed. "What—"

"Not here. Unless you want a scene in front of all your friends."

Duvall, turning red beneath his feathered velvet cap, nodded and signaled the clown to follow. They went into Duvall's home study. Bozo closed the door.

"Okay, where is he?" Duvall demanded as he moved toward his desk.

Bozo fired a pistol, striking Duvall in the back just above the kidney. The attorney staggered. A second shot caught him right between his shoulder blades. He fell forward across his desk.

Moving quickly, Doug Patout pulled on a plastic glove over the white cotton one that went with his costume. In his oversized red clown shoes, he moved to where Pinkie was sprawled across the desk, arms and hands extended in front of him. He had landed on his cheekbone, one side of his face turned up, his open eye registering the surprise he must have felt at dying so unexpectedly and so ignominiously, shot in the back like a fool.

Patout opened the lap drawer of the desk. In a plastic tray, along with paper clips, a couple of ballpoint pens, and a book of postage stamps, lay a loaded snub-nosed .38, a Saturday night special. "A no-class weapon for a no-class guy," Patout said, whispering into Duvall's ear.

He took the revolver from the drawer and placed it in Duvall's right hand, positioning the dead man's fingers around the weapon as though he'd been about to fire it.

Patout stepped back and checked the scene. What was he overlooking? What could trip him up? Duvall had legions of enemies, any number of whom could have come to the party disguised, enticed Duvall into his study, and then when an argument ensued, Duvall had been reaching for his weapon, when said enemy got to him first.

No more than fifteen seconds had passed since they entered the office. Even with the silencer, the shots had made sounds, but they would never be heard above the party noise. Patout was confident no one would remember the last costumed guest Duvall had been seen with, and even if they did, the man behind the Bozo the Clown makeup could never be identified.

Finally satisfied that he hadn't overlooked an incriminating detail, he removed the plastic glove and stuffed it into his pocket, then moved toward the door.

And then he stopped, realizing that he *had* overlooked something. Duvall hadn't bled a drop.

Bozo the Clown spun around in a swirl of polka-dot taffeta just as Duvall fired the .38.

The hollow-tip bullet mushroomed inside Patout's abdomen. Clutching his belly, he fell to the floor.

"I highly recommend Kevlar," Duvall said, steering his black velvet slippers clear of the lake of blood forming around Patout as he approached. "You never know when some gutless traitor is going to shoot you in the back." He aimed the barrel of the pistol at Patout's head.

"Mr. Duvall!" Someone knocked hard on the door, then flung it open. "She's gone, Mr. Duvall!"

"What?"

"I just checked the room, like you asked me to. The door was still locked, but she's not in there."

"Did you look out on the balcony?"

"Not there, sir. The windows were still locked."

"That's impossible."

"I'm sorry, sir, but it—"

"Get out of my way." Duvall pushed the man aside. "Finish up here."

With his cape flaring out behind him, Henry VIII ran out to search for his wife.

Doug Patout looked up into the face of a man he'd never seen before, but whom he knew was the last face he would ever see.

Chapter Forty-Two

Burke, dressed like the pirate Jean Lafitte, kept to the shadows at the side of the house until he reached the backyard. He glanced at the gazebo where he'd first seen Remy. A couple were necking beneath the vine-covered dome and didn't notice when he vaulted the fence. On his way inside, he picked up a half-empty glass an invited guest had left behind and strolled in as though he'd been out for a breath of fresh air. The rooms were thronged with people, all costumed and masked for the occasion. He waylaid a waiter—a steroid-popping bodybuilder by the looks of him—who was dressed as a sumo wrestler. Burke had to shout above the party racket to make himself heard. "Mr. Duvall is looking for his wife. Have you seen her?"

"I don't think she's come down yet."

Behind his small black mask, Basile rolled his eyes. "The boss is going to be pissed if she doesn't get her ass down here before this damn thing's over. Thanks."

He patted the bodybuilder's meaty shoulder and began

elbowing his way through the crowd. Remembering the layout of the house from his previous visit and keeping on the lookout for Duvall or bodyguards, he headed toward the main staircase, which was also a high-traffic area. He had expected the second floor to be deserted, but there were people waiting in the hallway for their turn in the powder room.

Pretending to be waiting for the facility himself, Burke moved along the corridor, nonchalantly studying the paintings on the wall, admiring the furnishings, until he reached the door of the master bedroom. It seemed like another lifetime when he'd passed himself off as a priest and hidden the wireless bug. That was before he really knew Remy. Before he regarded her with anything except contempt. Before he loved her.

The door was standing ajar. He pushed it open, glanced in, and saw that the suite was empty.

"Damn!"

"Something wrong?"

He turned. Little Bo Peep was smiling up at him. Strawberry blond curls framed her face beguilingly, but her sultry expression was more in keeping with the flushed bosom that swelled above her low bodice. "Uh, yeah. Mr. Duvall sent me after his wife. She's not where she's supposed to be."

"How sad," she said, pouting. "You've lost her, and I've lost my sheep." She reached out and stroked the leather scabbard strapped to Burke's hip. "Nice sword."

"Thanks. Have you seen her?"

"It's so long and stiff. I bet it could hurt a girl."

"Have you seen her?" he repeated, emphasizing each word.

She dropped her hand. "Jeez, you're a barrel of laughs."

"Maybe some other time. Right now my job depends on finding Mrs. Duvall."

"Okay. I saw her going downstairs with a group just as I came up to use the powder room. At least I think it was her. She was dressed like Marie Antoinette."

"Thanks." Burke sidestepped her and bolted downstairs. From the vantage point of the second step from the bottom, he glanced across the sea of people, trying to sort out the masquerades. Seeing no one who resembled the ill-fated French queen, he plunged into the throng, rudely pushing his way through the people, searching each crowded room. Determined to pack as much enjoyment as possible into the last few remaining minutes of Mardi Gras, Duvall's guests were deliriously making merry.

Burke's progress was impeded by a Red Baron flying ace who was mauling a giggling gypsy girl. A drunken mime made playful grabs at Burke's sword, and a large woman in a toga tried to dance with him.

"Mission accomplished."

Burke came around.

Holding a tray of drinks on his shoulder, the sumo wrestler smiled at him. "I see you got her to come downstairs. After talking to you, I saw Mrs. Duvall pass through here."

"You're sure? Marie Antoinette?"

"Yeah, I'm sure. Same costume as last year."

"Which way'd she go?"

* * *

The panniers were almost as wide as the aisles of the greenhouse. Remy batted them down as she made her way along the aisle in darkness. Knowing that Pinkie probably had spies posted at every exit, and fearing that she would encounter him, she hadn't felt really hopeful that her plan would work until she was well beyond the house, racing along the path toward the greenhouse.

It wasn't until she'd seen him dressed as Henry VIII that she remembered the elaborate costume stored in the rear of her closet, complete with white wig, mask, shoes, faux jewelry, even the beauty mark to paste on her cheek. Once she was dressed, she waited for a crowd to collect outside the second-story powder room, which was inevitable with so many guests in the house.

Then, slipping from the master suite unnoticed, she had joined a group of ladies as they descended the stairs. The new bodyguard, engaged in bawdy conversation with Little Bo Peep, hadn't given Remy a second glance. He had probably been shown a picture of her; he hadn't been looking for Marie Antoinette.

It was pointless to try to use any of the telephones inside the main house. There were drunken guests in every room. Even if she dialed 911, she couldn't have made herself understood without shouting to the dispatcher and calling attention to herself.

But there was a telephone in the greenhouse. It was in a small closet at the rear of the structure where the climate controls were located. For that reason, the enclosure was off limits to everyone except Pinkie. She needed that telephone for only one call. One. She had only to dial a single number. Seven digits.

She pulled open the closet door.

"Hello, Remy." Pinkie was kneeling over what appeared to be a floor safe, previously covered by tiles and unbeknownst to her until now.

Upon seeing him, she froze. But only for a heartbeat.

Then she turned and tried to run. But Pinkie caught her wrist, wrenched it, and shoved it up between her shoulder blades as he came to his feet. Then he roughly pushed her through the open doorway.

He was breathing heavily. His feathered cap was slightly askew. Sweat had loosened the spirit gum holding his fake beard in place.

"The delectable Marie Antoinette," he breathed in her ear. "Reputedly she was a whore, too. Did you know that, Remy?"

"I'm not a whore."

"A senseless argument, my dear. One for which I'm afraid I haven't got the time right now. Thank you for making it so convenient for me to find you. You were the next item on my list of things to be seen to, after I disposed of some records in this safe."

She probably could have wrestled her arm free, but she didn't attempt it because of the pistol being pressed against her temple. If she moved, he would have no compunction against killing her.

"Because one of my key men inside the NOPD tried to kill me a few minutes ago," he went on, "I suspect he was trying to eliminate the man who could finger him as a traitor. Namely me. Which also leads me to deduce that the shit is coming down, to put it in the vernacular."

"You don't know the half of it."

"Basile?"

"Him. District Attorney Littrell. The attorney general."

"Your lover has been one busy boy."

"Killing me won't get you out of this."

"No, but at least Basile won't get the spoils."

The three flowerpots nearest Pinkie exploded, shower-

ing him with fern root, bits of clay, and fragments of what
had been prizewinning cattleyas.

"The next one's for you, Duvall, unless you drop the
gun and move away from her."

* * *

Burke had left the house at a run and searched the im-
mediate backyard area. The necking couple had left the
gazebo. No one else was in sight. Was the waiter wrong
about Remy's leaving the house by a back door? Or was it
a trick? Had he been set up?

Scanning the yard again, he spotted the greenhouse.
Remy had referenced it numerous times. Avoiding the
paved path, he took the most direct route across the grass.

The evening was cold, so the glass walls of the greenhouse were foggy with condensation from the warmer
air inside. Even then he didn't stop to question the wisdom of barging in there before first determining what
he would find. He pulled the door open and ran in. He
saw nothing at first, but he heard Remy's shocked cry.
Seconds later, Duvall pushed her through the door of a
small enclosure.

Burke didn't stop to consider calling for help, or waiting for backup to arrive. He didn't think about letting the
system take over from here. Because the system had failed
him before.

Say a SWAT team swarmed the greenhouse and arrested Duvall by the book; he could afford a defense
attorney as unscrupulous as himself. Evidence had been
stockpiled against him. Eyewitnesses like Roland Sachel,
who had already tired of prison, were ready to testify
against him in exchange for early parole. But depending

on the judge and jury and the competency of the prosecutor, it was possible he would walk, just as Bardo had.

Even if he were convicted and sent to prison, life behind bars wouldn't stop him from terrorizing Remy and Flarra. He could order them killed from a cell block as easily as he could from his fancy office.

Those were sufficient reasons for handling Duvall alone. But none was the main reason. The night Burke had sworn to Kev Stuart's memory that he would avenge his death, he hadn't promised to see that the system carried out the rightful punishment. He had promised to carry it out himself.

So, crouching down beneath the level of the lowest metal shelves, he duckwalked forward until he had an excellent vantage point. When he fired those three warning shots into the flowerpots and issued his warning to Duvall, it was a cursory nod toward legality and civil rights. Burke had every intention of killing him.

But first he had to buy time enough to get Remy out of the way.

And, of course, Duvall was aware of that. He laughed at Burke's dramatic warning. "Go ahead and shoot me, Basile. She'll die first."

"You can't count on that."

"I don't have to. Just the possibility of it will keep you from pulling the trigger. You don't want another situation like Stuart."

A curtain of crimson rage descended over Burke's eyes. His fingers turned white around the pistol. He wanted to blast this bastard, this scumbag who had stripped Remy of her self-respect and all hope of independence, who had kept her in bondage with shackles of oppression and fear.

"You're a burnout, Basile. A head case," Duvall taunted.

"Shut up."

"I don't mind killing the cunt," Duvall said conversationally. "She deserves it. But I don't think you want another snafu on your conscience, do you? So lay down your pistol, and then I'll release her."

"Don't do it," Remy cried, speaking for the first time. "Do what you know is right."

"If you hit her, I bet you'd blow out your own brains next, wouldn't you, Basile? You couldn't live with knowing you had made another mistake and killed her, just like you killed Stuart."

"I said, shut up." Sweat was rolling off his forehead into his eyes, making them sting. His vision turned cloudy. His hands, too, were perspiring so copiously he could barely maintain his grip on the pistol.

Duvall's eyes narrowed. His fingers tensed around the revolver in his hand. Basile knew there was no way in hell that a man like Duvall, a man without a conscience, was going to back down from a standoff. He knew Burke's sore spot, and he would probe it. He would pour acid into it.

He said, "Stuart messed his pants when you shot him, did you know that? Bardo told me."

"Shut up!" Burke screamed, his voice cracking.

"He said Stuart died stinking to high heaven."

"I'm warning you, Duvall."

"Bardo said it was disgusting, the way he stank."

"Shut up, shut up," Burke moaned.

"Proud of yourself for making your friend die that way, Basile?"

"Stop!"

"He had a nice wife, too. I saw her at the trial. You

made her a widow. And now you'll get to watch Remy die."

"No!" Burke dropped his pistol and raised his hands to cover his ears. He slumped against the metal post supporting the shelf of orchids, sobbing.

"I knew you were gutless. Kev Stuart died because—"

But Duvall stopped in midsentence. His eyes rolled toward each other, as though to look at the hole between them. Another appeared an inch above the first. Then he fell backward onto the tile floor.

Basile stood up and walked over to him. Looking into the dead man's open eyes, he said, "Kev Stuart died because I didn't miss. Something you obviously forgot, asshole."

Remy moved up beside him. He placed both arms around her. "Flarra's safe."

"Bardo didn't—"

"He never got to her."

She went limp with relief. For several long moments, they clung to one another, then he nudged her toward the door. "I've got to call."

She glanced down at Duvall only once, then turned away. "Thank God he fell for your emotional collapse."

"So you knew I was faking it?"

"Of course. I was a little worried when you dropped your gun."

"I was a little worried about that myself. It was a risk I had to take."

Hand in hand, they walked across the yard and entered the house. None of the celebrating guests took notice of them. All were dedicated to cramming as much partying as possible into the last few minutes before midnight.

"The only room not open to guests is the study," she

said to Burke above the revelry. He motioned for her to lead the way.

She opened the door of the study, but recoiled when she saw the clown lying on the floor in a pool of blood.

Burke pulled her back into the foyer. "Call nine-one-one. Tell them to get in touch with Littrell."

Mutely she nodded and began pushing her way through the crowd. Burke entered the study, closing and locking the door so none of the guests would venture in, see the bodies, and cause a panic.

He stepped quickly to the young man in the dark suit and felt for a pulse. He was dead.

Then he crouched down beside the clown. Pain had etched lines into the white greasepaint. The eyes, heavily exaggerated by makeup, were closed and still. The large red smile was smeared and looked grotesque.

Burke wasn't at first sure if he were still alive, but then his eyes fluttered open. His lips moved, and he spoke in a thready voice. "Basile?"

Burke exhaled slowly. "Hey, Doug."

"I'm bleeding out, aren't I?"

Burke glanced down at Patout's hand. The white glove was saturated with blood. It also had soaked the baggy costume and had formed a red ocean around him. "I'm afraid so."

"Duvall," he said in a thready voice. "But at least I took the other one out."

The pistol with which he'd shot Duvall's man was still in his inert hand. Basile didn't disturb it. This was a crime scene. "I got Duvall," Burke told him.

Patout closed his eyes. "Good. Call...call...for help."

Burke stood up and moved toward the door, but when he reached it, he didn't open it to summon help. For several moments, his hand tightly gripped the doorknob, then decisively he released it and returned to Patout, hunkering down nearer him.

"Help me, Burke."

Gently, Burke removed the red bulbous nose and peeled the fiery red wig from Patout's head. "Can't do it, Doug."

Doug's fluttering eyes found his. As he stared into Burke's calm face, his shallow breathing whistled through his lips. "You know."

"That you were the mole in our division? Yes."

"How long?"

"Since the day you murdered Mac. And it was murder, Doug. Mac didn't come looking for me to turn me over to Duvall, as you said. He came to tell me that there was a better, cleaner way to get to Duvall if only I exercised a little patience.

"I played a hunch this morning, and it turned out to be right. I spoke with Littrell and then to the attorney general. It seems that soon after the A.G. took office he assembled a special team to investigate police corruption.

"Mac was part of it. He went through the police academy, worked his way up through the ropes, but all in preparation of infiltrating Narcotics and Vice and sniffing out the traitor. You, Doug. Mac was close to nailing you. You must have sensed the heat and shot him before he could share his suspicions with me.

"He might have been going for his gun in that fishing shack, but it wasn't to kill me. He only wanted to bring me in and, with the A.G.'s sanction, give me the skinny. He also wanted to sit me down and break it to me gently that the man I considered my friend was in fact a cop as dirty as they come.

"You know what the worst of it is, Doug? What I hate

the worst? Is that you laid your own crimes on Mac." Burke thrust his face close to the dying man's. "Why, Doug? Why Duvall, for chrissake? Why? For the money?"

"Cowardice," he wheezed.

"You're no coward."

"The guy I shot. Remember?"

"Our rookie year?" Burke had a dull recollection of the incident. "He was armed and went for his weapon when you tried to arrest him. It was a clear case of him or you."

Patout shook his head a fraction. "It was a throwdown. I panicked, shot him too soon, covered it." He paused to take several gurgling breaths. "He was Duvall's man. Duvall knew the guy used knives, not guns. He wouldn't have died with a pistol in his hand, and Duvall knew that. He's owned me ever since." A tear streaked through the white makeup. "I was a good cop. I wanted to be chief."

"It never would have happened, Doug," Burke said sadly. "If it hadn't been Mac, somebody else would have caught on to you."

"You."

"Yeah, me. Only I figured it out too late."

Patout let the pistol slip from his fingers and used most of his diminishing strength to grip Burke's loose pirate shirt. "How'd...how'd...you guess?"

"I didn't. You told me yourself."

Patout looked at him with confusion.

"After you shot Mac," Burke explained, "you told me that calls to drug dealers had been traced back to him, even the call that tipped them the night Kev was killed. That was a lie, and I knew it."

He bent nearer so that Patout wouldn't miss a single word. "A drug dealer is scum. But a cop who plays their game is scum shit. The bad guys were beating us at every turn with the help of one of our own. Internal Affairs didn't do shit because so many of them are dirty, too. The D.A. was playing politics and taking his sweet time. I suppose the A.G.'s team was working on it, but very covertly. It appeared that nothing was happening toward catching the son of a bitch who was selling us out to Duvall.

"How many raids had to go south before something was done? Ten? Five? Maybe only one. Maybe only *one* more failed bust would spur somebody to take action. Of course, who could guess that that one bust would cost Kev's life? I sure didn't.

"See, Doug," he continued in a quieter voice, "you lied to me that day in the shack when you told me that Mac had tipped the dealers that night. I knew it wasn't Mac. Because it was me."

Patout groaned. His head lolled to one side, but he didn't take his eyes off Burke.

"I tipped them, thinking that a failed raid, even on a chickenshit operation that wasn't very significant, might be enough to get an investigation underway. My brilliant plan backfired. I had no way of knowing Bardo was inside that warehouse. The one time I compromised my standards, the one time I played dirty, Kev Stuart was killed."

Moving nearer still to his dying friend, he whispered, "I've got to live the rest of my life with that on my conscience." He worked Patout's fingers from the cloth of his shirt and pushed his hand away. "But you're gonna die with it on yours."

Patout whimpered.

Burke glanced at the clock. "Two minutes until midnight, Doug. Fat Tuesday will be over, and you'll be dead." He cleared his throat and rubbed the tears from his eyes. "Then, I'll atone."

Epilogue

She's lovely, Burke."

"Yes, she is."

He and Nanci Stuart were sharing the glider on Dredd's *galerie*. It was a hot, still, humid Labor Day. They were resting in the shade while Dredd was giving the others fishing lessons at the end of his pier.

Burke wondered about the origin of the hunk of meat Dredd was using for bait. To his knowledge no one had investigated the disappearance of the two hit men Duvall had dispatched with Gregory James.

"What I mean is," Nanci said, "Remy's lovely on the inside."

"I know what you meant. That's what I meant, too."

She laughed, reminding him of the old days when Kev was alive and the three of them gathered in their kitchen for coffee and friendly teasing. "All the same, it hasn't escaped your notice that your bride is gorgeous."

He smiled with guilty pride, like a little boy who'd just

hit his first home run—through the neighbor's window. "No. That hasn't escaped my notice."

He watched as Remy listened intently to Dredd, followed his instructions with the determination of a neophyte, then smiled happily when he complimented her.

God, he loved her. He loved her so much it frightened him. Sometimes it hurt. Each day eclipsed Duvall's influence a little more. Soon it would be only a dark memory. Remy was evolving into a confident woman, secure in herself and in his love for her.

"She seems to enjoy her work at the gallery," Nanci remarked.

"She loves it. And she's good at it. Last week I attended a private showing. When she discussed the paintings with her clients, I didn't know what the hell she was talking about, but they were hanging on to every word."

"You're proud."

"Damn proud," he said earnestly. Just as sincerely, he added, "Thanks for being her friend, Nanci. Your friendship means a lot to Remy. She's never had a friend before."

"It's not an obligation. I like her."

He leaned forward to set his empty soft-drink can on an upended barrel and, in the process, knocked a collection of picture postcards to the plank flooring. He bent down to pick them up.

"Does Dredd have a pen pal?" Nanci asked.

"In a manner of speaking. An old friend of ours."

The postcards had been mailed from all over the country, dated about a week apart. None were signed. All were from Gregory James. The messages were brief, never more than a sentence or two, and would have been cryptic to anyone who didn't know the circumstances behind the young man's flight from New Orleans. He'd also alluded to Duvall's death and the relief that learning about it had brought him. Basically, the cards were sent to let them know that he was safe and thinking hard about the direction his life would take from here on.

The most recent card bore a postmark from Santa Fe. The sum total of the text was *St. Luke 15:11–24.* Dredd had looked up the scripture to find the parable of the prodigal son.

"He's been away for a while," Burke told Nanci. "But I get the idea he's working his way back to us."

"Hey, I caught one!"

The shout drew their attention to the pier, where Flarra was holding up her catch for the other fishermen to envy and admire. David Stuart, Nanci's oldest, offered to take the fish off the hook for her. Nanci confided to Burke that Flarra had made deep dents in her sons' conviction that all girls were icky and ugly and stupid.

"Before they met Flarra, they had vowed never to have anything to do with the opposite sex. She's weakened their resolve."

"She likes them, too. Poor kid never has had a family beyond Remy. She's really terrific, though. Smart as a whip. Funny. Looking forward to going to a coed school this fall." Chuckling, he added, "She even likes me. Hounds me all the time about when I'm going to get Remy pregnant."

"Remy confided that a baby is in the plan."

"We're doing our damnedest," he said, feeling his lips forming a smile. It was ridiculous how often he smiled these days.

"I'm so glad for your happiness, Burke."

"Thanks."

"Speaking of which…" She pulled her lower lip through her teeth. "I'm seeing someone."

"No shit? That…that's great, Nanci."

"You really think so?" she asked timidly.

"If he's everything you deserve, yeah."

"Well, I don't know if he's everything I *deserve,*" she said demurely, then broke into a wide smile. "But he's awfully nice. A well-established businessman. His wife died of cancer a few years ago. He loved her like I loved Kev, and that's a good sign, don't you think?"

"Definitely. How is he with the boys?"

"So far so good. And he looks great from the rear in a pair of blue jeans."

"Now you're talking."

"But of course he'll have to pass the acid test."

"Dare I ask?"

"Meeting you," she said.

He felt his teasing grin slowly dissolve. She was serious. "Why should my opinion of him matter that much?"

She reached across the space separating them and clasped his hand. "Remy's my new friend, but you're my best friend. Your opinion matters a lot to me." They gazed at each other meaningfully, then she stood up and dusted off the seat of her linen shorts. "I notice Peter is becoming frustrated. Time for a pep talk."

As she left him to join the others, Burke was too moved to speak.

He went inside the store, ostensibly to get another soft drink, but actually what he did was brace his hands on Dredd's countertop and stare down through the cloudy glass at the dusty candy bars and packages of beef jerky.

Several minutes later, the screened door squeaked open. "Burke?" Remy came to stand beside him. She placed her hand on the small of his back. "Everything okay?"

He acknowledged her concern by turning his head and giving her a wan smile. But he couldn't hide his eyes from her. "What's wrong?" she asked, alarmed.

"Nothing."

"You're sad?"

"Actually I'm happy." He wiped his damp eyes on his sleeve and told her about Nanci's beau. "It choked me up, to know that she values my opinion."

"Implicitly," Remy told him. "Her words to me exactly the other day when we had lunch."

News of Duvall's death had been a lead story that circulated far beyond state lines. It was followed by expanding reports of corruption in the NOPD and city hall, and the special task force that had exposed it.

Having heard this news, Joe had called Burke, who affirmed that this was the police matter he'd been involved in. It was now safe for Joe's family, and for Nanci Stuart, to return home.

On the eve of Doug Patout's funeral, Burke had confessed to Nanci his complicity in her husband's death. They had cried together, and she had thanked him for telling her. It had been a cathartic experience for both. Even so, Burke's misjudgment continued to haunt him.

"After what I did," he said now, "I don't understand how Nanci can forgive me, much less still think of me as her best friend."

"Burke," Remy said, moving nearer and placing her arms around him. "The only one who hasn't forgiven you is *you*. You've been appointed by the attorney general to ferret out all forms of corruption in the NOPD. District Attorney Littrell doesn't make a move without consulting you first. You're respected and admired." She laid her hands on his chest. "And deeply loved."

"I need you close," he whispered, drawing her against him and resting his chin on the top of her head.

"If I can forgive myself for the years I spent with Pinkie Duvall, you can forgive yourself your one mistake, can't you?"

He tipped her face up and kissed her, giving himself over to the taste and warmth and feel of her mouth until she angled her head back and murmured, "Make love to me."

He glanced over his shoulder and looked through the window toward the pier, where the others could be heard talking and laughing. "What, now?"

"Um-huh."

Needing no more encouragement than that, he swept her along through Dredd's awkward arrangement of rooms until they were stretched out on the narrow bed where she had lain before, their clothing strewn about like hurricane-driven debris. He kissed her mouth, throat, breasts. But when he would have entered her, she amazed him by seizing the initiative and doing something she'd never done before.

At first he whispered feeble objections, but soon he was too distracted by the onslaught of sensations to protest. Groaning her name, he buried his fingers in her hair. His hands followed the motions of her head as she made love to him with her mouth.

Then she straddled him, taking all of him inside her. It was mind-blowing, the way she rode him, the way her hips ground against his thighs, the way her mouth melded with his as, together, they came.

Lying quietly, lazily, sweatily, knowing they should get

up and dress and rejoin the party before their absence was noticed, they remained as they were.

"You listened, didn't you?" she asked softly.

"Hmm?" he murmured, still immersed in incredible pleasure and lacking the energy to say more.

"You eavesdropped on Pinkie and me."

Suddenly wide awake and flushed with embarrassment, Burke cleared his throat. "Uh, yeah. I planted a bug in the bedroom."

"Why?"

"I told myself I might learn something about Duvall's operation. But that was an excuse. The truth is, I was obsessed with you. I hated the thought of you with him. But at the same time, it was a vicarious..." He sighed with self-disgust. "Jesus, I must be a sick bastard."

"No, no you're not." She hugged him tighter and for a time they were quiet.

Then Burke asked how she had guessed about the bug.

She raised her head and gazed down at him, lifting damp strands of hair off his forehead. "You've avoided certain intimate acts that you think would repel me. You're afraid they would remind me of Pinkie." She smiled ruefully. "Burke, nothing we do together could remind me of him, or of anything I saw or overheard or experienced in Angel's house. It's not the same. With you, everything is for the first time. It's new. Clean. Right. I take joy from loving you. It's not the same at all."

He took her hand and pressed her palm against his mouth. He wanted to tell her how much he loved her, but, for the second time that afternoon, he was too moved to speak.

Besides, she already knew.

A rising star TV journalist determined to get the exclusive of her lifetime—by any means necessary.

An infuriating private investigator who wants her out of his family's life—but finds her impossible to resist.

A catastrophic interview that puts them both in mortal danger.

#1 *New York Times* bestselling author Sandra Brown delivers relentless suspense, staggering twists, and heart-pounding romance in her tantalizing new thriller.

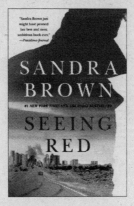

Please turn the page for a preview.
Available now.

Prologue

Did you think you were going to die?".

The Major pursed his lips with disapproval. "That question wasn't on the list I approved."

"Which is why I didn't ask it while the cameras were rolling. But there's no one here now but us. I'm asking off the record. Were you in fear of your life? Did dying cross your mind?"

"I didn't stop to think about it."

Kerra Bailey tilted her head and regarded him with doubt. "That sounds like a canned answer."

The seventy-year-old gave her the smile that had won him the heart of a nation. "It is."

"All right," she said. "I'll respectfully and graciously withdraw the question."

She could pass on it because, after all, she'd got what she'd come for: the first interview of any kind that he had granted in more than three years. In the days leading up to this evening's live telecast from his home, he and she had become well acquainted. They'd engaged in some lively discussions, often taking opposing views.

Kerra looked up at the stag head mounted above his mantel. "I stand by my aversion to having the eyes of dead animals staring down at me."

He chuckled. "Venison is food. And keeping the herd thinned out is ecologically—"

"I've heard all the justifications from other hunters. I just don't understand how anyone could place a beautiful animal like that in the crosshairs and pull the trigger."

"Neither of us is going to win this argument," he said, to which she replied with matching stubbornness, "Neither of us is going to concede it, either."

He blurted a short laugh that ended in a dry cough. "You're right." He glanced over at the tall gun cabinet in the corner of the vast room, then pushed himself out of his brown leather La-Z-Boy, walked over to the cabinet, and opened the paned-glass front.

He removed one of the rifles. "I took that particular deer with this rifle. It was my wife's last Christmas present to me." He ran his hand along the bluish barrel. "I haven't used it since she died."

Kerra was touched to see this softer side of him. "I wish she could have been here for the interview."

"So do I. I miss her every day."

"What was it like for her, being married to America's hero?"

"Oh, she was super-impressed," he said around a chuckle as he propped the rifle in the corner between the cabinet and the wall. "She nagged me only every other day about leaving my dirty socks on the floor rather than putting them in the hamper."

Kerra laughed, but her thoughts turned to the Major's

son and his aversion to his father's fame. She had felt obligated to invite him to appear on the program, perhaps in the final segment. Using explicit language that left no room for misinterpretation, he had declined. *Thank God*.

The Major crossed to the built-in bar. "So much talking has made me thirsty. I could use a drink. What would you like?"

"Nothing for me." She stood and retrieved her bag from where she'd set it on the floor beside her chair. "As soon as the crew gets back, we need to hit the road."

The Major had had a local restaurant prepare and deliver a cold fried chicken picnic supper for her and the five-person production crew. After they'd eaten, packing up the gear had taken an hour, but when all was done, Kerra had asked the others to go gas up the van for their two-hour drive back to Dallas, while she stayed behind. She had wanted a few minutes alone with the Major in order to thank him properly.

She began, "Major, I must tell you—"

He turned to her and interrupted. "You've said it, Kerra. Repeatedly. You don't need to say it again."

"You may not need to hear it again, but I need to say it." Her voice turned husky with emotion. "Please accept my heartfelt thank you for... well, for everything. I can't adequately express my gratitude. It knows no bounds."

Matching her solemn tone, he replied, "You're welcome."

She smiled at him and took a short breath. "May I call you every once in a while? Come visit if I'm ever out this way again?"

"I'd like that very much."

They shared a long look, leaving the many insufficient words unspoken, but conveying to each other a depth of feeling. Then, to break the sentimental mood, he rubbed his hands together. "Sure you won't have a drink?"

"No, but I would take advantage of your bathroom." She left her coat in the chair but shouldered her bag.

"You know where it is."

This making the fourth time she'd been to his house, she was familiar with the layout. The living area looked like a miniature Texas museum, with cowhide rugs on the distressed hardwood floor, Remington reproductions in bronze of cowboys in action, and pieces of furniture that made the Major's recliner seem small by comparison.

One of the offshoots of the main room was a hallway, and the first door to the left was the powder room, although that feminine-sounding name was incongruous with the hand soap dispenser in the shape of a longhorn steer.

She was drying her hands at the sink and checking her reflection in the framed mirror above it, making a mental note to call her hairdresser—maybe a few more highlights around her face?—when the door latch rattled, calling her attention to it. "Major? Is the crew back? I'll be right out."

He didn't respond, although she sensed someone on the other side of the door.

She replaced the hand towel in the iron ring mounted on the wall beside the sink and was reaching for her shoulder bag when she heard the *bang*.

Her mind instantly clicked back to the Major. Taking the rifle from the cabinet. Not replacing it in the rack. If he'd been doing so now and it had accidentally discharged... *Oh my God!*

She lunged for the door and grabbed hold of the knob, but snatched her hand back when she heard a voice, not the Major's, say, "How do you like being dead so far?"

Kerra clapped her hand over her mouth to hold back a wail of disbelief and horror. She heard footsteps thudding around in the living room. One set? Two? It was hard to tell, and fear had robbed her of mental acuity. She did, however, have the presence of mind to switch off the bathroom light.

Holding her breath, she listened, tracking the footsteps as they crossed rugs, struck hardwood, and then, to her mounting horror, entered the hallway. They came even with the bathroom door and stopped.

Moving as soundlessly as possible, she backed away from the door, feeling her way past the sink and toilet in the darkness, until she came up against the bead-board wall. She tried to keep her breathing silent, though her lips moved around a prayer of only one repeated word: Please, please, please.

Whoever was on the other side of the door tried turning the knob and found it locked. It was tried a second time, then the door shook as an attempt was made to force it open. To whoever was trying to open it, the locked door could only mean one thing: someone was on the other side.

She'd been discovered.

Another set of footsteps came rushing from the living area. The door was battered against with what she imagined was the stock of a rifle.

She had nothing with which to defend herself against armed assailants. If they had in fact murdered the Major, and if they got past that door, she would die, too.

Escape was her only option and it had to be now.

The double-hung window behind her was small, but it was the only chance she had of getting out alive. She felt for the lock holding the sashes together, twisted it open, then placed her fingers in the depressions of the lower sash and pulled up with all her might. It didn't budge.

Several blasts sounded in rapid succession, shooting at the lock.

Because silence was no longer necessary, Kerra was sobbing now, taking in noisy gulps of air. Please, please, please. She whimpered the entreaty for salvation from a source stronger than her because she felt powerless.

She put all she had into raising the window, and it became unstuck with such suddenness that it took her aback for perhaps one heartbeat. Another shot was fired and the bullet struck the porcelain sink and ricocheted into the wall.

She threw one leg over the windowsill and bent practically in half in order to get her head and shoulders through. When they cleared the opening, she launched herself out and dropped to the ground.

She landed on her shoulder. A spike of pain took her breath. Her left arm went numb and useless. She rolled onto her stomach and pushed herself up with her right arm. After taking a few staggering steps to regain her balance, she took off in a sprint. Behind her she heard the bathroom door crashing open.

A blast from a shotgun deafened her and sheared off the branch of a young mesquite tree. She kept running. It fired again, striking a boulder and creating shrapnel that struck her legs like darts.

How many misses would they get before hitting her?

There were no city lights, only a sliver of moon. The darkness made her a more difficult target, but it also prevented her from seeing more than a few feet ahead of her. She ran blindly, stumbling over rocks, scrub brush, and uneven ground.

Please, please, please.

Then without warning, the earth gave out beneath her. She pitched forward, grabbing hold of nothing but air. She was helpless to catch herself before smashing into the ground and rolling, sliding, falling.

Chapter 1

Six days earlier

Trapper was in a virtual coma when the knocking started.

"Bloody hell," he mumbled into the throw pillow beneath his head. His face would bear the imprint of the upholstery when he got up. *If* he ever got up. Right now he had no intention of moving, not even to open his eyes.

The knocking might have been part of a dream. Maybe a construction worker somewhere in the building was tapping the walls in search of studs. An urban woodpecker? Whatever. If he ignored the noise, maybe it would go away.

But after fifteen seconds of blessed silence, there came another knock-knock. Trapper croaked, "I'm closed. Come back later."

The next three knocks were insistent.

Swearing, he rolled onto his back, sailed the drool-damp pillow across the office, and laid his forearm over his eyes to block the daylight. The window blinds were only partially open, but those cheerful, skinny strips of sunshine made his eyeballs throb.

Keeping one eye closed, he eased his feet off the sofa and onto the floor. When he stood, he stumbled over his discarded boots. His big toe sent his cell phone sliding across the floor and underneath a chair. If he were to bend down that far, he doubted his ability to return upright, so he left his phone where it was.

It wasn't like it rang all that often anyway.

Holding the heel of his hand against his pounding temple, and with one eye remaining closed, he managed to reach the other side of his office without bumping into the bottom drawer of the metal file cabinet. For no reason he could remember, it was standing open.

Through the frosted glass upper half of the door he made out a form just as it raised its fist to knock again. To prevent the further agony that would induce, Trapper flipped the lock and opened the door a crack.

He sized her up within two seconds. "You've got the wrong office. One flight up. First door to the left off the elevator."

He was about to shut the door when she said, "John Trapper?"

Shit. Had he forgotten an appointment? He scratched the top of his head, where his hair hurt down to the follicles. "What time is it?"

"Twelve fifteen."

"What day?"

She took a breath and let it out slowly. "Monday."

He looked her up and down and came back to her face. "Who are you?"

"Kerra Bailey."

The name didn't ring any bells, but it would be hard to

hear them over the jackhammer inside his skull. "Look, if it's about the parking meter—"

"The one in front of the building? The one that's been flattened?"

"I'll pay to have it replaced. I'll cover any other damages. I would have left a note to that effect, but I didn't have anything on me to write—"

"I'm not here about the parking meter."

"Oh. Hmm. Did we have an appointment?"

"No."

"Well, now's not a good time for me, Ms...." He went blank.

"Bailey," she said, in the same impatient tone in which she'd said *Monday*.

"Right. Call me, and we'll schedule—"

"It's important that I talk to you sooner rather than later. May I come in?" She gestured at the door, which Trapper had kept open only a few inches.

A woman who looked like her, he hated turning down for anything. But, hell. His head felt as dense as a bowling ball. His shirt was unbuttoned, the tail hanging loose. He hoped his fly was zipped, but in case it wasn't, he didn't risk calling attention to it by checking. His breath would stop a clock.

He glanced behind him at the disarray: suit jacket and tie slung over the back of a chair; boots in front of the sofa, one upright, the other lying on its side; one black sock draped over the armrest, the other sock God-only-knew-where; an empty bottle of Dom precariously close to rolling off the corner of his desk.

He needed a shower. He really needed to pee.

But he also really *really* needed clients, and she had "money" written all over her. Her handbag, literally so. It was the size of a small suitcase and covered in designer initials. Even if she had been looking for the tax attorney on the next floor up, she would have been slumming.

Besides, when had he ever been known to say no to a lady in distress?

He stepped back and opened the door, motioning her toward the two straight chairs facing his desk. He kicked the file cabinet drawer shut with his heel and still got to his desk ahead of her in time to relocate an empty but smelly Chinese food carton and the latest issue of *Maxim*. He'd ranked the cover shot among his top ten faves, but she might take exception to that much areolae.

She sat in one chair and placed her bag in the other. As he rounded the desk, he buttoned the middle button of his shirt and ran a hand across his mouth and chin to check for remaining drool.

As he dropped into his desk chair, he caught her looking at the gravity-defying champagne bottle. He rescued it from the corner of the desk and set it gently in the trash can to avoid a clatter. "Buddy of mine got married."

"Last night?"

"Saturday afternoon."

Her eyebrow arched. "It must have been some wedding."

He shrugged, then leaned back in his chair. "Who recommended me?"

"No one. I got the address off your website."

Trapper had forgotten he even had one. He'd paid a college kid seventy-five bucks to do whatever it was you do to get a website up. That was the last he'd thought of it. This was the first client it had yielded.

She looked like she could afford much better.

"I apologize for showing up without an appointment,"

she said. "I tried calling you several times this morning, but kept getting your voice mail."

Trapper shot a look toward the chair his phone had slid underneath. "I silenced my phone for the wedding. Guess I forgot to turn it back on." As discreetly as possible, he shifted in his chair in a vain attempt to give his bladder some breathing room.

"Well, it's sooner rather than later, Ms. Bailey. You said it was important, but not important enough for you to make an appointment. What can I do for you?"

"I'd like for you to intervene on my behalf and convince your father to grant me an interview."

He looked at her, thinking that she appeared to be sane. He would have said *Come again?* or *Pardon?* or *I didn't quite catch that*, but she had articulated perfectly, so what he said was, "Is this a fucking joke?"

"No."

"Seriously, who put you up to this?"

"No one, Mr. Trapper."

"Just plain Trapper is fine, but it doesn't matter what you call me because we don't have anything else to say to each other." He stood up and headed for the door.

"You haven't even heard me out."

"Yeah. I have. Now if you'll excuse me, I gotta take a piss and then I've got a hangover to sleep off. Close the door on your way out. This neighborhood, I hope your car's still there when you get back to it."

He stalked out in bare feet and went down the drab hallway to the men's room. He used the urinal, then went over to the sink and looked at himself in the cloudy, cracked mirror above it. A pile of dog shit had nothing on him.

He bent down and scooped tap water into his mouth until his thirst was no longer raging, then ducked his head under the faucet. He shook water from his hair and dried his face with paper towels. With one more nod toward respectability, he buttoned his shirt as he was walking back to his office.

She was still there. Which didn't come as that much of a surprise. She looked the type that didn't give up easily.

Before he could order her out, she said, "Why would you object to the Major giving an interview?"

"I wouldn't. I don't give a crap. But he won't do it, and I think you already know that or you wouldn't have come to me, because I'm the last person on the planet who could convince him to do anything."

"Why is that?"

He recognized that cleverly laid trap for what it was, and didn't step into it. "Let me guess, Ms. Bailey. I'm your last resort?" Her expression was as good as an admission. "Before coming to me, how many times did you ask the Major yourself?"

"I've called him thirteen times."

"How many times did he hang up on you?"

"Thirteen."

"Rude bastard."

Under her breath, she said, "It must be a family trait."

Trapper only smiled. "It's the only one he and I have in common." He studied her for a moment. "You get points for tenacity. Most give up long before thirteen attempts. Who do you work for?"

"A network O and O—owned and operated—in Dallas."

"You're on TV? In Dallas?"

"I do feature stories. Human interest, things like that. Occasionally one makes it to the network's Sunday evening news show."

Trapper was familiar with the program but he didn't remember ever having watched it.

He knew for certain that he'd never seen her, not even on the local station, or he would've remembered. She had straight, sleek light brown hair with blonder streaks close to her face. Brown eyes as large as a doe's. One inch below the outside corner of the left one was a beauty mark the same dark chocolate color as her irises. Her complexion was creamy, her lips plump and pink, and he was reluctant to pull his gaze away from them.

But he did. "Sorry, but you drove over here for nothing."

"Mr. Trapper—"

"You're wasting your time. The Major retired from public life years ago."

"Three to be exact. And he didn't merely retire. He went into seclusion. Why do you think he did that?"

"My guess is that he got sick of talking about it."

"What about you?"

"I was sick of it long before that."

"How old were you?"

"At the time of the bombing? Eleven. Fifth grade."

"Your father's sudden celebrity must have affected you."

"Not really."

She watched him for a moment, then said softly, "That's impossible. It had to have impacted your life as dramatically as it did his."

He squinted one eye. "You know what this sounds like? Leading questions, like you're trying to interview *me*. In which case, you're S.O.L. because I'm not going to talk about the Major, or me, or effects on my life. Ever. Not to anybody."

She reached into the oversized bag and took out an 8x10 reproduction of a photograph, then laid it on the desk and pushed it toward him.

Without even glancing down at it, he pushed it back. "I've seen it." For the second time, he stood up, went to the door and opened it, then stood there, hands on hips, waiting.

She hesitated, then sighed with resignation, hiked the strap of her bag onto her shoulder, and joined him at the door. "I caught you at a bad time."

"No, this is about as good as I get."

"Would you consider meeting me later, after you've had time to . . ." She made a gesture that encompassed his sorry state. "To feel better? I could outline what I want to do. We could talk about it over dinner."

"Nothing to talk about."

"I'm paying."

He shook his head. "Thanks anyway."

She gnawed the inside of her cheek as though trying to determine which tactic to use to try to persuade him. Regarding that, he could offer some salacious suggestions, but she probably wouldn't go that far, and even if she did, afterward he'd still say no to her request.

She took a look around the office before coming back to him. With the tip of her index finger, she underlined the words stenciled on the frosted glass of the door. "Private Investigator."

"So it says."

"Your profession is to investigate things, solve mysteries."

He snuffled. That was his former profession. Nowadays he was retained by tearful wives wanting him to confirm that their husbands were screwing around. If he managed to get pictures, it doubled his fee. Distraught parents paid him to track down runaway teens, whom he usually found exchanging alleyway blow jobs for heroin.

He wouldn't call the work he was doing mystery-solving. Or investigation, for that matter.

But to her, he said, "Yeah. I'm a regular Sherlock Holmes."

"Are you licensed?"

"Oh, yeah. I have a gun, bullets, everything."

"Do you have a magnifying glass?"

The question took him aback only because she hadn't asked it in jest. She was serious. "What for?" he asked.

Those pouty lips fashioned an enigmatic smile and she whispered, "Figure it out."

Keeping her eyes on his, she reached into an inside pocket of her bag and withdrew a business card. She didn't hand it to him, but stuck it in a crack between the frosted glass pane and the doorframe, adjacent to the words that spelled out his job description.

"When you change your mind, my cell number is on the card."

Hell would freeze over first.

Trapper slammed the office door behind her, plucked the business card from the slit, and flipped it straight into the trash can.

Eager to go home and sleep off the remainder of his hangover in a more comfortable surrounding, he snatched up the sock on the armrest of the sofa and went in search of the other.

After several frustrating minutes and a litany of elaborate profanity, he found it inside one of his boots. He pulled on his socks, but decided he needed an aspirin before he finished dressing. Padding over to his desk, he opened the lap drawer in the hope of discovering a forgotten bottle of analgesics.

That damned photograph was there in plain sight where he couldn't miss it.

But whether looking at it, or acknowledging it in any manner, or even denying its existence, he was never truly free of it. He had lied to Kerra Bailey. His life was never the same after that photograph went global twenty-five years ago.

Trapper plopped down into his desk chair and looked at the cursed thing. His head hurt, his eyes were scratchy, his throat and mouth were still parched. But even realizing that it was masochistic, he reached across the desk and slid the photo closer to him.

Everyone in the entire world had seen it at least once over the past quarter century. Among prize-winning, defining-moment, editorial photographs, it ranked right up there with the raising of the flag on Iwo Jima, the sailor kissing the nurse in Times Square on V-E Day, the naked Vietnamese girl running from napalm, the twin towers of the World Trade Center aflame and crumbling.

But before 9/11, there was the Pegasus Hotel bombing in downtown Dallas. It had rocked a city still trying to live down the Kennedy assassination, had destroyed a landmark building, had snuffed out the lives of one hundred ninety-seven people. Half that number had been critically injured.

Major Franklin Trapper had led a handful of struggling survivors out of the smoldering rubble to safety.

A photographer who worked for one of Dallas's newspapers had been eating lunch at his desk in the city room when the first bomb detonated. The blast deafened him. The repercussion shook his building and created cracks in the aggregate floor beneath his desk. Windows shattered.

But like an old fire horse, he was conditioned to run toward a disaster. He snatched up his camera, bolted down three flights of fire stairs, and, upon exiting the newspaper building, dashed toward the source of the black plume of smoke that had already engulfed the skyline.

He reached the scene of terror and chaos ahead of emergency responders who would soon be scrambling to evacuate the area for blocks around and to set up street blockades to keep out anyone who wasn't search-and-rescue or medical personnel.

The photographer began snapping pictures, including the one that became iconic: Franklin Trapper, recently retired from the U.S. Army, emerging from the smoking building leading a pathetic group of dazed, scorched, bleeding, choking people, one child cradled in his arms, a woman holding on to his coattail, a man whose tibia had a compound fracture using him as a crutch.

The photographer, now deceased, had won a Pulitzer for his picture. The act of heroism he had captured on film during his lunch hour immediately earned him and the photo immortality.

And, as Trapper well knew, immortality lasted for fucking ever.

The story behind the photograph and the people in it wouldn't come to light until later, when those who were hospitalized were able to relate their individual accounts.

Though, by the time the tales were told, the Trappers'

front yard in suburban Dallas had become an encampment for media. The Major—as he came to be known—had been ordained a national symbol of bravery and self-sacrifice.

For years following that day in 1992, he was a sought-after public speaker. He was given every honor and award there was to be bestowed, and many were initiated and named for him. He was invited to the White House by every subsequent administration. At state dinners he was introduced to visiting foreign dignitaries who paid homage to his courage.

Over time, new disasters produced new heroes. The fireman carrying the toddler from the Oklahoma City bombing overshadowed the Major's celebrity for a time, but soon he was back on TV talk show guest lists and the after-dinner speaker circuit.

Then three years ago, it came to a screeching halt.

He now lived very privately, avoiding the limelight and refusing requests for public appearances and interviews.

But his legend lived on. Which was why journalists, biographers, and movie producers emerged now and again, seeking time with him to make their particular pitch. He never granted them that time.

Until today none had ever sought out Trapper's help to gain access to the Major.

Kerra Bailey's audacity was galling enough. But damn her for snagging his interest with that remark about the magnifying glass. What could he possibly see in that photograph that he hadn't seen ten thousand times?

He longed for a hot shower, an aspirin, his bed and soft pillow.

"Fuck it." He opened his desk's lap drawer and, instead of reaching for the bottle of Bayer, searched all the way to the back of it and came up with the long-forgotten magnifying glass.

Four hours later, he was still in his desk chair, still reeking, head still aching, eyes still scratchy. But everything else had changed.

He set down the magnifier, pushed the fingers of both hands up through his hair, and held his head between his palms. "Son of a bitch."